MORGAN

Unnatural Fire

A Countess Ashby de la Zouche
Mystery

f 493256.

This novel is entirely a work of fiction. The names, characters and incidents portrayed in it are the work of the author's imagination. Any resemblance to actual persons, living or dead, events or localities is entirely coincidental.

HarperCollins*Publishers*
77–85 Fulham Palace Road, London w6 8jb

The HarperCollins website address is:
www.**fire**and**water**.com

This paperback edition 2001
1 3 5 7 9 8 6 4 2

First published in Great Britain by
Collins Crime in 2000

isbn 0 00 651452 9

Set in PostScript Linotype Janson
and Adobe Caslon by
Rowland Phototypesetting Ltd,
Bury St Edmunds, Suffolk

Printed and bound in Great Britain by
Clays Ltd, St Ives plc

A note on dating

Due to the changeover from the Julian to the Gregorian calendar and the loss of eleven days in 1752 (which took place in order to complete the changeover) some things may seem strange to the modern reader.

The most obvious difference is in references to the astrological sign of Libra, which then began in early rather than late September.

It is also worth pointing out that in the late seventeenth century the New Year was commonly welcomed in on Lady Day at the end of March, although more modern thinkers were already advocating the revolutionary idea of changing years on 1 January.

Thank yous

Dennis William Hauck at the *www.alchemylab.com* site for help with the chemistry of alchymy.

Contents

ONE

Conjunction

The joining of two opposite components,
the subtle and the gross,
or the fixed and the volatile.

'Take this down . . . "At the stroke of 8 o'clock this morning, while the night-watch Charlies still slept in their boxes, the Honourable Marmaduke Smallwood tied a knot with tongue which he can never untie with his teeth. To wit, he married a common Covent Garden trollop, here, in the chapel of His Majesty's Prison of the Fleet . . ." Got it?'

Her patchy wig now askew and her heavily painted make-up starting to smear, Lady Anastasia Ashby de la Zouche, Baroness Penge, Countess of Clapham, thrust both her hands through the grille and gripped tight, the better to keep her place at the front of the heaving crowd.

At sixty years of age, her ladyship was in prison for debt. It was not the first time. She owed her druggist a mere trifle of six shillings, and the vile man had had the temerity to slap a writ on her.

It wasn't like this when Charles was king. But the darling man had been dead for fifteen years. And meanwhile Society had collapsed. Anybody could get on now.

Merchants lorded it. A title meant next to nothing. English Society was ruined.

To make matters worse, a Dutchman was on the throne. A Dutchman! A midget to boot. King Charles was six foot four, but this nasty little flat-lander was all of five foot.

It was hard for the Countess to adjust to this new way of life, and impossible for her to take to this king. She, like most English people, detested the Dutch. After all the English had been at war with them for years. And now here was Herr Van Nincompoop, otherwise known as William of Orange, sitting on the English throne.

But as Society had changed, becoming more and more obsessed with money, profit and wealth, the Countess herself had been driven into the marketplace to survive.

Taking her cue from a number of successful women, she *wrote* for money.

She had had a play, a heroic tragedy entitled *Love's Last Wind*, performed at Lincoln's Inn Theatre. To save her embarrassment she had composed it under the nom de plume 'The Aetherial Amoret'. Despite an outstanding cast including Thomas Betterton, Elizabeth Barry and Anne Bracegirdle, it had closed on the fifth day. Her profits were nil.

' 'Twas run down by the sparks of the Town,' the Countess had explained to her friend the Duchesse de Pigalle, who was unable to attend the first performance due to a chin-cough, the second due to a quinsy, and subsequent performances were impossible because she had an attack of flatus and any other thing she could think of to escape the ordeal of sitting through two and a half hours of the Countess's rhymed verse.

2

'Young people!' the Countess elucidated. 'The brisk buffoonery and the false glittering of a youthful fancy will turn to ridicule our most delicate conversations.'

'Harrumph!' said Pigalle. 'So zat is zat! Now you know you can write a play, you need not to do it again.'

The Countess had taken the hint, given up all hopes of becoming the new Aphra Behn and turned instead to journalism. She plied her scurrilous little pieces of tittle-tattle, or blasts against quacks, or fashions, or new plays and sold them to whoever would buy.

As fortune fell, the day the debt collector thumped on her front door Lady Ashby de la Zouche happened to be between engagements, and her funds were exceedingly low.

'I bought the drugs because I was ill of an ague, don't you see?' she screamed at the bum-bailiffs who had been sent by the druggist to take her into custody. 'Is the man a simpleton that he thinks I can earn money when I am sick?'

One of the bum-bailiffs applied a hairy hand to her fore-arm. She brushed it off. 'When I am fit again, *then* I can pay him. But for the instant . . .'

At this moment the four gnarled arms of the bum-bailiffs picked her up and dumped her in the back of a cart bound for the Fleet Prison.

Hence her present confinement.

Now that she had been in prison a day and a night, she was undaunted by her surroundings, and did not appear at all troubled that she was rubbing shoulders with some of the dirtiest and smelliest people in London. She stood proudly confident of her superiority. Why, at one time she had been the mistress of a king.

Good old, dead old, Charles.

She cut a fine picture for a woman of her age. After all, most women of her age were dead. She was smartly dressed, her clothes of the finest fabrics, in the latest fashions of 1670. The only trouble was, it was now 1699.

'All of human life is here,' she exclaimed, wafting her chubby little hand at the turnkey when she was deposited at the prison door. 'Perfect writer's fodder.' She stepped daintily through the wicket gate. 'Let me drink in the atmosphere.'

She inhaled the stinking air (infused with foetid sweat and unwashed clothes; with rancid breath from hundreds of mouths full of rotting teeth; with rat droppings, and human excrement; with damp and rot and piss), then spent the whole night awake in the hope of finding a tit-bit juicy enough to expedite her instant release. Some aristocrat, maybe, confined for debt, or a well-known man of the cloth locked up for drunkenness or debauchery.

As chance would have it she was luckier than that.

Within the prison there was a chapel, a chapel which had different rules to the other chapels and churches of London. The ministers of this chapel were busy all the hours the law permitted them performing marriages for those who, for one reason or another, couldn't wait the tedious weeks required for licences and banns. First thing this morning one of the happy couples was a low-life woman and a well-known toff. News of a clandestine wedding of this nature would earn her enough for her release.

She raised her voice above the hubbub. 'Bride and groom brought here by jesting friends, whole party rolling drunk. 'Tis certain none of them will remember by lunch-time the events of last night and this morning . . .'

It was still early morning and the grille to the street was busy. Measuring only two foot by four, the aperture, criss-crossed by heavy iron bars formed the only inlet to light from the street and the only outlet for the putrefied stench to escape.

Prisoners, debtors in the main, clamoured round the tiny space, thrusting out hands to catch idly tossed coins, their desperate eyes searching the street for familiar faces, each inmate living in hope that somehow today they would find the money to discharge their debts and be free.

Elbowing a feeble old man in the ribs for better access to the grille, her ladyship started to yell. 'The bride, all pretty in pink, will be known to readers as the very complaisant assistant in the sex shop at the sign of the Civet Cat and Three Herrings in Half-Moon Passage; the groom, I may remind readers, is heir to half of Hert-fordshire.'

In the shivering cold of the street Godfrey, Lady Ashby de la Zouche's ancient steward, scribbled frantically on to an old scrap of paper. 'Got it, ma'am,' he said, licking his pencil.

The scrum behind her pushed and squeezed until the Countess feared she might be crushed to death, while groping hands reached over her shoulders and under her arms trying to get to the front.

'You've 'ad yer turn, Madame Stuck-Up Hoity-Toit,' yelled a male voice some feet behind her.

Undaunted she sucked in another lungful of acrid air and rattled on. 'Take it to Mr Cue, the printing shop under the sign of The Laughing Painter in Shoe Lane.

5

And come back here with the money and . . .' At that instant, before she could finish her sentence, a group of lusty men succeeded in prising her ladyship from the grille and sweeping her backwards through the mob.

'. . . AND GET ME OUT OF HERE . . .' she bellowed in the general direction of the grille and Godfrey beyond it.

She was rudely dumped in a puddle of what she presumed was urine, and, primly lifting her skirts, stepped delicately out of it again.

'Fan me, ye winds, but that was a tight squeeze!' she exclaimed, and waddled demurely to the chapel door to take up her post again. Who knows, maybe more covert nuptials would be taking place later in the day. Folk streamed into the place, all marrying on impulse.

A chubby, sweating priest flopped down on the bench beside her, fanning himself with a copy of the Order of Service.

'Heavy day?' inquired the Countess ingenuously.

The priest sighed and nodded. 'When isn't it?'

'It's quite a place, the Fleet Prison, don't you think?' The priest nodded.

'Of course, a lady of my position seldom finds herself in such an abode.' She nudged him in the ribs and winked. 'But it was a mistake. I shall be released shortly, when they realise their error.'

The Minister of the Lord went on fanning himself.

'Had some pretty famous inhabitants here in its time,' she gabbled on. 'There was William Wycherley, the dramatic poet, you know – *The Country Wife*?' The priest's face was inscrutable. 'Bit coarse, his work, cuckolds and eunuchs and things. And there was that damned Puritan and woman-hater, Prynne. You don't happen to be a Puritan, do you?'

The priest shook his head. 'Church of England.'

'I could tell at a glance,' she smiled. 'There was a clergyman, like yourself, banged up in here too. John Donne. "Go and catch a falling star" you know . . . Marvellous poet.' She leaned back against the greasy wall. 'You yourself, in your office of chaplain, must see some celebrated personages . . .' she left the sentence dangling enticingly.

'You're looking for scandal!' snapped the priest rising from his short repose. 'Well, it'll cost you.'

Her ladyship plunged her hands deep into her pocket and rattled them about. She fingered eight pence. Not enough to last her the rest of the day, what with turnkey and tipstaff's fees, the cost of meals and bed – albeit that the bed consisted of a piece of sacking spread out over the flagstoned floor. She daren't risk it. She jumped to her feet and flung herself round at him, in counterfeit outrage.

'Scandal!' she whooped. 'All of my acquaintance know that I have always abominated the very word! I was simply expressing an interest in your work.'

'Work!' He peered at her over his half-spectacles. 'I just say the words, join their hands, and take the money.'

Her ladyship gulped. Was this a man of the cloth? 'But I thought . . .'

'You didn't think. I'm trying to earn enough in fees to get myself out of here, madam. The same as you.' He strode back into the chapel.

*   *   *

7

In the keeper's office near the entry gate, quite a different piece of commerce was taking place. Amid the stacks of books, the papers, the chains and locks and keys, sat the keeper himself. His breeches were down and on his lap, bouncing up and down, was a woman with a particularly large and white bosom.

'Oh, you're so big. What a man!' she cried, glancing down over his shoulder at the lists of incoming and out-going prisoners spread out on his desk.

Damn, those weren't what she wanted.

'Oooh, you are the master,' she wailed, reaching out and swiping her hand across the desk to shift things about a bit. 'You stud, you tomcat.'

'Body parts,' he grunted into her wobbling bust. 'I need you to mention body parts.'

'Thighs,' she moaned. 'Bosom.'

His snorting instantly became faster.

She pulled back a little in the vigour of her activity. She didn't want him to come so soon. Not until she had the information she needed.

Alpiew did not usually give her favours freely, but had decided that her present circumstances demanded excep-tional action. She liked an active and exciting life, but for the last few years it had been a constant repetition. First she would get a small job, like selling at a market stall, dressing the players, pouring strong waters in a tavern, or handing out towels in a bagnio. During these escapades she had made many friends around Covent Garden: prostitutes, brothel keepers, link-boys. Then she would say something she thought was funny but which was taken the wrong way and next thing she knew she was dismissed from the job. More often than not her anecdote recounted some sexual pass which had been made by the master of the establishment where she was currently working. They all did it. It was the fault of her bosom, she knew that. She'd never quite understood what these men saw in her snowy breasts. As far as she was concerned, they were simply an impediment to lying on her front or running fast. But all the men she ever worked for got a passion for them and thereby the wretched things inevitably landed her in trouble.

As she bounced, she remembered, with a pang of sadness, her youth, living as maid to a real lady. She'd been with her since the Great Plague had killed both her parents when she was five. Then the great lady had taken her in. She'd spent the happiest fifteen years of her life there, until her breasts suddenly tumbled out of her body and her ladyship's husband took a shine to them, and next thing you know, she was out. Since then it had happened again and again.

Once a man had had a fondle, and she'd made a joke about it and found herself back on the street, it didn't take long before her money ran out. Then she'd lose her lodgings and next thing she'd wind up in here. She'd use her ingenuity, more often than not call upon her friends in Covent Garden to have a whip-round, get out and start all over again.

'You've stopped talking,' snorted the keeper. 'Come on, body parts . . .'

'Arms, hands, ears, nose . . .' Alpiew's eyes surveyed the desk. 'Mmmm . . .' Where the hell was it? 'Navel, legs, feet!' Invoices, wages . . . she read. 'Toes, fingers!' Ah. Eureka! Her eyes focused on the document she wanted to see: 'Fleet Marriages for first week of March'.

She scanned down the list. 'Jones, Smith, Brown . . .'

'Body parts,' he squawked into her cleavage. 'Not men's names.'

'Oh yes . . . Bosoms, breasts, bubbies.'

It was Molly Cresswell who had suggested she make an attempt at this, her new enterprise. Mr Cue, the printer in Shoe Lane, was looking for someone witty to ferret out gossip for his paper, the *London Trumpet*. 'Well,' said old Ma Cresswell, 'there are few in London wittier or nosier than you, Alpiew, you little baggage.'

Bad luck for her that her landlord had got her thrown in here before she could try her hand at ferreting out some gossip. But having arrived in the Fleet Prison, Alpiew realised she could use it to her advantage.

She was still peering over the keeper's shoulder, nearing the end of the Fleet marriage list when she saw it: the Honourable Marmaduke Smallwood. Bravo! Not many people would be privy to that juicy bit of information. Married in the Fleet! And to the slut from the sex shop! Watch out Mr Cue! Now that she had got what she'd come for, she wanted this dull little episode of sexual congress to finish.

'Shoot!' she shrieked. 'Bottom, arse, fanny.' Then she looked down into the keeper's face. 'Cunt, cunt, cunt, cunt,' she shouted, and meant every word of it.

Her ladyship knew that the staff at the Fleet Prison were not renowned for their scrupulous honour. The money would be coming in to effect her release, and she wanted to make sure it didn't disappear into the breeches pocket of the keeper.

So, having given Godfrey an hour to get to Mr Cue's and return to the wicket gate, she decided to loiter near the keeper's office. She dawdled in the corridor outside, within sight of the main gate.

At the sound of an urgent clang, two turnkeys slid open a grille.

'Who goes there?' said one.

'Money for a prisoner's release,' came the reply. It was a strangely high voice, not Godfrey's (unless he'd had a very bad accident en route). Her ladyship puffed with pride. It was probably one of the printer's runners.

A scrawny but petite hand thrust an envelope through the aperture, and one of the turnkeys took it.

Her ladyship took up her position and watched the envelope carefully as it was carried to the keeper's door. She'd seen the mountebanks and prestidigitators doing their tricks in Covent Garden. She knew how quickly a full envelope could go up a sleeve and be replaced with an empty one.

Three loud knocks and the keeper opened.

'Prisoner's release money,' bellowed the turnkey.

The Countess poised herself, leaning forward, ready to claim her release, when, like a whirlwind behind her, a swish of skirts sped along the corridor and then some woman pushed her out of the way. Her ladyship teetered for a moment and then crashed to the floor in an inelegant pile.

'That'll be for me, darling,' said Alpiew, beaming at the keeper.

As her ladyship scrambled to her feet, the keeper looked down into the envelope.

'Banker's promissory note,' he read, 'drawn against the account of Cue the Printer, for the release of . . .'

The Countess stepped forward, giving Alpiew a shove in the ribs. 'Me!' she squawked.

Alpiew, outraged by this blatant hoax, grabbed at the Countess's hair. It came away in her hand, being a rather patchy red wig.

The Countess's hands flew to her grizzled and practically bald pate and she screamed, lashing out to grab at Alpiew's bodice string. As Alpiew retaliated, striking out in the general direction of her ladyship's skirts, her bosom tumbled from its confinement. Instantly her hands pulled back, demurely to cover her snowy breasts and prominent pink nipples.

Both of the turnkeys and the keeper stood transfixed at the wonderful sight of the pair.

In the brief hiatus, the Countess took one final lunge at Alpiew, who staggered backwards. Then, brushing herself down in triumph, her ladyship stepped forward to claim her release from the keeper. 'I am Lady Anastasia Ashby de la Zouche, Baroness Penge, Countess of Clapham, and I claim my release,' she announced firmly.

Alpiew, on the floor, frantically stuffing her bosoms back into the corsets from which they had escaped, looked up, and a tear sprang to her eye.

'Your ladyship?' she stammered. 'Lady Ashby? Can it be you?'

The Countess glanced down at the tumbled slut, and smiled with as much grace as her black teeth and gummy maw allowed. 'How lovely to be recognised. Yes.' She beamed graciously in the general direction of Alpiew, making sure the men were aware of the moment. 'It is I, Lady Anastasia Ashby de la Zouche, Baroness Penge, Countess ... etcetera, etcetera ...' She turned again to the keeper. 'Anglesey House, German Street, St James's ...' She stretched out her hand for her release papers. 'I think you will find everything is in order,' she announced, still coyly smiling.

Alpiew was on her feet now.

'Your ladyship? It's me. It's your own lost Alpiew, madam. Don't say you have forgotten me? Your kidnapped orphan?'

The Countess turned and peered at her. 'Alpiew? Can it be my own dear Alpiew? It can't be true ... ? I thought you were dead ...'

'No, madam. Abducted, but alive.'

The two women fell into each other's arms and, with much sighing and wiping away of tears, re-acquainted themselves after an absence of almost twenty years.

'Oh, Alpiew, Alpiew,' sighed the Countess.

'Oh, my lady,' crooned Alpiew.

'This tender, darling little child,' said the Countess, pointing towards the forty-year-old woman in her arms, 'was my very own personal maid for years and years,' she cried. 'She was practically a daughter to me. Till one night, she was vilely kidnapped by robbers, along with my vast and irreplaceable collection of silver and plate, and I have never set eyes on the pretty darling again, till this instant.'

'Oh, madam, madam,' wept Alpiew. 'What sagas I can tell you of that dreadful night, and how I woke bound and gagged and locked up in a chest and placed on a buccaneer's clipper bound for the New World.'

13

'Captured by privateers and pirates!' the Countess wailed. 'My poor Alpiew . . .'

The keeper coughed to regain attention. 'Excuse me, ladies, but have you lost all interest in your imminent release?'

Instantly the Countess regained her composure and stepped forward. 'Of course not, you buffoon. Just give me the papers and I shall take my instant leave of you . . .'

The keeper presented her with the release paper. 'To release one female, aged about forty, going by the name: *Alpiew*. Signed George Cue, Esquire.'

The Countess grabbed the paper and scanned it. Her jaw dropped. 'But this is . . .' For once she was lost for words.

'Mine,' said Alpiew, stepping forward and snatching the document from her ladyship's hand.

The turnkey was already at the wicket gate, ready to open it with a brown key bigger than St Peter's.

Alpiew took a few steps and turned back to the Countess. 'I won't forget you, madam,' she said and stepped out into the street and freedom.

By now, the Countess had regained the power of her jaw and it flapped up and down. 'The little dissembling villain, that perfidious, treacherous jade . . . I'll give her New World when I get out of here, I'll show her! Ingrate . . .'

The turnkeys stepped forward and took hold of her.

'She has cozened me, yet again.' She wriggled and squirmed in their strong grasp and she was whisked up the dank corridor. 'She mumped me of my snip! Once more! 'Tis certain she ran off with the plate herself. Certain. And my husband. Stole him too. Phough! The canting little nimmer. "New World" indeed. When my foot hits her backside she'll be heading for the New World all right . . .'

Alpiew chewed on the inside of her cheek as she glanced through the contract. A fortnightly scandal sheet, to fill two sides of foolscap. Pay: seventeen shillings cash.

She glanced up at Mr Cue, who was gazing steadily at her. If she wasn't wrong there was a keenness in his eye. He was eager for her to sign.

'Make it twenty shillings and it's a deal.'

Twenty shillings, thought Alpiew would just do, get her a nice lodging, with a bed and everything, and enough money to keep her in food and firewood.

'Twenty shillings!' exclaimed the printer. 'Am I King Croesus that you expect so much?'

'I ain't never heard of that cove, Mr Cue, but if he was willing to pay proper money for good scandal, then yes. One pound per week.'

Mr Cue shook his head. 'Funds won't run to it, I'm afraid.'

Alpiew rose from the rickety chair in the printer's front office. This was facing, she realised. She'd seen her ladyship do it often enough when playing at basset. 'One must face,' she had explained to Alpiew as a young girl, 'when one knows one is on to a good thing. If your hand is good, you face.'

Well, her hand was good. That was sure.

Mr Cue opened the door for her.

God's wounds, he was letting her go! This was not how it was meant to be. He was meant to agree to her demand. She held up her head and walked steadily towards the open door.

'Eighteen shillings and sixpence,' he said as she stepped over the threshold into a brisk chill wind.

Eighteen and six, thought Alpiew. So no firewood.

She paused. She'd seen her ladyship in this situation too. If he was coming back at all, it proved he was interested. 'Twenty shillings,' she said, striding out into the yard.

He followed her and stood by the door with his hands on his hips. 'Eighteen and six and not a farthing more.'

'Twenty,' cried Alpiew, moving into the street. She was about to turn back. Winter didn't last all year, after all. Eighteen and six was better than nothing. She could live without a fire in the grate. At the moment she didn't even have a roof over her head. If it was this cold now, how icy would it be by nightfall? And without the job she'd be sleeping on the street tonight.

She turned, and was surprised to find herself face to face with a fat sweaty woman in a mob cap.

'Seventeen shillings, and get on with it,' bellowed Mrs Cue, the printer's wife and business partner, her sleeves rolled up, her face red, her hands black with printing ink. 'Seventeen shillings, Mrs Alpiew. We need the copy, writ in a fair hand by Friday of each week. Here's the contract. Sign.' The hot sweaty woman held out a large sheet of paper and a dripping quill.

'I need time to read this,' said Alpiew, wishing she'd snapped up Mr Cue's offer of eighteen and six. Dealing with his wife was not something she could manage. She'd never known how to handle women, particularly indignant ones.

'Don't push your luck, Mrs Alpiew,' said Mrs Cue, gesturing her husband back to work at the press. 'You're on probation. We need juicy tit-bits, and fast. There are others panting for this job. We picked you only because your use of a fit young street urchin to get your information to us was more efficient than the creaking ancient retainer who brought the rival's story.' Alpiew thanked her lucky stars she had seen the child touting for trade through the grating. She'd given him threepence she'd been saving in case she needed a dry bit of floor tonight, and promised him six more if he got to the Cues before anyone else. 'What is your address? We will need that too.'

'Address?' Alpiew racked her brains, following Mrs Cue into the office. What to do? 'Why should you need my address?'

'Queries, of course. Last-minute queries. And perhaps we may get to hear of things you might . . .' Mrs Cue tapped her nose, leaving a grey smudge. She dipped a quill into the inkwell and held it out '. . . follow up.'

Alpiew slowly started writing her name, playing for time. Mrs Cue began tapping her foot.

'I suspect a little hesitation there, my girl.' Mrs Cue grabbed the top of the quill, sending ink spraying across the page. 'No address; no job,' she said, hoiking the quill out of Alpiew's hand. 'Who's to say you won't dance off with the money and we never see you again?'

Alpiew could see herself back sleeping on the streets. Bugger the firewood, she'd be lucky to get any food at this rate.

'Of course I have an address.' She racked her brain. She couldn't even remember any street names. A is for

. . . 'Anglesey House, German Street, St James's,' she said. The words were out before she remembered where she'd heard them.

Mrs Cue spluttered and guffawed. 'St James's? A slut like you? Sleeping with King Billy, are we?'

'His Majesty King William, if I may remind you, Mrs Cue, is only recently bereaved. No. I am staying with my old friend and mentor, Lady Ashby de la Zouche, Countess of Clapham.'

Mrs Cue shot her husband a look. 'Funny,' she said. 'She was after this job too.'

'I know, Mrs Cue.' Alpiew now understood why her long-lost mentor had attacked her so vehemently. 'We work together. We are a partnership.'

Mrs Cue nodded, still sceptical. 'Well, I'll bring the signature money round there for you this afternoon. In person. All right? About four.'

'All right.' Alpiew tried to disguise a gulp. Now there was divine justice! She'd got the job, but the Countess would get the money. 'I'll see you there,' she croaked. 'At four of the clock.'

Alpiew stood for a moment, leaning on the stout oaken palings, watching the coal-barges ply up and down the Fleet Canal. Rosy-faced lightermen battled with lumps of floating debris and chunks of ice to get their boats out on to the river to load or unload their cargoes into the clippers and sailing ships moored in the deep Thames water.

She thought back to the dreadful day all those years ago when she and her ladyship had parted company.

Her ladyship's husband was a foxy cove. Short, with a

pointed beard like Good King Charles the first, what lost his head. He swaggered around, all five foot two of him, winking at the lasses and making filthy insinuations behind the Countess's back. The cook had a word for him. 'Sir Pompous Braggadocio', she called him. He was a sort of merchant, Alpiew knew, though he never seemed to go to work. Something to do with ships and the West Indies, by all accounts. Made enough money, but it was common knowledge that his titles and all his finery were bestowed upon him as presents from the other Good King Charles, the second (the beheaded one's son) to her ladyship.

Although Alpiew was her ladyship's darling, his lordship had never paid much attention to her as a child.

It was her ladyship who had taken her in and fed and clothed her, and taught her to read and write. She had given her the name Alpiew, because the orphan child had been brought to her in the middle of a game of basset, a few minutes after her ladyship had won a very large sum of money on a call of 'Alpiew', which meant something to do with sevens and trumps, but Alpiew herself had never quite got to the bottom of the word, not being much of a card-player herself.

Down on the canal the men on the lighters were calling to each other, their voices muffled by woollen scarves. The river was starting to ice over, they were saying. Tonight would be a cold one. Had to rush, or the ships would be frozen in the town quays.

It was a cold night too when his lordship had come up into Alpiew's tiny bedchamber and demanded she come down instantly to the dining room. He needed her assistance.

Her ladyship, she knew, was out playing cards with her friend the Duchesse de Pigalle.

Alpiew pulled her mantua on and, without stopping to lace, threw a light wrapper over it, descended the shadowy steps and marched into the dining room.

His lordship was there with a handful of shady-looking rogues, their faces all covered, like the boatmen on the canal today, with scarves and hats pulled low over their eyes. The only illumination in the room came from the dying embers of the fire. The men were busily piling all the silver and plate into huge sacks. Reflections from the metals sparked and twinkled in the dancing red light.

'Tell her ladyship, when she returns from her evening's gaming, that I am gone to seek my fortune,' said his lordship with a smirk. 'She's too old for me. Forty i' faith, and fat with it.'

Alpiew dived for a sack bulging with silver, which he had slung over his shoulder. 'Then begone with you, sir,' she said, 'but leave her ladyship's precious things behind.'

His lordship grabbed at Alpiew, tugging the sack from her grasp. As he did so his hand lighted on her fateful breast and she was undone. Undone, in more senses than one, for indeed she'd pulled on her clothes so hastily she was all but unlaced at the back. Out tumbled one white breast, then the other. Every eye in the room was upon them.

His lordship gave a low laugh and took a step forward. 'What am I thinking of, gentlemen?' he leered. 'There are more precious things in my wife's possession than cold metal.' He waved a hand towards a burly-looking fellow, two yards in height. 'Bag her up too, Tom, this jilt is coming with us.'

Alpiew struggled like a wild thing, but it was to no avail. Though in the skirmish she managed to lose her shoe, tug out a long lock of hair and cut herself on a broken piece of glass, leaving a smear of blood on the wainscot. She tried, but did not have time to imprint the word 'HELP' upon the wall. She got as far as 'HE', which at least left a clue, before she was knocked unconscious.

That night she awoke to find herself on a ship at sea, bound she knew not where.

Alpiew gazed down at the murky canal water and shook herself back into the present. At least in wintertime you could stand here and dawdle. In the summer you'd suffocate from the stench.

What a position she was in! Behind her lay Shoe Lane and the printer's job, ahead of her the Fleet Prison, and her only means of pulling it off: Lady Ashby de la Zouche.

She had decided that she must honour her debt and indeed her promise to the Countess and go halves with her on the writing job. But to procure the job at all at least one of them had to be in the Countess's house in a few hours' time.

Her first thought was that she must effect her ladyship's release.

She crossed the bridge and walked briskly up through the Fleet Bridge market, past the brawling concert of fish-women and stallkeepers selling puddings and pies. She was starving hungry and the smell of pastry and bread inspired her stomach to let out a low growl.

A quack was trying to off-load a cart of ominous-looking green bottles: 'It cures all symptoms – sinking of the spirits, palpitation of the heart, twisting of the guts, intermitting fevers, hot and cold fits, consumptions, violent colics, and the green sickness,' he shouted, waving one of his bottles in the air. 'And brings away worms of all sorts of lengths and shapes, and leaves the body in perfect health.'

Alpiew made a sharp left turn and crossed the street leading to the prison.

Running to avoid an oncoming hackney carriage, she collided with a large fat woman. Alpiew knew her as a market-woman from Covent Garden. ''Ere, Mrs Alpiew, Simon the pot-boy from the Frying Pan and Drum was after looking for you.'

Alpiew thanked her for the information and scurried along to the prison.

She spoke to the turnkeys through the peep-hole in the main gate, but they refused to tell her the Countess's circumstances. As far as Alpiew knew she might have debts of hundreds of pounds.

She trotted round to the prisoners' grille and lingered there for a while, peering through, scanning the rabble inside clawing at the bars.

'Give us a penny, lass . . .'; 'Help free a man who has seven children to support . . .'; 'Give us a flash of your petticoats . . .'

Alpiew stooped to get a better look inside.

'Phwor! There's a lovely pair o' bubbies . . .'

A group of rowdies at the grille started cat-calling and whooping out innuendoes.

Alpiew yanked the front of her bodice up a bit.

'Countess!' she yelled. 'Lady Ashby de la Zouche!'

The men got noisier. Alpiew realised she was never going to get through to her ladyship this way.

She made for St James's, the Countess's home.

When she arrived at the German Street front door about an hour later she leant against the link-post and looked up at the façade. What a place! It was even bigger than the house her ladyship had lived in when Alpiew was her maid-servant. Maid-servant, that was it! With a house this size no doubt her ladyship had a large equipage. Someone inside must be able to help.

She strode up to the elegant front door and stood under the portico straightening down her skirt before ringing on the bell.

She waited. She heard shuffling footsteps inside, then nothing.

She looked down at herself. Maybe someone had looked out of the window and seen her, and taken her for a beggar. She rang again.

A rustle, and then the door opened a crack.

'Yes?' The voice was grumpy, male and old. She could see little else but a couple of wrinkles and one bloodshot eye.

'It's about her ladyship,' whispered Alpiew.

'Not here,' croaked the man. His thin lips revealed only gums. Then the door slammed in her face.

She battered at it for a few moments before giving up.

Alpiew left the house and walked along the way to the thronging Hay Market. The clock struck the half hour.

She passed a barber's shop displaying the sign: 'Money paid for Live Hair.' She fingered her tresses, piled high up on her head. She could sell her hair! Why didn't she think of it before. It wouldn't be the first time she'd pranced around London like a Covent Garden slut who'd been taking the mercury cure for the clap. She flushed hot, thinking of her escapade with the keeper this morning. It wasn't her usual way, giving sex to men. She crossed her fingers and prayed to the Lord that he hadn't given her a dose of the pox, or got her a belly-full. A baby was the last thing she needed.

Farriers and provender merchants chatted idly around her as she gazed at the barber's shop window. 'Gone to Lunch' said the sign on the door. So she couldn't sell her hair just yet.

The market was closing down for the day. Half past two.

A grazier was stacking bundles of hay on the back of his wagon. The horse, snorting puffs of white steam into the frosty air, pawed the earth waiting to be off back to the country.

Alpiew leant against the tethering post and tossed things over in her mind. She'd wait for the barber to come back and, while she was waiting, think things through and see if she could come up with a better plan.

It was quite simple. She had the chance of an income, *if* she could free the Countess.

The horse nuzzled her neck. Alpiew raised her hand and stroked the velvety muzzle. 'What would you do, old boy?' she whispered.

To free the Countess, she needed money. How much money she didn't know. How to get it was an even harder conundrum.

She stroked the horse's mane. 'Farewell my gaudy hopes!' she cried to no one in particular.

To get money that quickly there were only two ways she could think of: to steal it, and risk being thrown back into gaol with little chance of release, or to prostitute herself.

'Oh, there you are!'

Alpiew turned to see a young man smiling down at her. 'Oh hello, Simon,' she said. 'What did you want me for?'

'I was wondering if you could cover for me tonight?'

Alpiew furrowed her brow. 'Can you pay me in advance?'

Simon shook his head. 'Only with bachelor's fare, I'm afraid, bread, cheese and kisses.'

Bachelor! That was it! Why didn't she think of it earlier.

'Simon, my boy. You have to help me.'

'But I . . .'

She slapped him heartily across the back. 'Take no more than an hour of your time.'

Simon looked at her with a worried expression. With Alpiew he knew things were rarely straightforward.

'Wh-what do I have to do?' he stammered.

'Simple, Simon,' said Alpiew, glancing up at the clock. 'We've only got a few minutes to spare.' She grabbed his arm and started to run. 'Come on.'

'Why the rush?' Simon panted, stumbling along at Alpiew's side.

'Canonical hours stop at three,' she shouted to him as though it was the most logical reply on earth.

'Canonical hours?' he screamed, alarmed. 'But what have Canonical hours to do with us?'

'Not much,' she replied, leaping over a mangy dog which lay in her way. 'But it's the only time of the day we can get married.'

*   *   *

25

Alpiew and Simon arrived at the Fleet at three minutes to three. She looked up at the big clock outside. 'Perfect timing.' She bit on the inside of her lip. 'Now, quickly, Simon, start counting.'

'But I don't want to marry you . . .'

Alpiew slammed her palm across his mouth.

'Shut your jabbering maw and you'll survive,' she said, banging frantically on the prison gate with her free hand. 'Come on: one, two, three . . .'

A turnkey opened the small hatch.

'Yes?'

'We've got three minutes, mister, I need to get to the chapel quick.'

As the chains clanked and the wicket gate was opened to let them in, Simon began to whimper. Alpiew gave him a kick.

'Trust me,' she whispered. 'You'll come to no harm. Just keep counting! Thirty, thirty-one, go on . . .' Then she turned and smiled at the turnkey who was escorting them along the passageway leading to the chapel.

Please God let her be there, thought Alpiew, not run off to the privy or somewhere in the bowels of the gaol.

'Sixty-five, sixty-six,' chanted Simon.

'Less than two minutes,' said Alpiew to herself.

They passed the prison tavern, crowded, as usual, with guffawing men. As they rounded the corner Alpiew saw the Countess. She was sitting on a bench outside the chapel door, lurking, pretending to be interested in her fingernails.

'One hundred and forty-four, one hundred and forty-five . . .' whispered Simon.

Alpiew gasped, stumbled and fell to the floor in a

flounce of petticoats. 'My ankle!' she screamed and the Countess peered down at her. 'Simon, love, please go on ahead and tell the kind priest I am right behind you, please to prepare for an instant service of marriage.' She looked up at the turnkey, 'I beg you, sir, could you accompany him? I will be up on my feet straightway and fit to hobble down the aisle. I fear my beloved thinks I have trapped him into marriage and will dissemble to the priest . . .'

The turnkey shrugged and disappeared into the chapel after Simon.

The Countess had taken a few steps forward and was standing over Alpiew, squinting down at her. 'I thought it looked like you!' She raised her fist and fell upon Alpiew, showering her with blows. 'You verminous, swindling minx! You viper, you serpent that I have fostered . . .'

'Hold your peace, please, my lady,' hissed Alpiew. 'I am here to release you and present you with a contract. All I need is a short letter from you. We have less than a minute.'

Alpiew speedily told the Countess the entire position they were both in regarding the Cues' job, and how they could bring it to a successful denouement.

Within the minute Simon was standing beside her, smiling from ear to ear and telling her how the priest had said no. 'Canonicals stop at three, sharp, he told me.'

Alpiew feigned disappointment. She'd seen this same scene happen to couples, day after day. The priest was a stickler for the old Canonicals. It was his pernickety nature she had been depending on.

She turned and gave the Countess a sly wink. The

27

Countess lowered her eyelids and pursed her cherry-painted lips in reply.

It was exactly five past three, when, with little ceremony, the turnkey pushed Alpiew and Simon out of the prison gates.

'There we are! I told you that you wouldn't come to any harm,' said Alpiew, elaborately rubbing her hands. 'Now if you'd care to stroll round to the side with me, Simon, we can expect delivery of a letter through the prisoners' grille.'

The letter, written hastily in the Countess's usual scrawl, explained to Godfrey that Alpiew was to have access to the house, where she was to receive Mrs Cue in the front room. Godfrey would then take the money Mrs Cue gave Alpiew to the prison and effect the Countess's immediate release.

By six o'clock Lady Anastasia Ashby de la Zouche, Baroness Penge, Countess of Clapham was re-established in her London home. By seven she and Alpiew had struck a deal which suited them both: they would work as a partnership, routing out stories and writing them for the Cues' paper. The money they would split two-thirds in the Countess's favour, but in exchange for the lion's share of the cash, the Countess would give Alpiew free accommodation at Anglesey House.

TWO

Imbibation

*The feeding of a process
by the gradual and continuing addition
of some substance.*

But Anglesey House was not all it seemed.

Built in the latter years of the seventeenth century, it had a wonderful façade, rising three storeys, with superbly ornamented sash windows. Entrance was through a panelled door, encased within an elegant portico with acanthus-topped white Corinthian pillars.

Once inside, a visitor would see an airy hall with a number of doors to each side.

Via the first door on the right one entered the front parlour. Crimson silk brocade faced the walls, ornamented with carved limewood panelling, and a delicious chimney piece over which hung a portrait in oil of the Countess in her younger days, painted with his usual satin-inspired flair by Sir Peter Lely.

There was not much furniture in the room, just an ebony inlaid dresser and a few easy chairs in mahogany padded with red velvet, but it was well made and comfortable.

Alpiew and the Countess sorted out the details of their

deal together, seated on easy chairs in front of the unlit fire in this room, while Godfrey plied them with steaming dishes of chocolate.

Once Alpiew had signed and sealed, the Countess took her by the hand and led her through the rest of the house.

'We have much catching up to do, little Alpiew,' said the Countess. 'First you must see the reality of life here.' She waddled across the hall and threw open another door.

The room was empty and stripped of all ornament, even the wall coverings were gone and the ceiling plaster was peeling and lay in small fragments on the bare floorboards.

'I fell on hard times and needs must when the devil drives. So I used my ingenuity. Stripped the place of furniture first, sold it all off, piece by piece, and thus kept the wolf from the door.'

Alpiew whistled.

'Things went from bad to worse after his lordship vanished,' wheezed the Countess, hauling herself up the wooden staircase. 'Lucky for me, when our old house in the Strand was repossessed by his creditors, the King did not forget me, and kindly gave me this place. It was only a few years before the darling old cove turned up his shoes and went to meet his maker. The timing was rather fortuitous for me. If I'd gone broke a few years later I'd have had to petition his brother. But that big sulk, James, wasn't a patch on him. Terrible Papist hypocrite.'

In all the upstairs rooms the ceilings were down, and patches of black mould spread across the flaking walls. From the top floor one could quite clearly see the stars and the occasional bird flying past.

Alpiew shivered, beginning to think she'd got the worst end of the bargain regarding her free accommodation.

The Countess opened the door to the top room and announced: 'This is Godfrey's bedchamber.' The room was freezing, bare and dilapidated as all the others.

'But . . . ?' Alpiew thought her way round the house. Godfrey may sleep in this room, but where was her ladyship's chamber? She had seen no room with a bed in the whole house.

'Godfrey is a miserable old fart.' The Countess closed the door behind her and started her descent of the rickety staircase. 'But he's loyal. I don't know many grooms who'd stay on to serve you even when the horse is sold off, and you don't have the cash to pay them.'

She turned and smiled at Alpiew. 'And I get lonely, too. Nearly all of my friends have popped their clogs – not that any friend of mine would be seen dead in that noisome Dutch item of footwear – and I always think having Godfrey in the house is rather like keeping a grumpy dog.'

At the end of the tour the Countess led Alpiew down a dark corridor towards the back of the building and proudly flung open the door leading into the kitchen.

Here Alpiew was struck at last by the warmth. The room was white, with a big iron cooking fire set in a large open fireplace. The fire roared, belching heat into the room. On one side of the room there were pieces of furniture one would not usually see in a kitchen: Comfortable chairs, bookshelves, footstools, a card-table and two large truckle beds.

A washing line hung from the ceiling, and piles of books and papers littered the floor.

31

'This is where we *really* live,' announced the Countess majestically. 'Cosy, isn't it?'

The tallow candles, positioned on ledges and tables round the room, guttered in the cold draught from the hall.

Godfrey growled from the corner. 'When you've shut the door, it will be.'

'As you can see, I ran out of money years ago,' the Countess said, clicking the door shut behind them and waving Alpiew into an easy chair close to the fire.

'But how did it come to this? A woman of your prosperity?'

'Ah, Alpiew,' sighed the Countess, moving towards the wooden table. 'The greatest prosperity is not always the most durable. High living, little saving, pilfering servants and hard luck combined can reduce the richest of beings to penury.' She waved her chubby hand around to indicate the room. 'But we live comfortably enough. To tell true, now that I've lived in the kitchen for three years I cannot imagine why others don't do the same.'

She sawed three slices off the end of a bun loaf and skewered them on a strange pronged piece of metal. 'This was used by the park-keepers round Rosamund's Pond to stab up the leaves. I prigged it. It's so useful for batches of toast.' She wafted the instrument in front of the open fire.

'Why don't you sell the place?' asked Alpiew, totting up in her mind how many hundreds a house like this would fetch. 'It's a very big house. Salubrious area . . .'

'It's only a lease, my dear. Granted to me, for the duration of my life, by Old Rowley.' She sighed and leaned back in her chair. 'Darling old boy. Now *there* was a king for you. Tall, rugged, handsome, funny, sexy and . . . well, everything a king should be. A genuine Man of Parts.' She exhaled. 'Unlike the little Dutch dwarf who rules over us now. Each time I contemplate . . .'

'Shall I prepare another dish of chocolate?' asked Godfrey, staggering alarmingly to his feet. Naturally bone-idle, he rarely offered his services, but he would do anything rather than listen to the Dutch monologue again. Once her ladyship got on to the faults of King William and his countrymen there was no getting her off the subject.

Pulling a little leather drawstring purse from her pocket and plunging her podgy fingers inside, the Countess gave a winsome smile. 'Godfrey,' she announced, 'let's celebrate. Run along to Mrs Pickering's shop in St James's Court and fetch us a bottle of primrose wine.'

When he had shuffled out, the Countess turned to Alpiew, her face tight. 'It's a long walk down to Pickering's when you're as slothful as Godfrey. So while we wait for his return with a bottle of good cheer, you can tell me exactly what happened between you and my husband.' The Countess kicked off her shoes and put her feet up on the cast-iron fender. 'I gather you eloped with him. So maybe you know where he is?'

Alpiew was aghast. How could her ladyship have thought such a thing for all these years?

'No, your ladyship. No, no and no again!' Alpiew told her the whole story: how she was woken from her slumber and witnessed the theft, how she was gagged and bagged and driven off in a cart with all the sacks of booty. She told her how she'd been loaded on board, about the voyage and how she arrived weeks later in the New World.

'They freed me from my bonds as soon as we hit the open sea,' Alpiew was rattling the story off as fast as she could. 'And lucky for me, it was the sea that saved me. His lordship was horrid seasick. And I used the time while he was indisposed to befriend the captain and several of the crew. I played them all off one against the other, and between them the sailors defended my honour for the rest of the journey.'

The Countess let out a sound like 'Harrrumph!'

'It's true, your ladyship.' Alpiew pleaded with her. 'I beg you to believe me. I didn't like the man. I hated the fact that he'd stolen from you, and when I escaped from him my only desire was to return to London and your service.'

She didn't tell the Countess that her long-lost husband, Lord Peter Ashby de la Zouche, was a womanising liar and a professional thief. She didn't recount the conversations she had overheard on board ship, where he had boasted of how he ran a group of footpads and house-breakers in London, and that he was coming to the New World to expand his business interests by burgling the rich plantation owners. 'Remember the Lady Cleveland jewellery case?' he said to a group of open-mouthed seamen with a self-deprecating smirk. 'That was me. The Peterborough House Burglary?' He gave an insouciant shrug and grinned. 'Do you know my secret, boys?'

The sailors shook their heads.

'Simple. Follow the Eleventh Commandment: "Thou shalt not be Found Out."'

Alpiew went on to tell the Countess how, within

minutes of the ship docking in Jamestown, Virginia, she had run off and then, after many struggles and a tempest-tossed voyage home by way of Hibernia, she had arrived back in London three years later. She alighted at Queens Hithe Dock and made her way instantly to the Strand to her ladyship's old house and found it demolished.

'That's right. They knocked it down a few years after I moved out.' The Countess was calmer now, and sat back in her chair. Alpiew's story had the mad ring of truth. 'It was bought by a property developer who had an idea to build a row of shops in a sort of mall, where shoppers could promenade without the hindrance of wheeled traffic. Silly nonsense! Never catch on. Mind you, there's a very good mantua-maker there, I'm told.'

'So I took to living on my wits, your ladyship,' Alpiew was about to continue with tales of her exploits in and around Covent Garden, when she heard Godfrey's shuffling step in the hall.

'I bought some ham,' said Godfrey, flapping his arms out of his coat, and scraping the frost from his eyebrows. 'Out of the change.'

Godfrey poured three glasses of wine and carved the ham and some hunks of bread while the Countess and Alpiew worked on their plan of action.

'Maybe we should have someone on permanent guard at the Fleet Chapel...' posed the Countess, looking at Alpiew, who in turn looked at Godfrey.

'Oh no,' he snarled, baring two green teeth. 'Not me. I ain't going in no prison. Have me exported to Nova Zembla, rather.'

'*De*ported.' The Countess shot him a look. 'And don't think I wouldn't...' She opened her mouth, exposing a semi-chewed bullet of meat. 'Phough!' she said, grasping her wine glass and taking a hearty swig. 'Are you sure, Godfrey, this is not the lost limb of Lot's wife? I've never known ham so salt.'

'Good for working up a thirst on a cold night,' said Godfrey, topping up the glasses.

'And why, sirrah, would we want to do that and have to face the ice of the privy all night long?'

'It appears to me' – Alpiew quaffed a gulp of wine and decided to drag the subject back to the week's work – 'that as far as the scandal-sheet project goes, we have arrived at a kind of full stop . . .'

A loud thud interrupted her.

'What was that?' She gasped and jumped up from her chair, remembering the dilapidation of the rest of the house, and imagining the ceiling would fall in at any time.

'Front door,' snarled Godfrey, taking up a lit candle-stick and shuffling across the kitchen.

'We sold the bell, you see,' explained the Countess quickly. 'Base metals can fetch a tidy sum.'

The thud recurred.

'And Godfrey rigged up a sort of drum made from an old sherry cask.' She furrowed her brow, causing a large crack to appear in the white make-up on her forehead. 'But who can it be calling on me at this late hour?' She rose and smoothed down her dress, wiping away small specks of white from her withered cleavage, while listening at the door. 'A woman,' she hissed. 'I heard your name mentioned, Alpiew. Who knows you're here?'

Alpiew shook her head. 'No one.'

The Countess inched the door open and squinted

through the draughty crack into the dark hallway. 'Mmm, well-appointed, elegant mien, gracious bearing . . .'

'Her physog?' whispered Alpiew, raising on tiptoe to see over the top of the Countess's frizzled red wig.

'Can't see it,' the Countess edged closer to the door. 'Her hood falls low and keeps it in shadow. But her voice trembles, and methinks the lady is crying.'

Godfrey advanced towards the kitchen, the candlelight flickering along the hall.

'Milady,' he called, 'and Mistress Alpiew. A lady to see you.' He scampered round the door, and whispered very fast: 'She's young, rich, handsome, upset. Says she has work for you . . .'

The Countess and Alpiew exchanged a look.

Alpiew grabbed the candlestick from Godfrey. 'What did you leave her in the dark for then?'

After a mumbled introduction in the dim hall, the Countess ushered the mysterious lady to an armchair, while Alpiew applied the solitary tallow candle to four beeswax ones in gilt mirrored sconces in the front parlour.

'A job, you say?' smiled the Countess, lowering herself gingerly on to an upholstered chair on which she knew the seat had gone. She smiled weakly as she landed. 'Do forgive us. The staff are all off sick. No fire!' Her breath came out in a white cloud.

The mysterious woman shuddered.

'I need to be assured of complete secrecy,' the woman said. Her voice was low and very quiet. 'I come to you on a very delicate matter.'

Alpiew was busy costing the woman's clothing. A blue and white satin dress. The blue was powdery, delicate, expensive-looking. The woman was obviously well off, though not of the upper classes. Probably a rich merchant's wife, Alpiew thought. Maybe in tea or spices or some fashionable trade.

'It is my husband, Beau,' said the woman in a muffled voice. 'Formerly loving, nay doting upon me, of recent days he neglects me, his wife of seven years, whole days and nights, nay sometimes whole weeks together, under pretence of riding into the country to see his relations.'

'And these relations,' Alpiew leant forward trying to get a better view of the woman's face. 'Where are they to be found?'

'He has *no living relatives*, unless they have arrived from the Indies with no warning. For so far as I know, he has only a brother living, and the man works for the Carnatic League in a place thousands of miles away on the Indian coast, called Madras.'

'Ah yes, dear old Madras!' The Countess nodded sagely. She'd never heard of the place.

'But in the meanwhile I have discovered terrible things: many valuable pieces of small furniture I had are disappeared. I must find the harlot who has stolen from me . . .'

'A harlot has broken into your house and stolen your furniture?' said Alpiew, indignant.

The Countess waved her to be quiet.

'I believe my husband is stealing from me,' the woman whispered. 'And that he is doing so to keep some strumpet in high style, and it is to her loathsome bed that he disappears on his nocturnal absences.'

'Why do you come to us, madam?' asked the Countess, slightly perturbed that anyone should think her an expert on the subject of adultery or, for that matter, harlots.

'I asked Mr Cue, who is an old friend of my father's, if he knew anyone good at searching out scandal. He told me that this very day he had engaged you for that exact purpose.'

'You want us to write about it in the paper?' said Alpiew, incredulous.

The woman grabbed hold of Alpiew's arm, and pulled her close. 'No word of this matter must ever come out. If it does I will cut your throat.'

She let go, and Alpiew staggered back, making a mental note to keep clear of the woman's grasp in future.

'Treachery and profligacy are not in the character of my Beau. I love him as I love virtue and happiness. I want him to return to my arms. Despite the anguish caused by his ungrateful, negligent and contemptuous treatment of me, I would like him to repent his transgression and return to me. Either that or . . .' The woman paused to wipe a tear from her cheek.

'Or . . .' The Countess held her breath.

'That he be gone. Gone forever. Never to return.'

Alpiew let out a silent whistle. 'You don't want us to . . . ?' She daren't finish the sentence.

The woman pulled out a purse and removed two golden guineas.

'I want you to follow him. Follow him day and night. Follow him to his whore, that I may at least know the name of this *thing* who is my rival for his love.'

The Countess's eyes were transfixed by the glimmering coins. 'And . . . ?'

'I give you one now.' She held up a single coin, as though it was communion bread. Faster than a lizard's tongue the Countess's hand whipped up and snatched it from her slender fingers.

'The other,' the woman said, dropping the second coin back into her purse, 'you get when you bring me information of the whore.'

The woman rose, causing all the candles in the room to gutter for an instant.

'One moment,' said Alpiew. 'It may be necessary to take chairmen or hackney coaches, to follow your husband into taverns and dine at ordinaries and other places which cost money. Who will pay for those items?'

'Make a list of expenses, with receipts, and I will reimburse you in full.'

The Countess smiled. This enterprise was sounding better and better. 'How may we know him, this husband of yours?'

'He has the form of an angel, his voice is like celestial music. He is tall of stature, his mien and carriage upright and noble. His name is Beau. Beau Wilson. His only flaw, if flaw it can be called, is a small scar high on his right cheekbone. A scar won at sea, loyally defending his king at the battle at La Hogue.' She handed a piece of paper to the Countess. 'This is the address of our town house. You may suppose that any elegantly attired man of my former description emerging from the front door will be my husband.'

Mrs Wilson was in the doorway now, ready to leave. 'You must not communicate with me at all. Any pieces of news or informations you may garner, you will keep to yourself. I will come here and interview you after a few days.'

When Mrs Wilson had gone, the Countess and Alpiew

extinguished the candles in the front room and returned to the warm kitchen to discuss the project.

'The lady was very pretty,' said Alpiew, standing with her back to the fire and gulping down the primrose wine. 'Why would a man dance after a harlot if he had such a pretty wife at home?'

'Pretty, say you,' exclaimed the Countess, pursing her lips and lifting her eyebrows, and thereby causing another chunk of make-up to land in her cleavage. 'She may look pretty to you, but I'd wager she's naught but paint and plaster.'

'Talking of wagers . . .' said Alpiew and demanded to see the money.

'I am keeping it safe.' The Countess patted her skirt and lowered herself into an easy chair in front of the fire. 'Godfrey, pour us another bumper of wine.'

Alpiew snatched up the bottle. 'I'll do it quicker,' she stooped to fill the Countess's glass first then topped up Godfrey's and her own. Then she walked over to the other side of the kitchen and bent over the candlestick on the dresser. She opened her fist, revealing the coin which she had filched from the Countess's pocket.

'It's a fake,' she declared. 'I know. I've seen them at the theatre. Simply wood, gilded.'

Alarmed, the Countess stabbed at her skirts, grabbed for her empty purse and then lowered at Alpiew. 'Once a bung-napper, always a bung-napper!' she announced to the air. 'I am in partnership with a professional pickpocket!'

Alpiew put the coin to her mouth and bit hard. 'Ouch!' She reeled back, holding on to her teeth. 'Well, I'm wrong. It's bona fide gold, all right.' She tossed the golden guinea into the air for the Countess to catch. 'Congratulations, your ladyship! We're in business.'

At dawn Alpiew and the Countess were stationed in a mercer's shop doorway opposite the Wilsons' home, near Ludgate Hill.

They watched a variety of servants and deliveries go into the house, but no one came out. The sun rose. The Countess started to yawn. '"No Trust by Retail",' she said, reading the sign over the door. 'Strange words to put in gold capitals.' She read some of the signs in the display window: '"Garden Silks, Italian Silks, Brocades, Cloth of Silver, or Cloth of Gold, Geneva Velvet, English Velvet, Velvets Embossed."' She turned to Alpiew whose eyes were firmly fixed to the Wilsons' front door. 'Rather poetical, don't you think? Lovely chunkering rhythm.' She read on, beating out a rhythm against her skirt. '"Fine Thread Satins, striped and plain, Mohairs, Sagathies and right Scotch Plaids."'

She started to jig a little. 'If only we had a fiddler! They'd make excellent words for a jig.' She sang and danced on the spot. 'I myself was quite a dancer once, you remember, Alpiew. That's what drove the King mad about me. "Fine Thread Satins, striped and plain, Mohairs, Sagathies and right Scotch Plaids."'

She was executing a rather complicated piece of foot-work when Alpiew elbowed her in the ribs. 'Might this be him?'

The Countess staggered and grabbed at Alpiew to regain her balance. They both peered across the road at the open front door.

In the doorway stood a tall man, placing a feathered hat over his long black wig.

'Handsome fellow,' observed the Countess. 'Can you see the scar she talked of?'

'Were I a basilisk I might be able to.' Alpiew rolled her eyes. 'Otherwise, at this distance, it would require use of a reflecting telescope.'

In the hallway behind the man there was a flash of satin. A woman came to the door to kiss him goodbye.

It was their mystery visitor from the night before, Mrs Wilson. She glanced over her husband's shoulder in the direction of Alpiew and the Countess, who, both astonished at being seen, crashed into one another in an attempt to appear like casual window-shoppers.

Mrs Wilson closed the front door and her husband set off at a brisk pace. Falling in close behind trotted the Countess and her trusty partner, Alpiew.

Beau Wilson strode along Ludgate Hill and through Lud Gate.

'God help the poor wretches within,' said the Countess as they passed the small lock-up prison within the gatehouse.

Before them, dwarfing the figure of Beau Wilson, loomed the massive, though incomplete edifice of St Paul's Cathedral.

'Almost thirty-five years they've been at work on that place,' grumbled the Countess, hoiking up her skirt to leap over a pile of horse-dung in the road. 'And still no sign of the steeple!'

The two women weaved their way through mountainous stacks of massive grey stones, mounds of lengths of timber, bubbling pots of hot pitch and gangs of dusty labourers scratching their heads and staring alternately up at the building and back to their raw materials.

As the two women rounded the busy corner of the cathedral churchyard Alpiew grabbed the Countess's arm.

'Look! He's turning to look at someone.'

Beau Wilson had stopped in his tracks and was looking sideways across the churchyard. He was smiling.

Alpiew and the Countess dived towards one of the many booksellers' stalls and held books in front of their faces while they followed his gaze.

As soon as she set her sight on the object of Beau's interest, the Countess clapped a hand across Alpiew's eyes.

It was an old man, stark naked but for his waist-length hair and carrying a lusty cudgel.

'Not a fit sight for you, young girl,' she said.

Alpiew shook herself free. 'I've seen him a hundred times. It's the Naked Man of Pest House Fields. He is always going about thus.'

Alpiew gave a sidelong glance. Beau was browsing at a bookstall further along the row, riffling through a stack of pamphlets.

'In dishabillé when the weather is cold enough to ice the Fleet Ditch?' The Countess was still watching the naked man. 'Is he an escaped inmate of Bedlam who so exposes his bare skin to the sharp pinches of so frosty a season?'

'He's a man of good learning, I believe. A kind of self-willed philosopher. He believes wearing clothes makes people catch cold. Stops the humours or vapours escaping . . .'

'Pish! Ridiculous whimsy! I'll wager you he has few proselytes.'

In disgust, the Countess focused on the book she had open before her. She shrieked and threw it back on to the cart as though it were hot coals.

'Phough! What smutty stuff is this?' She started urgently to leaf through the many pamphlets before her. Alpiew grabbed her arm and yanked her away from perusal of a debauched book entitled *Aretino's Postures* full of prints of naked men and women *in flagrante*.

'Come away, madam. You can see those another day. Our quarry is upon the move again.'

'I have no desire whatsoever to see such immodest filth,' panted the Countess, trotting across the road into Cheapside. 'Considering we were on hallowed ground, I've never witnessed so much debauchery in one morning.'

'Make way there,' yelled a gouty-legged chairman. In his chair lolled a painted lady.

'Off to her morning exercise,' said Alpiew, stepping briskly on to the pavement.

'Something we're having quite enough of,' wheezed the Countess. 'Never walked so far in all my life.'

The shops were opening up along Cheapside and Alpiew and the Countess wove their way through coster-mongers calling their wares: 'Have you brass pot, kettle skillet or frying pan to mend?' 'Two a groat and four for sixpence, mackerel!' 'Pippins, pippins, good English pippins.'

Relentlessly ahead of them the green feather bounced up and down, heading in the direction of the Royal Exchange.

Past the men selling cures for corns, glass eyes for the blind, teeth for broken mouths and plumpers for sagging cheeks, marched Alpiew and the Countess in pursuit of the green feather. They saw it make a sudden sharp right turn into Birching Lane.

'Where in the devil's name is he leading us now?' gasped the hobbling Countess, now grabbing on to Alpiew's skirts for speed.

On the corner the two women squeezed through a crowd of sallow-faced men speaking in high voices and gesticulating wildly. 'Mincing Italians!' spat the Countess, looking up to see Beau Wilson vanish into a door.

'Eureka!' she huffed. 'We have him cornered.'

Alpiew inspected the sign-board swinging above the door: 'The Amsterdam Coffee House.'

The Countess was leaning against a stone horse trough, trying to get her breath back. 'Amsterdam! Dutchmen again! The water-rats of Europe, who love nobody but themselves.'

Alpiew bit the inside of her cheek. 'How can we get into a coffee house? It's for men only. Unless . . .'

A few minutes later Alpiew was inside, offering her services at the bar. While she waited for the manager to come she scanned the room for sign of Beau and his green feathered hat.

The man was sitting alone at a table in the corner with a copy of this morning's newspaper.

The bar lady was pulling the levers on a puffing coffee-engine, which dangled over the fire swinging on a blackened iron tray. She was preparing a cup for Beau.

'He's a handsome cove,' said Alpiew, nodding in the direction of Beau's table.

'Mmm,' said the bar lady, pouring some of the black liquid into a cup. 'Don't know how they can drink this filthy Mohametan's gruel.'

'I agree,' nodded Alpiew, screwing up her face. 'Horrid soot-coloured ninny-broth. Does he drink a lot of the stuff? I abominate a man whose breath stinks of coffee.'

'Only on lecture days,' said the bar lady, laying the cup on to a tray, and moving out to set it down before Beau.

Alpiew waited on the bar lady's return. 'I don't know how you can bear it,' she said as the woman approached, wafting away a cloud of smoke which belched from an adjoining table at which four men sat puffing intensely on briar pipes. 'They smoke like dragons in this place!'

'Ay, my friends all tell me I look like a kipper after a day's work here, I am so well smoked.'

'And the lectures,' said Alpiew. 'I suppose they cough through those?'

'Oh, no,' laughed the bar lady, washing out a cup in a big wooden bowl, and placing it on the drainer. 'The lectures happen at Gresham College, up Broad Street. Mid-day, usually. Gives me a bit of a rest.'

Alpiew glanced out through the window at the street clock. They had an hour in hand.

'Do you know,' she said to the bar lady, 'I can't understand how you put up with it: the coffee, the smoke! I already feel as well cured as a piece of streaky back bacon, and I've only been in here a few minutes.' She slid down from her stool. 'Tell your master, I'll not bother him for work. It wouldn't suit me. I suffer from a dreadful chin-cough.'

Alpiew pushed through the swinging doors out into the street.

'I might get a set of those plumpers.' The Countess was puffing her cheeks in and out, like a toad. 'What do you think? Would I look younger if my cheeks were fuller?'

Alpiew looked at the Countess who already looked fairly full-cheeked to her. 'I wouldn't buy a thing from those dreadful mountebanks,' she replied. 'Except food.'

'Thank the gods for that. I'm feeling pretty sharp-set,' said the Countess, who was now lolling perilously across the icy trough. 'We've been marching around for miles at this dreadful lark; it's hours since breakfast and my stomach is crying "cupboard"!'

Alpiew nodded. 'We have some time before Mr Wilson attends a lecture at Gresham College. While he is inside, I can go seize us a bit of prog.'

'Gresham College, eh!' sneered the Countess. 'Otherwise known as Wiseacres' Hall.'

Alpiew trotted off to fetch a couple of apples, while the Countess kept watch.

'He's very handsome,' said Alpiew, munching, on her return. 'His wife was right.'

'Too handsome to be wholesome,' leered the Countess. 'I'll wager he is a great friend to his glass, before which he admires the work of his tailor for hours on end. My husband, on the other hand, was a real man.'

Alpiew tried not to roll her eyes at the very thought of *that* pompous little popinjay.

But the Countess was on a roll. 'This fellow, Beau, is in love with himself and his own shadow. No more soul than a goose, I suspect, and if I was Mrs Wilson I wouldn't spend two groats pursuing him.'

A large bull-headed man, dressed for City not Court, pushed his way into the coffee house.

'Now there's a real man,' said the Countess, pointing with her apple. 'Broad shoulders. Looks tough, strong. The other fellow is too busy keeping his complexion clear and his wig full of bounce and shine.'

Alpiew took in the mien of the man who had entered. He looked like a real thug to her, broken nose and all.

'I am as cold as a sorbet at a frost fair.' The Countess shifted uneasily on the trough. 'There must be more comfortable ways of making money.'

Alpiew was beginning to doubt whether her partnership with the Countess could continue. They'd only been at work for a couple of hours and the woman was already moaning. Alpiew tried to think of the golden guinea sitting in the Countess's pocket. She started to hum a merry tune to keep up her cheer.

'And another thing,' snapped the Countess. 'Music today isn't what it was in my day, either. Since the untimely death of Mr Purcell, who do we have composing? Mr Blow! Mr Finger!' She let out her familiar harrumph.

'There's your answer,' Alpiew gave a smirk. 'If you're cold. Blow Finger!' She held her hands up to her face and blew, interspersing her puffs with notes from the tune she had been singing. The Countess couldn't help but laugh.

'You're a better tonic than any elixirs for sale at Doctor Megrim's shop at the sign of the Pestle and Mortar,' she said, shaking her head. 'Blow! Finger!'

The pair sat, swinging their legs from the trough and blowing merrily into their cupped palms.

The coffee-house door swung open again and the thug-like man came out, his hat pulled down over his face, and marched briskly away.

A few minutes later out came Beau, who strolled away in the opposite direction.

Alpiew and the Countess brushed themselves down and followed him.

Gresham College was thronging with people. Alpiew and the Countess stepped through a crowded little brick court and came into a spacious quadrangle where groups of ruminating philosophers stood in huddles gesticulating wildly and all talking at once.

'It sounds like a house-sparrows' convention.' Alpiew was on tiptoe, watching the green feather find his group.

A wizened man in an academic gown stepped in front of them and barred their way with a long staff.

'No women admitted to lectures,' he challenged.

'Why is that?' the Countess parried.

'Because their brains are too small to understand experimental philosophy.' The official smirked.

'Don't be so ridiculous,' said the Countess. 'I imagine most women have bigger brains than yours, for instance! And for the record, I have attended many lectures at the Royal Society in the past. I personally witnessed Mr Boyle weighing air!'

The official looked puzzled. 'But no women . . .'

'. . . are admitted to the Royal Society, yes, yes, so they say in all the literature, but I assure you, sirrah, I was there. The apparatus Mr Boyle used in his elaboratory consisted of a large pair of bellows, a fire, some scales and a set of fragile glass bottles. One, incidentally, was dropped by some clumsy fellow and Mr Boyle had to start afresh . . . He demonstrated by means of a J-shaped tube filled with quicksilver, and what with you and your fellows' abhorrence of a vacuum . . .'

She would have gone on, but the official banged his staff down on the wooden floor.

The men around her fell silent and all eyes turned to see what announcement he was about to make. Others in the hall, seeing that he was simply having an argument, picked up their conversations again and the Countess continued her eye-witness account. 'Mr Boyle also showed me some of his fantastical collection of oddities. The abortives in pickle, skeletons, shell-flies from the Indies, and the rest.'

'But, madam,' the official pressed on, 'the gravity of the subject matter of this lectu—'

'And talking of gravity, Mr Isaac Newton, the Master of the Royal Mint, is my next-door neighbour in German Street. Maybe I should get a letter from him? I see him often enough, darting around the garden, taking care in case another apple should land on his head.'

The official was shifting from foot to foot. The Countess was not going to give up now.

'I've also played around with your roguish magnets, and seen how a paper of steel filings pick themselves up and stand pointing, like the bristles on a hedge-hog, and a parcel of needles can be made to dance a country jig as though the devil is in 'em.'

Some of the men around her were laughing, others clapping the Countess.

She gave a coy little curtsey and bobbed up staring

impertinently at the official who was now reduced to a stuttering, flapping heap.

'So you see, I've had more practical encounters with experimental philosophy than you have, and surely it can do no harm,' she cooed. 'If, as you say, I won't understand it, well and good. Then it will be a waste of my time, don't you agree, and therefore no loss to you.' She flapped her hands about, head cocked to one side, as though to say, 'Get out of that one, you cross-biting cully!'

The official surveyed the smiling, nodding men who surrounded him.

He sighed and cleared his throat. 'You can stand at the back,' he whispered. 'But the slightest whiff of trouble and you're out.'

The Countess smiled graciously and sailed through the hall in the general direction of the green feather. Alpiew was at her heel.

A young man in a fair wig and baby-blue velvet vest stopped the Countess to congratulate her.

'Did you really see the great Boyle?' He couldn't hide his enthusiasm. 'What was he like?'

He was with a friend, a slim man in black, who stepped back and bowed to the Countess before moving off. 'I'll see you inside.'

'Sorry about that!' The blue boy blushed. 'Doesn't much like the company of women, I'm afraid. So tell me all about Boyle.'

'Oh yes, fine fellow!' The Countess was cool. Apart from the details she'd given she hardly remembered a thing about it as she had been so bored. 'It was a magnificent display. I have rarely been so absorbed.' A tube full of mercury moving two inches, she thought, what a fuss these men made over nothing! She gave another coy smile. 'I am so looking forward to the lecture today,' she said, attempting to change the subject from Boyle.

'Yes, the imminent eclipse of the sun.'

'Mmm, planetary motion,' sighed the Countess. 'My favourite!'

'There are those who say that it will bring us within a cat's whisker of the Day of Judgement, as it occurs not only at the vernal equinox, but also falls so close to the end of the century.'

'Yes,' the Countess nodded earnestly. 'Seventeen hundred. A fateful time.'

'And Saturn will be in opposition to Mars, and Mars to Star Regulus.'

'Are you going by the new or old calendar?'

'I'm sorry?'

'Do you favour the Protestant's Lady Day or Pope Gregory's new calendar which starts the New Year on January the first?'

While the Countess and the young man chatted, Alpiew was keeping an eye on Beau. He was standing in a circle of men, all looking intense and talking earnestly.

'New calendar, of course,' said the boy in blue. 'We are scientists. We have not been entering the New Year at the end of March since 1666.'

'Funny – you don't look old enough.'

'Not me personally. Scientists and . . .' The man leant forward and whispered in her ear. 'And many of us here are also Fellows of the Philosopher's Stone. The Hermetic Art. We're hoping the specific nature of the date will bring us to a maturation, maybe even a sublimation.'

'I see,' whispered the Countess with a wink. 'You're

53

so right.' She hadn't a clue what he was talking about.

The doors to the lecture room were opened and the audience flooded in.

The Countess and Alpiew positioned themselves at the back behind a brass rail, from whence they had a good view of Beau Wilson, who sat five rows from the front.

A wizened old man staggered up to the platform, and started to speak:

'The causes, properties and several natures within the axioms which govern planetary motion can be assessed by referral to divers ephemeritical tables . . .'

The Countess and Alpiew exchanged a look. Two hours of this!

'But in reconciling the differences among learned men: Aristotle and Descartes, Cardon and Copernicus, the Christian and the Arab, and while the views of Copernicus conflict with Galileo . . .'

The two women slumped back against the bench and prepared themselves to be bored out of their wits.

'Yes,' said Alpiew, strolling along the road some two and a half hours later, 'I'm with Descartes. The problems with vortices . . .'

The Countess wondered why she'd ever had the child Alpiew educated if she was going to apply her brains to such piffle.

'Where is he going now?' The Countess was squinting ahead at Beau's green feather, which was turning into a doorway with two other men. 'Let's hope it's an ordinary. I need my luncheon. I'm sick as a cushion and want nothing but stuffing.'

The two women pitched up at a maroon door with gold lettering.

'Pontacks,' read Alpiew. 'It looks like an ordinary.'

'Ay, it looks like an *expensive* ordinary.'

'But Mrs Wilson said she would pay our expenses . . .'

The Countess pushed through the door.

The room was small but well laid out. The maroon wall coverings and golden sconces gave the place an elegant air and a large gilt mirror at one end of the room made it seem twice the size.

They took a small table near enough to Beau Wilson to overhear his conversation.

While they waited for the menu they heard the men at his table talk of gold and silver and base lead, of sal ammoniac, and aqua fortis.

'Perhaps he has no woman at all,' said Alpiew. 'It seems to me that experimental philosophy is his mistress.'

The Countess leant forward. 'Not experimental philosophy. Alchymy!' she hissed. 'Listen. They are trying to make gold from base metal.'

'How do you know about alchymy?' asked Alpiew.

The Countess gave a shrug. 'The theatre, of course. Alchymists as characters always get a good laugh.'

A waiter bowed and presented menus.

'Is this more scientific garble?' Alpiew glanced down the list of available dishes, trying to make it out. 'I can read, milady, as you know, but I can't make out any of these words . . .'

'French,' snapped the Countess. 'I'll see how much of my *petit peu* of Français I can remember.'

She looked up at the hovering waiter.

'*Je ne say quoy*?' she said, pointing at an item on the list.

55

The waiter pinched his fingers together and kissed them.

'*Delicieux*, madam!'

'Good, we'll have that, then. He's saying it's delicious.' She smiled at Alpiew then ran her eyes down the list. 'Ah, and *les poussins deux jours dehors des oeufs* for me.'

The waiter bowed, took the menus and vanished into the kitchen.

'*Oeufs* are eggs,' mouthed the Countess. 'Just to be on the safe side.'

A laugh came from Beau's table and Alpiew caught the last few words. 'He believed that the malicious effects of the stars would spoil his projection.' The men were still safely upon alchymical art.

'Milady, I have been thinking . . .'

The Countess was gazing round the walls at the lovely little landscape paintings. 'Mmmm.'

'What about Mr Cue's job? We can't spend our whole time chasing after this cove. This task is naught but a one-off; our future income lies with Cue.'

'I wouldn't worry. We'll drive our quarry to ground by nightfall, I don't doubt. Tomorrow morning I'll wager we will be collecting a second guinea to match this one,' she patted her pocket. 'Then we'll be laughing. We can open an account with the newfangled banking company at the three crowns in the Strand, and live high on the hog.'

The waiter carefully placed two dishes in front of them.

'Anyway, I am enjoying this pursuit.'

The waiter poised his hands in place to remove simultaneously the two silver dish-warmers.

Alpiew gave him a beaming smile. To think that only yesterday morning she was banged up in prison, and today dining in a fancy ordinary.

As the waiter strolled off, carrying the two silver covers as though they were a pair of cymbals he was about to crash together, the Countess and Alpiew looked eagerly down at their plates.

On one lay a row of snails in a muddy green sauce, on the other two little new-born chicks with a lump of parsley butter melting down their tiny heads.

'This is a jest, I hope?' Alpiew started moving the snails about with her spoon. 'Snails?'

'I don't think so,' sighed the Countess with a grimace. 'And now I remember these are "two days out of their eggs", not two-day-old eggs.'

Unable to face the thought of putting this stuff into their mouths, however hungry they were, both women slid the food around their plates until it was appropriate to ask for the bill.

The men at the next table, having talked of nothing but furnaces and elaboratories during the whole meal, were clearly winding up and ready to go.

The Countess looked down at the bill. They had only had one course, but the total came to one guinea.

'I hope she meant it when she said she'd pay our expenses.' The Countess plunged her hand into her pocket and pulled out the guinea. 'For now we're broke again.'

'And still hungry,' groaned Alpiew. 'Nothing could get me to eat snails, your ladyship. These Frenchies are queer maggoty coves to eat such stuff and then charge a king's ransom for it.'

The rest of the afternoon the two disgruntled women trotted here and there in the footsteps of Beau Wilson. They followed him while he did a spot of shopping – a new cravat and some dressing powder for his peruke. Eventually they dragged miserably behind him in the direction of Ludgate Hill. As it was past seven, the women were hoping that he was heading for home, but he stalked right past his own front door and went on briskly along Fleet Street.

By the time he turned down into Salisbury Court the shops were all long closed and it was proving to be a cold moonless night.

Alpiew grabbed the Countess by the arm as she turned off the busy thoroughfare into a dark unlit alleyway. 'We can't follow him down there, milady. It's Alsatia. Where all the criminals live, immune from prosecution.'

'Oh, phough!' spat the Countess, pressing on. 'The laws were changed last year. They can be arrested here as well as anywhere now. No harm will come to us. You'll see.'

Alpiew still tugged at her arm. 'Truly, madam, the area has not changed. Why not wait till I run back and get us a link-boy to light our way at least.'

The Countess hesitated for a split second. 'We have no money to pay him. Come along. Our quarry is already out of sight.' She plunged on away from Fleet Street down the dark lane.

Alpiew trotted along at her side, muttering to herself, to keep up her own spirits as much as anything. ''Tis a vile verminous place inhabited by a lawless colony of hell-cats planted here by the devil as a mischief to mankind.'

The Countess was not in the mood for chit-chat. 'Hurry along. We can't lose him now. And think, Alpiew. Why is a gentleman of means entering a low-life area like this? A place renowned for hazard? This, believe me, Alpiew, is where we will discover the denouement to Mrs Wilson's mystery.'

'Then hold tight on to me, madam,' said Alpiew, gripping hard to her ladyship's elbow. 'For, speaking for myself, I am heartily frighted.'

The narrow street was dark, and at each window dark silhouettes moved in the smoky light of single tallow candles and rush lights. In entrances to even darker, narrower alleyways dusky figures lurked, some engaged in copulation, others in criminal acts of unspecific nature. All around them there was the hum of whispering voices.

Beau's footsteps were still marching ahead. And, holding each other's hands tightly, the two women trotted along in his wake.

An ale-house door opened and a thing barely recognisable as a woman staggered out. She wore no stockings, and a dirty smock. Her face, pock-marked, patched and smeared with dirt over the white make-up plastered on, wore a bitter sneer. 'Out of my path, you whores,' she shouted in the direction of Alpiew and the Countess.

The slut stumbled into the arms of a swarthy-looking fellow who was nipping nimbly across the road with a black expression on his face. His body recoiling in disgust and fear, he thrust her away. 'You coney catcher, lay off me!' he growled, throwing her to the ground before running on, looking around to the left and the right.

'He looks as though the dread of the gallows has drawn

59

the lines in his countenance,' whispered the Countess, as the surly man vanished into a dingy alley.

They heard the woman moaning in the gutter behind them. 'You nasty offspring of a dunghill, a pox take you.'

'Quick,' Alpiew tugged at the Countess's arm. 'It's so devilish dark it is hard to make our fellow out, green feather or no. I'd hate to find ourselves following the wrong cove up one of these dead-end lanes.'

They teetered along in the dark, clutching each other and muttering prayers under their breath.

'He's almost at the river,' puffed the Countess. 'He can go no further than that. He must be heading for Dorset Garden.'

'The playhouse, madam? But it's long closed down.'

'I know,' wheezed the Countess, her step increasing. 'What better place for assignation than an empty deserted theatre?'

The Countess and Alpiew sidled furtively along the long side of the building, keeping close to the wall.

The slopping of the water could be heard ahead of them. The tide was high.

The Countess held up her hands to Alpiew, and whispered close into her ear. 'Voices!'

A droning hum of male voices undercut the lapping of water.

Alpiew raised her finger to her lips, indicated to the Countess to stay still, then crawled along the ground. When her face reached the corner of the building she held back. She could hear more clearly but still could not make out any conversation. Just the odd word: 'Break the Rules . . .' 'Forgive . . .'

She inched forward, and peeped round the corner. She

had a pretty good view of the quayside, but still could not quite see the two men, who sounded as though they were tucked in under the arches of the theatre's façade. Anyone looking in her direction would see only something like a cornerstone or mud-scraper on the ground.

The purring voice continued: 'Kill you . . .'

At this word Alpiew thrust her head forward just in time to see the shadow of a large man lurch forward towards Beau, who appeared to be sitting on a low stone post at the far side of the quay. The large man whipped a piece of black fabric like a large handkerchief over Beau's eyes and knotted it behind his head.

'Into the row-boat,' commanded the man in a lowering tone. He yanked Beau to his feet and, gripping him by the arm, marched the stumbling gallant along at his side.

Alpiew had to control herself from leaping to her feet and running to save Beau, but what chance would she have against this huge bully?

The two men lurched down the river stairs and Beau climbed into the boat. The towering man seized the oars and started to row.

As the boat pulled away from the quayside, the Countess ran round into the colonnade at the front of the theatre and, squeezing herself behind a column, watched the little boat scull away into the black, fast-flowing waters of the Thames.

'Can you swim?' Alpiew was clambering to her feet, brushing herself down.

The Countess glowered. 'Don't be stupid. In those waters you'd be dead within minutes. Either of cold or putrefaction, otherwise you'll be swept away by those vortical currents you're so interested in.'

'There's nothing else we can do then,' sighed Alpiew. 'We've lost him for the night.'

'Ay,' said the Countess, half disappointed, half delighted. 'Home and supper. There's naught else for't.'

Alpiew paused. 'Oh, my ladyship!' She shook her head, and wiped away a tear. 'I keep thinking as though this business is all a game, or a play we're watching. But Beau Wilson is real flesh and blood like you and me . . .'

The Countess asked her to make her point.

'He's a good-looking fellow, and he never did us no harm. I am frighted, your ladyship. It may be that not only have we lost him for the night, but forever.'

THREE

Revivification

*The bringing of a mortified matter
back to life, or reactivating it.*

Godfrey was curled up near the roaring fire, deep into a book, when the two bedraggled women arrived home.

'I still can't think what we're going to tell the wife,' said Alpiew. 'I should have gone to his aid.'

'A caudle cup for three, Godfrey,' sighed the Countess, flopping into an easy chair.

'Cordial water, I think is nearer the mark,' said Alpiew hopefully. 'It is possible we might have been able to save him.'

Godfrey emitted a low grumbling sound and reluctantly lay down his book. Alpiew looked to the Countess, who shook her head. Take no notice. 'The question before us is simple.' The Countess leant forward, pulled off her little white gloves and held her hands out to warm before the fire. 'What to do? Shall we inform the constables? Rouse up a magistrate from his bed?'

Alpiew sighed. 'How could we explain ourselves? Why were we in Alsatia? Why were we following Beau Wilson?'

'Yes, yes. Where has he been taken, by whom? I can see that if we told the night-watch they would suspect we were not in our right minds.'

'Especially if they realised we were only released from the Fleet yesterday.'

Alpiew lifted her skirts and raised her feet towards the warmth.

'But we must tell his wife,' said the Countess, scratching her neck. 'Beau Wilson is obviously in grave danger for his life.'

Godfrey pushed towards the fire and, with a clatter, pulled a pot of hot milk from the hook upon which it had been suspended.

'If he is not dead already.' Alpiew bit on the inside of her cheek. 'But as for going to Mrs Wilson's home, I say rather you than me. The woman was quite explicit in her instructions. We are *not* to go to her house. And at this time of night 'tis no matter, for no servant will open the door to us, let alone listen to what we have to say. They will take us for a pair of tipsy trapes's.'

'But . . .' The Countess accepted the steaming cup of hot milky drink from Godfrey and blew on it. '(How I love a cup of sack posset before bed!) We may not have much time.'

Godfrey trundled back to the steamy milk pot and hoisted it back over the fire.

'I'd like to know who it was that took him.' Alpiew scratched her head. 'And why.'

The Countess shrugged. 'Probably the husband or lover of the strumpet.' She applied her lips to the little pipe protruding from the posset jar and sucked. Then passed the jar to Alpiew.

Godfrey flopped down again into a low chair with his book.

The three sat in silence for some minutes, Alpiew looking down with some disappointment at the caudle cup, before drawing in a mouthful and passing it along to Godfrey.

She ran all the possibilities through her mind. Perhaps Beau was taken for debt, or for some misdeed. Or the kidnapper was working for the husband of Beau's strumpet. Maybe he was the strumpet's pimp?

'What are you reading, Godfrey?' asked the Countess, bored now, pushing the spine of Godfrey's book so that she could see the title. Godfrey snatched the book away and turned his back on her.

'Pshaw!' gasped the Countess. 'Look what the worm-eaten numps is reading! Jeremy Collier's *Immorality and Profaneness of the English Stage*! Harrumph!'

'I agree with everything he says,' mumbled Godfrey, waving the book in the air. 'You only have to see the effect these new stage plays have on youth. Sex! Violence! No good can come from it.'

'You are a secret Puritan, Godfrey, and I won't have such thoughts aired in my house.' She huffed again. 'I've put up with you reading Quarles and Prynne and other material offensive to my sensibility, but enough is enough. Collier indeed! You'll be joining the Society for the Reformation of Manners next, with all those jealous wives who, though they have no desire to romp with their husbands themselves, resent the poor fellows having a bit of pully-hawly elsewhere.'

Alpiew sat up with a start. Could the wife have anything to do with it? How hard she had seemed when she said that if Beau was found guilty she had wished he would be 'gone forever'.

Perhaps she had arranged for him to be kidnapped!

Alpiew sank back into her seat. No. If Mrs Wilson was behind the kidnapping why would she have employed them to witness it?

'Surely you went to the theatre as a young man, Godfrey?' The Countess had risen to Godfrey's bait. 'With your lady-friends, perhaps?'

'When I was young Oliver Cromwell shut all the theatres down, and a good thing too.'

'All right then,' snapped the Countess, slurping at the posset spout. 'So what did you do for fun in the good old days?'

'We didn't have fun.' Godfrey grinned his toothless grin. 'It was banned.'

'Luckily for me,' sighed the Countess, 'I was in France during the "Troubles".' She gave a little cough, and spluttered into the cup. 'Infant that I was.'

'You only have to walk the streets today,' snarled Godfrey. 'Look at the place! All these bands of youths upsetting chairs, pulling knockers off doors, insulting women. Young men in their gangs: the Scowrers, the Tityre-tus and the rest of them. It wasn't like that in my young day. It's all because of the theatre.'

'Godfrey, my dear, you do not grasp the real problem,' sighed the Countess. 'There will always be gangs of youths on the rampage. Young men have ever behaved in a wild and unruly manner and they always will. The theatre is irrelevant to the argument. Young *men* are the problem. *Pluse sa chonge et* also *plus est la* same thing . . . or something French I can't quite recall . . .'

the Countess fizzled out and Godfrey returned to his book.

'Pigalle always says it.' The Countess scratched her wig. '*Pluse sa chonge*, something, something, French.'

'I have it!' exclaimed Alpiew. 'I shall turn Huguenot!'

The Countess span round and peered at her. 'Huguenot? Not while you're sleeping under my roof.'

'French,' Alpiew explained. 'We must inform Mrs Wilson of her husband's misfortune first thing in the morning. Then she can do whatever she thinks fit.'

'But pardon my stupidity, what has a Huguenot to do with Mrs Wilson?'

'Listen: "*Morbleu! Tettebleu! Ventrebleu! Mort de ma vie!*" You see, I know all their canting terms. Milady Wilson does not want to see me or you, but she will surely come to the door for a young French lady selling Spitalfields silk ribbons.'

The Countess gave Alpiew a nod and downed the remains of the cup of caudle in one.

'Good girl, Alpiew.' She held up the cup for Godfrey to recharge. 'Then we'll be free to press on with some juicy stories for the *Trumpet*.'

At the first stirring of the Town, Alpiew, having done a deal with the keeper of a Spitalfields French ribbon shop, rang the bell to Mrs Wilson's front door.

Some yards behind her and across the street the Countess lurked in a doorway.

A servant opened.

'*Bon jour!*' Alpiew smiled. '*Sacré bleu*, but I have some bargains for ze lady of ze 'ouse!'

Looking puzzled, the servant disappeared into the hall, leaving Alpiew at the front door. She gave a quick turn to wink in the Countess's direction.

A few minutes later Mrs Wilson, pale and drawn, stood in the doorway. A brief shudder of alarm ran through her when she recognised Alpiew. 'I told you not to come here.' She spat the words out under her breath.

Alpiew spoke over her: 'All manner of ribbons, madam, deep scarlet knots, and cherry, lemon and silver gauze . . .' Her accent had dropped altogether. She suddenly remembered it. '*Morbleu*, but zey are belle.'

Stony-faced, Mrs Wilson was running her fingers through the ribbons in Alpiew's basket. 'Well?'

Alpiew lowered her voice. 'He didn't come home last night, did he?'

Mrs Wilson shook her head.

'And I know why . . .'

Mrs Wilson froze and met Alpiew's eye.

'Your husband has been kidnapped.'

'Kidnapped?' With shaking hands Mrs Wilson picked up a strip of silver ribbon. 'How much is this one?'

'It is very belle, no? Three pence to you, madame,' said Alpiew aloud. 'Blindfolded and bundled on to a rowboat at the wharf by the Duke's Theatre.'

'I like the scarlet,' said Mrs Wilson, tears gathering in her eyes. 'When?'

'Last night,' whispered Alpiew. 'It was a huge man did it. Strong built. Rough.'

Suddenly from behind her came a loud cry. The Countess yelling at full pelt: '*SACRE BLEU*, Alpiew!'

Alpiew span round to see her partner, arms akimbo, mouth flapping up and down, white-faced through the paint, looking for all the world as though she had seen a ghost.

Alpiew followed the Countess's gaze across the street.

Striding along Ludgate Hill, smiling at all in his path, came Beau Wilson, his green hat feather flapping gracefully in the breeze.

Mrs Wilson sighed the name Beau, then looked sharply at Alpiew. 'Begone, you tawdry slut,' she snapped, shoving the ribbon back into the basket. She lowered her voice to make a quiet threat. 'No more of your theatrics, hussy, or I shall have you finished off.'

And with that remark she slammed the door in Alpiew's face.

Turning, Alpiew saw that Beau Wilson had stopped, and was engaged in conversation with the Countess.

'You were at the lecture yesterday, were you not?' he said with a relaxed grin.

The Countess, still lost for words, nodded her reply. 'Most interesting discourse, was it not?'

Beau smiled. 'I thought it was rather dull.'

Seeing what was afoot, Alpiew decided to lurk at the other side of the street. It would help their pursuit if at least one of them retained their anonymity.

The Countess was trying desperately to wipe a large drip from the end of her nose. Beau dug into his breeches pocket and produced a handkerchief. 'You can have this.'

The Countess looked at it in horror. Handkerchiefs were worth money. What might he want in return?

But Beau merely raised his hat and bidding the Countess 'adieu' marched up to his front door and let himself into his home. He seemed happy and for all the world as though he had spent a comfortable night. There was no hint of the dramatic scene the two women had witnessed. No bruises, no cuts. It was as though Alpiew and the Countess had dreamed the scene last night in the cold darkness of Dorset Garden wharf.

When Beau had disappeared into his house, Alpiew gave a sharp whistle, shaking the Countess out of her reverie of astonishment.

'What's going on?' she whispered, pulling the Countess into an adjacent shop doorway.

The Countess had wiped her nose and thrust the handkerchief into her pocket.

Alpiew shook her head. 'He looked as happy as a skylark on a summer's day.'

'It's a deepening mystery,' said the Countess, now transfixed by the strange items on display inside the shop. 'What is this place?'

'An apothecary's,' Alpiew replied. 'But where can he have been taken, and how is it that he is now free, and *why, why, why?*'

'I don't like the look of those things,' said the Countess, still fixed on the large glass vessels, full of bubbling foul-coloured liquids. 'She didn't give you any more money I suppose?'

'Of course not.' Alpiew tutted. 'We look half mad to her now. All we can do is wait here till he comes out again and follow . . .'

They stood, gazing into shops, strolling up and down to keep warm in the icy wind, until after two o'clock.

Then Beau, nicely muffled up in a great cloak, swept out from his front door and marched briskly in the opposite direction to yesterday's walk.

'Let us pray he leads us to more salubrious areas this afternoon,' said Alpiew, diving on to the road behind him. 'And no more mysterious escapades in Alsatia.'

After a brisk five-minute walk along Fleet Street, Beau Wilson turned up a short road which led them to the Lincoln's Inn Theatre in Portugal Street.

A crowd was swirling in the road outside, people hallooing each other and calling greetings.

Beau clapped his hand on the back of an old fellow in a grey wig.

A chair unloaded its cargo of a large fat woman with her pet monkey, momentarily blocking their sight of Beau. As she paraded past them into the theatre they could hear Beau laughing.

'Lucky we have those few spare shillings from the Cues' money with us,' said the Countess, squatting down on a tethering post. 'It looks as though we are about to spend an afternoon at a play.'

Alpiew groaned. 'I hate the theatre.'

The Countess saw Beau and his elderly companion move nearer the door.

'I wonder what piece is to be performed?' The Countess moved towards the door and scanned the list of presentations. 'Oh deuce, no! *Xerxes* by Colley Cibber.'

Alpiew was looking over her shoulder. 'No, madam, that was last week. Today it's *The Double Dealer*.'

The Countess threw a glance in Beau's direction. 'How appropriate.'

Beau strolled into the building. The Countess and Alpiew followed.

'The usual scrum,' said the Countess, shoving her way through a knot of laughing women.

'At least it is warm in here,' replied Alpiew as she elbowed herself to the auditorium door. 'And doesn't involve walking.'

A path was made behind them for an elegant woman who had just descended from an expensive-looking coach, complete with grand liveried equipage. A little blacka-moor child in pink satin pantaloons and striped vest-jacket, a ravishing pink and gold turban sitting proudly on his little head, marched behind her, carrying her skirts, shooing people aside.

'Madam Hoity-Toit,' said the Countess, staggering back out of the woman's path. 'New money,' she growled under her breath.

Beau went for a bench seat in the pit, so the Countess and Alpiew took seats in a side box where they could have a good view of him.

Page-boys in the theatre's livery were lighting the chandeliers over the stage, and the orchestra was playing a merry tune. The music ended, a tapping from the wings and the audience fell into a hush.

The Countess leant forward in delight as Anne Brace-girdle came on to the forestage to speak the prologue.

> *'Moors have this way (as story tells) to know*
> *Whether their brats are truly got or no . . .'*

Alpiew was thinking hard. Perhaps that was it! Maybe Mrs Wilson could not beget Beau an heir and he had gone the clandestine route to procreate?

Anne Bracegirdle swept the boxes and the men in the pit with a winsome smile.

'Whatever fate is for this play designed,
The poet's sure he shall some comfort find:
For if his muse has played him false, the worst
That can befall him, is, to be divorced:
You husbands judge, if that be to be cursed.'

The Countess dug Alpiew in the ribs. 'Apposite, apposite!'

To whoops of applause Anne Bracegirdle swept off the stage and two actors emerged from the side doors to open the play.

'Ned, Ned, whither so fast? What, turned flincher! Why, you would not leave us?' said one.

'Where are the women?' replied the other.

Alpiew looked down at Beau, and glanced briefly round the auditorium. She was aware of the strange smell peculiar to the theatre: a mélange of perfumes, some heady, some musky, some all flowers and powder. She could smell violets, and sandalwood, lily of the valley and patchouli, attar of roses, freesia, honeysuckle and musk. The theatre was not full, but it was what the players called 'a good house'. The boxes were all taken. Her eyes suddenly met the large appealing gaze of the little blackamoor servant.

Last night had been warm, but not the most comfortable of her life. She had shared with the Countess, who growled in her sleep. And as for the noises emanating from Godfrey's bed . . . She didn't like to think too hard on that. Most of all she'd lain awake worrying about the pretty, dark-haired man whose wife did not trust him. Her head was full of thoughts of murder and mayhem till the sound of milk pails and carts in the street outside signified oncoming dawn. And here was the cove, smiling, content and free and sitting not three yards from her. While the players bustled on and off she was tempted to shout out to him: 'Where were you last night, Beau Wilson?'

As the players left the stage for the interval, orange girls heaved into the pit with their baskets and started calling their wares. 'Fine China oranges; juicy ripe oranges . . .'

Many of the audience got up to go out into the cold street to smoke a pipe or stretch their legs. Some only had a single-act ticket, and planned to come back another day to see the other acts.

Beau stayed on his bench, chatting with the old fellow in the grey wig and Alpiew tried to work out what the old chap did. A doctor perhaps, or a lawyer.

'Quite good,' said the Countess to Alpiew. 'I enjoy a good Congreve . . . "Tho' marriage makes man and wife one flesh, it leaves 'em still two fools."' She chuckled to herself. 'Very apropos.'

'I wasn't listening,' Alpiew said, still gazing down into the pit. 'I was keeping my eyes on him.'

'And?'

'He was watching the play.'

'Did he blush at any of the marriage barbs?'

Alpiew shook her head.

'Looking lustfully at any particular actress? Bracegirdle? I know she makes out she's a virgin, but from my experience of working with her, I should think she's no more a virgin than I am . . .'

Alpiew shook her head. 'He laughed at Mrs Verbruggen, but who doesn't?'

'Pish! With haunches and posteriors that size I think the whore's wise to go for laughs.' The Countess pursed her scarlet lips and remembered the cruel barbs Mrs Verbruggen had made upon her own play, throwing the script to the floor, calling it a thousand names and stamping upon it.

She lifted her hand and shoved her wig slightly to the side. Pox on the trollop. She'd soon come up with some scandal on her and get her revenge.

Both Alpiew and the Countess stared disconsolately in Beau's direction.

'I wonder what did happen last night?' said the Countess under her breath. 'He looks none the worse for his fluvial escapade.'

Alpiew sighed. 'Indeed, madam, he seems positively blooming.'

Beau was waving his hand in the air. A nearby orange seller caught his eye and squeezed along the row towards him. He handed her some coins and she passed over two oranges.

Alpiew grabbed the Countess's arm. 'Did you see that?' she said, excited. 'Watch!'

Beau Wilson handed one orange to his elderly friend. He then looked briefly down at his own and, pulling down the peel with a magician's dexterity, made a fist and put it in his pocket.

'It's a note,' gasped Alpiew. 'Didn't you see? It was tucked under the skin – he's put it in his pocket without reading it.'

'At last,' hissed the Countess. 'An assignation.'

But at that moment the orchestra struck up and the players strode back on to the stage. Mrs Anne Bracegirdle as the heroine, Cynthia, was quizzing Susannah Verbruggen, who played an eccentric coquette, Lady Froth.

'Indeed, madam!' Anne Bracegirdle gave a snort. 'Is it possible your ladyship could have been so much in love?'

Susannah Verbruggen rounded on her. 'I could not sleep; I did not sleep one wink for three weeks together.'

Every line was worming its way into Alpiew's head, bending her thoughts on Beau and his wife this way then that . . .

'How, pray, madam?'

She watched the two actresses seeming to tease each other.

'Oh, I writ, writ abundantly,' Mrs Verbruggen's voice gave its familiar swoop. 'Do you never write?'

Who had written the note, wondered Alpiew? And why all that subterfuge with the orange?

'In love and not write!' boomed Susannah Verbruggen.

Alpiew decided to look round the audience, try to get all their faces stored in her head, just in case. Maybe Beau was sitting only yards away from the person who had made the assignation.

Alpiew glanced down for a moment to Beau's seat.

He was gone!

'Your ladyship . . . your ladyship . . .'

The Countess was riveted to the stage.

Alpiew leapt from her place, tugging on the Countess's arm and pointing down to the pit.

Aghast, the Countess followed Alpiew, clambering over others to get out of the theatre.

All around them the audience shushed and tutted. To leave at the intervals was usual, to rush out noisily a few minutes into an act, unforgivable.

The two women clambered down the front steps and

dived out into the street. They looked up and down and across. No sign of Beau.

Alpiew stamped and let out an oath. 'What shall we do? We've lost him again.'

The Countess had started to run off along Portugal Street towards Drury Lane.

'Hold, madam, what if he went the other way?' Alpiew stood on tiptoes at the top of the steps flapping her arms up and down as though she was making an attempt at flight, as the Countess turned and limped towards her. 'Fiddlesticks and fie,' she called into the frosty air.

The Countess flopped down. 'Maybe he's still inside,' she said, hopefully. 'Or perhaps he's gone back to the tiring rooms to watch the actresses undress.'

'You're right,' gasped Alpiew. She remembered her own days dressing the actresses, and sometimes serving them with drinks in the summer. The tiring rooms were always crowded with young blades trying to get a glimpse of the Bracegirdle bosom, or somewhat more than a glimpse from the lesser actresses. 'You stay here, milady, and keep your eyes on the audience as they leave. I'll go round behind stage. I know some people here. I used to dress.'

Happy to be able to see the end of the comedy, the Countess sidled into the auditorium and squeezed into the back row of the pit.

The Countess glanced round at the boxes. There were pretty women, flighty-looking women, women who positively oozed availability. But perchance *the* woman had fled during the interval.

The blackamoor boy caught the Countess's eye. Pretty

little creature, thought the Countess. Though not so pretty as her own dear Cupid had been. His mistress looked rich. Haughty and rich. The Countess hoped that the woman treated the child with kindness.

'Let secret villainy from hence be warned;
Howe'er in private mischiefs are conceived . . .'

Verse! The end of the play was upon them. The Countess stood and positioned herself by the door to make a hasty exit should she see anything.

'Torture and shame attend their open birth;
Like vipers in the womb, base treachery lies,
Still gnawing that, whence first it did arise;
No sooner born, but the vile parent dies.'

The audience clapped and hoorahed, and yelled 'Ancora', though they could not surely mean it. Even she didn't fancy sitting through the whole thing twice in a row.

Out came that brazen tart Verbruggen to speak the epilogue.

The Countess scoured the heads before her. If only she could see some tell-tale sign to give them a quick story for the scandal sheet. It would make losing Beau a second time not seem quite so dreadful.

'. . . But though he cannot write, let him be freed
At least from their contempt who cannot read.'

Mrs Verbruggen smiled, blew kisses into the audience and tripped off the stage.

While the applause died down, the Countess placed herself on the steps to watch the audience leave. When there were naught but a few stragglers she moved back into the auditorium, hoping that Alpiew had had more luck behind the scenes.

After a few minutes, Alpiew emerged through the side doors to the stage.

'Nothing,' she said, climbing down into the pit. 'Not been there, never been there, no one's ever heard of him.'

She slumped next to the Countess on the back bench. Some of the orange girls had returned with brooms to clear up the peel.

'Hold!' cried Alpiew to a girl with a large broom, diving forward towards the bench where Beau had sat. She crawled about on her knees under the green baize-covered benches for a moment or two, then surfaced dusty but empty-handed. 'Nothing.'

She turned to the girl with the broom. 'I'm looking for a note. I thought he might have dropped it.' She took a closer squint at the orange girl's face. 'Were you the one who sold him the orange?'

The girl nodded.

'So,' Alpiew said quietly, bidding the girl come closer, 'tell me: Where did you get the orange?'

'It was one of me own.' The girl was on the defensive. 'I never stole it.'

'No, no,' said Alpiew. 'I don't suggest that you did. But then how came there to be a note tucked into its skin?'

'Oh, that,' said the girl, slopping the broom lazily across the floor. 'A few folk do it. To pass messages, you know. Assignations.'

'Mmm,' Alpiew was listening, encouraging. But the

girl was obviously afraid to talk. She dived to her knees and started frantically grabbing at pieces of withered peel on the floor.

The Countess, seeing that something was afoot, had crept forwards and hovered a few yards away. 'Did a lady give you the note,' she cooed quietly floorwards, 'to give to the handsome gentleman?'

The girl shook her head violently. 'No! No woman.'

'A man then?' said Alpiew.

The Countess flung herself on to her knees, trying to help the girl clear the floor of peel and pith. 'Clever deduction, Alpiew. I'm surprised Mr Newton hasn't hired you for his assistant.'

'What kind of man?' Alpiew took the cue from the Countess and was holding open the rubbish sack.

'Big,' said the girl, looking about her and lowering her voice. 'Square cut. Frightening.'

'Was he at the play?' Alpiew was trying to recall the images of the audience. 'What colour jacket?'

'No,' the girl was firm. 'He came and went before the play started. I had to have time to fix it in the orange-skin, see.'

'You can't remember anything more about the man, then?' asked Alpiew.

The girl shook her head, and the Countess grabbed her whisk broom for a final brisk go at the floor.

'You won't find the note,' said the girl, looking at the Countess with dismay. 'Otherwise how would he know where to go?'

The Countess rose and carefully and deliberately handed the girl her broom. She was smiling, displaying her black teeth in an ingratiating grin. 'Silly me! Without

the note he'd never know that today's meeting is at . . .'
She shook her head and clicked her pudgy fingers as
though trying to shake out a lost thought.

'St Paul's.'

'St Paul's,' laughed the Countess in a tinkly voice.
'Dear old St Paul's!'

'You read the note?' said Alpiew, trying to keep her
voice calm. 'You can read?'

Alpiew was astonished. Most girls at this station of life
could not read. Alpiew herself had been lucky that the
Countess had taught her.

'I didn't mean to read it. I didn't even want to. But
you can't help seeing things when you're trying to stuff
them into an orange's skin. And when things are letters,
and you know your letters, you can't help reading 'em.
They just sort of leap out at you. And you know what
they say, see. Just by looking at them.'

'Reading's a funny thing, isn't it?' laughed the Countess. 'When you can't do it, you can't, then suddenly you
can't not. I do so sympathise! Reading! Pish to it!'

'It started as a joke,' the girl simpered. 'But some fellow
last year thought it was fun to teach me the alphabet,
and it's been terrible ever since. Those cursed letters!
They're everywhere, talking to you.'

'And they said "St Paul's"!' The Countess looked sym-
pathetic. 'Those naughty letters!'

'I preferred it when they just looked like black lines.
Life was easier then . . . Now everywhere I go it's "Exit"
and "No credit" and all sorts of things I don't care to
know.'

'Maybe you should move to Smyrna,' said the Countess. 'They have different lettering there.'

The girl looked up, hopeful again. 'Smyrna! Is that a coffee house?'

Alpiew wanted to end this method of inquiry instantly. 'Anything else?'

The girl peered at her. She'd lost the track.

'Anything else what?'

'On the note? Anything else.'

'9,' muttered the girl. 'St Paul's 9.'

'Nine!' cooed the Countess. 'You poor little thing, how dreadful for you. You know your numbers too?'

At that the girl burst into tears.

It was after eight when the Countess and Alpiew passed through the West Gate of St Paul's Cathedral. A few men were putting away their tools, pulling covers over the cauldrons and other building implements. The booksellers were all gone home and their stalls shuttered up.

'Pity,' sighed the Countess. 'We could have had another peep at all that filth while we waited.'

In attempting to step over a puddle Alpiew slid for a couple of yards and only regained her composure by grabbing at the Countess.

'Ice,' said the Countess. 'I'll wager the naked man we saw here last time won't be doing his rounds tonight!'

The two women climbed on to the long wooden bridge which led up to the West Portico of the church.

'I suppose they'll put steps down there,' said the Countess, gazing into the moat-like depths below. 'I fancy we are like the creatures going into the Ark.'

Once inside they were both astonished by the space

of the new cathedral. The Countess looked up. 'The pillars seem disproportionately large.'

'All the better for us to hide behind,' said Alpiew, 'when our cove arrives.'

'It's so nice to be early. Where shall we choose to station ourselves?' The Countess looked around. 'Where is the best quarter for an assignation?'

Alpiew darted her eyes round the huge hollow space. 'I shall reconnoitre, milady. You wait here.'

In the middle of the aisle stood an old man, head thrown back, gazing upwards to the stars.

'Do you work here?' asked the Countess in as reverent a voice as she could muster in this cold.

'No,' said the man, not moving. 'See up there!' He pointed up through the gaping hole in the church's roof. 'The stars and planets. Maybe even God Himself.'

'Mmm,' said the Countess with a shudder, silently dashing out a little prayer for forgiveness for all her sins.

'They say Heaven is only six miles, straight up,' said the man. 'If we had a magnifying optic strong enough and pointed it straight through that hole we might be able to glimpse Him. And do you know what the fools are going to do?'

The Countess muttered a bewildered 'no'.

'Fill it with a cupola and top it with a three-hundred-foot spire. 'Twill be the highest spot in London. Higher even than the Monument to the late Fire.'

The Countess inhaled, trying to sound impressed. 'It will certainly be an impressive church.'

'Church!' laughed the old man. ''Tis no more like a church than is my dog's kennel, ad's heart. It's more like a goose pie than a church. And this embroidered hole in the middle of the top is like the place in the upper crust where they put in the butter.'

The Countess gave him a sideways glance, and hoped she was safe in his company. Perhaps the fellow was escaped from Bedlam. 'Horrid smell,' she said.

'Brimstone, probably,' the old man spoke in a matter-of-fact tone. 'Not so long ago it used to be a stable,' he went on, still craning up to look at the Heavens. 'Oliver Cromwell kept his horses here. God walked out then, and he'll not come back. It's a heathenish place. No church.'

Alpiew puffed across the Nave and stood near the Countess.

'The girl must have got it wrong. They wouldn't have arranged to meet here tonight.'

'Why's that?' the Countess replied, keeping her eye on the old man.

'It's always locked up at night. It's open now because there was a fire here this afternoon. The organ room burned down. They're only here to clear up after that.'

'That'll explain the smell,' said the Countess.

'A judgement from the Heavens,' said the old man.

'No. A plumber's torch,' answered Alpiew.

'St Paul's. Nine.' The Countess scratched beneath her wig. 'What else could it mean?'

'St Paul's, new built,' said the old man. 'Now that's in a square packed with trulls and strumpets, but it's not a goose pie.'

Alpiew grabbed the Countess's elbow and jerked her away. 'I am half-mad, to be sure, madam. He means St Paul's, Covent Garden, a much more likely site for an assignation with a whore.'

Both women were running now, down the rickety wooden bridge.

'What's o'clock?' The Countess was gripping the rail and teetering along at full speed.

Alpiew turned back to the cathedral and looked up at the clock. 'Ten minutes to nine.'

'We'll never do it.' The Countess puffed. 'Covent Garden's miles away.'

Alpiew slipped across the same puddle. 'Pox on this ice,' she called. 'Have we enough pennies for a hackney carriage?'

The Countess plunged her hands into her pocket. 'Two pennies.'

'Then we'll go as far as that takes us.' Alpiew rushed out through the West Gate into Ludgate Street and yelped at passing hackney carriages.

They trundled by, along with chairs and private carriages pulled by puffing horses, snorting clouds of breath into the frosty night. Ahead of them all along Ludgate Street boys trotted back and forth with flaming links, lighting pedestrians along the street.

'It's the wrong time,' Alpiew cried back into the blistering cold wind. 'These folk are all coming home from dinner.'

The two women dashed along, walking faster than most of the carriages.

Five minutes later they were crossing the Fleet Bridge. The dark canal beneath them was silent.

'Frozen over,' said Alpiew.

'Me too,' replied the Countess, puffing clouds of steam like a plump wizened little dragon in a green mantua.

Alpiew was still waving her arms at every passing carriage. Suddenly one pulled in.

'Where to, ladies?' The driver leaned down.

'As far along in the direction of Covent Garden as we can go for two pennies,' said Alpiew, handing the Countess up into the coach.

'Somerset House,' the driver yelled back into the cab. 'The hackney carriage queue.'

Alpiew and the Countess didn't speak in the darkness of the cab. They used the time to get their breath back and to prepare themselves for the next dash, up Brydges Street and into Covent Garden.

The driver took their two pence and deposited them at the entrance to one of the streets running to Covent Garden Piazza.

Up the street they ran, clutching their skirts, darting in and out of revelling youths. At this time of night the area was very crowded. Men were on the trail of taverns, bagnios and sweat-houses and prostitutes; women were either on their way to or from work – as actresses, coffee-house wenches, tavern keepers, sweat-house women, and every type of prostitute from the doorway knee-tremblers to sophisticated flagellants and kept-women.

'Phough!' panted the Countess. 'Look at those two –' pointing at two very tall painted dames – 'they look like men in women's clothing.'

'They are,' huffed Alpiew. 'They do a roaring trade, I'm told.'

'Pshaw!' gasped the Countess. 'Perhaps Godfrey's right. The flesh-pots are upon us.'

Alpiew turned into the square, shoving through a throng of men gaping into a doorway.

'What's going on there?' asked the Countess, running backwards to have a longer squint.

'It's Mrs Birch's Elysium House of Flogging. They're plucking up their courage – to enter or not to enter?'

'Flogging?' The Countess stopped in her tracks. 'There's somewhere to visit for our column. Maybe we should send Godfrey in there to smoke out the clientele . . .'

Alpiew rushed back and yanked the Countess into movement again. 'My lady, we are already three minutes late for this assignation. I heard the bells strike the hour as we alighted from the coach.'

The Countess gathered up her skirts and stumbled through the drunken hordes in the square.

A crowd of rowdy youths was dancing round the central column, throwing their wigs into the air, trying, without luck, to crown the globe on the top of the pillar. 'Three cheers for the Tityre-tus,' they yelled.

Link-boys dashed in and out of the crowds, touting for trade.

Prostitutes of all shapes and sizes minced and teetered around the square, some sitting on tethering posts, others lolling against the huge columns of St Paul's Church.

'Phough!' The Countess wrinkled up her nose, and squeezing past a row of painted doxies seated on the steps of the church she asked: 'What is this smell? Civet cat?'

'No. Perfumes.' Alpiew was at the doors rattling at the handle which turned and turned in her hand.

'It's a false door, dearie,' said a tall thin prostitute in green, whose face was so spotted with patches she looked as though she was in the later stages of the plague. 'The altar's right behind it.'

'So how do you get in?' Alpiew was rubbing her fingers together in impatience.

'You don't,' snapped the prostitute. 'The church is locked at night. Too useful for trade. The minister didn't like it.'

Alpiew stamped and screamed. 'So tell me, where would a person go if they have an assignation at St Paul's?'

''Ere! You maw-wallop!' Another prostitute stepped out of the flickering shadows. 'You're on our turf. Get your poxy little snapper away from here. You're queering our pitch.'

The Countess hoiked herself up to her full five foot two. 'I beg your pardon! I am Lady Anastasia Ashby de la Zouche.'

'I don't care what you've caught, dearie,' snarled the tart. 'Just shove off. And take this clap-ridden trollop with you.'

'This is my woman, Alpiew. We have arranged to meet a gentleman friend of my late husband . . .'

Alpiew was pulling up her sleeves ready to throw a punch at the woman who had insulted her.

The Countess pulled her back. 'Come along, Alpiew, we can make our inquiries elsewhere . . .'

They emerged from the portico and peered through the railings.

'Your ladyship,' Alpiew gasped. 'There he is! Look. In the churchyard.'

A few yards away from them, to the side of the church, leaning forward, his head in his hands, Beau Wilson sat on a grave, alone.

The Countess and Alpiew ducked and crept along the

length of the railings, to the gate from the piazza into the churchyard.

'Locked.' The Countess shook her head. 'What are we to do? Keep watch from here? How did he get in?'

'There's a gate at the other side. In Bedford Street. It's obscured from our vision here, by the church.'

The two women stood huddled in the gate, faces squeezed up to the freezing railings, peering through into the darkness.

'Fan me, ye winds,' the Countess hissed. 'Behold our prey!'

From the shadows at the far end of the churchyard, gazing in Beau's direction, came a woman. Tall, thin and graceful, she was elegantly dressed . . . but for one thing.

'Why is she wearing a vizard mask?' whispered the Countess. 'She's no Covent Garden punk. Look at the cut of her clothes. She's a lady of quality or I'm a Dutchman!' She spat at the very thought.

'Come on,' said Alpiew. 'It's a dash, but let's go for the entry in Bedford Street. We could go round in a couple of minutes.'

'No,' said the Countess. 'One of us' – the Countess nodded towards Alpiew – 'must stay here . . . To keep an eye on immediate developments. Which is the way?'

Alpiew pointed the Countess to turn at the Unicorn, go the length of Henrietta Street and turn to make the third side of the square into Bedford Street.

The Countess trotted off into the night.

Alpiew looked again. The woman was standing still. But Beau slowly stood up and turned to face her. He took a couple of steps and stumbled.

Alpiew heard him swear under his breath. He steadied himself by grabbing on to a headstone, and walked gingerly forward.

'Alpiew, my life, my joy, my darling sin, how dost thou?'

Alpiew span round. It was Simon.

'You're in your cups, Simon. Should you not be at your post down with the pots?'

'Alas, I am dismissed, Alpiew.' Simon wrinkled up his face and was about to cry.

Alpiew was still trying to dart looks through the railings into the dark churchyard. 'There's always call for pot-boys, Simon. Look how many taverns there are in this square alone. Do the square. Knock from door to door. You'll get employ. Go on.'

Simon did not move, but his face unwrinkled.

'No time like the present.' Alpiew flapped her arms, indicating he should go. 'Along with you. Try Mother Lovejoy at the Blackamoor's Head. Say I sent you.'

Simon shuffled from foot to foot, and then finally moved off.

Alpiew applied her eyes to the railings, but after gazing into the flaming flambaux of the piazza the churchyard seemed blacker than ever. The Countess must have got round into the churchyard by now.

Alpiew peered into the black. Suddenly she heard a thumping noise, followed by a sound like a cat's late-night wail, then nothing but a rustle of clothing.

A few moments later she heard the familiar tread of the Countess's feet clipping along the flagstoned path.

'Alpiew!' The Countess's voice came from near the spot where Beau had been sitting. 'Did you make out what happened? Quickly. Make your way round.'

Alpiew gathered up her skirts and ran as though the devil was after her.

She turned into the back gate to the church and scampered along the alley leading to the churchyard. Heavy footsteps were running towards her. Whoever it was filled the space, and when he reached Alpiew he pushed her to the ground.

She heaved herself up and tried to get a good look at the disappearing figure. But it was too dark and he too quick. He had turned the corner before she got a chance.

She dragged herself to her feet and stumbled along the alley. As she burst into the churchyard she heard a loud scream. A woman's voice.

She cursed herself for not having borrowed a link from one of the boys in the square to light her way. All was silent, but for the noises of carousing wafting through the far railings from the adjacent busy square.

Alpiew reached the side of the church and slid herself along, keeping flat to the wall, peering towards the gravestones.

She could see nothing but the stones. No sign of Beau, or the mystery masked woman, or of the Countess.

She stopped, holding her breath, to listen. She could make out a faint whimpering.

'Milady?' she whispered. 'Are you all right?'

'No,' came the reply. 'I've fallen and twisted my ankle. Fetch help.'

Alpiew dashed to the Covent Garden railings, near to where she had recently been standing, and thrust her face through. 'Help, ho!' she called. 'Fetch the watch! My lady is injured.'

Hoping one of the square's revellers was sober enough to hear her, she clambered back over the gravestones towards the Countess's mutterings.

'I'm all wet,' said the Countess. 'My hands are all wet where I fell.' The Countess was splayed out on her back, like a tortoise. 'I seem to have stumbled over a bundle of clothes some fool left here.' She was tugging at an adjacent headstone, trying to pull herself up from the frosty grass.

Alpiew grabbed her from behind to help her to her feet and then to seat herself on a neighbouring grave. 'Did you see the woman?' she asked.

'She had gone before I got round here,' gasped the Countess. 'The errant husband, Beau as well, I think. I heard a man running away though. Heavy footsteps, you know.' She bent down and rubbed at her ankle. 'I'll never be able to walk on this leg. Curse this darkness! I can't see a thing.'

In the distance, at the Bedford Street entrance, a flaming torch bounced along, with a couple of hats lit beneath it.

'Here comes assistance, my lady.'

Alpiew looked back along the path. 'Look, madam, what's that?' She pointed down at something glowing on the grass. The Countess followed her gaze.

'Fireflies,' she said.

'In this cold?' Alpiew took a few steps away and retrieved the object. 'It's a piece of cloth, madam, but bewitched,' she said, inspecting it carefully. 'Throwing off light as though the devil were in it . . .'

Behind Alpiew the two officials marched along the churchyard path, their link held high. 'Where's the lady?'

said a man's voice. 'I am the Covent Garden beadle, and this here is my constable. We'll help her to a carriage.'

The beadle in his long cloak stepped on to the grass, lighting his way with the flaming link.

'I'm so sorry, sir. I missed my footing and alas . . .' She swept her hand down to indicate her sore leg.

'What's your name?' asked the beadle in the rather patronising tone used by officials towards elderly women.

The beadle put out his hand, and the Countess stretched out hers to grasp it.

'Lady Anastasia Ashby de la Zouche, Baroness Penge, Countess of Clapham . . .'

Alpiew gasped first. Then all eyes followed the same path. First to the Countess's outstretched hand, her white glove smeared with red, then along her wrist to the blood dripping from her lace cuffs, then following the drops of the gore to the ground, where, at the Countess's feet, lay a knife. Next to the knife was a face, Beau Wilson's face. His eyes were bound by a black cloth and his face was white. His body was sprawled out alongside a lichen-covered tomb. The life was drained out of it, and from ear to ear, his throat had been cut.

The beadle and constable exchanged a look, then both stepped forward, the constable pulling a length of rope from his pocket.

'Madam Aspidistra Zela Douche, or whatever your name is, in the name of King William, I hereby arrest you on the most grievous and capital offence of murder.'

FOUR

Resolution

*This occurs when substances which are mixed
become violently separated.*

Alpiew made good use of her heels before the last slip
was tied to the knot round the Countess's wrists. Darting
in and out of the tombstones in the dark, she bent low
to cover herself and scuttled out to the street and into
the busy piazza. It was a reflex with her, for she had run
from the law so many times in the past.

Panting, she checked over her shoulder to be sure her
escape had been effected successfully then ducked into
the Blackamoor's Head, hoping that Simon was still
there.

He was. She grabbed him by the elbow. 'I need you to
follow the constables who are escorting my mistress . . .'

'But . . .'

'. . . find out where they take her, then run along and
give the news to Godfrey at her house in German Street.'

'But I'm waiting to be seen by Madame Lovejoy . . .'

Alpiew held him by the chin and looked earnestly into
his eyes. 'This is a matter of life or death, Simon.' She
had walked him to the doorway and now she shoved him

out into the street. 'Go. Run. They'll be going down Bedford Street. Shoo.'

She clapped her hands after the boy, then slumped down on to the pavement as he ran off into the night.

What to do? What scurvy fortune! What a living nightmare.

There was only one punishment for murder: death. How could the Countess prove she didn't kill that wretched, handsome Beau Wilson?

Alpiew took a deep breath and clambered to her feet, as two drunks loomed perilously over her.

Jostled by men looking for prostitutes, she made her way across the piazza, her head down in case the beadle or any of his men were still looking for her.

Prostitutes! A vizard mask was what she needed, then she could operate safely.

'Aagh!' she screamed in the ear of a nearby prostitute. 'Look over there!' She pointed at a man she'd never seen before. 'My master. Out looking for a whore.'

The prostitute's eyes darted a glance at the man.

'If he sees me he'll rush off, I suppose, thinking I'll tell madam . . .' Alpiew looked up at the woman. 'What can I do?'

The man was eyeing up the prostitute. Alpiew turned her back from him and raised her hands to her face. 'Help me! How can I get away without being seen?'

The prostitute, seeing that she was about to lose a customer before she even got him, tugged loose the mask which dangled on a ribbon from her waist and thrust it towards Alpiew. 'Get out of here,' she hissed. 'You're killing my trade.'

Alpiew clapped on the mask and dived away from the

portico as the man lurched forward to make a bid for a quick bit of pickle-me-tickle-me. She crouched by the railings and peered into the graveyard through the eye-holes of the mask. A number of watchmen with link-boys in attendance were moving about in the flickering light. A gang of tough-looking men had wrapped Beau's body in a sheet and were lifting him to take him away.

The beadle read from a crumpled piece of paper. 'Here's where to take the body . . .'

No doubt they would take it to his wife.

'Chale House, Angel Court . . .'

Yes, his home address.

'Where's that then?' asked one of the bearers with a grunt as he took the weight of the body.

'One of those smart courts between Ludgate Hill and Old Bailey,' replied his colleague.

Alpiew shuddered at the words Old Bailey. Beau Wilson was dead, and the Countess was found with his blood on her hands. Murder. A capital charge.

'Lucky he had this receipt in his pocket,' said the beadle flicking the piece of paper. 'Mind you, "one gallon decayed urine" – funny thing for such a well-dressed fellow to be buying.' He crumpled the note and tossed it aside. 'Still, round here . . .' He gave the men a knowing look. 'Folk get up to all sorts of bizarre activities.' He scratched his groin and then lifted his arm. 'Each to his own, I say. Onward!' he called, and the little procession set off.

Alpiew waited till the last link was carried along the passageway out into Bedford Street, then she made her way round into the empty churchyard.

She bent low and scanned the grass. She picked up the

receipt and pocketed it, then sat down on the tombstone where the Countess had been sitting.

It was time to build up a picture of the whole business.

It was of prime importance to get the Countess released. Alpiew knew all about the justice system, and knew that, with no money to back her, her ladyship didn't stand a chance.

The one certain way to get her freed was to find out who *did* kill Beau Wilson.

So what did she know of him?

Firstly he had a wife. A wife who did not trust him, suspected him of dalliance. A wife who had said if she found her husband guilty of infidelity she wished him 'gone . . . Never to return.' A wife who had an icy temper. After all, she had threatened to slit Alpiew's throat. And now someone had done just that to her husband.

What else? What of Beau? He was a relentlessly cheerful person, always waving and smiling at folk in the street; liked revolting French food; walked very fast with a long stride; attended lectures at the Royal Society; in the twenty-four hours they had pursued him he had made two mysterious assignations, the first of which had him taken on to a Thames row-boat blindfolded, and the second, also blindfolded, had led him to meet his own death.

Returning home after the row-boat incident he had appeared nonchalant, had even approached the Countess to chat about the Royal Society's lecture the previous day. At the theatre he had also seemed calm and collected. Not frightened. He watched the first act and left at the interval, but there was nothing unusual about that, many people came to see the second act a different night, or didn't bother if they'd not enjoyed the first. The orange seller who'd passed him the note tucked into orange peel had thought nothing of it. It was a common practice.

What of Beau's associates?

First there was his suspicious wife. Alpiew didn't trust her a bit. It was a well-known fact that most murders occurred within families.

She had frequently seen the thick-necked thug in places where she had encountered Beau. He went into the Amsterdam Coffee House, but didn't stay long enough to eat. Surely it was his silhouette she had seen down at the Dorset Garden quayside too. She had not seen him but more than likely he was also the man who had pushed her down tonight. Behind the vizard mask Alpiew's face was filmed with sweat. She pulled the mask back and reached into her pocket for a handkerchief.

She shook it out and a strange light flared up before her. It was the charmed glowing handkerchief she had picked up before she and the Countess had found Beau's body. She shoved it back into her pocket and left the churchyard.

Down on the Strand Alpiew pushed into a brightly lit bar and inspected Beau's receipt. It was issued by the apothecary's shop opposite his home. On closer inspection it was not a receipt, but an unpaid invoice. Across the bottom was scrawled in a spidery hand: 'For your immediate attention.' Beau had bought one gallon of decayed urine, and beneath this was a row of indecipherable symbols.

Alpiew turned the note over. On the back of the invoice there were two words writ in a clumsy hand. '*Alles Mist!*'

It was incomprehensible.

She folded the invoice and tucked it down her cleavage, the safest place she knew, and the one advantage of a large bosom.

She began to realise how tired she was – every bone and sinew in her body ached with cold and exhaustion. But now was not the time for sleep. She hurried out of the tavern and ran along the Strand. She wanted to see how Mrs Wilson took the news of her husband's death.

Those fellows would be taking their time carrying his body. First they'd repair to the watch-house and send out for a cart, then secure the body, then hitch up a pony and head east. Because of the sensitive nature of their cargo they would also avoid main thoroughfares, thus lengthening their journey. No doubt they would stop off for a pint or two along the way. Alpiew knew if she kept up a brisk pace she could be there before them.

She secured the mask and strode out in the direction of Ludgate Hill.

She thought of the Countess as she walked. No doubt they'd roused a Justice of the Peace and he would by now have written a notice instructing some gaoler to take her into custody until a trial could be arranged. Sometimes that took months. Sometimes the whole business was over and done with in a week.

When she arrived in Angel Court, the Wilson house was in darkness. Alpiew sank back into the shadows of the apothecary's doorway and waited.

She let her eyes close and drifted in and out of sleep. As a result she had no idea what time it was when the burly figures of the constable's men lumbered up to the door with Beau Wilson's corpse. The beadle had obviously done his business of incarcerating her ladyship and was with them to break the news to Mrs Wilson.

He rapped three times on the door.

After a minute or two Alpiew saw a candle trail its flickering path down the main staircase. A maid, she presumed.

There was a sound of bolts being shot back and the door opened a crack. The beadle whispered a few words and the maid shut the door. Alpiew watched the candle make its way upstairs again. Moments later a number of candles were lit on the landing and Alpiew saw Mrs Wilson's shadow coming downstairs. The front door opened again.

Alpiew had a good view of Mrs Wilson, lit by the links of the corpse bearers. The beadle made an obsequious bow and muttered a few words. Mrs Wilson's face stayed in repose for a few seconds, then her eyes darted past the beadle towards the cart carrying Beau's body.

Her face contorted as though to scream, and she plunged past the beadle and, still in silence, ran to the cart and clambered up on to it, pulling at the sheet which draped her husband's body.

The jerky movement of the sheet being pulled away caused Beau to move, his face falling sideways. His hand too fell from the side of the cart and swung like a pendulum across the wheel.

'He's not dead, you see,' said Mrs Wilson, pulling his head up into her lap and kissing his lips. 'He's just cold.' She pulled his other hand towards her and started rubbing it. 'Just cold.'

She looked to the men who had escorted the body. 'You are dismissed. Thank you for bringing him home. You can go now.'

The beadle put his hand up to the distraught woman, but she snarled at him, thrusting him away. 'Go, go, go. You're not wanted here.'

Beau's head lurched back, exposing the full extent of his fatal wound. The knife had lacerated his windpipe and sliced through both tendons. Mrs Wilson looked down and saw the reality: the heavy head swinging on little more than the spine and a flap of flesh, and screamed and screamed.

Her maids and footman rushed out and, after a few words from the beadle, gently coaxed her down from the cart and back into the house.

'I'll send for the doctor,' the footman informed the beadle. Other lackeys were carrying Beau's body into the house.

'I have to speak to her,' puffed the beadle. 'This is a case of murder and we must speak to her. The miscreant is already arraigned by the Justice of the Peace and held safely under lock and key . . .'

'Come back in the morning,' said the footman. 'I must help my mistress.'

The body was inside, and Alpiew could see it being laid out on the dining-room table. Lackeys, carmen, bootboys were hovering in the eerie light of a single taper. Beau's valet was hurrying round the room, lighting sconces and candelabra as the footman stepped back into the house and slammed the door behind him.

'Not even an offer of a drink,' grumbled the beadle, 'after all our efforts.'

The men and their cart rumbled off again down Ludgate Hill.

Alpiew crossed the road to the Wilson house. Mrs

Wilson's reaction had certainly *seemed* genuine enough, but it would be interesting to know what the household servants made of their master's untimely death.

The dining room was now brilliantly illuminated, but no one thought to close the curtains. Alpiew, face hidden behind her black vizard mask, could see quite clearly and with only a pane of glass between her and the room she could hear well too. 'Criminy!' said the valet. 'He's been well and truly dispatched.'

'Prinked up to the peruke as usual for one of his mystery outings . . .' Another male servant.

'Perhaps the cuckold who got his horns from our late master thought he needed teaching a lesson.'

The men let forth a strange sombre giggle.

An old woman, probably the cook, started to sob. 'But he was kind enough to us . . .'

'Go and fetch some water from the kitchen, Abigail,' said the valet. 'We've got to get him cleaned up.'

The sobbing woman left the room, and Alpiew tried to inch her eyes up to the window.

The men started to talk between themselves.

'Madam knew,' said the coachman, pointing his finger towards the ceiling. 'She'd paid someone to follow him. I took her there. St James's.'

They broke off as a young serving maid flung the door open and rushed into the room. She hurtled up to the table, took a look at Beau's miserable remains, and screamed, throwing herself violently on to the corpse, her hands gripping his face. 'That bitch!' she howled. 'That bitch did it. I knew she would.'

The valet stepped forward and grabbed at her, pulling her off Beau's body. 'Betty, leave off.' He nodded towards the ceiling and shook his head, adding in a low tone: 'Not now.'

Betty, her face smeared with Beau's blood, turned and snarled at him.

'You go to hell, you traitor!' She turned back to Beau's corpse. 'Just let me get my hands on her. I'll finish her off too, for killing him.' She stretched out her hand and gently stroked Beau's marble cheek. 'I'll avenge you, sir. You know I will.'

Alpiew realised she had not taken a breath for nearly two minutes and sucked in air in a huge gasp. This was very much more exciting than the damnable theatre.

Unanimously the servants looked towards the window. Alpiew ducked out of the light, turned and walked briskly away, just as the footman stepped forward and drew the curtains.

'I demand my instant release,' squawked the Countess. 'You may think I'm a silly old fool that you may take advantage of, but I know my rights.'

The Countess was yelling through the bars at no one in particular. She was in a cell in the Charing Cross lock-up. The keeper had reluctantly taken her in and had now returned to his bed.

'It's a mistake. Why would I murder the man? He was my stipend,' she croaked. At this rate her voice would give out before morning, or so the keeper hoped.

The Countess let out another bloodcurdling shriek, and slumped back against the grimy cell wall.

Debtors' prison was one thing; being held on a murder charge quite another. She knew the form. Being dragged before a judge and jury who only needed the forces of law to say you'd done it, and you'd be guilty of having done it. It was true that an expensive lawyer could get even the guilty off, but, despite the law's motto, in most cases the reality was 'Guilty till proven innocent.'

And how was she going to prove herself innocent? She'd had the man's blood on her hands, the murder weapon and corpse at her feet.

She cursed Alpiew. Taking to her heels like that! Deserting her in her hour of need.

She'd probably never see the wench again.

Meanwhile how to get a message out? How to get help?

'Milady?' She heard the hoarse whisper and recognised Godfrey's voice at once. It seemed to be emanating from a ventilation grille at floor-level, so she crouched down to speak.

'Godfrey? It's me. They've locked me up for murder. It's all a mistake, but I'll need help.'

Godfrey grunted. 'Help costs, madam. And we ain't got a bean.'

The Countess's head whirled. 'Try the Cues,' she said. 'Make out Alpiew and I are researching some huge scandal for them. Earth-shattering. Political. High places. Anything. Make it sound dramatic.' Godfrey did not reply. 'Where is Alpiew, by the way?'

'Not seen her, madam. But she sent some boy to tell me you was banged up in here.'

The Countess somewhat revised her opinion of Alpiew. 'Tell her when you see her to get me out of here. And warn her to lay low. I overheard them talking. They're on the lookout for her too as an accessory. It would be a disaster for both of us if she's caught.'

Godfrey let out another low rumble.

'Meanwhile, I need a book,' she hissed. 'Very important. It's huge and brown and currently propping up some wonky piece of furniture in the kitchen.'

'Not very light reading, madam, if you don't mind me saying.'

'In fact I do mind you saying, Godfrey. That book may be my redemption.'

'I don't think a book . . .'

'It's not your job to think, Godfrey,' said the Countess. 'Just get that book to me.'

Alpiew walked all the way back to German Street in record time.

What a day! And tomorrow she would be very busy. She had to find out who killed Beau, and thus release the Countess. Where to start, though? She had the apothecary's invoice in her pocket. She could visit him, which would serve a double purpose as it would give her another opportunity to watch the goings on at Chale House.

But first Alpiew knew she would need to get some sleep at last. She crept into the kitchen. Evidently Godfrey was out. She undressed and tucked herself up in the truckle bed in the warmth then lay in the dark and fell to misery thinking about the Countess.

Her thoughts flew to Mrs Wilson, the sight of Beau's corpse and the dramatic scene with the maid, Betty. Maybe this maid was the whore Mrs Wilson was after? The girl's emotional outburst was beyond the realm of duty and, come to think on it, none of the other servants seemed particularly surprised by her deluge of tears.

The other servants hadn't given much away, but Alpiew now knew that all of them thought Beau was a philanderer. And of course their duties would mean they had suspicions of his behaviour: The chambermaids must know he regularly stayed out all night, the valets knew he primped himself up, the chairmen knew he had something to hide, or why did he choose so often to go by foot, or take a hackney carriage when he was paying them to carry him about town? So what the Countess and Alpiew had suspected from the outset of the case appeared to be true, with the added mystery of Betty and her promise to take vengeance on Mrs Wilson.

Tomorrow, Alpiew decided, she would visit the apothecary and ask him a few questions. After all, his receipt was her only lead. While she was there she might try to chat up one of the Wilson household.

Finally, somehow or other, she'd get a message to her ladyship, reporting on progress.

Just as she was finally drifting off to sleep, Godfrey came crashing in.

'Got to bring her a book,' he grumbled. 'Some fancy thing, called *Coke upon Littleton*.' He got down on to his knees and surveyed the kitchen at floor-level. 'You'll have to get out of bed.' He looked up hopefully at Alpiew. She pulled the sheet higher to cover her thin night-shirt.

'Can't lift the bed and you,' he added, pointing down at the book under one of the bed's legs.

Alpiew let out a violent puff of air and pulling the sheet to her neck climbed off the bed. Godfrey wiped away a glob of dribble which was drooling down his chin, then tugged out the book, which left the bed at a most dangerous angle.

'Let's have a look at it, then.' Alpiew held out a hand from behind the sheet. Godfrey tossed the book in the air, hoping Alpiew would have to drop the sheet, but she caught it and sat again in one smooth movement.

'Mmm,' she said. 'All in Latin. Must be a law book. I thought it would be.' She glanced up at Godfrey who was still slobbering down at her. 'Oh, go to your bed, you drivelling feeble nincompoop!'

Godfrey's mouth fell open even wider, but he staggered back with a snarl. 'Well, you'll have to give it to her tomorrow then.'

'And how am I going to do that? Being held on a murder charge is not a tea-table assembly, you know. They're not going to let me in there and just hand her a book.'

'No, they're certainly not. They'll collar you there and then.'

Alpiew looked at him. 'What do you mean?'

'They came here looking for you.' He shuffled off his greatcoat and slumped down. 'Well, I suppose it was you they meant: "Buxom wench, brown hair, blue eyes . . ."'

Grabbing the sheet, Alpiew loomed over Godfrey where he sat. 'I hope you told them you knew of no such person.'

Godfrey shrugged, eyeing up her upper torso. 'Not that buxom anyway. Seen bigger in my time. Told them I should be so lucky . . .'

'So I'd better find somewhere else to stay tomorrow.'

She looked round the kitchen. She'd be sorry to leave here. It was warm and really rather comfortable. 'Where does the Countess go when she needs to hide from creditors?'

Alpiew knew it was worth asking. Many houses still had priest's holes left over from the Commonwealth, when it was against the law to be a Catholic, and priests had to be hidden so that they could perform clandestine ceremonies: masses, baptisms, weddings.

'She usually holes up with Pigalle, that froggy female friend of hers.'

The Duchesse de Pigalle! The last Alpiew saw of her the woman was dressed in men's riding gear and fighting a duel with a young man in Hide Park.

But that was twenty years ago, before Sir Peter had abducted Alpiew to the New World.

Furious at the memory, Alpiew glared at Godfrey. 'And the book? How will you get that to her ladyship, then?'

'I was going to slip it to her tomorrow,' puffed Godfrey, pulling off his ancient boots. 'When they move her from the Charing Cross lock-up to Newgate Prison tomorrow afternoon.'

Alpiew spun round. 'They're moving her?'

'Of course they are!' Godfrey was in nothing but his vest and socks now. 'You can't swing a cat in those lock-ups, you know.'

Alpiew bit her lower lip and flopped back in her bed, which for want of the book to maintain its equilibrium, deposited her back on the floor.

Alpiew grabbed at a nearby stack of papers, and thrust a large manuscript entitled *Love's Last Wind* by the

Aetherial Amoret under the short leg. 'Right! So she'll be paraded through the open streets,' she whispered. 'Now we're talking business.'

Next morning Alpiew was outside the apothecary's waiting for it to open for trade. She had risen early and stopped for a chat with some friends at the Hay Market. A certain carter owed her a favour, and later today she would be calling it in.

There seemed to be much activity at the Wilson house, but that was only to be expected, upholders and other funerary merchants would be plying their trade, seamstresses for the shroud, cabinet makers for the coffin, jewellers with mourning rings, printers for the funeral invitations . . . The funeral! Now that would be interesting. Who would turn up, send flowers?

The Wilson door opened again and a man in dark brown clothing stepped inside.

'Can I help you, mistress?' In the shop doorway the wiry little apothecary stood holding the door open with his walking crutch, and cocking his head. He had only one leg.

Alpiew spun round as the man hopped back into the shop and nipped behind the counter. She pulled the invoice from her cleavage and stepped into the shop.

'I need to know about these things.' She spread the invoice on the counter.

'I'm still owed for them.' The apothecary had pushed a pince-nez on to the bridge of his thin hooked nose. 'What's going on over there, anyhow?' he said, indicating the Wilson house. 'Someone won the lottery?'

Alpiew shook her head. 'No. There's been a bit of trouble. Could you tell me about this invoice?'

'You new? Not seen you hereabouts before today . . .' The apothecary took a sharp intake of breath through his yellow teeth. 'I'm owed money by him for weeks. Don't know why I let him have this stuff on tick . . .'

Alpiew smiled. 'I'm here to make sure all the bills get paid. I simply need to know what they're all for first.'

The apothecary took the scrap of paper and started writing, black ink spraying over the counter from his scratchy feather pen. 'Simple elaboratory equipment, actually.' He peered at her above the lenses of his pince-nez. 'Usually used in metalwork.'

As he slid the paper across to Alpiew, behind her the door pushed open and the man in brown she had seen formerly enter the Wilson house rushed into the shop. He was panting and flustered.

'Saline solution. With mustard . . .' He pushed his wig back and wiped the sweat from his forehead. 'An emetic, antidote to a poisoning. Quickly!'

He shouted the last word and the apothecary jumped back out of his way.

'What's happened?' Alpiew glanced through the window across the road. The front door was open and some of the male servants she'd seen the night before were standing in the street flapping their hands and talking anxiously between themselves.

'She's taken poison. Mrs Wilson is dying.'

'Which poison?'

'How in God's name should I know?' The man was yelling now, hysterical.

The apothecary leant forward and grabbed the brown

man's jacket. 'Tell me which poison. I may have an antidote.'

'I don't know. I'm just the lawyer.' The man wiped his head again. 'She's been vomiting in the night. Covered in it. But she's unconscious. White. Deathly. Barely breathing.'

'Tell me what to do, sir,' snapped Alpiew to the apothecary, shoving the piece of paper he had given her down her cleavage. 'I'll do it.'

The apothecary limped out from behind the counter. 'Fetch a sample of what she took, however small, and bring it to me. Quickly.'

Alpiew darted from the shop towards the house, yelling at the servants as she rushed past. 'What did she take? The apothecary needs to know.'

No one moved.

She grabbed hold of a tall boy in a dark curly periwig. 'Come with me. Show me the way!'

'It's nothing to do with me.' The boy shook Alpiew off, screaming. 'I don't work here. I'm just her lawyer's footboy! I don't even know her.'

Alpiew swung round to the others on the step. 'Quickly!' She dragged the valet by his cravat into the Wilson house.

The pair ran up the stairs and into Mrs Wilson's bedchamber. Beau's widow lay still on the bed, her pale face strangely tinged with shades of green.

There was a drinking cup by the bed. Alpiew grabbed it and dashed back to the apothecary.

The lawyer was now sobbing. She handed the item over the counter and after staring into it and sniffing, rubbing the silvery powdered dregs between his fingers, he announced: 'Antimony. Last thing you need is an emetic. Get her standing up. Walk her about. Gastric lavage. Water, water and more water. Then get on your knees and pray.'

Alpiew watched as the lawyer stumbled across the road, gathering his 'footboy' (as he had described himself) before going inside. The footboy was protesting, pulling back.

'Why would a woman like that take her own life? She has everything!' The apothecary was also gazing over the road at the Wilson house.

'Her husband was killed last night,' Alpiew said in a low voice. 'Murdered.'

The apothecary let out a hissing noise. 'Ah well,' he said. As though that explained everything.

A girl sidled past the shop, looking into the window, blocking their view. Alpiew suddenly realised who it was. Betty! Mrs Wilson's maid. She was in a great hooded cloak and carrying a bundle under her arm. And she wasn't actually looking into the shop, Alpiew realised. It was more as though she was averting her face from the Wilson house across the road. Trying not to be seen. Alpiew bid the apothecary good-day and rushed from the shop, to see the maid Betty turn into Ludgate Hill in the direction of Fleet Street.

Keeping a good distance between herself and the maid, but never losing sight of her, Alpiew followed her down past St Bridget's churchyard and along the narrow road behind the Bridewell Prison.

Then the girl ducked into an alley maybe only a yard across. Alpiew knew where they were heading. Back into the dingy, dangerous dives of Alsatia – Salisbury Court, whence Beau had led them a merry dance the night he appeared to have been kidnapped.

She let the girl go just out of sight, confident that she could still follow her by the clacking of her shoes.

The clacking stopped. Alpiew darted into the alley, just in time to see Betty's cloak disappear into a low oak door.

Alpiew ran up and applied her eye to the keyhole but it was too hard to see. From the look of the street it was a storehouse. Part of the Thames wharves. This alley was yards from the water's edge.

The only windows were two barred small semicircular lights at ground-level. Alpiew stooped to try to get a glimpse inside. The windows though were heavily barred, and Alpiew suspected that it wasn't only grime which prevented her being able to see through them. The lights had been painted black on the inside.

A bell started ringing. Probably the noonday bells at the Bridewell, thought Alpiew.

She jumped up in alarm. Noon! She had things to do which would not wait. She hoiked up her skirts and ran.

The Countess climbed up on to the small wooden cart. Rope had again been applied to her wrists, and despite the fact that her wig was at a perilous angle, her every attempt to straighten it had knocked it further off kilter.

The Newgate officers climbed on to the front of the cart, and with a click of the tongue one of them shooed the horse along.

The Countess scanned the crowd shoving along the busy Strand, trying to see Godfrey. She *must* have that book. It was a comprehensive study of English law and contained many successful appeals against charges of murder and mayhem.

The cart rocked along. A few people stood and stared, some even cat-called, but the Countess looked imperiously down at them from under her skewed wig and continued her search for Godfrey and her precious law book.

Suddenly the cart lurched to the right and, turning into Shoe Lane, left Fleet Street.

'Why are we turned?' demanded the Countess. 'Surely the usual way is up the New Canal.'

'Not today, love,' snarled the officer over his shoulder. 'Too icy. Dangerous for the pony near all that water. Never get her out if she fell in.'

'And you'd go down like a stone,' laughed his companion.

The Countess sucked in her cheeks and tried to ignore his rude remark. But worried that the Cues might be standing outside their print shop, or coming along the street, she kept quiet and hung her head the whole length of the street.

At the top of Shoe Lane the cart turned into Holborn. Still no sight of Godfrey or the book. She hoped the man had wit enough to see that the route had changed and he wasn't waiting like a ninny in the wrong place.

She peered down the canal sides as they crossed Holborn Bridge, but of course she realised, with her eyesight, she couldn't have seen him even if he was there.

The cart rumbled relentlessly towards Newgate, at the conduit turning into Snow Hill and past St Sepulchre's churchyard. The Countess shuddered. Tombstones to her left and looming ahead the grisly red-brick façade of Newgate Prison. Still no Godfrey. The drivelling fool was probably still at home, snoring, or snuggled up to the stove reading his copy of that Puritan swine Prynne's *Histrio-Mastix or The Players' Scourge*, 'Wherein it is largely evidenced by divers arguments that popular stage-playes are sinfull, heathenish, lewde, ungodly spectacles.' Ridiculous book. She picked at her rope manacles. As if going to see stage plays led to a life of crime!

'Uh oh,' groaned the driver, pulling up the horse and causing the Countess to lose her balance. 'What a mess!'

Ahead, blocking the whole of Snow Hill at its entrance to Newgate Street, a hay wagon had spilled its load. A group of men were piling the hillock of hay back on to the wagon, using a pitchfork and bare hands.

'We've got to get through,' yelled the driver. 'Murderer on board.'

The hay men glanced up in the Countess's direction. 'Oh yes?' One sneered, bending again to return to the job in hand. 'Better help us then, and it'll be done quicker. It's this ice,' he added, sliding his feet to demonstrate the perilous footing.

The second official reluctantly climbed down and started grabbing handfuls of hay and tossing it up on to the wagon.

'Your ladyship!' The Countess peered ahead. Beyond the pile of hay, Godfrey was leaping up and down, waving a large brown book in the air.

The Countess cursed under her breath. That was certainly not the way to keep a low profile! Now she'd never get the book. Then she realised it wasn't even the right book. The idiot was holding up her copy of the tragedies of Shakespeare! Bombastic and barbarous baloney by a bald, bearded Warwickshire sheep poacher. How was that going to help get her released?

She staggered to her feet to shout at him, when someone tugged at her skirt from behind and she tumbled off the back of the cart and landed on the ground with a heavy thud.

Before she had a chance to open her eyes and curse, someone had ripped off her wig and plonked a huge black gentleman's peruke on her practically bald head. Next thing she was propped up on to her feet and a large green gentleman's riding cloak was thrown over her shoulders. Then she was briskly frogmarched forward past the prison cart and through the hay.

'Keep walking,' whispered Alpiew, also decked out in a heavy hooded cloak. 'Don't look back. Walk like a man. They're not looking for a man, remember.'

The Countess increased the size of her strides and lifted her shoulders and had already passed the cart before the Newgate officer noticed she had gone.

He twisted round, saw his cart was empty and raised a holler, leaping down and rushing behind the cart, looking under it, peering back along the street the way they had come.

'Murderer at large,' he yelled. 'Elderly woman in pink, blood-stains down the front. Moth-eaten red wig. More paint than a shop-front. Find her!'

He looked down at his feet where lay something resembling a dead rat. He stooped to pick up the Countess's wig. 'Elderly *bald* woman,' he screamed. 'No wig at all!'

'Duck!' hissed Alpiew as an official-looking man ran from the prison door towards the cart.

'Lady Ashby de la Zouche?' the official called to the cart driver.

Alpiew and the Countess turned up a side street and strode away from the scene.

By the time they had reached the Duchesse de Pigalle's apartments in Arlington Street, St James's, just round the corner from the Countess's own house, Alpiew had untied her mistress's wrists and told her of the goings-on at the Wilson household.

'And the creature, Betty? She, I presume, had a month's mind for Mr Wilson?'

'Perhaps,' said Alpiew, remembering how, without any foundation but her own loyalty to the household, the same had been said about her own relationship with the Countess's errant husband, Sir Peter.

'But just enough love for him to make her attempt to kill the wife, suspecting her to be guilty of his murder? Is that it?'

Put that way it all sounded wildly far-fetched. But Alpiew was sure something was afoot, and that that something definitely concerned the maid Betty.

'This antimony stuff?' puffed the Countess. 'What exactly is it?'

Alpiew shook her head. 'I didn't have time to stay chatting at the shop, you know,' she said. 'I had to follow that girl to the place in Salisbury Court.'

'So what was the invoice all about then?' The Countess was busy ordering all the facts in her head. 'For what purpose did Beau Wilson want fermented urine, or whatever you said it was?'

'The invoice?' Alpiew dug into her cleavage. 'I never had time to look. Too much going on.'

They stood on the doorstep of Pigalle's house. The Countess pulled on the bell, while Alpiew unfolded the tattered scrap of ink-sprayed paper the apothecary had given her.

' "Item: one gallon decayed urine",' she read aloud. ' "Item: one German glass retort. Item: one pound pure sand. Item: seven drachmas of cinnabar . . ." '

The door opened and a foreign-looking satin-turbaned servant with long mustachios stood looking down at them.

'Gentlemen!' he sneered with a contempt bred of long familiarity with the bizarre. 'Can I 'elp you? I *presume* you are come to see Madame La Duchesse?'

But Alpiew and the Countess had forgotten they were wearing gentlemen's perukes and cloaks, and anyhow were too engrossed in the invoice, as Alpiew read out the final article on Beau's shopping list. ' "Item: two scrupulii of antimony." '

FIVE

Decoction

*The digestion of a substance
in the flask without the addition
of any other material.*

Olympe Athenée Montelimar, Duchesse de Pigalle, was in mourning. Swathed from head to foot in black satin, as she stepped forward dolefully to welcome her visitors, her carrot-coloured hair seemed to light up her face like a garish halo.

'My darling Ashby!' She strode towards the Countess, her hands outstretched, ready for the Countess to step into her arms. 'I knew you'd come to me.'

The Countess ducked out of her path, and pressed herself hard against the door jamb. She held her hand out. 'Stand back, you lesbian,' she declared in a firm voice.

Pigalle raised her shoulders and shook her head in a Gallic way. 'But I thought . . .'

'Because I am attired as a man, it does not necessarily follow that I am a convert to the ways of Sappho.' The Countess moved into the darkened room. 'Why are all the curtains drawn, and the candles lit? It's only mid-afternoon.'

She turned to face her old friend with a sudden and rather unbalancing sweep. As she teetered she grabbed on to a nearby table to steady herself and found herself eye to eye with the corpse of a tattered red squirrel.

'It's George, I'm afraid,' swooped Pigalle in an impenetrable French accent, bending lovingly over the open casket. ''E died last night. It's been a bad week for me. On Monday a rat got my nightingale, yesterday my darling jackdaw flew off with my favourite earrings and hasn't returned, and now . . . George.' She reached out a long knobbly finger and stroked the mangy cadaver. 'I think it was an ague.'

Blinking in the darkness Alpiew looked around her. She'd never seen anything like it. The room was the most ornately decorated place she'd ever encountered. Swags of silk and satin draped every sumptuous wall. Gorgeous oil-paintings of a beautiful woman in various stages of undress hung over the fireplace and on the wall opposite the shuttered window. On another wall hung a guitar. The furniture was red and gold. Every surface was covered with a hundred things: a large conch shell, a necklace, a clock, a cabbage, a jar of paintbrushes, a pair of tom-toms, a sleeping cat, a stuffed crocodile. The carpet resembled a thick woollen blanket of flowers and ribbons with white polka dots. But on closer inspection Alpiew discovered these to be bird excrement.

'We need sanctuary,' said the Countess, matter of factly.

'Not your creditors again, darlink?'

'Worse than that, I'm afraid, Olympe, dear. I'm wanted for murder.'

Pigalle beamed in a wild red-lipped leer. 'Why didn't

you say so? How marvellous!' She clapped her hand in the direction of the moustachioed footman. 'Azis! Set out ze card-table. We have four for basset.' She looked sympathetically towards the Countess. 'Who was it, darlink? Zat swine of a husband of yours?'

'But, madame,' Azis coughed in the direction of the dead squirrel, 'the ceremony for . . .'

'Oh, yes, of course.' Pigalle banged the lid on the squirrel's box and carried it over to the fireplace. 'Goodbye, faithful servant,' she cried, and with a nonchalant toss flung the little coffin into the flames, before marching back to take a seat next to the Countess, who was now perched primly on a red velvet-covered sofa. 'So tell me ALL . . .'

While Azis and Alpiew set up the chairs and put out the cards the Countess explained the events of the last few days to the Duchesse.

'So who do you think did it?' said Pigalle rising from the sofa at the end of the saga, ready to take her place at the card-table.

'It's an open-and-shut case, in my opinion.' The Countess rubbed her hands together. 'It was the wife.'

Pigalle started shuffling the cards.

'Or the maid,' piped Alpiew.

The Countess hovered by her chair. 'I don't have any money.'

'Of course not, darlink. I take notes of credit.' Pigalle thrust out her hand. 'Azis! My mask.'

Azis took the red-sequinned vizard mask which hung from the door handle and passed it to his mistress. She clapped it on. 'It's important zat I wear a mask so you can't see from my face whether I am winning or losing.'

She spread out her hand of cards, then slammed one down on the baize top. 'I face.'

Alpiew shifted in her seat. What a bind they were in. While they were here they couldn't start discovering the real culprit, but if they ventured out they were in danger of being apprehended for the crime. She laid down a seven of clubs.

'What you both need, my friends, is a Tyburn Ticket,' squawked Pigalle. 'It is ze latest thing. All my friends want one. It goes like this: First you catch a highway robber, then you turn him in, then zey give you the Tyburn Ticket, then you are immune from ze gallows.'

The Countess shuddered and she clasped at her scrawny neck, thereby giving Pigalle just enough time to get a good look at her cards.

Alpiew rolled her eyes ceiling-wards and laid down a three of hearts. It would be harder to catch a high-way robber than it would be to find out who killed Beau.

'All this talk of poisoning, it's like old times. Do you remember, Ashby, back in Pareee? Everyone there was at it. Poison was almost a national pastime. And when zey caught the guilty ones zey burned zem alive, and we all went to watch, and our clothings were ruined.'

The Countess laughed. 'Covered in smuts! Oh, Olympe, dear, those were the days!'

'And we all loved King Charlie, didn't we?'

The Countess let out a winsome sigh. 'Indeed we did.'

'I remember, you were a devil.' Pigalle gave her friend a little nudge and had a closer look at her cards. 'Remember when you wrote on your bed-head "Leroy was Here"! Oh how we laughed.'

'Leroy?' said Alpiew, re-sorting her cards and flinging down an ace.

'French, darlink! *Le roi*! Ze king.' She glanced at the table. 'Oh, an ace. Zat beats a king.'

Azis was sweeping up the cards, ready to re-shuffle.

'It's all so different now.' The Countess knew she had lost this hand, and passed her cards over.

'*Au contraire*, my friend, *nothing* 'as changed,' snapped Pigalle, furious at having lost a hand to a domestic. 'Today it is all verbiage. Everyone at court *spouts* piety, *alors*, but when ze darkness comes zey are all rousting each other, like always.'

Azis had dealt a second hand.

Pigalle picked hers up and started furiously sorting. 'I have a box tomorrow for ze theatre. Benefit performance for Monsieur Finger, ze musician. Ze famous Italian castrato, Sigismondo Fideli, will be singing. Would you like to join me?' She slammed down a knave.

The Countess jumped up and down on her chair, nodding. 'I would adore to.'

This was too much for Alpiew, who leapt to her feet. 'May I remind you, your ladyship, that we are wanted on the capital charge of murder? And unless we can prove that we are innocent we will be on the run for the rest of our lives.'

The Countess bit her lip. Living here in this lovely place, with a friend who remembered the old days, sounded like heaven to her.

'And sooner or later,' added Alpiew, reading the Countess's mind, 'if we stay here they will find us, and then they will march us to Tyburn where we will be hanged by our necks until dead. I face.' She deposited her winning hand on the table-top.

'Ze girl is right,' declared Pigalle, flinging down her cards. 'You must sleep 'ere tonight, but when it is dark, you must go to zis woman, Mrs Wilson, and see if you can get her to confess . . . Before she . . .' Pigalle made a grotesque face indicating a state of death.

'It's almost dark now.' Alpiew raked in the money she had won, including a credit note from the Countess.

'No, no,' shrieked Pigalle. 'Much best after midnight . . . later. When all the Charlies are asleep, and ze beadle and his constables in their cups. Just before dawn is best.'

The Countess gave her a sideways look. 'How do you know this?'

'So many times I have clambered in through windows to recover love-letters written in a rash moment.'

'I face,' said Alpiew, turning up a knave of diamonds.

'Oh, and I would suggest a decent gentleman's set of breeches under zat cloak.'

The Countess looked flustered.

'I can lend you some of mine,' smiled Pigalle. 'I have some gorgeous male vestments. They will suit you, darlink.'

A tattered parrot in the corner let out a wild screech, and the monkey which till now had been asleep on a sideboard leapt up and clambered up the curtains.

'I mase,' said the Countess. 'Pigalle, sweetheart, I'm so hungry I can't think straight.'

'Why didn't you say?' Pigalle leapt up from her seat. 'I have a perfect little supper for us. Azis, heat up ze fromage pecan, *s'il vous plaît.*'

Alpiew shuddered. More French cooking. Still, she had money in her pocket, they had a comfortable place to sleep and sometime after midnight she and the Countess would creep out and confront Mrs Wilson.

Mrs Wilson woke with a start.

The Countess put her finger to her mouth. 'It's us, Mrs Wilson,' she whispered. 'Your employees.'

Mrs Wilson sat bolt upright. Alpiew had drawn the curtains and the first streaks of dawn were visible over the rooftops.

After what had turned out to be a delicious dinner of quails grilled with cheese washed down with a glass of Asti Spumante ('I get it shipped in specially, darlink, from Piedmont'), both the Countess and Alpiew fell into a deep and profound sleep and hadn't woken until the milk pails were rattling outside their windows.

It was still dark when, wearing their gentlemen's attire, the two women had made their way across the city to Angel Court. They climbed in through a downstairs window, and crept up the stairs. Alpiew showed the Countess the way to Mrs Wilson's bedchamber.

'Why are you here?' Mrs Wilson wiped the hair out of her eyes. 'I thought . . .'

'You thought,' said the Countess, adjusting her heavy peruke, 'that I was in prison. But as you see, I have been released.' She strolled casually round to the side of the bed and perched herself on a blanket by the foot-post. 'So tell me true. Was it you? Did you engage us to mask your own crime? Have your husband murdered, being then certain that Alpiew and I would be the first to stumble across his corpse, and therefore the Justice's suspects? Was that your plan?'

Before Mrs Wilson could speak, Alpiew, who was now crouching at the other side of the bed, whispered into her ear: 'Who is your accomplice? The big man who was also tailing your husband? Is he your lover?'

'Or,' added the Countess, 'did you employ him to follow us?'

'To make sure we would be there at the right time?' hissed Alpiew.

The grey light was filtering into the room now and showed Mrs Wilson's pale complexion. She did not speak.

'Why did you employ us, Mrs Wilson? Tell us the real reason you paid us to follow your husband.'

'I told you everything before.' Mrs Wilson leant back against her pillows. 'I suspected my husband was seeing another woman. I thought he was giving her money. Why else are we in debt everywhere?'

Alpiew raised an eyebrow as she glanced round the well-appointed room, furnished in the latest style.

'I was a wealthy woman. I brought my husband a substantial dowry. My lawyer tells me now I've nothing but this house and its contents. My husband, when I married him, was a successful merchant. Yet his strongbox is full of nothing but notes of debit.'

'So you had him killed to stem the flow?'

'I did not. I did not have him killed. I loved him. He was my life.'

'You let the authorities arrest me, and did nothing to free me.' The Countess leaned back. 'We did our part,' she said. 'Perhaps you might explain your position regarding our employment to the authorities so that they will leave us be.'

The room was almost light. Alpiew rose and glanced anxiously out of the window. Servants were scurrying back and forth carrying water pails, milk jugs, loaves of bread. 'Write it for us. Write a letter in which you say you were employing us to follow your husband, but you believe us to be innocent of his murder.'

Mrs Wilson shook her head. 'I cannot do that.'

'Because you are the guilty one?' The Countess loomed over her. 'You must. Or we will arrange for the constables to be told that you said to us just two days before he was killed that you wished your husband dead.'

'I did not.'

Alpiew swung round and faced her. 'You said if he had another woman that you wished "That he be gone. Gone forever. Never to return."'

Mrs Wilson shook her head.

'Only a few words,' said Alpiew, pulling items from her pocket. 'Here's pen and paper. Now write.'

'It's impossible.' Mrs Wilson bowed her head. Alpiew thrust the pen into her hand.

Mrs Wilson started to cry. 'But I cannot write. I do not know my letters.' She let out a desperate sob. 'I know you didn't kill my Beau. But nor did I. You must believe me. I loved him. He gave me to believe that he loved me. I wanted to have his child, and move to a house in the country and be away from all this hurry and scurry. But now it will never be.'

Alpiew and the Countess exchanged a look.

'Was it guilt made you take poison?'

'I took no poison. I almost died that night out of grief.'

Alpiew laughed in her face. 'Madam, I can assure you, you did take poison. You took a measure of pure antimony. I was with the apothecary who identified the matter in your bedside cup to your lawyer.'

'No.' Mrs Wilson looked very puzzled. 'That cannot be. I was ill because I was so upset.'

'No, madam.' Alpiew shook her head. 'I assure you it was poison.'

'I took the powder before I heard that Beau was . . .' Her words broke off and again tears brimmed in her eyes. 'I took the powder as I did every night.' Mrs Wilson tugged open a drawer next to her bed. 'I took the powder Beau had prepared for me.'

The Countess raised her pencilled-in eyebrows. 'Beau prepared the sachet of poison for you?'

'Not poison. I took the same each night. He always prepared the powder himself. To strengthen me, so that I might become pregnant and bring us an heir.' She pulled a crumpled paper from the drawer.

The Countess took the wrapper, a piece of white paper, empty, but folded to hold a powder, and marked with a ♀.

'It's the sign for woman,' said Mrs Wilson quietly. The Countess inspected the paper closely then pocketed it and peered into the drawer. It was full of the usual female things: pins, brooches, ribbons, powder, rouge, some Spanish papers and a pot of flesh-tinted addition. She congratulated herself on her correct surmise that Mrs Wilson wore paint.

'There seem to be no others, madam. Yet you talk as though there was a regular supply.'

'Indeed there was. Beau would prepare the stuff in

batches, and wrapped it in a paper which my maid Betty brought to me each evening.'

Alpiew, still on the lookout at the window, spun round. The mysterious Betty! What had she to do with this affair? 'Why should anyone want to murder your husband?' she asked. 'Apart from you, that is.'

'That I do not know. Everyone loved him. Even the servants. Betty made no secret of her adoration of him. He was a wonderful man.'

Alpiew raised her eyebrows. Betty again! She'd seen a display of that adoration with her own eyes, and knew that even if Betty was wild about Beau, she held nothing but contempt for his wife.

'Whoever borrowed my Beau for occasional nights,' sighed Mrs Wilson, 'has now taken him from me forever.' She took the Countess's hand and squeezed it. 'I am truly sorry that by employing you I have embroiled you in this living hell. Now all I ask is for your continued help. Please, Lady Ashby de la Zouche, please help me to find Beau's killers and to bring them to justice.'

The Countess shuffled backwards a little.

Mrs Wilson threw back the covers and opened a small casket on the table beside the bed. 'I will pay you richly, I swear. But I can only pay you if you bring me results.' She drew out a small drawstring purse. 'Here's five guineas to cover your costs. Find out who killed Beau. And why.'

'But you say you have nothing but debts, madam. How will you be able to pay us handsomely?'

'Now that Beau is dead I will have money enough . . .'

A sudden banging at the front door made Alpiew jump back from the window.

'Oh Lord, madam, it's the constables. Someone must have seen us climbing in.'

Mrs Wilson looked from Alpiew to the Countess and back. 'You haven't been released at all, have you? You are on the run . . .' She reached out and grabbed the Countess by a plump arm. 'If you help me, I will help you.'

The Countess nodded, leaping from foot to foot as though she could dance herself away from this trouble-some spot.

Mrs Wilson pulled back a tapestry wall-covering beside the bed. She grabbed the Countess by the shoulders and pushed her through a small hidden door.

'What's this? A priest's hole?'

'It's my garde de robe, fool! Quickly.'

Alpiew followed into the tiny room and both women cowered behind the racks of mantuas, gowns, cloaks and riding jackets. Alpiew had a quick root round and dis-covered a tiny casement window at the end of the rack of clothing.

Through the tapestry curtain they could hear rapidly advancing footsteps on the stairs then Mrs Wilson's bed-chamber door being flung open.

'Mrs Elizabeth Wilson?' boomed a male voice.

Mrs Wilson's voice was clear. She must be standing at the other side of the curtain. 'Yes.' Her voice quivered slightly.

'Are you alone?'

There was a pause. Alpiew hoped that Mrs Wilson was not giving the constables a treacherous glance in the direction of the garde de robe.

'Where were you between nine and ten of the clock

on the night your spouse Beau Wilson met with his fate?'

'I was here, at home.' Mrs Wilson walked away from the curtain, and the bed creaked a little. She had obviously sat down on it.

Alpiew mouthed to the Countess pointing to the tiny window. 'I'm going to try . . .' She slowly unbolted the catch and lifted her leg up to the sill.

'We have received information that you were seen walking briskly from St Paul's churchyard a few minutes before the constables came across your husband's slaughtered corpse.'

'No, no.' Mrs Wilson's voice was now shaking. 'I swear I was here, at home.'

Alpiew's legs were both outside now, and she was squeezing her bottom through the gap.

'And where is your paramour?'

'I have no paramour.'

Alpiew swivelled round and prepared to drop to the ground. She gave a little wave before slithering out of the window and out of the Countess's sight.

'That's enough. Constable, tie her hands.' A sudden scurry of feet. 'We are taking you to a Justice of the Peace, where we will be bringing grave charges against you.'

'But . . .'

'Yeouch!'

The Countess winced. It was the sound of Alpiew hitting the ground.

'What was that?' Footsteps moved towards the curtain. 'So, who have we here?' The curtain was flung back, the door opened and then the rack of clothes parted revealing the Countess, crouching. She teetered forwards.

'Your gentleman friend . . . ?' The constable tugged the Countess out of the garde de robe by her cloak, and looked her up and down. 'Oh, the devil, Mrs Wilson. What scurvy rogue is this?'

''Tis no gentleman friend, sirrah. 'Tis a woman.'

'Each to his own taste . . .' The constable was taking in the picture before him: The smiling Countess, her tubby little body squeezed into gentleman's attire, her peruke fetchingly covering one eye. 'So, Mrs Wilson, would you care to effect the introductions?'

The Countess pulled off her peruke and opened her jacket, exposing the contours of her considerable bust beneath the linen shirt and steinkirk. 'Mrs Wilson is right, Constable. I am no lady's paramour. I am Lady Ashby de la Zouche.'

The constable's men were laughing into their sleeves.

'Well, well.' The constable coughed. 'Just the woman we were looking for. Clever escape you effected yesterday, madam.'

He turned and signalled to his friends, who had tied Mrs Wilson and thrown a cloak over her shoulders to cover her dishabillé. 'Take her down, boys.'

'Well, Lady Whatsit. I am here to tell you that due to informations given by various bystanders who saw a tall, elegant woman running from the scene . . .' The constable ran his eyes up and down the short squat figure of the Countess. 'It seems, therefore, you are no longer under suspicion. That your story about falling across the corpse has been believed by the Justice of the Peace. So you are free to go. Though perhaps you might like to explain to me what you are doing *here*.'

The Countess thought quickly. 'I knew the only person

who could arrange for me to be freed was Mrs Wilson. I came here to ask her to . . .'

The constable gave her a smile and clapped her on the shoulder. 'So when it comes to trial you are saying that you will give evidence against Mrs Wilson?'

The Countess nodded. 'I will give evidence, yes.' She was sure that Alpiew would be in a good position by now, and prepared to follow the inevitable strange procession leading Mrs Wilson to the Justice of the Peace and thence to whichever lock-up or prison was appointed for her incarceration.

'You are living at your own lodgings?'

The Countess gave a brisk nod. 'I will be found at Anglesey House, yes.'

'Then you may go.'

Alpiew had had a rough landing on to a small gorse bush and lost her periwig. She rushed across the garden and, shoving the wig back on to her head, she turned the back-door handle and strode into the hall with all the authority of one who was supposed to be in the house.

The cook, who had been listening on the stairs and was now gossiping in the hall with Beau's valet, stood staring at her. Alpiew tipped the brow of her hat and said in her deepest voice: 'I'm with the constables, madam,' then walked straight to the front door through which she briskly exited.

She hovered on the road outside, where she had watched when Beau's body was brought back, until, to her surprise, the constables bundled Mrs Wilson out of the house.

She hesitated for a moment. What to do? Follow Mrs Wilson, or see what had happened to the Countess? She decided to follow the constables.

She lingered in a doorway while Mrs Wilson was bundled on to the steps of the Justice's house and heard him order that she be detained at the Fleet. When she had heard this news she hurried back to Chale House.

The Countess was peering into the windows of an India house on the corner of Ludgate Street when Alpiew found her.

'Look at these Japan work trays! Beautiful, and only a guinea apiece.'

Alpiew glanced over her shoulder at the sumptuous display of pictures, fans, china, and other fashionable impertinences.

'Come, Alpiew,' the Countess flashed the five guinea pieces in her palm. 'We have some money, let us sit among all this modish nick-nackatory, and take a dish of tea, while we chew over the cud.'

Alpiew was all hurry and go. 'But, madam, surely we cannot . . .'

The Countess grabbed her by the wrist and yanked her into the shop door. 'What can we do now in such a hurry? Our chief suspect is detained and our best plan is to actually *have* a plan. Draw up a list of clues.'

They took a table at the back of the shop and sipped their tea, watching with amazement as customers came in and paid over two guineas for items as small as sandalwood fans, paper nosegays and stoneware grout cups.

'So could Mrs Wilson have been the woman in the graveyard?' The Countess chomped a small round biscuit. 'Think hard, Alpiew. The constable says she was there. Could it have been Mrs Wilson behind the silver vizard mask?'

'I think not.' Alpiew shook her head. 'Too tall. Too elegant.'

The Countess slurped from her tea dish. 'I agree. I believe the Wilson woman is telling us the truth. Though I'm not sure it's the whole truth and nothing but the truth. Do you think she can write?'

'They say every chambermaid in London can write now, but that doesn't mean that every merchant's wife can too.'

Two Quaker women, bowing at everyone in sight, and checking the prices on items in a nearby display gave Alpiew a smile which was more like a threat. 'I think they want our table,' said Alpiew.

The Countess threw them a magisterial look. 'Let them sing for it. Continue, Alpiew.'

'If Mrs Wilson wanted to rid herself of her husband – and remember we heard her say today that since he was dead she would have money – even if she was not physically there herself, it is still possible she hired another to do the dirty work.'

'Taking the powder . . .' The Countess looked towards the Quakers, dropped another biscuit into her mouth and, crunching loudly, continued: '. . . to make herself ill to cast away suspicion from herself.' Popping another biscuit into her mouth, she stopped mid-chew, crumbs flying. 'But would it do that? Surely the poison trick only made her seem more guilty. As though she regretted what she had done.'

Alpiew sighed. 'So that is that, then. She is guilty and we will not be paid more than this five guineas?'

The Countess shook her head. 'No . . .'

A hovering waitress snatched away the tea dishes. 'Anything more?' She inclined her head in the direction of the Quakers. 'Only there's a queue for this table.'

The Countess glared. The Quakers bowed in unison. 'Bring us the menu,' she snapped. 'We want more. The ladies who wait could surely browse among the nick-nackatories on sale in this establishment.'

The girl moved off. The Quakers huffed.

'I'm not being rushed by followers of some weird new cult. If Mrs Wilson is guilty and we can discover her accomplices to the Justice perhaps we will earn a reward. Similarly, on the small chance that she is in fact innocent, then eventually she will pay us. We can't lose.'

The serving girl thrust the menu at the Countess and gave her a surly glare. Alpiew clearly heard the words 'bizarre', and 'unnatural' from the direction of the Quakers.

'Another pint of bohea, if you please.' The Countess thrust the menu back whence it had come and raised her voice. '*And* a plate of ratafias.'

'So what have we, milady? Let us deduce the facts.'

'What have we, indeed?' The Countess counted on her fingers. 'Suspects: Mrs Wilson, the tall elegant lady in the mask and the big thug who rowed Beau away.'

'You have missed one.' Alpiew cocked her head in thought. 'It is the maid Betty I am suspicious of. I'll wager she knows more than anyone the truth of the matter.'

She reminded the Countess how she had seen Betty running from the house the morning Mrs Wilson was taken ill. 'And remember I told you how passionately she threw herself on Beau's body.'

The Countess sighed. 'So many mysteries: who wrote the note that we saw him take from the orange?'

'Well, Mrs Wilson would be the obvious.'

'But she just said she couldn't write.'

'Ah, yes.'

'And the powder. If it was the usual powder, then we know why she took it, but if it was another, who did the switch?'

A waiter arrived with a pot of tea and a plate on which stood two glasses of a dark red liquid. Although early in the day, the girl had obviously had enough.

'What are those?' The Countess peered at the glasses.

'Two ratafias, madam.' The waiter placed them on the table.

'Ratafias?'

'Yes, madam, two ratafia wines.'

'Not wine, you blockhead,' sighed Alpiew. 'My lady wanted ratafia *biscuits*. Why would she ask for a *plate* of ratafia wine?'

'All right, all right.' The Countess waved her hand. 'We'll take the wine, but please bring us some ratafia biscuits as well.'

The Quakers were now openly disapproving.

Alpiew caught their look and whispered. 'We can't drink strong waters at this time of the morning . . .'

'Why not? We can drink whatever we want, whenever we want without their approbation.' The Countess took a sip, holding up her glass, as though toasting. 'Mmm! Delicious!'

Alpiew bit her lip. 'Confusion, confusion!' she

muttered, watching the waiting girl scribbling out their bill in order to appease the puffing Quakers. The Countess sipped at her ratafia wine. 'Mrs Wilson's got a few more questions to answer. But best if we leave her to rot a while in the Fleet, and in the meantime I suggest we find the elusive Betty and smoke her out.' The Countess tossed back the rest of her wine and took a swill of tea. 'Come along, Alpiew, drink up, drink up. 'Tis my opinion, you know, that Quakers are the most designing, deceitful sect of creatures in the world, who assume more pride and exact more homage from their seeming sanctity, than the truly pious.' She made sure to raise her voice a little.

Looking at the glass of ratafia, Alpiew screwed up her face and shook her head. 'It's too early for a fortified wine, madam. I'll get a megrim.'

'No problem, my dear.' The Countess downed the second ratafia in one gulp, and grinned wildly. 'Pray ladies, put off that sanctified aspect and try to look like a pair of inhabitants of this world. 'Tis soon enough you'll be in the next.' She strode across the shop to the cash desk, and stooped to speak to the cashier. 'I find myself amazed to see two such proud, sanctified sisters amid all this lovely stuff which they consider mere trash and trumpery.' While the Countess paid, the serving girl arrived at the table with the biscuits. Alpiew took them straight from the plate and crammed them into her pocket as she left the shop.

It was only when a pair of boys trundling along with an empty chair stopped to laugh at them both that Alpiew and the Countess looked at one another and remembered they were still dressed in male clothing. Remembering the outrage on the faces of the two Quaker women, they threw back their heads and laughed until they ached.

The blackened out windows of the Alsatia warehouse gave no clue as to whether Betty, or indeed anybody was inside.

After returning to German Street to change back into their usual female clothing, Alpiew and the Countess had called in at Chale House asking for Betty, but the sobbing cook told her she'd not been seen since yesterday morning, before Mrs Wilson was 'taken bad'.

'When I saw her scuttling past the apothecary's shop,' Alpiew told the Countess as they walked away in the direction of Salisbury Court.

The alleys of Alsatia didn't look so bad by daylight. But the characters who populated it seemed even worse up close. 'Lying, fraud, impudence and misery are drawn in all the lines of their countenances,' whispered the Countess, as they trotted briskly through a small square packed with loitering fellows puffing on pipes and swigging from black bottles. 'Nothing but devilism in every feature.'

The two women linked arms, their eyes darting, and turned into a narrow alley.

'It stinks worse than a urinal in August.' The Countess held a handkerchief to her nose and looked about, noticing wizened women peeping from behind the ragged curtains of upstairs windows. 'Perhaps Betty belongs to the criminal fraternity which inhabits this dreadful place.'

'Maybe,' said Alpiew, 'she was stealing from the Wilson house. Taking all those bits of furniture that Mrs

Wilson said had gone missing. She was certainly hurrying something away under her cloak yesterday morning.'

A tall, dark man jostled them out of his way, and spat a gob of phlegm on to the cobbles.

'I have never known a place peopled by such an abominable race of degenerate reprobates,' murmured the Countess, wrapping her cloak tighter about her. 'Like bats and owls they skulk in their obscure holes by daylight, emerging at night to exercise their villainy. It's the nearest London gets to Sodom, I imagine.'

'This is the place I saw her go into.' Alpiew was trying to peer through the blacked-out ankle-height window.

'What treasure trove will we discover behind these walls?' The Countess moved along to the little Gothic door and tried peeping through the keyhole. 'There's a candle lit,' she hissed at Alpiew. 'Someone is inside.'

The Countess grabbed the handle. 'Then there's nothing else for it,' she cried and pushed at the door, which, to her surprise, opened. The two women tumbled down a short wooden flight of steps and landed in a heap on the stone floor.

Although from the outside this cellar, situated so near the wharves of the Thames, looked to be a dank cold place, they found themselves in a cluttered room of unusual warmth. Shelves lined the walls. Upon them stood row upon row of jars, bottles, books, mortars, boxes. On the long counter which ran the length of the far wall there were piles of spoons and pestles and strange glass vessels and copper basins. In one corner a small brick stove belched out heat and an orange glow. In the other a tatty grey curtain was pulled across. Probably hiding a close-stool, thought the Countess. Dotted around the room, which was obviously in use as an ela-boratory, were pieces of substantial furniture. An expen-sive-looking easy chair, an oak chest inlaid with ivory, a pretty little escritoire, a footstool.

In the centre of the floor was a crumpled woollen blanket and a feather pillow.

'Phough!' exclaimed the Countess, waving her hand about. 'What is that abominable smell?'

Alpiew raised her fingers to her lips. She had noticed a scurry of fabric disappear behind the curtain. With a swift motion she yanked it back. Crouching on the floor, pressed tight against the wall and curled up as though against injury, cowered Beau Wilson's maid, Betty. She looked dishevelled and tear-stained.

'Hey day! What have we here?' exclaimed the Coun-tess, hauling herself to a standing position. 'The quarry is cornered.'

Like a hunted animal Betty flung herself towards the steps and the open door. But as she passed Alpiew grabbed at her hair, and the Countess blocked the way. Betty's arms flailed out, hitting the Countess, grabbing at her clothing. She was not going to be captured without a struggle.

'Is this the love nest you shared with Beau Wilson?' taunted the Countess while Alpiew started a hair-pulling contest with Betty. Suddenly with a wail Betty let go, and fell to the ground sobbing.

Alpiew took the opportunity to pin her down by sitting on her, while the Countess trotted up the steps and closed the door to the street.

But closing the door plunged the cellar into darkness, for the agitation of the fight had blown out the candle.

The only illumination was an orange glow coming from the brick stove. The Countess made the slow careful descent of the stairs in the dark.

'So, Betty,' said Alpiew, gripping Betty's wrists and pinning them to the floor, 'did you kill him?'

Betty stopped wriggling and started quietly to cry, tears spilling down her cheeks and dripping on to the floor. 'Of course I didn't? Why would I? He was everything to me.'

The Countess was trying to find the candle while bumping into the furniture. 'Everything?'

'He held my future in his hands.' Betty lay perfectly still now, her voice cracked and thin. 'I adored him.'

'And what was Beau Wilson to you?' The Countess almost hummed her question, feeling along the worktop for the candle. 'Was he your lover?'

'How could that be?' Betty sobbed again, shaking her head. 'Of course not. I was just a maid and he a gentleman.' She rolled again into a tight ball. '*She* killed him. I know she did.'

'Did she indeed?' The Countess nodded at Alpiew, who was still sitting upon the little maid. This was good. And what's more the Countess had found the candle. Now she only needed to find the tinder-box. 'You seem very miserable about it all, Betty. And no wonder! How alone you must feel at this time.' She stooped down and stroked the girl's hair. 'No one who understands your point of view.' She turned to Alpiew and snapped. 'Stop being so cruel, Mistress Alpiew. You are not in a theatrical production of *The Rival Queens*, so stop playing at Roxana fighting with Statira and help Mistress Betty to her feet.'

Alpiew was mystified. She'd never heard of the play, let alone seen it, but she had heard about the famous scene so popular with the crowds and actresses alike where two barnstorming leading ladies fought each other tooth and claw for the love of Alexander the Great (on two occasions really stabbing each other with the prop daggers), and helped Betty to her feet.

'He was a lovely man, Mr Wilson.' The girl sobbed on. 'So kind. So gentle. Wouldn't hurt a fly. No one was ever so kind to me as he was.'

'Fetch the blanket, Alpiew.' The Countess helped Betty to a chair. 'Poor Betty has had a nasty shock.'

While Alpiew wrapped the blanket round Betty's shoulders, the Countess, her eyes now accustomed to the light, glanced round the room, which had all the trappings of a workshop, with its great earthenware jars, strange metal contraptions and containers, lengths of tubing, and shelves of books and more jars.

'What is this place where you have taken refuge?' asked the Countess. 'It must be very uncomfortable, living here.'

Betty's eyes darted around, as though worried that the Countess may have seen something she shouldn't.

'It's an elaboratory, madam,' she said. 'I worked here for Mr Wilson.'

'Did Mrs Wilson come here a lot?'

'Mrs Wilson? No, never.' Betty wiped the tears from her cheeks. 'No one knew about the place. Just Mr Wilson and me. I was his assistant. He was training me, like an apprentice, you know.'

'It's very strange for a girl to be apprenticed in a place like this, isn't it?' Alpiew was puzzled. 'A vinegar works, an oil shop, a brewery, yes, girls are trained up to work in places like that, but if I'm not wrong, this place must be connected with the new experimental philosophy, and the fair sex are not so welcome in that brave world.'

The Countess was fingering a glass jar half-full of bright green powder. 'What did this work of yours entail?'

'I helped him mix . . .' Betty shook her head. 'I promised him. I swore I would not tell a soul.'

The Countess lowered herself on to a small brown leather footstool and perched upon it at Betty's feet. She grabbed Betty's hand and started patting it. 'I know, I know. Poor Beau was always trying to hide all knowledge of his discoveries, but what's the point now, eh? Alpiew and myself . . . I am the Countess Anastasia Ashby de la Zouche, by the way.' She nodded towards Alpiew. 'My maid Alpiew.' She kept up the rhythmic hand-patting. 'We were trying to protect Beau, because we knew he was in trouble, isn't that right, Alpiew?'

Betty's lips were quivering. She was still unsure.

'Beau, Mr Wilson, arranged for Alpiew and me to accompany him to the lecture at Gresham College a few days ago. Even though we are women! As you know he took no notice of silly prejudice, and encouraged *us* too, you see. Because it was *so* important to him, this project, which cost him so much money, and almost his marriage. And his life . . .' She waited to see Betty's response. But the girl was still beadily watching her. 'And now we are all in this together, because he is . . . gone.' The Countess broke off and burst into racking tears.

Alpiew stood gaping at her mistress. Where had all

that come from? Betty grasped the Countess's hand and gripped it hard.

The Countess wildly searched her memory for words from the deadly boring scientific lecture.

'Had he suddenly come to a projection? Or was he still merely at the calcination stage? Something had happened, that is sure. The afternoon of the theatre, when he got the note . . .'

'You know about the note?' Betty's eyes lit up. 'Then you must know who killed him. That note sent him to meet his death . . .'

'She must have been desperate,' cooed the Countess. 'Finding all her money gone . . .'

'Oh, I think she had money enough.' Betty's eyes narrowed. 'She was rich. That was the whole point. He would never have done it otherwise.' She stood up and strode across to a chest of drawers and, pulling open a drawer, revealed a great pile of golden guinea coins. 'Here is the proof.' She sifted her hands through the glittering coins. 'She gave him all this on the day she killed him.'

'She gave him all that?' Alpiew stared at the drawer. 'There must be over a hundred guineas. So why did she tell us she was destitute?'

'You've *talked* to her?' Betty turned and glared at Alpiew. 'Where is she? Bring me to her.'

The Countess cocked her head. Something wasn't quite adding up here, and Alpiew was on the verge of cobbling up their inquiry. 'Alpiew, dear, let me ask the questions while you light a few more candles about the place. It's awful dark. Now, Betty, I need you to tell me about the powders you prepared for her.'

'Who?'

'Mrs Wilson.'

'Oh.' The turn in Betty's inflection gave the Countess all she needed to know. There were two 'she's: Mrs Wilson – and another.

'Mr Wilson made the stuff up and I wrapped them in papers.'

The Countess struggled up from the low pouf, to discover that both feet had gone to sleep. Grasping the bare brick wall for anchor, she teetered in Betty's direction. 'The powders were prepared here, I suppose?'

Betty nodded. 'What have the powders to do with it?'

'Someone tried to kill Mrs Wilson too, didn't they?' She searched Betty's eyes for any give-away flickers. 'Show me the stuff you prepared for Mrs Wilson.'

Betty pointed up to some high shelves crammed with hundreds of labelled bottles and jars. 'Venus. That's the one.' Hoiking up her skirts she clambered on to the worktop and reached up for the jar, a large pretty earthenware vessel in blue and white delft. 'Mr Wilson made up the receipt himself. It's for women.' She blushed as she placed the jar on the top and jumped to the floor. 'Married women, I should say, for I believe it's to do with procreation and such. I was not to take the stuff. On strict orders.' She opened a drawer and displayed a sheaf of papers marked with a ♀. 'It's a sign for "Woman", Mr Wilson said. Venus was a woman, you see.'

The Countess was looking Betty up and down, mystified.

'It's part of the teaching,' Betty explained. She took a paper, opened the jar and took a scoop of the brown powder within, which she levelled off with an iron

146

spatula. Then she tipped the powder into the centre of the paper, and with the deftness of a conjuror folded the paper so that no powder could escape. 'One sachet ready for consumption.' She held the finished product up for the Countess to see.

'You're quite an expert.' The Countess took the powder and inspected the neatly folded back. 'Beau, Mr Wilson, knew what he was doing when he took you as his apprentice.'

Alpiew had illuminated the cellar and was now taking a good look round. It was strange. Although the worktops were rough wood, the shelves dirty, the walls black with soot, every piece of furniture was elegant drawing-room stuff in perfect condition: an ornate oak and wicker easy chair, a fine barley sugar-legged side-table, a mahogany escritoire, a pair of silver wall sconces.

'It's a fine elaboratory, to be sure,' said Alpiew, prodding at a huge metal machine. 'I would be glad to make a few experiments here myself. Did Mr Wilson study the writings of Mr Newton?'

'Isaac Newton?' Betty's face lit up. 'Oh, he idolised him.'

'I know Mr Newton personally,' leered the Countess. 'He is my next-door neighbour.'

Alpiew was now checking the titles of all the books on the worktop. 'So this place was a secret. Am I right? That would be important in a business like this.'

'And Mr Wilson brought this nice furniture here from Angel Court?'

'He needed something to write on, and somewhere to sit.' It was a relief to Betty to have someone she could talk to. 'So I carried it here piece by piece.'

So that explained the mystery of Mrs Wilson's disappearing furniture.

'I was not strong enough to smuggle a bed here, so he made do with blankets and a pillow.'

Though her back was to them, Alpiew stopped moving. She didn't want to hear the Countess's response to that one.

'You both slept here from time to time?' The Countess was rubbing her foot, as though she was only vaguely interested in the reply.

'I never slept here. Never.' The Countess was fingering the blanket at her feet. 'Until last night.'

'Why suddenly last night?' Alpiew swung round.

Betty snatched the blanket up and folded it. 'Because I was frightened. After what happened to Mr Wilson, I thought they might come looking for me.'

'Why didn't you leave right away, when they brought Mr Wilson's body home?'

Betty threw up her arms. 'You've seen the streets round here. I would have been too frightened in the dark.'

'But Mr Wilson stayed here with *her* some nights?'

'She didn't know where he worked.' Betty furrowed her brow. 'No. He stayed here when the process needed watching, and on other nights he stayed at home.'

'Always at home?'

'Except . . .' Betty's lips tightened. 'Except for the six times he went to her.'

'Six? How do you remember so well?'

'It was twice each month, since January, that he went to her.'

'And this other woman of his,' ventured the Countess, 'did Mrs Wilson know about her?'

'Oh no!' Betty was adamant. 'But I think she was beginning to suspect something was going on. Mr Wilson told me he believed she'd taken on some superannuated old crows to follow him about.'

The Countess checked herself before reacting. 'Did you ever find out the name of this other woman of his?'

'No.' Betty moved across to the counter and started stacking books in methodical piles. 'But I wonder whether Mr Wilson ever knew it either. The whole thing had to be kept secret.'

'There are a lot of secrets, Betty, aren't there?' The Countess pushed up her sleeves. 'Come along, Mistress Alpiew, let us help Mistress Betty.'

Alpiew moved over and stood on Betty's other side. The Countess put out her hand for a rag to wipe the top down. 'And that is the problem when one is trying to bring Mr Wilson's murderer to justice.' The Countess gave her portion of the counter a frantic rub, turned and smiled at Betty, handing the rag to her. 'But at least the law is in action, for this morning they have arrested Mrs Wilson.'

Betty gasped. 'Arrested her?'

Alpiew nodded.

'Arrested Mrs Wilson? For what? Not . . .'

'Why,' the Countess shrugged, 'for killing her husband, of course.'

Betty put her hands to her mouth, then turned and indicated the chair for the Countess to sit.

'I will tell you all I know, Countess. If you're trying to help madam, I must help you.' Betty leant back against the counter. She spoke briskly, each phrase well considered, and frankly spoken. 'Mr Wilson worked with me, here, in his elaboratory. We studied the hermetic arts.' She wafted her hand to indicate the equipment, the jars, the stove. 'It is an expensive business, as you can see, and he ran up considerable debts. His wife knew nothing of this. In order not to bankrupt himself and his wife with him, he undertook a certain task for a lady. Who the lady was, or what he was required to do for her, I do not know.'

'So how were these meetings organised?' Alpiew knelt on the floor at the Countess's feet.

'He would receive a note, warning him of the time, the place of an assignation. So far as I knew, he always met a man. I glimpsed him once. A rough, thuggish fellow. Then he would go with this man and do whatever it was that he did. When he came home he brought the cash. Always coins, never bills of exchange. That was part of it, the anonymity, he called it, which was "vital", he said, "to the enterprise". He would give these coins to me, and I would wrap them up like a parcel of washing and bring them here to the elaboratory, so that he could pay his creditors without his wife ever knowing that he had debts.'

'So this place was like a secret office and his personal bank as well as an elaboratory?'

'It was a place where he could escape the humdrum of City life, he said.'

'And you and Mr Wilson were never . . .' Alpiew left the sentence dangling. Betty flared into a fury. 'Never. I was Mr Wilson's apprentice. When he made the great alchymical discovery, I would make my name as his chymical assistant . . .'

'And you are certain this place is secret? No one else ever came here except you and Mr Wilson?'

Betty nodded again.

'Not even Mrs Wilson?'

'It was to be a surprise for her,' said Betty. 'When he reached projection, or even sublimation, then he was going to tell her. For then he would be truly rich.'

'And projection, sublimation would entail . . . ?'

'Turning base metals into gold, of course. The chymistry runs through several phases, and at the ultimate part of the process the gold would start to emerge.'

'And your part within the process was . . . ?' Alpiew leant forward.

'I took notes. I described each process, the heat, the ingredients, the results. Here –' Betty turned and pulled a small green leather book from a shelf – 'this was his log-book. All our work was noted here.'

The Countess flicked through what seemed to be page after page of meaningless hieroglyphics. She looked up and smiled at Betty. 'May I borrow this?'

Betty grabbed back the book and thrust it deep into her pocket.

'Now that Mr Wilson is no longer able . . .' The Countess put her fingers to her lips and threw Betty a quizzical look. 'Perhaps we could enlist the help of Mr Newton?'

'Not even for Mr Newton.' Betty patted her pocket. 'The book does not leave my side.'

The Bridewell clock struck the hour. In one swift move the Countess rose from the chair and moved towards the door. 'Time flies, Mistress Betty. Will you stay here?'

Alpiew had slid along the counter and pocketed the sample paper marked with a ♀, which Betty had prepared earlier. She was tempted to prig a pocketful of golden guineas too, but the Countess had already reached the top of the steps.

'I think he knew something...' Betty gasped, as though trying to get this last piece of information off her chest before she was left alone again. 'He'd been with *her* the night before. In the afternoon he went off to the theatre to get his next assignation note. He left the play before the end and came home and told me...'

The Countess was teetering dangerously on the top step. 'Told you...?'

'That he had made a great discovery. A discovery so important that it would shake the whole of Society, and the knowledge could make him a very, very rich man.'

Alpiew was at Betty's side. 'And the discovery was...?'

Betty raised both arms in despair. 'That I will never know. He left his home to come here alone for a short time, and then...'

'And then...?' Alpiew and the Countess spoke in unison.

'He went to the assignation to make his demands. And it was there that he was murdered.'

Alpiew strode along the quayside kicking stones into the murky waters of the Thames. The Countess perched on a riverside capstan. At noon the river was busy: Lightermen were plying their sea-coal laden vessels up and down to the Fleet to unload, western bargemen steering full barges out to the docks at Tilbury and back, row-boats traversing the river to the south bank with assorted passengers – priests, overdone molls, soil-stained gardeners and scarlet-coated soldiers. All the watermen yelled abuse at each other across the water so that the river was as noisy as any street.

'So what do you think?' Alpiew turned back and looked at the peeling façade of the boarded up Dorset Garden Theatre. 'Is Mistress Betty telling us the truth?'

'I can't see that we'll get anything at all from the gobbledegook in that log-book.' The Countess strained to see into the distance to the opposite bank of the Thames. 'I don't even think it was writ in English. Strange hieroglyphics. Impenetrable stuff.'

Alpiew skipped back to the water's edge. 'I like puzzles. I'll go back there some time, and see if she'll let me have a squint.' A lone oarsman in a small row-boat was passing the wharf. 'Where do you think Beau went that night with the blindfold?'

The oarsman yelled up to Alpiew from the water: 'Need a boatman, Madam Rainbow?'

Alpiew shook her head. 'No thank you, you nasty fellow.'

'I'm a professional.' The boatman pulled off his short-skirted doublet and pointed at the badge on his sleeve, to show in whose service he rowed. 'Much like you, if I'm not mistaken.'

'Hold your tongue, you old swabber,' bellowed the Countess. 'Turn your oars to the shore and you shall have our custom.'

While he manoeuvred the row-boat into the steps, Alpiew helped the Countess down to the water's edge. 'You see, Alpiew, we can deduce where Beau might have been taken.'

The Countess peered towards the boatman, who was

standing, one foot on land, one in the well of his vessel, and yelling abuse at a passing barge which had caused a wake to rock him. 'Meanwhile, Alpiew, my dear, let us gird up our tongues to deal with this saucy water-rat.'

'Ay, I wonder the river-men get any trade at all,' sighed Alpiew. 'To get anything out of the fellow we must put up with a torrent of river wit.'

' 'Tis their custom,' said the Countess with a shrug. 'Just as the players do nothing but flatter each other, so the watermen deal in insults, which somehow pass for friendly discourse.'

'Where to?' The waterman, beaming, so glad was he to have custom on such a blustery day, held out his hand to assist the Countess.

'My lady has had a little trouble with her husband,' whispered Alpiew. 'So it's more of an inquiry than a ride.'

'Some lousy rogue of a wicked reprobate cuckolded you then, Grannum?'

The Countess puffed, ready to give as good as she got, but Alpiew squeezed her arm as they both plopped gently down on to the cross bench.

While the oarsman steered the vessel out into the middle stream, Alpiew pressed on.

'She's sorely wounded by the affront, and she wants to know where she can discover the notorious strumpet who has laid siege to her darling.'

'Where did he go from?'

Alpiew pointed back to the receding façade of the abandoned Dorset Garden Theatre.

'I'd need to know which night, and what time.'

Another boat passed carrying a parcel of gardeners

making their way to the City. Both boatmen knocked each other's oars.

'You lousy crew of worm-pickers and snail-catchers, watch where you're going.' The Countess's oarsman shoved at the other boat with his oar.

'Three nights ago, around nine o'clock.'

'Three nights ago?' The boatman rubbed his chin in his hand. 'Mm, cold one was that. Lot of ice about. Surprised there were any boats at work at all.'

'There was one,' said Alpiew. 'I saw it leave here myself.'

'How many oarsmen?' asked the boatman.

'One,' replied Alpiew.

'How many passengers?'

'One.'

'And it was dark too.' The boatman picked up his oars. 'In my opinion, madam, they wouldn't have gone far. It would not be possible on that night.'

'Why's that?' said Alpiew, leaning forward.

'Tides, Mistress Top-Knot. The Thames is like the sea, subject to the whim of the moon, and we boatmen are ruled by its vicissitudes. Three nights ago at nine the tide would have made any journey pretty difficult unless he wanted to go round in circles eddying with the currents. And what with the ice, which threatened almost to shut the river down, I'm amazed anyone took to the water at all.'

'But I saw him get into the row-boat and leave the wharf.'

'In my opinion there could be only one point in taking the river at all on such a night . . .'

'Yes?' said the Countess.

'Like the chicken, old Grizzel,' the oarsman laughed. 'To get to the other side.'

'I don't know anything about poultry, sirrah, I just want to know where he can have been a-going, not to return till morning.'

'Well, Madam Scold, there's only two ways to cross this stately river of ours, and that's by London Bridge or by the water, and in my opinion if he took the water he would have been heading over yonder.'

He waved his oar in the direction of a set of steps on the southern shore.

'In that case,' said the Countess sitting back and almost toppling, as there was no back to the seat, 'take us to that place.'

The boatman took a few minutes to steer his craft across the river, shouting insults at every other boat within earshot, and they shouting more back.

'It's like a morning at Billingsgate,' muttered the Countess as they bumped against the pebbly shore.

'Here you are, Fustilugs, Marygold Stairs.'

Alpiew peered back to the Dorset Stairs. 'Too near,' she said. 'My feeling is that the river journey was a little longer, and would not have set down in vision of whence they had left . . .' She looked along the shore and saw that the bank took a sharp turn. 'Is there another place just out of sight?'

'And that would have to be up-river, and in the opposite direction to the bridge,' said the waterman with a knowing shrug.

'Why so?' said Alpiew.

'Now, mistress, if you were to row across nearer to the bridge, why not simply take the bridge?' Alpiew saw the logic in that and nodded her assent. The boatman plied his oars again. 'You'd have to be well built to have done it t'other night though, against the tide.'

Wielding his oars with some force he scudded along the shallow water. 'Just round the bluff of the land, there's Cupit's Stairs.'

The Countess's eyebrows shot up and her lips pursed so hard she almost dribbled. 'Cupid's Stairs!' She smiled and tapped her nose. 'I think you have hit it, great Neptune's slave. Take us there.'

'It's a bit of a struggle, this bit,' he explained, hauling at the oars. 'You're going against the tide, and upstream and against the wind today. Though as I remember it, there was no wind the other night.'

The Countess and Alpiew disembarked and clambered up the rickety stairs, the boatman close behind them.

'What desolate wilderness is this?' cried the Countess, surveying acres of fields and wasteland.

'This place?' The boatman stood with his hands on his hips. 'Why, you old vixen, this is Lambeth.'

'A pox on the place. Does anyone in their senses live here?'

'Not if they can help it. Excepting the Archbishop of Canterbury, that is.'

'God save me from visiting Canterbury if it's a more dismal place than this. And what in God's name is that stench?'

'That's the tanneries at Southwark.' The waterman laughed, and raised his arm to point along the shore towards the southern side of London Bridge. 'Stink worse than a pisspot in the chamber of a clapped whore.'

The three stood with their backs to the river and

surveyed the land before them, the Countess pumping her fan under her chin. A little lane stretched ahead, towards the south. The river side of the lane was lined with miles of timber yards, the land side with acres of marsh.

'If he landed here he must have been picked up in a carriage,' said Alpiew.

'Take me back to civilisation,' screeched the Countess, snapping her fan shut and scrambling down the stairs to the row-boat. 'I never knew such a bleak desert as this abominable Lambeth existed so close to my own dear London.'

'Back where you came from?' inquired the boatman.

'Where is that charming-looking place?' asked the Countess, indicating some elegant buildings surrounded by gardens on the other side of the water.

'That's Somerset House Gardens, madam.'

'Of course, of course. Perfect. Take us there.'

SIX

Disintegration

*The breaking down or dissociation
of a substance into different parts.*

Alpiew and the Countess sat shivering on a bench under
a mulberry tree in the gardens. Liveried servants rushed
back and forth along the tree-lined paths, weaving
through the elegant parterres leading between Somerset
House and the Royal Wardrobe in the Savoy carrying
boxes and parcels of items either going into storage or
coming out of it.

'It's hopeless,' sighed Alpiew. 'I think we should give
up. There is nothing we can do to discover the murderer
of Beau Wilson.'

The Countess cupped her gloved hands to her face
and blew on them. 'What leads do we have?'

'None,' said Alpiew, pulling her cloak tightly around
herself.

'No, no, no, Alpiew. We are bowed but not defeated.
One,' said the Countess, picking off a plump finger: 'who
was the man we saw at Dorset Garden Quay? Two: who
was the woman we saw in St Paul's churchyard? Three: is
it the same woman as the one Betty told us about who paid

Beau? Four: who tried to kill Mrs Wilson and why? . . .'

'Five,' added Alpiew: 'what was the huge discovery that Beau had made the night before he was killed?'

'And if you come to think about it – Six,' said the Countess; 'where was Beau taken after his journey in the row-boat?'

'Seven,' added Alpiew, warming to the counting: 'what was he hoping to make in the elaboratory?' She sighed and rose from the bench. 'It's absurd. We could go on forever and ever.'

The Countess's nose was beginning to drip. She plunged her hand into her pocket and pulled out a hand-kerchief.

'Eight,' said Alpiew, pulling a handkerchief from her own pocket: 'what is wrong with this kerchief that it glows in the dark, and to whom did it belong?'

'Nine,' said the Countess, holding her handkerchief out before her at arm's length: 'can you lend me a ker-chief? I cannot bear to use this as it was given me by Beau himself.'

Alpiew grabbed the handkerchief from the Countess and laid it on one knee, the 'bewitched' handkerchief on the other. 'Both the same! But one throws out light, and the other is an ordinary kerchief. Therefore I believe we can safely assume that the bewitched kerchief also belonged to Beau.'

She crammed both handkerchiefs into her pocket, while the Countess wiped her nose with her glove.

A coach pulled up in the street behind them and a group of men marched across the gardens and into Somerset House.

'The Queen lived there, you know. Queen Henrietta

Maria. Even after darling Charlie died. She moved back to Portugal a few years ago.'

'Madam,' Alpiew was in no mood for more reminiscence from her mistress, 'I love to hear about your past, but not when we have a murder to solve.'

'I'm sorry, but it makes one wonder, seeing such a lovely place, why subsequent queens have eschewed it. James's Italian Mary didn't use it, nor did William's Mary.'

Alpiew was glowering.

'All right, all right!' The Countess shifted uneasily on the bench. 'So, where have we got to?'

'No further on at all, madam. This is what we have: Beau Wilson was seeing some woman, name, address unknown. She was giving him money for doing something, we don't know what, and he was using that money to pay his debts. He meanwhile was training up Betty, his chambermaid and confidante, in the chymical arts, the pursuit of which had plunged him in debt, meanwhile keeping his beloved wife, who cannot even read or write, in the dark about everything.'

'Meanwhile this Betty was stripping his house of fine pieces of furniture to bring to a seedy warehouse in Salisbury Court.'

A cart rattled through the park. Two liveried boys trundled along towards it carrying large boxes labelled 'candlesticks' and 'napery'.

'We know too,' added the Countess, 'that he visited a lecture at Gresham College, took lunch in a filthy French restaurant . . .'

'Pox on the place,' Alpiew spat at the mere memory.

'. . . went off by row-boat perchance to a wilderness

called Lambeth, and arrived back at his home next morning, smiling and unscathed. He then attended a play at the theatre, where he was given a note . . .'

The Countess clicked her fingers. 'That's who we need to see again. That orange girl.'

Alpiew sighed. The orange girl had obviously given all she knew already. The Countess was angling for an afternoon in the warmth of the playhouse.

'Come, Alpiew!' The Countess rubbed her hands together and white clouds poured from her lips as she spoke. 'The theatre is the key! And so near.'

Alpiew groaned. Her worst nightmare. She'd prefer to stay in the cold till she became an ice-statue than sit through more of that ranting nonsense. Nonetheless, she lagged along behind the Countess in the direction of the Lincoln's Inn Theatre.

They arrived just in time for the performance. The audience were shoving in through the open door. The Countess's face lit up. 'Something is on today. Good. Then we may go in and observe in warmth.'

'Ashby, darlink!' the familiar French swoop revealed Pigalle, hoiking up her skirts as she stepped down from her carriage. She gripped the Countess's arm with a ferocious grip. 'My life is a tragedy! You must come and share my box so zat I can tell you all.' She clasped the Countess round the waist and steered her up the steps. 'I feel as though someone is making of me an April fish, but there are two weeks to go before the end of March so I know zat cannot be.'

'I'm sure it can't be that bad,' simpered the Countess as the three women took their place in the side box. 'What is on today?'

'You don't know of what you speak, Ashby. You are lucky, lucky, lucky,' wailed Pigalle, her fright of ginger hair trembling on her head. 'You have dear, sweet Alpiew to assist you, to dress you, to carry your trays and fix your drinks. Alas, I have no one!'

'But Azis?' The Countess smiled.

Pigalle's face blackened. 'You mean Aswas!'

'He's not dead, is he?'

'No,' glowered Pigalle. 'Worse. He left me. Poached by the wife of that upstart Alfons Van Keppel.'

The Countess shuddered. 'Gone to a Dutchwoman?'

'Don't talk to me about it,' Pigalle shivered in reply. 'Flems!' She hawked up and spat. 'Revolting creatures one and all.'

The orchestra came to the end of their overture and the scene slid back to reveal a small portly man in a long cerise velvet jacket and silver breeches. The audience rose to applaud. Pigalle leaned to whisper to the Countess. 'I adore Signior Fideli, don't you? What an artiste! And today accompanied by Finger! What a treat we are in for.'

A violinist in a brown suit came on to the stage and stood beside Signior Fideli. He raised his violin to his chin, Signior Fideli took a huge in-breath and started to sing:

> *When from old Chaos brisk light started out*
> *In number and measure the world moved about . . .'*

His pure voice soared up and up the scales, while the predominantly female audience leant forward in a rapture.

> *'Like volumes of music the spheres then began*
> *To refresh and enliven the spirit of man . . .'*

Alpiew's jaw was at waist-level. She'd never seen anything like it. A man stood on the stage and sang with a woman's voice. Well, actually, a voice higher than any woman she knew. She could never have reached that top D, even if a dray horse and cart ran over her foot.

> *'All the orbs in their turns still to pleasure advance*
> *And by their movements they teach us to dance,*
> *They teach us to dance and to love.'*

Eyes popping, Alpiew leant forward to whisper to the Countess. 'Is he a woman in a periwig?'

The Countess smirked at her ignorance. 'No, dear, he's the famous Sigismondo Fideli. He's the most celebrated Italian castrato in the world!'

'A famous Italian what?'

'Castrato! Castrato! He is a man, but he's had his stones removed.'

> *'The planets do their courses run,*
> *The moon and the stars dance to the sun . . .'*

'His stones? You mean . . . ?' Alpiew indicated her pubic area, while the Countess nodded with her tongue poking into her cheek, before mouthing: 'No testicles!'

Leaning forward, Alpiew screwed up her eyes and tried to get a better view of the man's breeches.

> *'. . . They dance and by their comfort prove*
> *The power of harmony and love.'*

Alpiew looked around at the audience. Everyone was transfixed. For a few minutes she watched the Countess and Pigalle both gazing at Signior Fideli with adoration writ across their countenances as though he was, well . . . as though he was a whole man.

Alpiew leant forward to whisper in the Countess's ear. 'I've just seen someone, madam. You enjoy the concert. I will wait for you at the door when it is over.'

Without taking her eyes off the chubby little man, the Countess nodded her approval.

Alpiew squeezed out of the auditorium and took to her heels. 'What a caterwauling!' she cried to an orange girl squatting on her haunches in the corridor and totting up her takings before the first interval.

'Signior Fideli?' cried the girl. 'Sure he is the charmingest creature. A voice like an angel.'

Alpiew scurried along. The world was gone mad. She whipped behind a curtain and nipped through the link door leading backstage into the wings.

A gaggle of adoring females crowded in the shadows at the side of the stage, leaning wistfully against the scenery and watching the singer as though in a rapture.

Alpiew shoved through them to get back to the tiring rooms.

In the green room a few actors, mere hirelings by the look of them, were slouching around drinking. Alpiew caught a few snatches of their conversation, which included the words, 'I', 'leading player', 'I', 'my years of experience', 'I' and 'me' and was grateful to be only passing through.

She pushed her way into the ladies' tiring room. A robust middle-aged woman was sitting under the high window sewing.

'Hello, Molly,' said Alpiew, sitting on the long

actresses' bench with her back to the worktop and mirror. 'How's things?'

Molly peered over the top of her spectacles. 'If it isn't my bonny Alpiew! Not after a job, are you?'

Alpiew wondered Molly did not know her better. 'Milady is attending the show.'

Molly pulled a face of sympathy. 'Now there's a mystery. Drury Lane puts on a show of tumbling and rope-walking and dancing dogs, which crams in the audiences. Then tops their success with the Kentish Strong Man . . . Did you see him?'

Alpiew shook her head. 'I hate the theatre.'

'No, no,' Molly grinned. 'This was something! Six foot tall, muscles like soup bowls studded all over him. And he could make these muscles jump up and down as though they had a life of their own. He lifted a weight of two thousand two hundred and forty pounds, snapped huge ropes asunder. It was amazing. And when he lifted up a horse . . .'

'A man lifted a horse?' Alpiew thought she might have misheard, but Molly nodded.

'A horse!' She lay down her needle and sighed. 'What a man! I wouldn't mind playing at pickle-me-tickle-me with him.' She started on her sewing again. 'So what do they book in here? A little fat Italian with no nuts, who can sing higher than a cat on heat, and the women all go wild for him.' She let out a heavy sigh and snapped the thread with her teeth. 'I don't know.'

Alpiew tossed her head back towards the green room. 'Why're *they* all in?'

'The actors? They're pretty disgruntled. They were all rehearsing this morning, and never went home.' Molly pulled at the loose thread and knotted it before choosing another colour thread from her sewing basket. 'It's been a poor season for plays. No one's happy. A lot of the actors were laid off altogether at Christmas. Unless they could jump through a hoop, or dance upon the high rope.'

'And none of the actors get paid while that eunuch's out there squawking.'

Molly nodded. 'And next week the management, in their wisdom, have decided to cancel the scheduled plays and bring in a Monsewer Balloon, dancing master to the French Dauphin.'

Alpiew's mouth fell open. 'The French dolphin? How can you teach a fish to dance?'

'Dauphin, not dolphin. It's French for prince. So another speciality act knocks down the actors' pay.' Molly sighed and pulled the thread tight. 'Still, they *are* actors.' She threw her eyebrows up, and tapped her nose with her thimble. 'Know what I mean? They've all actually got *real* problems but all they're moaning about is the size of their parts.'

'They should be grateful they're not Signior Fideli! He hasn't got any parts at all!'

Both women whooped with laughter, and had to cover their mouths in case the sound carried through to the stage.

'So what you after, then, gal?' said Molly, holding her thread between her teeth while she searched for a lost bead on her lap.

Alpiew leaned forward to whisper. 'I've got to find out about some fellow, big lump of a thing. He's using the orange girls to pass notes to certain people.'

'Rich women, I suppose? They all do that.'

'No.' Alpiew shook her head. 'He passed a note to a gentleman friend of my lady's, and that note lured him to a place where he was murdered.'

Molly gasped. A rousing bout of applause filled the dressing room. Molly waited for it to subside before speaking. 'That wouldn't be the young gentleman killed in Covent Garden the other night, would it?'

'You know about it?'

'We all do.' Molly pulled up the hem and turned the skirt inside out. 'Everyone here hangs about in the piazza at night. So when someone gets his throat slit . . .' She shrugged.

'Lovely dress,' said Alpiew. 'Whose is it? Brace-girdle's?'

'No, it's Mrs Barry's.' Molly shook the dress out, displaying its full gorgeousness. 'It was Queen Mary's wedding gown.'

'Queen Mary in a play?'

Molly shook her head. 'No the real Queen Mary.'

'King William's dead wife?' Queen Mary had died of smallpox at the age of thirty-two only five years earlier.

'Not that one, the Italian one, Mary of Modena, married to King James.' Molly stroked the dress, brushing a loose piece of cotton from the jewelled bodice. 'She gave it to Mrs Barry for teaching her how to speaka da ingleesh! She wears it whenever she plays queens. Which, as you know, is most of the time.'

Alpiew's only memory of Mrs Barry was once when she had taken a temporary job working backstage fetching and carrying. Alpiew's impression was of a sneering woman with a lopsided face, snapping her fingers and screeching,

'Dresser!' A real diva. So Mrs Barry now owned this ravishing dress which had once clothed a queen.

'The Queen gave her the gown she wore at her coronation too, can you believe it? And Mrs Barry tears a cat in everything she plays, so the dresses frequently need my attention.' Molly held the dress up in front of herself. 'Think I could make queen if I chatted up old William? He must get lonely banging about in all those palaces without a wife.'

'Don't know about that,' Alpiew laughed, 'but you'd be my own right royal friend if you could find out anything about that fellow who left the note for me.' Another screeched song came to an end amid a tumult of applause. Alpiew rose and kissed Molly on the cheek before wandering out through the side door to the street.

A gaggle of women were already clustered outside, waiting for the performance to end and Signior Fideli to come out so that they could maybe see him, talk to him, touch him.

'He is everything in the world one could wish!' A large woman in red was trying to lead a chant.

'*Almost* everything one could wish,' corrected her friend.

A pretty little blonde thing chirped up: 'They say there's a lady in the City has a child by him.'

Much laughter erupted from the crowd of assembled ladies. Alpiew slipped through with a scowl.

'Well, it must be charming to have a child by him,' reiterated the blonde.

'Madam I met a lady the other day with three!' It was the large red woman again, flapping her fan with excitement.

'All Fideli's?' The crowd was agog.

'All Fideli's, all in wax. Twopence the piece.'

Great laughter all round. Alpiew raised her eyebrows, wondering that women had so little to do with their time they could go chasing after this fat little male soprano.

'Oh, Gemini, who makes 'em? I must buy a dozen.' Every lady was fumbling for notebooks, scraps of paper, anything to write down the name of the shop selling Signior Sigismondo Fideli wax dolls.

Alpiew grunted and, turning the corner, made her way back into the theatre by the front entrance.

'I *must* have him,' hissed Pigalle.

The Countess's painted-on eyebrows shot up. 'Fideli?'

'Don't be ridiculous,' spat Pigalle, pointing at the little satin-clad moor in the next box. 'Him! Ze pretty bambino.' As before, the child was furtively smiling and winking at women in the audience, while his elegant mistress gazed at the stage.

'Don't flatter yourself,' whispered the Countess. 'He's promiscuous. He flirted with me in the same way at *The Double Dealer*.'

'I don't care about zat,' said Pigalle, leering in a revoltingly coy way at the boy. 'He is beautiful and would look delicious as part of my equipage. Especially now zat ze rat, Azis has gone.' Pigalle pondered methods she might employ to snatch the child, or lure him from his mistress with caresses or sweetmeats. 'And I could treat him every day with lovely surprises and presents, and shower him with love.'

Signior Fideli was building to a climax:

> *'Let us drink and be merry, dance and rejoice*
> *With claret and sherry, with music and voice . . .*
> *The changeable world to our joy is unjust*
> *All treasures uncertain, then down with your dust.*
> *In frolics dispose of your pounds shillings and pence*
> *For we shall be nothing a hundred years hence.'*

'Zat's it,' hissed Pigalle. 'I will offer her so much money for him, she cannot refuse.'

'Sssshhh!' The Countess frowned at Pigalle. She at least wanted to listen to Fideli. Pigalle seemed interested in nothing but the blackamoor boy in the adjacent box.

> *'So why should we turmoil in cares and in fears,*
> *Turn all our tranquillity to sighs and tears . . .'*

'One way or other, I will have him. It is love!' Pigalle turned away from the Countess to flutter her eyelashes again at the pretty moorish boy.

Alpiew had fought her way to the back, and shot the Countess a look.

> *'Let's eat, drink and play till the worms do corrupt us*
> *'Tis certain that post mortem nulla voluptas . . .'*

Fideli was getting the audience ready for a wild crescendo leading to the first interval. The words were depressing enough, thought Alpiew, but the heady smell of perfume – violets, lily of the valley and musk – made her feel dizzy.

> *'. . . Let's deal with each other that we may from hence*
> *Have broods to succeed us a hundred years hence.'*

'Not much possibility of that in *his* case . . .' Alpiew whispered, preparing to yank the Countess out as soon as the applause started.

Fideli was on the usual first reprise line:

'Have broods to succeed us a hundred years hence . . .'

Pigalle was still eyeing up the little moor as the Countess tottered to her feet.

'Have broods to succeed us a hundred years hence.'

The rest of the audience sprang up and started clapping and screaming 'Ancora!' Alpiew pushed the Countess through the door and they raced along the corridor towards the front door.

'Where is the fire, Alpiew?' The Countess tutted and straightened her clothing.

'Remember, milady, we have work to do.' Alpiew pulled open the door and they thrust through to the rapidly darkening afternoon.

As they descended the front steps, a hand slapped down on Alpiew's shoulder. Somewhat alarmed, she turned to find Mrs Cue grinning down at her. 'Mistress Alpiew! And how is the week's scandal coming along?'

Alpiew grinned inanely.

'Ah, Countess Ashby de la Zouche,' Mr Cue stepped forward and kissed her hand. 'What spicy tit-bits have you up your sleeve? Only a couple of days to your deadline, is it not?'

The Countess gulped. The Cues stood smiling expectantly. 'Alpiew has been investigating Signior Fideli's love life, haven't you, dear?'

Alpiew gave a wan smile. 'Women are collecting wax dolls of the castrated cove, I'm told.'

'Really?' Mrs Cue beamed. 'And who owns them? Duchesses? Ministers' wives? Who will all proclaim they bought them for their children. I hope you have something more salacious than *that* for us, Mistress Alpiew.'

'The whipping house . . .' The Countess was dredging her memory for details of the place. 'We saw some very interesting people going in there. Exceedingly high up in the government.'

Mrs Cue gave her a penetrating look. 'Oh really? Who?'

'Aha, Mrs Cue,' the Countess rubbed her hands together. 'Patience! Patience! You'll find out soon enough. Believe me, we're on to a *really* big fish.' She glanced around hoping for a visible clock. There wasn't one. So she wafted her hand in no particular direction. 'Ah, look at the time. We're late for our scheduled appointment with Madam Whiplash.'

She grabbed Alpiew's hand and they ran off along Portugal Street, turning briefly to wave at the Cues when they were out of earshot.

Back at Anglesey House, the Countess found Godfrey snoozing in front of the fire. Open on his lap was a large book. The Countess snatched it up and read the spine. '*A Feast for Worms* by Francis Quarles! Where does he find this rubbish?' The Countess hurled the book to the floor.

Alpiew picked it up. 'What is it?'

'Epithets for a good life: "He that begins to live, begins to die"; "He that hath no cross deserves no crown" and other such tedious moralising nonsense. Godfrey!' She gave her groom a shove. 'There is work to be done. Put on your coat and come with us.'

'Not *hard* work, I hope, milady.' Godfrey blinked and groaned. 'I can't carry coal or anything, milady. I've done my back in.'

'I wouldn't worry about that now.' The Countess handed him his hat. 'Whatever is wrong with your back I'm sure will be "corrected" soon enough.' She threw a smirk in Alpiew's direction. 'You will have a *spanking* good time. Now *whip* your gloves on, and we'll *thrash* along to Covent Garden.'

Half an hour later they were all three standing outside Mrs Birch's Elysium House of Flogging.

'I'm not going in there,' snarled Godfrey. 'I'm not having some buxom floozy fiddling with my bits.'

'No one's going to fiddle with your bits, I can assure you.' The Countess shuddered at the very thought of Godfrey's bits. 'A nice girl will simply tickle you with a whip. And you will find out who is her most famous client, and then we can all dine on rump steak for a week.'

Gritting his teeth, Godfrey gripped on to the architrave, while Alpiew and the Countess shouldered his wiry frame through the bead curtain into the dark entrance of the famed establishment.

A pair of pale hands with long talons gripped Godfrey and tugged him inside.

'Come along there, Master Timorous,' barked a woman in stentorian tones. 'Get you into my cell. What's your name?'

'Godfrey!' shrieked Alpiew and the Countess through the curtain.

'Well, Godfrey,' growled the dominatrix, 'you need to be punished. You've been a very, very bad boy.'

They heard Godfrey let out a yelp as he vanished into the darkness.

'Good,' said the Countess, wiping her hands. 'We can find a nice India shop and have a light snack and a dish of chocolate before his session is up.'

'Oh, no we don't,' said Alpiew, plunging her hand into her pocket. 'We're taking our sample to the apothecary to be tested.'

'What sample?'

Alpiew produced the powder she had filched from Beau Wilson's elaboratory. 'A replica of the powder which poisoned Mrs Wilson.'

'How did you get that?'

'Don't ask.'

The apothecary looked at the powder, sniffed it, put some of it on a piece of glass and wet it, held it up to the light, tossed some into a flame and finally tasted a little. 'Definitely *not* antimony,' he said.

The Countess and Alpiew had arrived at the apothecary's just in time to catch him before the shop closed for the day.

'But the stuff in her beaker definitely *was*.'

The Countess looked out of the window across at the Wilson house. The front door was open. Candles hung in sconces lit the hallway, throwing shadows out on to the dark street.

The valet sat on the front step smoking a pipe, puffing clouds of smoke into the already foggy evening air.

'So what is this stuff then, if not antimony?' Alpiew looked down at the dark brown powder.

'Not a notion,' the apothecary poked at it with a little metal probe. 'Seems to be an amalgam of various products. Look, you can see, some granules are smaller and of a different colour to the others.' He held up a pinch and sniffed it. 'If I'm not mistaken one of the ingredients is a powder of stinking arrack.'

'What?'

'A common weed. Grows on every dunghill in the nation. It has a secret magnetic virtue to strengthen the womb, and by sympathy moves away any diseases thereof. Also the head. It's known as a cephalick, and all cephalick herbs help the womb.'

'Might one take such a mixture to encourage conception?'

'Oh, certainly. If that is what it is intended for I would venture your other ingredients are the likes of calamint, pennyroyal, thyme, mother of time, bethany, dittony, burnet, feverfew, mugwort, sage, peony roots, juniper berries, gentian roots. Any of those.' He dipped his finger into the powder and took a tiny taste. 'Mmm. The last two would explain the dark colour. See how it goes violet when wet. That would be the gentian.'

'No poison, then?' Alpiew was disappointed. 'It is a genuine healthful powder?'

'Oh yes.' He indicated the shelves behind him. 'Such as I make up here myself. These powders are in great demand.'

'And the other stuff. That was a genuine poison, you think – no other use for it?'

'Antimony?' The apothecary scooped up the powder and folded it back into its sachet. 'No. Not to be taken in any circumstances. It's a metal, essentially. Used in the production of alloys and alchymical research.'

'And you sold some to Beau Wilson the day before he died?'

The apothecary nodded, flicking through the large invoice book on his shop counter. He placed his finger on an entry on the previous page. 'That's right. Two scrupulii.'

'So how did that antimony get into Mrs Wilson's glass and who put it there? That is what I must discover.'

Alpiew thanked the apothecary, took the sachet and left the shop, while he took up his crutches and limped round to lock the door after her.

She found the Countess sitting on the step where the valet had been. The front door was pulled to.

'Things are in a pretty sorry state here,' she said. 'The house was ransacked this afternoon, and the staff have received a message from Mrs Wilson's lawyer telling them she is destined to swing on the Tyburn Tree, and they'd better move on.'

'He says she's to be hanged?'

'Correct!'

'That's early days, isn't it, milady? The woman was only arrested this morning. And the house ransacked too! What was taken?'

'Some things of value, Mrs Wilson's jewellery, pictures, a clock, linen, plate and silver. But they turned the place over, made a terrible mess.'

'Where was everyone?' Alpiew pushed the door open. 'They didn't hear anything?'

'I gather when they received their dismissal they all got rolling drunk on strong liquors from the dead man's drink closet. So while thieves turned the place upside down, the loyal staff were all wassailing in the kitchen.'

The two women stood on the threshold staring down the corridor. Papers were strewn everywhere, the walls, once hung with paintings were bare.

They moved through to the kitchens. The valet was throwing things into a large bag. He looked up guiltily. 'If I don't take them, someone else will!' He exclaimed, presenting a blue paper roll containing a sugar loaf. 'And if not some*one*, it'll be the rats. They can sense when a house is empty, you know.'

The kitchen was in a bad way too. The work-table was littered with dirty drinking vessels and plates upon which the detritus of smoked tobacco mixed with congealed gravy, chairs were upturned, cupboards hanging open and empty.

'Is there no such thing any more as staff loyalty?' said the Countess, turning a chair the right way up and sitting on it.

'Not when the master's dead and the mistress doomed to die.' The valet rolled a stack of cutlery in a piece of green baize and threw that on top of the sugar. 'And we haven't had our wages for two weeks. So this is payment in kind.'

'Do you think your mistress killed your master?' Alpiew took a jar of spice and placed it in the valet's bag.

'I don't know what to think. Something's been going on. There was a maid here – Betty's her name – she knew about something. The master and some paramour, I gather. So mayhap the mistress found out too, and put an end to his frolics.'

He pulled open a drawer and rooted about for more things to filch. 'And now, if you wouldn't mind taking your nosiness elsewhere, I have things to do before I leave this cursed place.'

'I see.' The Countess rose. 'Well, may I wish you the best of luck in finding new employment. I hope your new mistress finds you as trustworthy as your last.' The Countess was already on the threshold. 'Come, Alpiew, we must leave the man to pack up Mrs Wilson's things.'

Alpiew shut the kitchen door behind them and followed the Countess along the hall. 'What do you think?'

'I think that the world's come to a fine pass, and that any society where self-preservation exalts over allegiance to others can only result in misery and hatred.'

'Come on, milady, Godfrey and I would stick by you.' She peered back at the closed kitchen door. 'Quickly, come, let's have a look upstairs.'

The Countess glanced into the front room, but Alpiew was already swinging round the newel post. 'Make haste, milady, while that sour-faced man is providing for his future, let's go up and see the bedchamber again.'

They tiptoed up the stairs. Mrs Wilson's chamber looked much more tousled than the hall. It had been truly ransacked. Lying in the centre of the floor was another powder sachet marked with the same symbol that Betty had told Alpiew meant woman: ♀. Alpiew picked it up and shook it. It was full. 'Get this checked too, why not?'

'Whoever committed this act of burglary seems to have concentrated their efforts in here, don't you think?' The Countess was poking about in the drawers which, removed from their chests, lay in stacks at the foot of the bed. 'Look!' She pointed at the garde de robe in which they had hidden early that same morning. The pockets of coats and cloaks were pulled out. All bags were inverted.

'I'd say someone was doing more than stealing in here.' The Countess looked at the pile of books, all open and flung down, as though each one had been riffled through. 'In my opinion, this room has been subjected to a methodical, if not exactly orderly, search.'

She looked at the bed. The pillows were slashed open, the sheets lay strewn about, and the mattress was cockeyed to the base. 'Looks rather like a bedchamber after a very interesting late-night frolic.' The Countess smiled to herself and remembered her nights with King Charles. 'A churning amour, to last all the night long.' She sighed. 'It's a long time since I was tumbled by those roaring delights.'

'Godfrey!' yelled Alpiew, with a very different type of sex on her mind. 'What's the time? He'll be beaten to a pulp by now!'

They arrived outside Mrs Birch's Elysium House, the flagellant's paradise, just as Godfrey staggered from the entrance. He looked shattered but serene, a combination which, in Godfrey, both Alpiew and the Countess found disturbing.

'Well?' The Countess stood before him, blocking his way.

'Well, what?' leered Godfrey.

'Need a link to light you home, mistress?' A small boy tugged at the Countess's sleeve, waving his flambeau in her face. 'It's a dismal, dank, foggy night, and folks cannot see two feet ahead of them.'

The Countess passed the boy a penny. 'To German Street,' she cried. 'By the fastest, most direct route.'

The boy led on. Godfrey lolled against the wall.

'Come along, Godfrey, fall in!' The Countess gave him a sharp poke. 'Are you drunk?'

Alpiew shoved Godfrey into action with a heave from her shoulder. 'You've had your fun, Godfrey. Now spit it out. Who was in there?' She was in no mood for a coy Godfrey.

Godfrey smirked and rubbed his nose. 'That would be telling now, wouldn't it?' He gave a rattling cough, which obviously passed for a chortle, and staggered along behind the wavering flame.

'Pull yourself together, man.' The Countess took hold of his sleeve, and linked her arm in his. 'You know something. I can tell from that leer. So who is it?'

'Sure, wouldn't that be telling?' Godfrey strode along with a new skip in his step.

The street was crowded, despite the smoky fog which hung in impenetrable swirls.

'I thought you had a bad back, Godfrey?' The Countess was panting, trying to keep up with him. The link-boy was taking his pace now from Godfrey.

'So, I do, Countess. And so what?' Godfrey laughed again until his laugh turned into a rattling cough. 'You'll be finding out soon enough who was in there.'

'Is it good news for us?' The Countess was almost begging. 'Boy! Boy!'

The link-boy stopped and turned.

'A little slower, pray. This smoky air is no help to perambulation.'

The boy raised his link and marched on. Smirking

serenely to himself, Godfrey followed now at a slower pace, the two women at his heels. 'Oh, yes, milady. Very good news for you.'

'Boy!'

The link-boy stopped again. The Countess held up her hand. 'One second, please.' She stood in front of Godfrey, blocking his way as they tried to pass through the row of blue posts at the end of the alley leading into Leicester Fields. 'Stand and deliver, Godfrey. This is no time to prevaricate. I must write this story up and despatch it to the Cues or there will be no supper.'

'Pointless waste of time, if you ask me,' Godfrey sighed and gave a world-weary shrug. 'But if I said Robert Smith is Mrs Birch's favourite client, would it mean anything to you?'

'No!' The Countess started flapping her arms, wafting the fog into swirling eddies. 'Who on earth is Robert Smith?'

'He's a prominent Member of Parliament,' said Alpiew, tugging Godfrey along the path towards the Countess.

'For Stratford-upon-Avon,' smirked Godfrey. 'In Warwickshire.'

'Enough geography, thank you.' Alpiew pushed Godfrey through the posts into the impenetrable white of Leicester Fields. 'That's good enough for us. Thank you, Godfrey. Off you go home.' Alpiew turned to the Countess. 'Let him sneer his smutty way back on his own, filthy rogue!' She called out to the link-boy. 'Turn about your flaming torch, my lad. For we are headed for the Fleet Prison.'

The boy winced.

Alpiew whispered to the Countess. 'We must go talk to Mrs Wilson. Keep her abreast.'

The Countess slumped down on to a blue post. 'Oh yes, Alpiew, that would be very useful! If you did not notice, it is night-time now. So we go to the lady on this dark and miserable night to tell her we are come to a full stop, while she looks forward to sleeping on a damp flagged floor, to dream all night of being hanged.'

Alpiew realised the Countess was right. They were no further on. If anything, things were even worse now than they had been this morning. Mrs Wilson's house had been plundered, for a start.

The Countess's mind was running along the same track. 'Wait one moment, Alpiew. You are right. She should be told about the mess at her house.' She glared down at the link-boy.

'Didn't you hear me? The Fleet Prison.'

'I'll need paying extra.' The boy held out his spare hand.

'Of course,' said the Countess, pressing another two pennies into his palm.

The prison grille was not as crowded as usual. The side streets round the Fleet were even worse afflicted with the acrid fog than Covent Garden. The smoke of thousands of fires belched from chimneys and tumbled down on the cold air, to hover at street level, trapped in the thick fog rising from the fetid canal.

The link-boy coughed. Alpiew coughed. The Countess coughed.

'The bills of mortality will be full of deaths from coughs and wheezes this month, no doubt.'

'Thank you for that piece of information, Alpiew.' The

Countess grabbed the boy's flaming link and thrust it hard against the prison grille. 'Hello in there? We needs must speak with Mrs Elizabeth Wilson. It is urgent.'

'Shove off, you poxy whore,' came the retort from the solitary prisoner looking out. 'You're past it, Grannum.'

The Countess squeezed her face against the iron. 'Phogh, you nasty dog that stinks of the drippings of other people's fundaments, I care not a fart for your insult. Put your wrinkled little pizzle back in the acorn where you keep it, you niggardly son of a whore, then pull up your breeches and go fetch me Mrs Wilson.'

With an astonished expression the prisoner ran off. Alpiew and the link-boy stood rooted to the spot, mouths hanging open, eyes wide. The Countess glanced at them, pulling her scarf over her nose. 'I don't want the putrid humours from in there rising and diving down into my lungs,' she mumbled through closed lips. 'You see, Alpiew, I have no intention of making an appearance in the bills of mortality for many a year.'

After a few minutes Mrs Wilson arrived at the grille. She looked beaten and weary.

'We need to know some things . . .' The Countess knelt so that she could talk more intimately. 'Did you have anything in your house which someone would now want?'

'Plenty,' snapped Mrs Wilson. 'Valuable paintings, jewellery . . .'

'Nothing written down? Beau's will, for instance? A piece of paper which someone would want to find, now that . . .' She let the sentence trail off.

The light from the flickering link caused the hatched

shadows of the grille to create a criss-cross pattern on the prisoner's face as she shook her head.

'The will is with the lawyer. Beau left everything to me.' She started to cry, silently. Her face betrayed nothing, but great tears rolled down her grey cheeks. 'Like furies, the ghosts of my past sins start up and terrify my restless imagination.'

'Sins?' The Countess leant into the grille.

'I have been hard. Treated people coldly. Even Beau. I wanted him to be a success. To be rich. I hated his failure.' She gave a little sob. 'I am guilty. I killed him. It was me.'

Alpiew had stopped breathing. She hoped the boy did not utter and break the spell.

Mrs Wilson stretched through and took the Countess's hand.

'Guilt gnaws at me. Guilt! The secret wound that bleeds within.'

'I know.' The Countess squeezed Mrs Wilson's hand in hers. 'I know.'

'If I had not wanted him to be something, someone . . .' She closed her eyes and let out a whimper. 'I should not have driven him into the arms of whoever murdered him. And death had not closed his eyes, nor laid his icy hand upon my Beau's heart.'

The silence was broken only by the faint crackling of the boy's link.

'I have sent a note to my lawyer, telling him it was my fault. I killed Beau.'

The Countess swallowed before she spoke. This was why the message that the woman was due to go to the gallows had come through to the household so fast upon her arrest. She was as good as pleading guilty to a crime the Countess felt sure she had not committed. 'Mrs Wilson, you loved your husband. He loved you. I will call myself a thousand fools before I let you go to the gallows for a crime you did not perpetrate, nor I believe could ever even have contemplated.'

Mrs Wilson did not respond. But the tears overflowed from her red eyes.

'Mrs Wilson, you must heed me.' The Countess turned back to Alpiew. 'Mistress Alpiew and I will do everything we can to save you. But, for Beau's sake, please do not resign yourself to Tyburn's fatal tree.' The Countess indicated to Alpiew to help her to her feet. 'Alpiew will now ask you a few questions. Allow us, at least, to try. Somewhere in this city the real killer of your beloved Beau wanders free. Think on that for a moment. If you allow yourself to hang for this crime, they will exalt in the triumph of having killed him and then having escaped their due punishment.'

Alpiew knelt down in front of the grille. 'Do you trust your maid, Betty?' Alpiew decided to be blunt and to the point with the inquiries.

'I do.'

'And your valet?'

'A self-seeking careerist.'

Alpiew couldn't agree more. 'Do you know if Beau owned or rented a property in an alley off Salisbury Court?'

'In Alsatia!' Mrs Wilson gave a sardonic smile. 'I should think not!'

'Did he have any interests other than his business as a merchant?'

'He meddled in the new experimental philosophy.'

'Do you know that experimental philosophy is an expensive hobby?'

'Not if you do not practise, but only attend lectures and so forth.'

'Where did he get the powders he gave you for your women's problems?'

'He made them up himself.'

'Practical experimental philosophy, Mrs Wilson. For which he needed equipment and premises.'

Mrs Wilson took this in. Alpiew could see the thoughts starting to run through her head.

'And that,' she added to see the effect, 'is where your missing furniture went.'

'Beau took it? Not to furnish the house of a mistress?'

'He had an elaboratory. In Bridewell Alley. A low cellar. Part of the old wharves behind the Dorset Garden Theatre. It was there that he practised experimental philosophy. And it is there that Betty went into hiding when you were taken ill.'

'Is she all right?'

Alpiew nodded. 'But she is frightened.'

'You will be seeing her?'

Alpiew nodded again.

'Ask Betty to come here and talk to me. Please.' Mrs Wilson closed her eyes and swayed.

The Countess stooped to speak again. 'You are tired, Mrs Wilson. We will return tomorrow. Go to bed now. Dismal as bed is in that place.'

Mrs Wilson gave a feeble smile and slowly moved off into the darkness of the Fleet Prison.

'So now, boy . . .' The Countess fished in her pocket.

'For a few more pennies would you light us to Salisbury Court?'

'Salisbury Court? That domain of barbarous and brutish savages? Late at night? In a fog? Without a man to protect me?' The boy screwed up his face and took to his heels. 'Not on your life.'

SEVEN

Digestion

*The slow modification of a substance
by means of a gentle heat.*

Alpiew and the Countess arrived at the elaboratory in one piece.

'Well, Alpiew, we have just undertaken one of the rashest, wildest and most desperate resolutions that ever was taken by man, or woman.' She pulled her hood back. 'When that nasty fellow came roaring out of the tavern towards us, I swear it put me into such a cold sweat that if I had been wearing a hat my hair would have lifted it right off.'

Alpiew suppressed a yawn. Despite the excitement of the walk she was exhausted. 'And the bells are chiming nine, milady. We have had a long day. And speaking entirely for myself I am exceeding fatigued.' She reached out for the door handle. 'Let us wind up this business in as short time as we can, and get home to our cosy kitchen, a cup of hot wine and a nice warm bed.'

As they entered the elaboratory Betty jumped back in a guilty manner from what she was doing. Alpiew caught the flurry of turning pages on the worktop as the girl flung herself round to face them.

'Mistress Betty,' the Countess smiled as she descended the stairs, this time carefully clutching the handrail, 'I hope we have not surprised you?'

The cellar was lit by a solitary candle on the worktop, throwing dancing shadows across the cavernous cellar. In the corner a cauldron bubbled over the stove. Betty's hands were black.

'Your mistress is to be hanged, Betty. How do you feel about that?'

There was a moment's silence before Betty started to sob.

'Well?' The Countess sank down on the easy chair. 'Have you any informations which may help us to get her freed?'

Betty wiped her sleeve across her forehead. 'There's nothing else I can tell you. I swear.'

Alpiew moved forward and glanced along the worktop. Some equipment was set up, a large copper machine with strange tubes leading down to a great empty bowl. Nearby a giant pestle was full of something lumpy and brown.

'You are continuing the experimentation?' Alpiew picked up a dusty black jar. It had no lid on it. She peered inside. 'What's this filthy stuff?'

'Charcoal powder.' Betty was standing in front of the main part of the experiment. 'I owe it to Mr Wilson to continue his work. Perhaps I will hit on the last discovery.'

Alpiew moved over to the corner and started poking about round the stove, picking up copper and lead vessels and inspecting them. 'What's this called?'

'Leave those alone!' Betty ran over and tugged a strangely shaped container from Alpiew's hands. 'It's a pelican. But it's strictly for use by those involved in the hermetic arts. The adept must be pure of soul.' She plonked the pelican firmly down on the flagstoned floor and stood in front of it. 'You are not an initiate.'

The Countess grabbed Betty's hand. 'And are you pure of soul, Betty? What will you gain from this experiment? Will you be able to free Mrs Wilson, or find the murderer of her husband? Or is it only money which interests you? Maybe you are part of the conspiracy which led him to his foul death.'

Betty was shaking her head. 'No! No! That's not right. I knew of it, but was not part.'

'Knew of it? Knew of what?'

Betty spoke slowly. 'Why should I want him dead? My life was sweet when he was alive. Now look at me.' She wafted her hand to indicate the grimy cellar. 'I live underground like a mole, only creeping out at dawn to forage about for food.'

'But why do you have to live thus?' Alpiew moved round the room poking and prying. 'The other servants are going on as normal. You could be like them, still sleeping in your cosy bed in Angel Court.'

'They stayed? After Mr Wilson was killed and an attempt made on Mrs Wilson? I don't believe it. They had no fondness for the family. None of them. They were modern servants. They worked for money, not loyalty.'

The Countess was delighted. How perspicacious of the girl to see that. 'So you didn't like the other servants?'

'I was brought up by my parents, who were old-style

servants. They chose their masters well and stuck with them.'

'How commendable.' The Countess stooped forward. 'Why don't you sit, my dear?'

Betty shook her head. 'I am too tired. I might fall asleep.'

'Something has been puzzling me, Betty dear. Something which makes me not quite believe that you are telling the strict truth.'

Betty looked down at her and shrugged. 'What?'

'Why did you bring the money Mr Wilson had been paid by the mystery lady here that morning, when you knew that Mr Wilson was dead?'

Betty's expression did not change.

'I understand why you did so on the previous occasions. And don't deny it, because Mistress Alpiew saw you come out during the commotion, with a parcel under your arm.'

Betty glanced back at Alpiew.

'So? Why not leave the money in the house for his widow, to whom it surely belongs?'

'I panicked. I was used to bringing it here in the morning when my household duties were done.'

The Countess clapped her hands. 'Not good enough!'

'The cash had to leave the house otherwise Mrs Wilson would find out what was going on.'

'More like it.' The Countess tilted her head in a quizzical fashion. 'And what *was* going on, Betty? You know very much more than you have told us, of that I am sure.'

'Mr Wilson was fierce about the business with the woman. He didn't want his wife to know.'

'About what?'

'His evenings. What he did for the money.'

'Don't you see, Betty, that now it doesn't really matter. Do you want your mistress to swing by her neck from a rope at Tyburn over a silly marital secret? Can it be that important?'

'But how will telling you make anything better?'

'Perhaps if we know what was going on we can find out who did kill Beau. Or maybe you think it was Mrs Wilson?'

'Of course I don't.' Betty stamped her foot. 'She adored him. Besides, she was at the house all evening. I was there too. She sat in her room. I could hear her crying.'

'Why was she crying?'

Betty was silent.

'It is clear that you know the reason. It doesn't matter if you were overstepping the mark, listening at doors, whatever you were doing, but you must tell us all that happened on that last day. It is the only chance of saving your mistress's neck.'

Betty sank down on to the footstool and put her head in her hands.

'The master came home from the playhouse. It was about four. He gave me the coins he'd got the night before, and I stored them away with my dirty linen, under my bed, as I always did. And when I came downstairs I heard them arguing. I stood on the landing and listened. I was frightened they might be arguing about me.'

'About you? Why should they quarrel about you?'

'I used to help Mr Wilson with the books, and things. Because I could read. She could not. It made her jealous and angry. Mrs Wilson has more of the new way of dealing with servants. She thinks you shouldn't befriend them, or talk to them except to boss them about. But Mr Wilson he came from a country family . . .'

'And he treated you like a friend?' The Countess knew all about this new style of household management, and didn't like it a bit. She was all with Mr Wilson. 'As I do Alpiew.'

Betty glanced over at Alpiew again. 'And then I thought that if Mrs Wilson discovered that I was practising at chymistry here with him, she would dismiss me from her service.'

'But . . . ?' the Countess whispered. There was a small silence, crowded only by the shadows dancing round the walls. Alpiew did not budge. She had found the shagreen log-book and was standing at the work-counter, quietly working her way through it.

'But their quarrel was not about me.' Betty spoke quietly. She was obviously distressed by the whole matter. 'Mr Wilson told her he had to go out again in the evening on business. She challenged him, accused him of having a mistress, a kept-woman, who he was going to leave her for. There was a bit of a scuffle between them. I heard a crash, and could tell from his voice that he was on the floor, picking things up. She went on shouting, saying she knew he spent all his money on this mystery woman, "his whore", she called her. Which was the wrong way round, you see? Poor Mr Wilson. He went into a fury, telling her that everything he was doing he was doing for her. And that he was going to make them both rich.'

'So did he tell her how he was going to do that?'

'Of course not.' Betty was pulling at the frayed edges of her sleeve. 'He didn't tell me how, neither. I thought it was the usual stuff but he told me no. He spoke of a fortune. Much more than he usually got.'

'Usually?'

'For what he usually did when he went missing from home.'

'And what did he do?'

'Sometimes . . .'

The Countess held up her hand. 'You have told us how he came here to work on his experimentation, but on those six nights you spoke of, what did he do then?'

'He received a note at some stage of the day. He had no warning about these. They were just passed to him wherever he might be: dining, seeing a play, wherever there were the sort of creatures who will pass a note for a penny.'

'And what was in these notes, Betty?'

'Time and place. The meetings were always the same day. But every time he was to go to a different place. There he was blindfolded by the man he called Scum.'

'Scum?'

'He didn't know what he was called, but he was a big terrifying low-life ruffian. So he called him Scum, simply for a name to use when we talked about him.'

'And when Scum had blindfolded him?'

'He would be bundled into some transport, usually a coach. But the second to last time it was . . .'

'A row-boat.'

'How do you know that?' Betty jumped up, startled. 'You're not . . .'

'We saw him. Alpiew and I. We were down at Dorset Garden Quay, just behind here, and we watched as he was blindfolded by this Scum, and shipped off.'

'The boat journey was very short, he said. A few minutes only. Then he was hauled out, dragged up some steps and thrust into a hackney coach.'

'How did he know it was a hackney coach?'

'Mr Wilson was convinced it was a different coach each time. Different smell, different seats. He said they smelled of public coaches. Scum paid the driver and whispered the instructions, and the sides were pulled down, so he could not see, and off he went into the night.'

'Didn't these hackney drivers think there was anything odd about carrying a man in a blindfold in their cab?'

'Oh, milady, what with masquerades and parties and other nocturnal romps?' Alpiew crossed over now to where the two sat, having read her fill. 'I would think not. The man wasn't squealing, and the driver got his fare up front. What would be the problem with that?'

The Countess sighed. Alpiew was right. 'So where did he go in these hackney coaches?'

'A place in the country. He could hear birds, and cows. And there he'd . . .'

'Yes.'

'Do something awful for money. Something awful with this woman.'

'By awful,' said Alpiew, 'I suppose you mean he did *the business*?'

Betty nodded. 'For money.'

'And who was the woman?'

'I don't know, because he didn't know. He never saw her.'

'Phogh!' The Countess threw her hands in the air. 'He did the business with her and never clapped eyes upon her physog?'

'Truly, madam. That's what he told me. The blindfold never came off. He was told by Scum that if he peeped it would be the end of him. Someone would cut his throat for him.'

'Where did this woman live?'

'He couldn't work that out either. When he was picked up by coach from the City it was a very long journey. About an hour.'

'In which direction?'

'How could he know? He was blindfolded, and it was dark.'

'If he couldn't see, how did he know the time?'

'Church clocks along the way. And latterly he started counting the time. He wanted to find out where it was he was being taken each time.'

'And was it always the same place?'

'Oh yes. He knew the feel of the floor, the creak of the boards, the layout of rooms and stairs as he was led about.'

'How did he first get this appointment, being paid for doing . . . that, with some woman who paid him for it?' The Countess was scandalised by the whole notion of a woman paying a man for sexual congress.

'He was sent a note one day in the theatre. It was signed only "A Lady of Quality". And she offered to sponsor his alchymical work.'

Alpiew was beside her like a shot. 'How did she know he did alchymical work if it was a secret?'

'I never thought of that.' Betty pressed her fingers to her temples in thought. 'There are a lot of men do it. It's like a great cobweb across London. They all know each other. Maybe another who had gone before, told the woman about him. I don't know.'

The Countess had risen and was stretching her legs. 'And so what went wrong? Why did the idyllic money-making scheme come to an end? Did Beau get too greedy? Or did Beau peep?' Alpiew suppressed a smile.

'I don't know. But whatever happened that last night, the night he went by row-boat, changed him. From then on he seemed very tense and excited. After the row with his wife he came here. To write up his notes, he said. Then he returned briefly to Angel Court to change his clothes before going out to the fatal meeting. It was then he told me that he had made a discovery so important that it could rock the nation and if he used the knowledge wisely it would make him immeasurably rich.'

Alpiew and the Countess were now looking at the alchymical equipment, wishing it could come to life and speak to them.

'You are right in what you both imagine I am trying to do.' Betty stepped over to the stove and pulled open a vent to bring it up to full heat. 'I am going through the log-book, trying to reconstruct his last experiments, to see if I too can discover that thing he had found.'

'Why the log-book?'

'It's where everything was written. A way of never losing anything. There were no scraps of paper, only this.'

'You seem very sure, Betty.' The Countess still thought something wasn't quite right. 'How can you be certain the secret lies in the log-book?'

'Where else could it be?' Betty was applying a set of leather bellows to the stove. 'He told me he was worried about his meeting, and that just in case he would leave me a message.' She pointed the bellows round the room.

'I've looked everywhere. There is no note. It must be in the log-book.'

'So there's nothing else for it.' Alpiew pulled up a stool. 'We must go through the book.'

'I'm working through the last few pages.' Betty indicated the equipment on the counter. 'This is a German retort. It is filled with sap of urine . . .'

The Countess unfurled her fan, flapped and flopped down on to the easy chair. 'I wondered about the stink.'

'On the stove is a lute which I must fill with water and into that we place the German retort.'

Alpiew rolled up her sleeves. 'And what are you hoping to produce?'

'Astrum Lunare Microcosmicum.' Betty started measuring out the charcoal powder. 'I need to produce it for the next stage of the experiment. It's a factitious self-shining substance.'

'What does that mean?'

'It's a sort of fire, which does not burn.'

Alpiew whipped out her bewitched glowing handkerchief. 'Like this?'

Betty gasped. 'Where did you get that?'

'It was in the churchyard near Beau's body.'

Betty inspected the handkerchief. 'It is the stuff, certainly. But it is his wife's kerchief.'

'And talking of his wife,' said the Countess from the comfort of her chair, 'why did you try to poison her?'

'Get out. I have told you.' Betty slammed the log-book shut and pointed to the door. 'I would never do a thing against either of them.'

'And what of this, then, Mistress Betty?' Alpiew

whipped out the sachet she had retrieved from Mrs Wilson's floor.

Betty glanced at it. 'Where's the other one?'

'Other one?' Alpiew laughed. 'You can make them up at will. You demonstrated that yesterday.'

'There should be two packets like this. Mr Wilson bought two on the same day as he bought that.' She pointed at the sachet Alpiew held.

'Mistress Wilson drank one of these that you made up for her, but as for the other . . .'

'No, no,' Betty screamed. 'Mrs Wilson didn't drink this. This is poisonous.'

'But this is the same stuff you make up for her each day.' Alpiew pointed up to the jar marked 'Venus'.

'It is not.'

Alpiew held up the paper. 'Look at it. It's the same as you showed us last time.'

'No, it isn't.' Betty opened the drawer and pulled out a paper. 'Let me show you.'

She folded the paper as she had done before, then turned it over and marked it with a ♀.

'Look.' She turned the paper again. 'This is the top fold, this the bottom. Give me that one.'

She took Alpiew's sachet, and turned it round. 'Top, bottom.' She turned it face-up, revealing the sign ♂. 'There! The sign for antimony.'

Alpiew peered at the two packets and could see the difference. It was clear once you knew.

'What a confusion. I am utterly in a maze.' Alpiew had almost forgotten the Countess was there, seated in the easy chair, now inspecting the empty wrapper she had taken from Mrs Wilson's drawer and had been carrying round in her pocket. 'This must be the second one.'

'Do you see?' Betty snatched it and lay it beside Alpiew's powder and her own. It was clear that both the empty and full wrappers which had come from Mrs Wilson's bedchamber were folded in the same way, and in the opposite direction to the ones Betty made up. They were both antimony.

'I prepared the drink for her as usual, in the afternoon. The powder had to infuse, you see, in a glass of wine, for some hours before she should drink it. In the fight he must have dropped the powders he had just bought, and she must have spilled the drink I had prepared, and then she must have made up another for herself with the wrong stuff.'

Alpiew was trying her hand at refolding the Countess's paper wrapper. 'Tell me, Betty, why not just write "antimony" on the front?'

'The folded packet is too small, and symbols are quicker. And if you can't read, then a symbol is clear.'

'Not in Mrs Wilson's case. She almost killed herself mistaking Venus for upside-down Venus, which happens to be antimony.'

'But why, Betty dear,' asked the Countess from her chair, 'did Mr Wilson want antimony in the first place?'

'That's obvious, isn't it?'

'Not to me, Betty,' the Countess let out a sigh, remembering the lecture at Gresham College. 'I am as ignorant of the new experimental philosophy as a Hottentot bred in a cave.'

Betty pointed up at a small empty jar. 'He wanted to make the star regulus.'

'Lost me again, I'm afraid.' The Countess peered up at the rows of mysterious bottles and jars, wondering why anyone wasted their time on such a ridiculous hobby.

'Sulfide of antimony. It's the new path to finding the philosopher's stone, and to being able to process base metal into gold. We were going to take the antimony, mix it with charcoal and heat it till the metallic element sinks to the bottom. This is the seed of antimony which is called the star regulus.'

'And then?'

Betty winced. 'I don't know. That's why I must work on this book.' She turned back to the stove where the water was come to a boil. 'Mistress Alpiew, help me lift this over.'

Alpiew took the other side of the German retort and they lowered it into the bubbling water.

'Now watch. This process is miraculous, and very beautiful.'

The three women gathered round the stove and watched as Betty applied the bellows to the stove. The coals glowed first red, then yellow, then almost white. 'It's coming now. Watch the liquid in the retort.'

The thick muddy mixture of decayed urine and charcoal powder started to bubble and strange flakes, like small pieces of lightning, began to rise up and spill over the sides of the retort into the boiling water in the larger lower lute. The whole room was illuminated with a bright yellow glow.

'We have distilled ourselves the spirit of the microcosm of the moon: Astrum Lunare Microcosmicum. Commonly called Phosphorus.'

Betty pulled out a long metal spoon and ladled a small pool of the luminous liquid for them to inspect.

'Well!' The Countess had risen from the chair, transfixed. ''Tis a prodigious phenomenon indeed, Betty. Who would think stinking old urine could come to such a delightful pass.'

Alpiew held up her bewitched handkerchief. 'It seems dim in comparison.'

'It fades with time, but recharges when it is exposed to the light.' She took Alpiew's handkerchief and used it to wipe up some drips from the flagstones. 'It is indeed prodigious, but also dangerous. While liquid it must be kept in water at all times. I could make myself a lamp with this stuff, to read by, as long as it is sealed in a jar.'

The Countess reached forward. Betty snatched the spoon away from her reach.

'No, your ladyship. If this stuff gets upon your skin, you will appear all aflame, even in the dark. And twill burn the skin most dreadfully.'

Alpiew held out Beau's recharged handkerchief. 'But it does not burn inanimate objects?'

The Countess was pulling her gloves on. 'This lecture on experimental philosophy is all very fascinating, Betty, but how does it help us to identify Mr Wilson's murderer?'

Like the Astrum Lunare Microcosmicum, the girl had been all aflame with excitement, but this reminder sobered her again.

'Give me a few hours with the log-book. I'm sure I will find something.' She looked up at the door. There was no light coming through the keyhole. 'It is late now, but I will work on into the night. Come and see me in the morning, and I hope I will have solved Beau Wilson's last riddle.'

The fog was even thicker and the danger was compounded by a fine layer of ice on the cobbles when they went out into the night. Alpiew and the Countess huddled together for the duration of the long walk home.

'It must be almost midnight,' whispered Alpiew as they marched up the Hay Market. They could hear the footsteps and coughing of other people throughout their walk, but could see no one through the impenetrable fog. 'There's many a man will not find his way home tonight,' said the Countess. 'Lucky we have each other to guide us back to our bed.'

'So much for Astrum Lunare Microcosmicum.' Alpiew steered the Countess into German Street. 'The most prodigious thing I can imagine in all the world is a roaring fire in the fireplace, a steaming cup of sack posset, and a plate of food on my lap.'

'A nice slice of juicy chicken.'

'A meat pie.'

'And then sleep.'

'Oh yes, sleep!' echoed Alpiew, pushing through the front door. 'Glorious sleep!'

They shook their cloaks and hung them up in the hallway.

'What a day!' Alpiew shuffled up the hall behind the Countess.

'I shall sleep like a new-born baby tonight, Alpiew.' The Countess flung open the kitchen door, but instead of going in, stood stock-still on the threshold and let out a gasp so loud it was all but a scream.

Alpiew rushed forward and stared over her shoulder.

Godfrey was standing by the table and in front of him, in an easy chair, puffing on a long briar pipe, his feet up on the fire rail, sat Sir Peter Ashby de la Zouche, Baron Penge, Earl of Clapham. The Countess's long-lost husband.

EIGHT

Mortification

The substance undergoes a kind of death,
usually through a putrefaction, and seems
to have been destroyed and its active power lost,
but is eventually revived.

'Going to join us in a glass of best Rhenish wine?' Sir Peter held up the long green bottle for all the world as though he'd never been away, let alone absent for twenty years. 'It's a frisky little wine, fairly trips across the tongue.'

'How did you . . . ? Why . . . ?' The Countess teetered forwards. 'I thought you . . .'

'Were dead, or in America?' Sir Peter stood up and swept the seat of the best chair ready for his wife to sit upon. 'Which amounts to much the same thing. Those American settlers! Think a pudendum is a place to store your puddings.' He swept open his arms ready for the Countess to enter them and be hugged. 'Come to your long-lost husband, my lass.'

Through the layers of white Venetian ceruse on her face (applied at the start of the week and topped up each morning; four layers to date) the Countess could be seen to blush. 'Peter! You came back. I knew you would.' She minced forward into his arms with a coy smile.

Alpiew couldn't believe her eyes. Her mistress was smitten again, like a young maid playing at romps with a new-found swain. And after all the terrible things she had said about him!

Alpiew looked at the little man in his turquoise velvet suit and lacy cuffs. He twirled the ends of his pointed Van Dyke beard and moustache (first cultivated when in exile in France during the Commonwealth and 'modelled upon our late martyred King Charles I') and grinned, exposing a couple of new gold teeth. A shiny and expensive-looking brown peruke hung in well-dressed and powdered curls over each shoulder. His hat, a wide-brimmed affair with a mass of multicoloured feathers, lay at his feet. 'So, Mistress Alpiew, you weren't scalped by the Sioux or burned for a witch by the English settlers?' He shot her a beady look.

'I have been back in London for many years, Sir Peter.' Alpiew gritted her teeth, she wasn't pleased at having to explain herself to this rascal. 'And I am happy to say that my mistress and I were recently re-united, to my enormous delight.'

Sir Peter held the Countess close, speaking over her shoulder, while gently stroking her back. Alpiew watched, fascinated. She had forgotten how short the man was, and was rather intrigued by his new fashion accessory – a large gold hoop earring.

'Couldn't believe my eyes when Godfrey staggered into that whipping place this afternoon.' Sir Peter gave a loud guffaw. 'I immediately asked about you, of course. Since you'd left the old place, dear wife, I had no way of finding you when I returned from the New World. But Godfrey told me everything . . .'

Alpiew wondered what Sir Peter was doing in the Elysium House of Flogging. He caught her look.

'That place is owned by a chum of mine, actually. Old army friend, you know.'

Alpiew knew Sir Peter had never served a day in the army in his life. 'Nice little earner, he's got there. Easy money too. Thinking of buying myself a cut of that. And thanks to that serendipitous visit I have newly discovered the wife whose company I have missed for so long.'

He held the Countess out before him and stared at her cracked face, faded crimson lips now smudged round the edges, black eye make-up running in rivulets down the crazed surface of her face-paint, her ratty red wig, as ever, askew. 'What a corker! You always were a beauty, my love, and now the Lord has seen fit to re-unite us.'

The Countess lowered her lashes and laid her head against her husband's chest as he folded her again into his arms.

Alpiew couldn't bear to watch. What was the horrid little man after?

'Lovely little pied-à-terre you have here, my dear.' Peter patted the Countess's back. Alpiew noticed the wink he exchanged with Godfrey. 'I think living here together we could make quite a splash.'

'Excuse me, milady,' Alpiew could take no more, 'but I have some further business relating to today's inquiries. May I take my leave of you, madam, till tomorrow?'

The Countess popped her head up from her husband's chest. 'But, Alpiew, aren't you going to stay here and celebrate? We can all be a family again, just like we were in the old days.'

Alpiew edged towards the door. 'There will be time

enough for that, madam, I'm certain. But tonight I must . . .'

Sir Peter screwed up his eyes and raised an eyebrow. 'What's this business of yours, then?'

Before the Countess could reply, Alpiew almost shouted: 'We're digging up some dirt on Robert Smith, the moralising MP with a big secret.'

'Ah, old Bob Smith!' Sir Peter chuckled. 'You should have come to me. I've got a dossier on him as long as your arm.'

'I'd like to see that, tomorrow, if possible.' Alpiew glared across the kitchen at Godfrey, who was smiling serenely into the fire. How could he have landed them with this? 'But tonight,' said Alpiew, 'I have to do one more thing.' She was holding the door open. 'I'll stay with a friend and call on you in the morning, milady.'

The Countess did not look up. She was in heaven and had no need of further company. Sir Peter gave Alpiew a sarcastic little wave. He was making it perfectly clear that he was glad she was going, which almost tempted her to stay.

After pulling on her cloak and scarf Alpiew left the house and stumbled along German Street cursing her way through the impenetrable fog. At this time of night there was only one place she could think of to take refuge, and that was Beau Wilson's elaboratory. At least she could be sure that Betty was up. She could even help Betty with her preparations. But whatever happened, it was warm there and she could eventually get some sleep curled up on a blanket on the floor.

Her hunger kicked in as she emerged from Leicester Fields, so she stopped off at the still busy Covent Garden

Piazza for a late-night snack from a food wagon before tackling the dangerous alleys of Alsatia.

By the time she was crossing Salisbury Court Alpiew realised it must be well after one o'clock. She strode along, trying to feel unafraid, for surely if you felt it, you must look it. Because of this she was oddly grateful for the fog, which felt like a protective blanket around her. Along the narrow alleys of Alsatia the same shadowy figures lurked in doorways, she heard the same squawks and moans coming from cracked windows and black stinking alleys, but everything was dulled.

She was nearing the turn for Beau's elaboratory when she saw floating towards her something like a huge glowing butterfly. But it was no insect, for the sound accompanying it was a thundering of running feet. The patches of lightness split in two, growing larger as they came closer. Alpiew stood very still. The thud of hurrying feet shook the very paving stone she stood on, then for a moment the dark shadow of a man emerged before her, wearing two luminous patches like a pair of badges on each glove. He stumbled into her, causing her to lose her balance and fall backwards into a foul-smelling doorway.

When she pulled herself up again, the man was gone. The fog dampened the sound, and it was as though he had completely vanished into the murk. But she was aware of a lingering scent. A scent strangely alien to this rough stinking place. It was of violets and lily of the valley and musk. Like the Lincoln's Inn Theatre. The scent which drifted into her nostrils reminded her of sitting that afternoon in the box at the theatre.

The fright had left Alpiew breathless and with a thudding heart. She stood in the alley a moment, getting her breath back, before scuttling along to the elaboratory.

To her surprise, despite the cold surging fog, the elaboratory door was ajar. Alpiew pushed it open and tiptoed down the stairs. The room was brightly lit. And all the light was coming from a large brilliant area in the corner near the stove. 'Betty?' Alpiew moved cautiously.

As she got nearer to the source of light, she realised what it was.

Betty's naked body was slumped into a half-sitting position, her head lolling motionless against the wall. Although she had a gaping dagger wound to her chest, this was not the most remarkable feature about her. Betty was painted from head to foot in phosphorus.

From the contorted expression on her face it was obvious that in her last moments she had suffered agonies. Betty was dead.

Her hands trembling uncontrollably, Alpiew bent down and closed the poor girl's eyes. She could see a pile of clothing in the middle of the floor. She threw it on the body for modesty's sake, but found that once Betty was covered the room was plunged into darkness, except for her glowing hand which the clumsily thrown clothing had not concealed. Alpiew stumbled over and kicked Betty's hand back under the clothes.

Then, still barely breathing, she moved to the worktop and lit some candles.

She knew that she and the Countess had been gone for over two hours now. So she started working her way round the elaboratory, always with her back to the corpse, looking for anything which had changed since they left.

The most obvious difference was Betty herself, and the pile of clothing, which she had been wearing, but which was now covering her corpse. Near the spot where the clothes had lain was a large bowl of milky-coloured water, smelling of soap. Alpiew dipped her finger in. It was tepid. Betty must have been washing herself when whoever did this unthinkable thing had disturbed her. Alpiew took a huge gulp of air. She couldn't bear to think of what had happened here.

She moved to the back of the room and inspected the bookshelves and rows of jars. Everything looked much as it had before.

There was water on the floor. This must have spilled from the vessel where the phosphorus had been made, when the murderer had thrown the contents of the lute over Betty. The lute itself lay upturned beside the body, slowly dripping on to the flagstones.

Alpiew could not control her shaking limbs and sat down on the easy chair. Then she leapt up and ran to the work-counter. Where was the log-book? She scanned the shelves for its distinctive shagreen cover. It was not on the worktop either, nor anywhere on the floor.

Perhaps Betty had put it away, out of sight? Alpiew checked through the counter drawers. They were stacked with pieces of tubing, knives, spoons, smaller pieces of equipment, and the stack of money which Beau had been paid by the mystery woman. The money was still there! Because Alpiew didn't know how much had been there in the first place, she could not be sure that some had not been taken, but why would a thief leave the lion's share behind? Whoever had been here tonight had surely not been after money. It had to be the log-book. Alpiew drew up a seat at the escritoire and pulled open a drawer. She rifled through a stack of bills. They were mostly from the apothecary and oil shops, a few for equipment and some pieces of copper, lead, iron and tin. Everything seemed directly linked to the alchymical experiments. She pulled the drawer right out and checked behind it. Nothing.

Alpiew searched for over an hour before admitting defeat. The log-book was not in the elaboratory. Whoever had killed Betty had taken it with him. So Betty's surmise was correct. The great discovery that Beau had made just before his death was somewhere in the book. And now that great discovery had brought about another death.

Alpiew shuddered. She was not sleeping here tonight. That was certain. But before she left she decided to have one final search of the room.

There was only one place Alpiew realised she had not looked. And that was Betty herself, and amongst her clothing. Perhaps, after all, the book was still here, in a pocket.

She stooped over the clothing hiding Betty, and thrust her hand deep into every pocket, trying not to disturb the garments and thereby reveal Betty's anguished dead face. The pockets were empty.

She had come to a dead end. She moved round the cellar, blowing out the candles one by one.

As the flickering glow of the last taper guttered to black she turned towards the exit. It was too dark to see. She was terrified she'd stumble, trip over the clothing, fall down on to the corpse. She turned back to face the stove to find a candle and the tinder-box.

Something in the corner near Betty's body was glowing. It was a few inches from the edge of the clothing, where Betty's hand had been before Alpiew tucked her up.

Glowing brightly on the flagstone floor was some writing. Betty had written something in the phosphorus which dripped from her fingertips. Alpiew got down on her knees and inspected the figures drawn in brilliant yellow light.

Betty's dying message was short but clear. The last thing she had written was a number: 33.

NINE

Lixiviation

*A process of oxidation,
by exposing the substance to air and water.
This forms vitriols.*

Alpiew made her way back to German Street, but could not bring herself to go inside. How could she sleep in there while that idiotic man rattled off his ludicrous stories? How could she talk to the Countess and not tell her what she had seen this night? She moved along the street and turned down Berry Street. She was not frightened any more, however dense the fog. Trudging uphill into James's Street she decided to take the short cut through Park Place into the northern parts of St James's Park. There would be some other stragglers there to huddle up with. She glanced up at the rear windows of the Duchesse de Pigalle's Arlington Street home. To her surprise the lights were blazing all over the house. Perhaps she was up and about at this late hour. It was worth a try. A bed in a madhouse was better than a bush in the park.

It only took a few minutes to hurry round the corner and knock on the Duchesse's door. If she was turned away with a mouthful of incomprehensible French insults, what difference could it make to her present misery? She banged the knocker.

The door was flung open almost instantly and the Duchesse loomed in the doorway swaying slightly. The mirrored candle sconces behind her illuminated her ginger hair so brightly that it seemed on fire.

'*Merde alors*!' she shrieked. 'Alpiew! *J'ai chié dans mes frocs*!' Behind her in the hallway a small gang of elderly men hovered, burbling. 'Are you all right, Olympe?' 'Who is it?' 'Take care . . .'

'These gentlemen are leaving, darlink. We have had ze most perfect game of hazard. Ze dice loved me tonight. Non, Sir Charles?'

A portly gentleman sidled up to the Duchesse and planted a juicy kiss on her cheek. 'Alack a day, you have clear cleaned me out, you saucy goose. I'll have to get five more ships back from the Indies before I can afford to play with you again, you sausage!' He slipped past Alpiew and on to the front step. 'Anyone for a march?' He bowed in Alpiew's direction before stumbling into the street. 'Can't see the nose on your face, gentlemen. We'll have to go home arm in arm.'

'Duchesse, I am more yours than my own.' A lean, hawk-like man took his leave with another kiss. 'I am sure I will sleep tonight without rocking.'

Alpiew thought they would never go, there was so much kissing and jesting.

As the last man was swallowed up by the fog, Pigalle turned to Alpiew. 'So, what is ze problem?'

'I am offering my services,' said Alpiew quietly. 'As a temporary replacement for Azis.'

'Marvellous,' cried Pigalle, taking Alpiew's arm in a

taloned grip and tugging her up the stairs, puffing out the candles as she passed them. 'Thank God for zat! Azis was my valet de chambre, my companion, my cook, my secretary, my equerry, my *everything*. I am lost without him.'

On the first landing the Duchesse, staggering about from an excess of wine, led Alpiew to a door.

'Zat is where ze rat lived. You can sleep in there!' Then she teetered off alone, blowing out the lights. She turned at her own door. 'I like a good, as you English say, hearty breakfast, Alpiew, please. But make no mistake, not "an English breakfast". How you Englanders partake of oysters, red herrings, anchovies, and whey before noon, is a puzzle to me. To break my fast I prefer ze eggs, ze toast, ze marmalade. At eight o'clock sharp, if you please.'

Alpiew slept in a black room. The walls were lined in black brocade, the curtains black velvet with black silk tassels, the furniture all black lacquer, even the sheets and blankets were black. It had much the same deadening effect as the fog, and made Alpiew curiously aware of each breath, each heartbeat. She slept badly, dreaming luminous dreams of Betty and the mysterious Astrum Lunare Microcosmicum.

She woke a few hours later at dawn to prepare breakfast for the Duchesse. She put the butter out to thaw on the kitchen table (the larder was as cold as an ice-house) and got the fire going in the dining room. When she could see streaks of light in the sky she made her way down to St James's market to buy some fresh hot bread. As she strode along the street her mind was a turbulent bustle of images: blood dripping from the Countess's sleeve, the fat little Italian singing at the playhouse, the black, black room, Betty's bright glowing body. She shuddered.

The market was the usual morning bustle. Alpiew felt so strange, partly from lack of sleep, partly from the shocks of yesterday, that the very normality of the market traders appeared quite startling. Betty's death had had a much more profound effect upon her than Beau's.

She bought half a dozen fresh brown eggs, the loaf and some mushrooms. She thought Pigalle could do without meat, for which she'd have to make the extra tramp to the Hay Market.

Spinning round and round in her head was the picture of Betty lying glowing in the elaboratory. She didn't know what to do. Should she share her information about Betty's death with anybody? Should she inform the authorities? She decided against it. With her luck and her recent implication in Beau Wilson's death, that was not a good idea. How on earth would she explain her innocence?

Betty's poor agonised face loomed before her on every stall displaying apples, cheeses, oranges, nuts. Alpiew thought back to the pathetic fears Betty had harboured earlier in the day. How ridiculously unimportant it was that she had been frightened to admit she had listened to a row through a keyhole. She thought of the white hand peeping out from under the clothes. What did 33 mean? Did it mean anything?

Her head swirling, she crept into Pigalle's house, and swept back the curtain leading to the Duchesse's kitchen.

'Hands up!' Before her in the shadowy corridor stood

a masked man, his rapier pointed at her chest, the brilliant point resting on her exposed cleavage. 'If you care for your life!'

Alpiew threw up her hands without question. The loaf, mushrooms and eggs crashed to the floor.

'Oh, *merde*! Alpiew, it's you!' Pigalle whisked off her mask. 'I'd forgotten I'd taken you in. I imbibed a lot of brandy last evening with the Prince di Ponce. He's a great friend of Fideli, so *naturellement* I had him back here for a nightcap. And his friends too. Fleeced zem all.'

Alpiew got on her knees and started to wipe up the mess of broken egg. 'What a waste!'

'Rubbish,' snapped Pigalle. 'We will eat zem strangled.'

'Excuse me, madam?'

'Strangled, strangle. You know, strangled eggs on toast, isn't zat a favourite here in London?'

Alpiew looked with some dismay at the dusty floor, which was skimmed with cobwebs, cat fur, and worse.

Once the pre-seasoned egg dish was served up, Pigalle, scoffing it in great spoonfuls, stood up. '*Sacré bleu*! I have omitted to inquire *how* you come to be here working with me? Is my friend Ashby sick?'

'Worse than that, I'm afraid.' Alpiew fished a large knot of fluff from her soggy toast. 'Her husband has come back. He's moved in and, what is worse, she seems delighted about it.'

'*Quel foutoir*!' Pigalle spat the well-masticated contents from her mouth back on to her plate. 'Has ze woman lost her head? Ze man is ze *roi des cons*, *non*? King of arseholes. And she is a *vache folle*, eh?'

Ladling the chewed food back into her mouth, for a

moment the only sound in the room was Pigalle eating. She wiped the plate clean with a slice of bread, and rose with a huge gesture.

'I must go to ze rescue of my dearest friend.' She swept her chair back and started pulling off her clothing and throwing it to the floor. 'Alpiew, I kiss you!'

Alpiew hoiked her dress up higher over her bust to cover her cleavage. She'd heard the rumours about Pigalle seducing chambermaids. Three weeks after being dismissed from Pigalle's service, one pretty twenty-year-old had been committed to Bedlam as it was said she spent every waking hour kissing a portrait of the Duchesse which she kept in her pocket.

'Come here, Alpiew.' As Pigalle lurched towards her, Alpiew braced herself. 'No, *ma petite chou*, I will not have my usual fencing practice in St James's Park zis morning. I need you to dress me in my most beautiful gown.' Pigalle rushed out of the dining room and strode up the stairs two by two. 'And while I am being dressed I will deliberate upon a plan of action.'

An hour later the Duchesse emerged in a scarlet gown which clashed mightily with her ginger hair. She carried a green velvet cloak, a hat to match and a pair of high pattens. 'Just in case of mud, dear Alpiew. There will be much of zat, and worse, where I am going today.'

Alpiew rushed out of the back door to the mews to tell the coachman to bring the Duchesse's best coach to the front, with horses fit for a day in the country.

'While I am gone you can clean up a bit. I'm not too fussy . . .' As Pigalle climbed up into the carriage she leaned back to talk to Alpiew, who was waiting by the front door. 'Organise a delivery of champaign from

Widow Bourne in St James's, and fresh fish for tomorrow from ze market, and then take the cats for a walk in the park. Their leads are hanging in ze hall.'

Pigalle slammed the coach door shut, and leaned out of the window. 'I will do my best, but, *ma foi, j'en ai ras le cul!* Think of us, darlink, we are going a long, long way. If I can persuade her to come with me, zat is.'

Alpiew stepped back on to the kerb, frightened the wheels would run over her feet. The driver cracked his whip and the horses lurched forward. Pigalle collapsed back on to the red velvet coach seats, which clashed with her dress, which clashed with her hair.

'Where are you going, madam? In case anyone asks?'

'*Sacré bleu*, darlink!' Pigalle hauled her face back to the window. 'It's *too* dreadful.' She held herself steady by the blind string as she yelled back down Benet Street at Alpiew. 'I am going to Acton!'

Alpiew tried to clean Pigalle's home as best she could. Anywhere she saw that the dust was opaque, she left it undisturbed. She made some order in the pantry, and scrubbed the floor where she had earlier dropped the eggs. Then she went round the house feeding animals. Some of the animals were so old it was difficult to tell whether they were alive or stuffed. When in doubt she left a little food out, hoping that such an eccentricity would pass for normal in this fantastic household.

She looked at the leads in the hall and hoped the cats had no supernatural way of telling on her, for she had no intention of taking them for a walk in St James's Park.

When things looked as though she had worked very hard, Alpiew wrapped her cloak about her and made her way to Angel Court. She was hoping to talk to the valet, to see if he had anything to add. If he was still there.

But as she feared, the place was locked up, shutters closed and no reply from the front or back doors.

She went into the apothecary to ask if he'd seen anything.

'They've all gone. Every last one of them. The creditors had a quick whirl round the place, so I doubt if there's any furniture left. And I hear the news is bad for Mrs Wilson, too. It's hard to think of a soft-spoken pretty woman like that being a cold-blooded killer, but, contrary to Monsieur LeBrun and his theories that the passions engrave themselves upon the physog, here we have a case of a picture of evil framed in a very comely face.'

'I was working for her,' Alpiew sighed and leant across the counter, looking down at the lengths of tube and glass vials in the boxes behind it. 'But I confess, now my work has come to a sort of full stop.'

The doorbell tinkled and a boy runner came steaming in.

'Good morning, Thomas!' The apothecary took a list from him and started making up the order. 'Have you got a bag for this stuff?' He read from the list. 'Blue vitriol.' He pulled a jar from a shelf behind him and started ladling spoons full of blue crystals into a piece of paper, which he then wrapped with the same deftness Alpiew had admired in Betty.

'Ah, caustic marine alkali. I think I'm out of that. If I have any it'll be on the top shelf. Could you run up the ladder for me?'

'You know that's beyond me, sir.' The boy limped back and displayed his misshapen limbs. 'Sorry.'

Alpiew found herself standing between a one-legged man and a boy with a withered hand and a club foot. Being the only person in the shop capable, she took the little step-ladder from the counter side and assembled it near the apothecary.

'You don't mind popping up and bringing me down that jar, do you? Top shelf, third along from the left.'

Alpiew hiked up her skirt and climbed the steps, holding on to the shelves for balance. She grasped the large brown jar, which was wedged to the ceiling and swung it down at the apothecary. As his hands reached up, the ladder started to wobble, then to sway. Alpiew dropped the jar, and swung round, gripping at dusty shelves to steady herself. Then, just as the ladder made its peace with gravity and stopped wobbling, Alpiew found herself eye to eye with a label. The label was on a great earthenware jar on the penultimate shelf. Written upon it in a bold strong hand was a number: 33.

'What is this stuff?' The tone of her voice frightened the errand boy, who darted for the door. 'Quickly, sir. You must tell me what this number thirty-three denotes?'

Alarmed at the sudden change in Alpiew's manner, the apothecary swiftly pushed his spectacles down and scrutinised the jar at which her finger was stabbing. 'That's no thirty-three. That's a chymical symbol.'

Alpiew leapt down and grabbed the apothecary by his jacket. 'Yes, yes. A chymical symbol – but for *what*?'

The apothecary pulled away, trying to brush himself down and calm this mad woman who stood fiery-eyed before him. 'Nothing special,' he said, pushing his spectacles high on to the bridge of his nose again. 'Just sul-phide of mercury. Although most people call it cinnabar.'

'How much further?'

Pigalle had succeeded in enticing the Countess away. Not because of the lady's reluctance to stay with her husband, but because her husband had left German Street very early in the morning for a business meeting and wouldn't be back till late in the evening.

'Business? Yes, yes, about the horse races at Newmar-ket, I shouldn't wonder,' said Pigalle, yanking her friend up into the coach. 'You didn't give him any money did you?'

The Countess gave a winsome nod. 'Only a few pounds.'

Pigalle rolled her eyes and walloped the roof of the coach with her fan, signalling the driver to move off.

'*Alors*, what a lovely day we can look forward to. I am told ze English countryside is beautiful in winter.'

The coach trundled along St James's Street, and with the flick of the whip the horses picked up speed as they turned into the road which led to the turnpike at Hide Park Corner. The driver paid his dues, and the coach went through the gate which marked the western boun-dary of Westminster.

The Countess gazed out at the tree-lined avenue. 'King's Road is too far out, don't you think, to be quite fashionable . . . ?'

'Zis isn't ze King's Road. Only the King and his special friends may use zat elegant highway. Remember, we do not have a pass nowadays.'

Both women let forth a heartfelt sigh.

'Now that Charlie is gone.'

'And ze flat-lander reigns.' Pigalle crossed herself and peered out. 'Zis road I believe is called Knightsbridge.' She pointed out of the window at a stretch of wooded land. 'Yes, look, there is Hide Park.'

The coach rumbled on along decent roads, then small lanes and finally on to what could only be described as dirt tracks.

'You haven't told me *why* we are going out of London at all, Olympe, dear.'

Pigalle tapped her nose, leaving a smudge of grey from her finger which had been fiddling with the dirty window catch. 'You remember ze charming little blackamoor at ze theatre?'

The Countess nodded. How could she forget the promiscuous little flirt?

'Well, he told me, when his lady was indisposed for a moment, zat zey live in Acton!'

'Acton?' screeched the Countess. 'Are we going to the ends of the earth, Pigalle? Phough, I thought you said a little day-trip.'

'A little way out, I know, but it will be an adventure!'

'Harrumph,' went the Countess, as expected. 'So what is the address?'

'Of zat I am not sure,' Pigalle shrugged. 'But, *ventre bleu*, there cannot be many great ladies living in a godforsaken place like Acton.'

'Of course there can, dear.' The Countess's lips were pursed and tight. 'It's all the fashion nowadays for the *haut monde* to want to swill around in pigsties, miles from civilisation, talking of nothing but fresh air and Nature.'

'You joke, no?'

'No, I do not joke. It's not the sixties any more, my friend.' The Countess shook her head. 'Dancing into the morning at a City ball and staggering home fuddled with drink in the early hours to a lovely elegant house in the heart of Town is no longer *à la mode*. Now we are in the nineties.'

Pigalle was gaping at her in disbelief, so the Countess made up her mind to continue her tirade.

'Today young people want to wander unfrequented rustic paths, not in an elegant park laid out with beautifully cultivated parterres, but in great open meadows crawling with insects and cows, with no music to speak of but silly birds singing. It is thought a great thing nowadays to converse with yokels in a country tavern rather than make gay conversation in a London salon. You may not believe it, dear, but rich people today *want* to live in the country!'

Pigalle let out a Gallic grunt. 'So how will we ever find him?'

'That's your problem, I'm afraid.' The Countess rubbed her hands together, preparing herself for a day of 'I-told-you-so's. 'Didn't the boy drop any hints?'

'Hints?'

'Is the house a mansion or a cottage? Has it a garden, a gate, a drive, a flock of pigs?'

'Nothing.' Pigalle slumped into the corner. 'It is a wild-duck chase.'

'You promised me a day of fun, Pigalle!' The Countess sighed and slumped into the opposite corner. 'Not a scavenger hunt out in the sticks.'

Pigalle perked up, looking out of the window, trying

to seem cheerful and undeterred from her errand. The coach rolled past a large roadside tavern. 'Oh, look, Ashby!' she cried gaily. 'Ze World's End!'

The Countess screwed up her eyes and sniffed. 'You said it, dear.'

The smell in the elaboratory was bad. The stove had gone out now, but the place was still warm.

Betty's body was already starting to decompose. God rest her poor soul.

But Alpiew knew she had to come here and follow her last clue. Trying not to think about the corpse in the corner, Alpiew clambered up on to the counter and ran her eyes along the shelves. Bottles and jars, all neatly labelled, some dusty with disuse, others sparkling new, stood on shelves two deep. There must be hundreds here. Alpiew rolled up her sleeves and started the inspection: amber-grease, sawdust, charcoal, iron filings. There had to be some cinnabar here. Thyme, mother of thyme, gentian, hops, vervain, sage, arrack, hellebore, assafoetida. Alpiew moved some bottles to inspect the second row on the top shelf: borax, gum arabic, turpentine, ivory shavings, snake skin, quicksilver, blood of a pigeon, ground stones of fox. Alpiew gulped. For what purpose would anyone want powdered fox's testicles? Lime – quick, lime – quenched, vitriol, litharge of silver, Glauber's salt, luna cornea, loadstone.

Footsteps thundered towards the cellar on the street outside. What if the killer was coming back? Alpiew held her breath and looked down for somewhere to hide. But the rhythmic tread tramped on past the cellar door.

Alpiew resumed her task. Plumbago, realgar, pyrites, ostracites, powder of algaroth ... Disturbed dust had irritated her nose. She let out an almighty sneeze, blowing dust from the shelves in all directions. She stooped to pull out her handkerchief and came eye to eye with a large jar of reddish powder. It bore the muddy label 'Cinnabar – pulverum'.

Alpiew jumped down and placed the jar on to the counter. Pulling out the cork stopper she peered inside. Lumpy earth-red powder filled the jar to the brim. She up-ended the jar and spilled its contents on to the worktop. Brushing the powder around she found what she was looking for. A piece of paper with one torn edge. It was the same size as the log-book, and had clearly been ripped from it. On it, in Beau's scrawled hand, was a long row of symbols. Nothing else. It was a clue, but what did it mean?

Just an equation:

$$☉: ♃ ♂ \; \text{⚏} \; = \; ♅ \; (♀/☉) \; (☉/†) \; \text{⚐} \; @ \; ● \; ♎$$

'After Kensington Palace we turn up a smaller road, cross two bridges, one of wood and one of stone and go through a place called Shepherd's Bush.'

'Shepherd's Bush?' squealed the Countess. 'Please don't go on, Pigalle. It doesn't make the place any better to know the name. To what depths of rusticity are we to stoop?' She suddenly turned and gripped Pigalle's elbow. 'Please, please promise me that we won't have to stop and talk to any shepherds. I beg you!'

'No, if you don't like.' Pigalle shrugged. 'Then if we get lost we will press on till Turnham Green.'

'Turnham Green! The riposte to that is too obvious, even for me.'

The two women passed the rest of the journey in stony silence, looking out at the dismal fields.

As they entered the hamlet of Acton the coach pulled in at an inn, with, creaking in the wind, a badly painted sign, The Cock.

'Here we ask ze questions,' said Pigalle, stooping as she strode through the undersized door.

'And avail ourselves to some pig's trotter soup, I suppose, and a firkin of ale.' The Countess waddled to a chair near a roaring fire and warmed her hands. 'Come along, Pigalle, you're to treat me, remember. Today is supposed to be my fun day out.'

Pigalle ordered them lunch. Slabs of bread with cheese and an onion. 'For some reason it's called a Ploughman,' said Pigalle, tearing at the bread with her long yellow teeth.

'Mmm,' said the Countess, pulling off a hunk. 'Tastes like one.'

They chomped in silence, staring into the fire. Pigalle was the first to push her plate away.

'I've asked my coachman to inquire, discreetly, about the child.' She quaffed some of the beer from an earthenware mug.

'What's he called?'

'I wish I could remember. It was one of those foreign names, *d'accord*. A good name for jokes on ze stage, I thought at the time. Adullah? Mahatma?'

'Well, if you don't know his name . . .' The Countess popped a crumb of cheese into her mouth and continued her gripe. 'In my opinion there were only two people who ever had any excuse for living in the country. And they were Adam and Eve.'

But Pigalle was not to be deterred. 'Owzat? Abenazah? Saladin? What was it?' She screwed up her face in deep thought. 'It's on ze tip of my tongue . . .'

'Yoovbinad?' suggested the Countess.

'Stop it, Ashby,' snapped Pigalle. 'You don't understand. It's love. I *must* have him.'

'Must, must, must. It's always "must" with you, Pigalle, have you noticed?'

'You can talk.' She continued her litany of stage moors. 'Oroonoko? Jaffeir?'

'You must 'ave me in your coach to the country, you must 'ave a monkey, you must 'ave a box at the theatre.' The Countess bit into her onion. 'Must 'ave a this, must 'ave a that.'

Pigalle sat up abruptly, banging her mug down so hard that beer swilled on to the table. 'You have hit it, my friend. Now we know how to find ze house. Zat is the boy's name. I remember now.'

'His name? His name is Zat? How very droll!'

'No, no. His name is Mustafa! Mustafa Roy.'

The Countess picked up. 'I see what you mean. Mustafa. So if he is Master Mustafa Roy, then his mistress must be Mrs Roy.' She leapt from her chair. 'Come on, Pigalle. It's mid-March. It will be dark before we finish this revolting lunch, and we'll never find him.'

The apothecary told Alpiew that the equation was gibberish.

'A real hobble-de-hoy of symbolism. I think an astrologer would be more use than me.'

He pored over the paper through his spectacles. 'I can make out a few things. Here . . .' He laid his finger on the first symbol and ran it along. 'Skull, quicksilver, copper, day. Later there's iron, and copper again. And gold pops up in the last bracket. After it a cross which is the sign for deadly poison.' He laid the paper down and removed his spectacles. 'That's as far as I can take you. The symbols look to be more astrological in form. This is something like a birth chart. Try a philomat.'

'A what?'

'A philomat,' said the apothecary. 'In common parlance, a dabbler in the astrological arts.'

'This is where we part company with ze coach' Pigalle thrust her feet into a pair of metal pattens and threw open the door.

'I do hope you are merely jesting.' The Countess glanced down at her pink satin shoes and grimaced. Outside the coach door lay nothing but sodden fields stretching as far as the horizon. Or rather, up to a great hedge which obscured the horizon from their present view. Behind the hedge could be seen the roof of a little house.

'It's not far, darlink. Look –' Pigalle was out and raring to go – 'just beyond zat long bush.'

'It *is* far, actually, Pigalle,' said the Countess, pointing down at her shoes, 'in your best satin slippers.'

Pigalle sighed, removed her pattens and handed them to the Countess.

'All right then.' The Countess snatched the pattens. 'As long as the coachman can lend me his arm.'

'No no, don't be silly, Ashby.' Pigalle was prodding the ground with her foot to see what the damage to her shoes might come to. 'He has a broken wheel to see to.'

The Countess gave a little sob of horror and turned to look at the coach, wondering how close she had come to catastrophe. 'But it is in perfect condition.'

'How can she refuse to help us?' Pigalle shot her a wink. 'Two ladies in distress.'

The Countess teetered out on to the pebbled lane. Pigalle's pattens were unusually high. 'I feel as though I am walking the slack wire at Bartholomew Fair,' she whimpered, clutching on to her friend's arm as they staggered on to the lumpy green meadow in the direction of the little house.

The Countess looked up and stood, swaying precariously, thrusting her finger out in the direction of a wooden stile. 'We must surmount that?'

Pigalle nodded and clambered over, bending back to help her friend. Then they took on the fields, stumbling over tufts of long grass, narrowly missing crusty cow-pats. They advanced towards a rustic gate and in the enclosed garden beyond caught sight of the elegant woman from the theatre. She had on a white and silver loose mantua, lined with rose satin, a Dutch straw hat was perched casually upon her loose hair, and pink ribbons hung from her sleeves.

'Typical Rich Rustic, you see,' snapped the Countess. 'It's the absolute end in fashion.'

The woman was carrying a wicker pannier and absently plucking weeds from the camomile lawn. She turned and, seeing the two dishevelled women walking towards her, headed briskly for her front door.

'Madam, please to help us,' the Countess called in as pitiful a whimper as she could muster. 'Our coach has broken down – see . . .' The Countess turned and indicated Pigalle's coach which now leaned at an unhealthy angle beyond the hedge.

'Let me introduce us, madam. I am ze Duchesse de Pigalle and this is my friend Anastasia, Lady Ashby de la Zouche, Countess of Clapham.'

'Baroness Penge . . .'

'Yes, yes, yes,' snapped Pigalle, firing an ingratiating smile in Mrs Roy's direction. 'Perhaps we could come in and sit by your fireside . . .'

'. . . and take a cup of chocolate while . . . ?' The Countess shot her a winsome smile and pointed back to the coach again.

Mrs Roy swished her skirt and came over to unlock the gate's padlock.

Under her breath Pigalle fired out the line of action. 'You divert her with small talk while I make overtures to the child.'

With a click, the gate opened.

'I'm sorry to disappoint you, ladies,' said Mrs Roy. 'But I am going fishing now. If however you would care to join me, I can gladly invite you in to share a little supper. But until I go fishing there will be nothing to eat.'

The Countess opened her mouth, but before she had time to utter, Pigalle gave her ankle a firm kick. 'We should be delighted. How I adore ze fishing!'

The two women sidled through the gate. Pigalle was

almost falling over herself trying to peep round for the little black boy.

'What a lovely place you have here.' The Countess stared at the pretty little red-brick cottage, faced with creeper and rose bushes, and wished she was back in the dilapidated squalor of German Street and civilisation.

'Do you prefer a rod or a net?'

'Whichever!' said the Countess, mystified by the exact meaning of the question.

'And Mr Roy, does he come fishing too?'

Mrs Roy paused before replying. 'Mr Roy works in London. He does not get many opportunities to come here.'

'I can imagine,' said the Countess in sympathy, with him rather than his wife.

Mrs Roy gathered up her skirts and tripped across the lawn. 'My servants will help us to the river.'

'A river!' said the Countess, dreading another cross-country hoik. 'What a novelty! Fancy there being a river in the country. One is so used to Old Father Thames, one doesn't think that outside Town . . .'

'Don't worry,' said Mrs Roy, 'it's only at the bottom of my garden.'

Mustafa, dressed today in the tweeds of a country squire, carried the box of flies and hooks, and a big lumpen girl with yellow plaits carried all the rods, baskets and tackle. A bench was conveniently situated at the water's edge.

The three ladies sat, while the two servants, Mustafa and the girl with flaxen hair, laid out the paraphernalia for an afternoon's angling.

'We catch excellent trout here. I believe I can't offer

you a diversion to better suit your temper. Can you imagine anything so pleasant?' The woman fastened a fly to the end of her line and cast in one firm shot. 'There are your rods. Cast, and let us wager who will catch the first fish.'

Pigalle and the Countess looked at one another and blinked in alarm.

'This day is so wonderful,' blurted the Countess, 'I am doubting whether I am awake or perhaps enchanted, I am so happy.'

Pigalle was making eyes at the little boy, who true to form, winked back.

The Countess pressed on with diversionary conversation. 'We sit here, with our lines and baits, to delude the poor harmless fish of the . . .' She cocked her head. 'What is this river called?'

'Stamford Brook, Countess.'

'Of course,' sighed the Countess, trying to untangle a knot of fishing line which was caught up with the beaded front of her gown. 'Dear old Stamford Brook.' She tugged the knot free, and the hook flew up and caught in her wig. She sat very still, aware that one tug could spell disaster. 'So tell me about Mr Roy.'

'Madam,' Mrs Roy's voice had a sharp edge to it, 'you are very curious, methinks, and will let me catch no fish. If we don't succeed at our enterprise, we will starve and there will be no supper.'

The Countess gave a sly look in Pigalle's direction, wanting her to help out in the conversation, but the bloody Frenchwoman was facing the other way, sorting through a large basket with Mustafa. She had no interest whatsoever in this over-primped specimen of a woman, and marked this up as one huge favour Pigalle now owed her in return. How could she keep going and yet not seem to be prying?

'That's a lovely dress you're wearing! Italian in style, am I right? I always wanted an Italian model myself, but my husband, well, you know what men are like . . .' She felt Mrs Roy stiffen. Lord, she had got on to husbands again! She touched the wide spread of Mrs Roy's skirt. 'Wonderful fabric. A satin moiré, is it?' She well knew it was nothing of the sort, but at least it diverted the subject from the wretched woman's absent husband.

'White damask, lined with rose taffeta. The train is half an ell long, the bodice silver moiré, and a muslin cravat with silk tassels. The ribbons are Spitalfields silk. About five yards of the stuff in all.'

Something was disturbing the water's surface.

'My word! Look!' The Countess leaned forward to look and the hook caught in her wig immediately tugged it to one side. She straightened up smartly. 'Can that be a fish on the end of your string?'

'Looks like a tiddler.' Mrs Roy got on her knees to peer into the dark water. 'The trout spawn at this time of year, so they're either huge or else you can net a full batch of small fry.'

The Countess used the moment to elbow Pigalle, who saw her predicament and tried to unravel the Countess's fishing line from her hairpiece. 'Have you lured the boy?' she hissed when close enough to Pigalle's ear.

Pigalle nodded.

'I had a lovely peach-coloured gown once,' said Mrs Roy, reclaiming her seat after casting her line again. 'Magnificent, it was. A *robe de chambre* in rose damask

from China, lined with yellow taffeta, an echelle of burgundy ribbons, ribbons on the sleeves, and behind a large
bunch of ribbons to mark the waist.'

Pigalle suppressed a yawn.

'I also had a steinkirk of mechlin lace, to conceal my
bosom, which went with it.'

The Countess gave the woman a sideways look. To
her there didn't seem that much bosom to hide.

'When we go inside I shall show you my lovely new
earrings. Indian brilliants with the odd ruby.'

'Oh, good,' said the Countess, referring to getting
inside to the warmth rather than seeing the earrings. 'I
can't wait.'

'What *happened* to ze rose-coloured dress then?'
Pigalle had packed up her line and was standing, ready
to trot.

Mrs Roy swung round. 'Why . . . somebody spilled
something on it. It's ruined.' She beamed a smile. 'But
no matter, my husband has promised me another to
replace it. Even finer than the last. I think I'll have eau
de nil this time, with olive ribbons and a sepia trim . . .'

'Yes, yes, yes,' said the Countess with some urgency.
'But look! I truly think there appears to be a very large
fish on the end of your – um – string.'

The astrologer's shop was quite the strangest place Alpiew had ever seen. Dried bats were pinned to the ceiling,
and silver stars lined the walls. In the corner stood a
human skeleton, and on the centre of the table, a black
lacquer affair inset with mother-of-pearl symbols and
ciphers (one of which Alpiew immediately recognised

from the torn page from Beau's log-book), stood a stuffed owl.

On the other side of the table sat an old man. He was hideous, bloated and purple and venomous-looking, like a monstrous toad.

As Alpiew entered he spread out a large pack of cards. 'Cut!' he ordered.

Alpiew hesitated in the doorway. 'I'm sorry to bother you, sir. But it's not a prognostication I'm after . . .'

'You want me to cast your nativity?'

Alpiew shook her head and fumbled in her pocket for the page. 'It's this. A puzzle my lady has been given. And we are confused as to its interpretation.'

She handed the page over, praying he would not expect an enormous fee for his time.

$$\odot : \text{♈} \; \text{♂} \; \text{♒} \; = \; \overset{\text{♂}}{\odot} \; (\overset{\text{♂}}{\text{♀}} \; /\text{☉}) \; (\odot/\dagger) \; \text{⚓} \; @ \; \bullet \; \text{♎}$$

The astrologer let forth a great puff, as though he was on the verge of deflating entirely.

'Ah, a reference to the fourth great eclipse of this year of our blessed saviour 1699.'

Alpiew crept forward. 'You can decipher it?'

Without lifting his eyes from the paper the astrologer indicated for her to sit. ''Tis now the year of Our Lord 1699; 5,648 years since the creation of the world, 4047 since the general deluge of Noah's flood, 321 years since the invention of the gun, 33 years since London was almost consumed with fire . . .'

Three years since the rat ate up the cat, thought Alpiew, wishing he'd get on with it.

'. . . 1699, a year in which this noble realm is blessed

with no fewer than four eclipses of the luminaries. The first, of the moon, is just passed, and near ten digits of that luminous body were obscured. It occurred five years to the day after the interment of our late Queen Mary, wife of the present King, but whether that is significant, I doubt.' He passed his hand above his head. 'This morning saw the second, an inferior affair of the sun, barely discernible. The third, a lunar happening, will be to us, alas, invisible, but to our antipodes it will appear total.' He looked up. 'Do you follow me?'

Alpiew did, vaguely, so she smiled and encouragingly let him go on.

'The fourth and last is an eclipse of the sun, on the thirteenth of September at about eleven minutes before noon. That is London time. I cannot speak for the Welsh or Cornish, and what have you. You know the cause of an eclipse, I presume? I can give it you briefly in an allegorical poem.' The man opened his eyes to a startling degree and started to perform for Alpiew.

'*Thus Cynthia –*'

He dropped the poetical mode for a second to explain: 'That's the moon –

'rose with an awful grace,
Slips on her veil and hides her revered face
And lest proud Solus – that's the Sun – *should the matter ask,*
She soon surprised him with her vizard mask.
When this grave pair thus play their antic tricks,
We mortals certainly must feel the effects.'

The astrologer rubbed his hands together. 'You see! Clear as a bell.'

On a foggy night and under water, thought Alpiew.

'Now this particular eclipse is celebrated in the beginning of the celestial balance, the sign of Libra, a constellation dominated by the goddess Venus. An important eclipse, this one, and visible to us, here in London. Notable too, as it occurs alongside an opposition of Jupiter and Mars from Leonis and Aquarius and will much aggravate the effects thereof.'

Alpiew gulped. What was he talking about?

'Mars, god of war, will be busy, for he is also opposing the Lion's Heart, the Basilisk, Cor Leonis.'

'Is that what it says on the paper?' asked Alpiew, nodding in the direction of the log page.

'Of course not,' huffed the astrologer. 'I was just telling you about the eclipses which occur during this year. Those last two symbols surely refer to this last, greatest eclipse of which I just spoke. You see, the blackened figure denotes eclipse, the last character in the set represents the sign of Libra, the celestial balance, commonly called the Scales.'

This process of discovery may be going to take some time, thought Alpiew, but at least the man seemed to think the note *had* a meaning. She leaned forward and tried to understand.

'Alas, alas,' crooned the old toad. 'I fear the terrible effects of this eclipse will be fatal to poor England, for if just a glance of it will bring a man to disaster, pray that Providence defends the whole kingdom from its malicious influence.'

Alpiew began to feel a little frightened. Perhaps the man knew what he was talking about. It sounded as though he was announcing the imminent end of the world, or something like it. Then with little ado, assuming a matter-of-fact air, he turned back to Alpiew's paper.

'The first character we see represents Nigredo, a kind of state full of gloom and decay, necessitating change. Next up comes Mercury, planet of communication, both mental and nervous co-ordination and transmission. Close by, too close for comfort, comes the fair Venus, planet of love, unity and feeling.' He turned the paper so Alpiew could better see. 'This fourth symbol represents a conjunction, this means that two planets are within a few degrees of one another. This is a powerful aspect, giving strong emphasis to the planets involved. Next comes the Cor Leonis, I spoke of. This is a star at the heart of the sign Leonis, hence Lion's Heart – do you still follow?' Alpiew chewed her lip and nodded. She did – more or less. She leaned in, and took a closer look. 'Could the upside-down Venus mean antimony?' She pointed at the symbol she recognised. 'I've encountered that one before.'

The astrologer screwed up his nose. 'Absolutely not. That is the earth, in this case sitting astride the sun. An unlikely concept.' He stabbed his finger back on to the equation. 'Within the first brackets we find Mars and Venus snuggling up together and a line dividing them both from the Sun – a smaller one than the last, but that may just be a slip of the pen, these quills aren't always as efficient as one could wish; the second brackets the Sun and what appears to be a dagger, or a cross. I would volunteer the hypothesis that this is the Latin cross, the *crux ordinaria*, *crux immissa* or *crux capitata*. The Latin word *crux* of course, derives from *cruciare*, meaning to torture. This form of cross is sometimes called "God's mark". You follow?'

Alpiew smiled in what she hoped was an intelligent way. She was trying to take it all in, and wished she'd made notes. The astrologer puffed and pressed on with his reading, poking his finger at each sign as he gave his interpretation. 'The said cross is followed by some alchymical sign I do not know, then a traditional printers' abbreviation meaning "at".' He slid the paper back towards Alpiew. 'The rest I have already told you. Eclipse Libra.'

Alpiew took back the paper and stared down at the signs. 'So what does it all mean?'

The astrologer sat back in his chair, took a long breath, placed his fingertips together in a line and raised his eyebrows. 'To tell you the truth, young lady . . .'

Alpiew leant forward in eager anticipation. The man puffed out again, then leaned forward and stared Alpiew directly in the eye. '. . . I haven't a notion.'

Mrs Roy's country table was laid in a stylish dining room floored with marble. The walls were hung with Indian pictures and the wainscot lined with Dutch ceramic tiles. In the corner of the room adjoining the handsome oak buffet was a small fountain with which the servant girl washed the glasses.

' 'Tis certainly well-rigged for a country house,' said the Countess. 'In such a far-flung place I imagined the waterworks would be exceeding primitive. But that little invention is perfectly the latest thing.'

'Yes,' agreed Pigalle. 'There are all the conveniences of a palace in this little house.'

Mrs Roy beamed. 'My husband is very attentive to my needs.'

The servant girl brought in the steaming fish, now killed, filleted and cooked and laid out on a great silver platter. Mustafa trotted behind with a bowl of potatoes and cabbage.

'Mmm,' Pigalle sniffed appreciatively as the dishes were laid down. 'Smells divine.'

'It's a lovely cottage,' said the Countess, piling her plate high. 'Have you lived here long?'

Mrs Roy smiled. 'Four months. I am a newly-wed.' She stroked her belly. 'I am hoping that the country air will help me produce an heir for Mr Roy.'

Pigalle was inspecting the underside of the delicate greyish-blue china plate decorated with ducks and rocks. 'But my word, this is genuine Carrack porcelain.'

'A present from my husband, to celebrate.'

'Celebrate?'

'A forthcoming event.' She rested her hand on her tummy.

'So Mr Roy has made the most of his weekends,' said the Countess, cramming a forkful of fish into her mouth. 'This is scrumptious. And you can mash up anything we leave and make a fine kedgeree for breakfast tomorrow.'

The servant girl, who had turned a ghastly shade of grey, put her hand to her mouth and rushed out of the room.

Pigalle's eyes followed her. 'Your girl. She is sick, no?' She grimaced. 'Perhaps in ze country pregnancy is infectious.'

Mrs Roy slammed down her knife and fork. 'That's it! That is it! I've had enough of your innuendo. I welcome you into my house and all I get in return is rudeness.'

She rose from the table and swished her skirt in a great arc behind her. 'Two has-been, rejected mistresses of a king long-dead and best forgotten. I am sure that by now your coachman has mended the wheel he no doubt took off in the first place so you could come here and pry. Go on! Get back to your smoky holes and leave me in the peace and tranquillity which I seek.'

Pigalle spluttered. The Countess was trying to get as much of the contents of her plate as she could into her mouth before they were ejected.

Mrs Roy turned on them with all the passion of Mrs Barry performing in a heroic verse-tragedy. 'And don't think I did not hear you trying to lure my little Mustafa away from me with tales of kings and princes and monkeys and parrots and cats on leads and money. But you cannot have him. He is mine. He was given to me, by my husband.'

She threw her napkin down on to the table with such force it knocked her fork from her plate with a clatter. A glass of wine tumbled in its wake and the stain spread slowly across the linen table cloth.

'Get out. Both of you. Go on! OUT!'

Pigalle was already at the door. The Countess at her heels.

'Out, out, out! You two senile old whores,' shrieked Mrs Roy in a wild hoarse voice. 'And don't come back.'

Alpiew sat in a tavern for some time trying to puzzle out Beau's equation using the knowledge she'd acquired during the morning.

In the afternoon during performance time she strolled

back to the theatre to see if Molly had got any news for her.

The streets were again crowded with the inamorati of Signior Fideli. Alpiew shoved through a further huddle of women in the tiring-room corridor and made her way to the green room.

Molly was sewing a piece of lace which had separated from the steinkirk it usually adorned. 'Alpiew,' she cried, throwing down the needle and thread, 'I have news of your ruffian.'

Alpiew perched on a stool.

'If he's the man we think he is, he was an actor here. A hireling. Only remained a few weeks, took a couple of three-line roles, stirred up a great deal of hostility and left.'

'How did you find this out?'

'Another orange girl, she's been with us for years, noticed him lingering to pass his note to that new girl who you chatted to. She recognised him straight away, and attempted to talk to him, ask him how things were going, and that sort of stuff. But he walked on, made as though he did not know her.'

'What was he like?'

'Oh, you know ... He was an actor. What more can I say? When you work in the servicing trade they don't talk to you as though you are human, so I had little to do with him when he was here, except for fastening buttons on his breeches, which in his case seemed to pop off very frequently.'

'Really! Why?'

'Because he was ...' Molly coughed, and suppressed a grin. 'Noticeably well-endowed in that area.'

Alpiew raised her eyebrows. 'As in all others.'

'Indeed. A bull of a man.'

'Might anyone know more? Actresses, for instance?'

'Try at the lodging house in Rose Court. He had a room there.'

'As they all do . . .'

'True.' Molly knotted and cut the thread and laid the steinkirk down. 'Some of them are bound to be there now, whining about the size of their roles in this and how their part in that has been passed to another, and how the audience of today have no taste in preferring Signior Fideli to them . . .'

They listened for a few moments to the song wafting in from the stage:

> '. . . *Let's deal with each other that we may from hence*
> *Have broods to succeed us a hundred years hence.*'

'It is rather amusing, do you not think?' Molly picked up a feathered headdress, and inspected it for damage. 'That a man with no equipment at all is screeching away and thereby earning a fortune, with multitudes of women throwing themselves at him, while a man of gigantic proportions couldn't even turn one head or keep a role of three lines . . .'

'Jack Fry! A dull unmannerly brute. Scum of the earth.'

'Funny, that's what someone I knew called him – Scum.' Alpiew was sitting in one of the bedchambers rented out to players in Rose Court. The room was small, scarcely allowing room to move round the sides of the bed, but it was cosy enough. From above there came the screechings and squallings of an almighty row between two women. Alpiew glanced up. 'They sound like to kill one another . . .'

The player threw himself back on the bed and yelped with laughter. 'Rehearsing, darling. They're going through some stock scenes. From the number of times they're running out of breath in each rant, I'd wager it's the dagger scene in *The Rival Queens*.'

'Oh,' replied Alpiew, none the wiser.

'They're practically amateurs, those two. A good player must be the master of all the passions: love, joy, grief, rage, tenderness and jealousy. They can only do rage.' The actor sniffed. 'But I have to say in them rage sounds more like petulance.'

Alpiew tried to drag the subject back to Jack Fry, her Scum.

'Oh, him!' The actor sighed, and pulled some fluff from his waistcoat. 'He drove us mad. Always moaning, thinking he was better than everyone else . . .'

Alpiew stopped herself from saying, 'Which actor doesn't?' instead nodding politely.

'He thought he should be taking Betterton's roles. Said the man was a superannuated old fool. Senile. Thomas Betterton! The greatest actor of our times! Can you imagine! Said the audience today wanted real men.'

Alpiew laughed. 'Not if the success of Signior Fideli is anything to go by.'

'Silly little Italian.' The actor winced and patted his breeches. 'I would do much for my art, but that far I would not go. It is not necessary. In my younger day there was a play . . .'

'But you're not a bit like Jack Fry,' Alpiew jumped in,

in case the actor was ready to launch into another tedious theatrical anecdote. At this rate she'd be lucky to get three facts by midnight.

'Oh, yes. Jack Fry! A real second-rater. Anyhow, the nasty fellow left the company after a row about perquisites with the triumvirate – if one may so describe two women and one man.'

'Why not?' said Alpiew, who didn't care what he called anything so long as he got on with telling her about Scum.

The actor sat bolt upright. 'The gender of the word Triumvirate is quite inappropriate. It pre-supposes three men, whereas our company is run by the tragedienne, Elizabeth Barry (a woman), the professional virgin, Anne Bracegirdle (another woman) and the greatest player of our era, Thomas Betterton. Two women and a man. Between them they manage the patent, and control the company. They choose the plays, the repertoire, the actors and they hog all the best costumes to themselves. I worry that when my time comes for promotion up the ranks . . .'

'They didn't like Jack Fry, then?' Alpiew took the opportunity to remind the player why she was here.

'Jack Fry! What a joker! He wanted more pay, bigger parts, to be included in the country exeats. You name it. Kept ranting that he should be made a journeyman actor, not just a hireling.' The actor was so excited he started fanning himself with a piece of paper from his side-table. 'I had a frightful run-in with him. I was playing the small but pivotal role of Osman, in *The Royal Mischief*. Terrible play! Written by some slip of a girl . . .'

Alpiew coughed, hoping it might do the trick.

'Oh, yes. Well your Jack Fry took the part of Acmat, a eunuch. Let me tell you Acmat is a *marvellous* role, marvellous. *I* would have been brilliant in it. But this Jack Fry fellow was forever jibing at me that we should swap roles for "better verisimilitude"!' The actor raised his eyebrows in horror and leaned forward in an intimate way. 'Do you see the implication, my dear?' He pouted his lips. 'He was trying to tell me that he was more of a man than I! I mean! He got me so cross I almost brained him with my ornamental trumpet.'

'And these exeats Jack Fry was not included in. What are they exactly?'

'The company goes to where the court is for the summer or to festivals – Oxford, Windsor, Hampton Court to play for the royals and the courtiers. I played on the –'

'Why would that be important to Jack Fry?'

'Oh, him! He fancied himself as much in real life as he did on stage. Thought his physique could win him a rich or titled wife who would see him provided for for the rest of his days. When the big three told him he was not suitable for such occasions he upturned a table, smashed a chair and told them they could shove their theatre up their portholes.'

Through all the theatrical chat, Alpiew was building a fair picture of the man Beau called 'Scum'. 'And this tantrum? I suppose Fry regretted it afterwards?'

'In no way.' The actor stroked a strand of stray wig hair from his cheek. 'In fact he smiled that vicious smile of his, packed his things and told us all to "go play with our parts", and that he'd had another offer.'

'Which was?'

'At first we all thought he must have joined up with

those philistines at the Drury Lane company (a third-rate ensemble if ever there was one, all tumblers, dancing dogs and overweight women performing on the slack wire), but it turned out: no.' The actor leaned forward and lowered his voice. 'One of the girls who dressed, and who I am told had had some kind of intrigue with the gruesome man, bumped into him one night in the piazza and he was really pleased with himself. Said he was earning a fortune as a lady's protector.'

'Really?' Now we are coming to the business, thought Alpiew. 'Who was that lady, did he name her?'

'Some elegant dame in the country, he said.' The actor assumed more of a sneer in his countenance than was his norm. 'Though I wouldn't believe a word that man uttered.'

'And the woman?' Alpiew was anxious to keep this subject on the line. 'What did she want of him?'

'Butling, sutling?' The actor shrugged. 'Who knows? One would have thought he was her paid paramour, the way he bragged.'

'There is no possibility that he was?'

'How should I know, darling? He was hardly going to talk love-life with his ex-paramour was he?'

'And this lady Jack Fry was being paid by, did he tell the girl where she lived?'

'Suitable name for a place to accommodate a would-be actor . . .' The actor licked his finger and stroked his eyebrow.

'Yes?' Alpiew had to control herself from getting up and shaking the information out of the man. 'Where is that?'

'Acton! Acton!' The actor smiled from ear to ear. 'Do

you get it? Acton. He could still say he was in Actin'.'

Alpiew did a bit of acting herself and laughed. 'And was he a good actor?'

'*He* thought so. No one else did. Though he had a certain *je ne sais quoi*.'

'Pardon?'

'He had a stage presence which was somewhat frightening,' said the actor grudgingly. 'He would have been admirable in those vulgar, uncouth displays by Mr Shakespeare (a verbose bumpkin from the last century), but he was no use whatsoever in the refined and elegant plays in which this country excels. Yes. I can see him as a brawling soldier in *Henry V*, a monster like Caliban or even a rough nobleman such as Hotspur in *Henry IV*. But Jack Fry could not play the genteel rakes and beaux of today's celebrated writers. Oh, no.'

The two sat in silence for a moment. A clock struck the half-hour. The actor leapt up and grabbed his livery cloak from the bed-post. 'Is that the time? I am late.' He threw his cloak around his shoulders with a well-practised flourish. 'I see Jack Fry best in that vile play, *The History of King Richard III*.'

Alpiew rose and sidled briskly round the edge of the bed. Pigalle would be expecting her home very soon. She would have to run all the way. 'As the King?'

'No, no.' The actor held open the door for Alpiew. 'As the murderer of the Princes of the Tower.'

TEN

Division

*The separation of a substance
into its elements.*

The Countess and the Duchesse sat in agitated silence all the way to Hide Park Corner.

'Is he well, ze husband?'

'Peter, why don't you call him Peter? It's his name,' snapped the Countess.

More silence.

As the coach came into German Street, Pigalle tried again to make the peace.

'It was a stupid idea to try and get zat boy. You are right.' She turned to face her friend. 'Ashby, darlink, I am sorry. Why do you not bring Peter round to my house for dinner tonight. We could make a four for cards.'

The Countess gave a little pout. 'And how are you going to do that, Olympe? Have you forgotten that Azis has left you? As *all* your servants do.'

Pigalle leaned forward and tweaked at the Countess's elbow. 'But now I have Alpiew.'

'Alpiew!' The Countess's jaw dropped, and her eyes

started out of their sockets. 'Yes, yes. This makes sense.'
The Countess puffed out her cheeks like a fish and tightened her lips to the width of string. 'A woman who would drag me through mud and mire to steal a moorish boy from some poor lonely country wife, would think nothing of stealing my dear pretty Alpiew from me.' She was on the verge of tears now. 'Alpiew, that precious creature, who is as near to me as if she was my own child.'

The coach shuddered to a stop. The Countess yanked the door open and stepped out. Forgetting that she was still wearing Pigalle's high metal pattens, she fell flat on her face. Pigalle jumped out to help her to her feet, but once up the Countess turned round and threw a hard slap across Pigalle's heavily powdered cheek. 'You are no friend of mine!' she spat. 'It is lucky for me that someone who really *does* care for me has managed to find me again, after all these terrible years of separation.'

At this moment Sir Peter and Godfrey came rolling along the street.

'Peter, darling.' The Countess stood in the position used in the theatre for imploring scenes. 'Please, beloved, save me from this thieving lesbian!'

'Pigalle, you old trout, how the devil are you?' Sir Peter grinned at Pigalle as he kissed his wife on the cheek. 'Why don't you join us? Godfrey's got the fire going in the front room, we could have a round or two of basset?'

Pigalle made her apologies, she had business, there were birds to be fed.

'Sorry, Pigalle, old girl. No apologies permitted today. Haven't seen you for too long.'

Pigalle looked towards the Countess, who was fluttering coyly in Sir Peter's direction. Worried for her friend's sanity, she acquiesced.

'But first I must fetch Alpiew. She is temporarily staying with me . . .' Pigalle took a deep breath. 'In order to give you two love-birds a bit of time together.'

With Alpiew in tow, Pigalle arrived at the Countess's house a half-hour later. The five sat round a folding card-table. Godfrey ripped open four new books of cards and dealt. The Countess was playing but, still in a fury with both Alpiew and Pigalle, set down her cards in sulky silence.

Sir Peter organised his hand with an enigmatic smile. 'Godfrey and I did some good work today, eh, Godfrey?'

Godfrey grunted.

'Got a nice little earner going. Down at the palace. Seven, I face.' Sir Peter slid two gold coins across the table.

Godfrey laid down the pack. Alpiew and Pigalle exchanged a look.

'It's a shame I forgot my mask. I always wear a mask when playing for money.' Pigalle spoke with her eyes down, fixed intently on her hand. 'Which palace? St James's or Kensington?'

'St James's today.' Peter grinned. 'Very successfully. Today St James's, tomorrow the world!'

'I'll make a paroli.' Pigalle laid down two gold coins. 'I mase as much more. Your card loses, Sir Peter, for two guineas. So tell me, what is your business at court?'

'Going to make me a fortune out of royal arseholes.' Sir Peter tapped his nose. 'A large amount of cloth fell into my hands.'

'Cloth?' said Alpiew, taking a sly sideways look at Sir Peter's cards.

'That's right, Alpiew. Sold it to the palace. I face.' He turned up a card. 'Quadrupled what I paid for it.'

Godfrey laid down more cards. 'Five wins, knave loses.'

Pigalle scooped up her winnings. 'And what is zis fabulous fabric? Ells of silver embossed brocade from ze Indies?'

'Couple of dirty old sails, which had, somehow or other,' he winked at Godfrey, 'got ripped up and ruined.'

'And you sold zat to ze palace? I knew ze Dutch had strange taste in upholstery, but . . .'

Alpiew slipped a card up her sleeve ready for later.

'Ducketts,' grinned Sir Peter. 'Stool ducketts. Who's going to mind using a dirty piece of sail to wipe their behind? I raise you a paroli.'

'Two guineas more.' Pigalle laid down a five of diamonds. 'I thought there were official purveyors for such things. Ze Royal Household, no?'

'Oh yes, that's right. But there's trouble in the Lord Steward's department. Much disgruntlement among the lower orders. And, you'll remember, Pigalle, old girl, I always say where there's moaners, there's money.'

'I don't know what they have to be moaning about.' Alpiew slid a few pence forward and laid down. 'It's a good job working at the palace. Secure.'

'Loss of perquisites,' said Godfrey. 'Used to get their meals free, and could sell on the unfinished candle stumps . . . And the leftover food from banquets.'

'But since the Dutch have taken over the purse-strings, all that's gone.' Sir Peter briskly sorted his cards and laid down a seven of spades. 'Trouble is, at the same time as stripping them of their perqs, they've forgotten to pay them. Some of the under staff are a year in arrears. So . . . Seven wins, five loses.'

'I see,' said Pigalle, watching her money slide across the table to Sir Peter's place while he placed a knave in the centre of the table. 'You sell cheap rubbish to zem, and zey invoice for ze usual price and pocket ze change.' She laid down an ace.

'I'll raise you a sept and leva.' Sir Peter laid out five guineas. 'For, you see, I am flush this evening! Today we put our toes in the water. Tomorrow we submerge ourselves.'

'Really?' Pigalle matched Sir Peter's money. 'You take on Kensington Palace?'

'Yes, and see what other items, fallen from the back of a dray-cart, we can shove their way.' He sucked on the top of his beard while he deliberated over his hand. 'They say Princess Anne has almost as large a household as the King himself. And both of them stuck out there in Kensington.' Sir Peter turned to his wife. 'I've never known you so silent, Ashby, dear. Are you ill?'

The Countess pouted. 'I am ill *served* by my friends,' she cried. 'What's more, I have spent the most horrid day imaginable.'

'Ace wins, knave loses.' Godfrey cut the pack and shuffled.

Sir Peter, Pigalle and the Countess laid down. Alpiew was arranging the card up her sleeve, getting ready to play it.

The Countess was preparing for a good long moan. 'Today my French so-called friend dragged me to a place of unimaginable horror. A nasty little spot in the middle of nowhere going by the name of Acton.'

'Ah,' said Sir Peter with a sigh. 'Acton! An arboreal delight!'

Alpiew's card tumbled out of her sleeve and to the floor. 'Acton?'

'Very verdant. Acton Green, so pertinently named.' Sir Peter rearranged his hand. 'Acton: green woods, their leafy bowers prettily sheltering all the main roads which run out to the west.'

The Countess was not to be deflected from her fury at Pigalle. 'Dragged all that way to see some wretched, insulting woman, who had no conversation but clothes and angling.'

'With a big thug of a footman?' Alpiew had laid her cards face-up on the table. Pigalle was making frantic mental note of them.

'What are you talking about, Alpiew?' said the Countess, amazed at having got such a reaction. 'There was no footman. Only a vomiting maid and a carbonadoed child.' She glanced down at the card lying on the floor at her feet. 'Alpiew, is that King of Diamonds yours or mine?'

In a complete fluster, Alpiew picked up the card and laid it on the table. 'I mase. But, milady, I must know about Acton. Is it a large place?'

Godfrey turned up the top of the pack. 'King wins.'

Oblivious to her win, Alpiew pressed the Countess. 'Tell me about Acton. Who did you meet there?'

'Please change the subject. Don't you see, it was bad enough going there, without having to talk about it all night.' The Countess helped herself to one of Alpiew's cards. 'Anyhow, why would you want to know about that uncouth countrified spot?'

Alpiew knew instinctively that she should not talk about the Beau Wilson case in front of Sir Peter, Godfrey and the Duchesse de Pigalle. She remembered too that she had not yet even told the Countess about Betty's dreadful fate nor the discovery of Beau's final message.

While Alpiew stared at the Countess, Godfrey was repeating over and over: 'You've won, Alpiew. Take your money.' Pigalle swiped the money across the table to Alpiew's place so that play could continue.

'Thank you, Godfrey. New cards here, please.'

'Countess . . .' Alpiew started, trying through subtle facial expressions to let the Countess see how serious the matter was. 'Milady, it is a matter of grave urgency. I need to talk to you alone.'

The Countess pursed her lips, and shrugged. 'Don't think I will forgive you so quickly for such a fatal betrayal.'

'My lady, you must help me. I have to speak with you privately.' Alpiew blurted out the first shocking thing she could dream up to get her attention: 'I'm pregnant!'

The Countess eyed Alpiew slowly, then gave a sly look in the direction of her husband before remembering he'd only been back a day.

'I *must* talk to you now, milady,' cried Alpiew. 'Out of the hearing of others. You are the only one I can turn to. You are practically a mother to me . . .'

With a demure bob towards the others at the table the Countess rose and took Alpiew's hand. 'Come, Alpiew, we will retire to the kitchen and let this dissolute scene of gay frivolity continue unabated.'

Once seated in front of the fire Alpiew blurted out the truth of the story. 'Oh, milady, I am sorry. But I had to get you alone,' she explained. 'You see, becoming pregnant is almost the only thing that hasn't happened.'

Alpiew hurriedly told the Countess of Betty's shocking death, of the 33 and the note in the bottle, of the trips to the apothecary and the astrologer, and how the large man they had seen in Beau's vicinity was in all probability this very actor who now worked for a rich lady in Acton.

'So you see, milady, we must go back to this Acton. Look round, ask questions, see whether anyone knows of him out there.'

'We could try the tavern. They do an excellent lunch called a Farmhand.' The Countess now felt as though she was an expert on the countryside and its ways, and was glad to share her knowledge. 'Or maybe that ghastly insulting woman would know of him. And even if she doesn't, we could take a bit of nice cold revenge. Come.'

She took Alpiew by the hand and led her back to the front room.

'Pigalle, my dear friend, Alpiew can stay with you to help you out for the next few days. And in return I would like to borrow your coach and coachman tomorrow.'

Pigalle was on a losing hand. 'Yes, yes!' She looked up from her cards. 'Curse on these spades,' she said, laying down a three. 'And when is ze baby due?'

Alpiew took her seat and picked up her hand of cards, which now mysteriously consisted of all the lowest cards in the pack. 'What baby?'

'An easy enough mistake to have made,' the Countess covered. 'I never taught poor Alpiew about "country matters". This afternoon some nasty fellow put his tongue in her ear. Poor girl is so simple she thought that would give her a baby. But I've put her right about the messy thing that really occurs. Now, Pigalle, you agree to the coach?'

Pigalle caught Alpiew's sly wink and supposed this must be some ploy of Alpiew's to distract the Countess with information about her husband. '*D'accord*! *D'accord*!'

The Countess turned to Sir Peter. 'And, dearest husband, we can drop you off at Kensington Palace to sell your wares. We passed it today. It is en route!'

The stink of tarry old sails filled the coach.

'I don't know that I'd like to clean my posterior with pieces of that,' said the Countess, fanning herself.

'We thought of selling off some blocks of ice from the Fleet canal to the Keeper of Ice and Snow, but it turns out they've been inundated with offers, and no one is in the mood to eat sorbets at this time of year, so –' Sir Peter kicked the sack full of material into the corner – 'when we've off-loaded these sails, my next venture will be horse-shit.' He clapped and splayed his hands like a magician at a fair. 'There's enough of the stuff lying around on the city streets. You can't cross the road at the Maypole in the Strand without getting your boots well and truly shitten. So all I need to do is get a bit of organisation going, ship it out to these parts and sell it to the gardeners. Look, they are setting out acres of ornamental gardens around here.'

'So, Sir Peter,' Alpiew was glad they were nearly at the palace, but tried to be polite in the meanwhile, 'where will you start today?'

'With the shit or the shit-rags?' He laughed at his own vulgarity. No one else did. 'With Princess Anne, I think. She looks a game bird. Bit bossy and not the prettiest girl in the kingdom, but I hear she's married to some big lump who can barely speak the King's English. Probably lonely. A little flirting in that direction should get us an order for ordure!'

Alpiew sighed. She'd been party to many of Sir Peter's previous fortune-making schemes, and had always hated his coarse sense of humour. Mercifully, the red brick of Kensington Palace loomed ahead. 'Here we are, Sir Peter. You'd better get out, or we shall be late.'

'Come along, you old lazybones.' Sir Peter gave Godfrey, who was snoring, a sharp elbow in the ribs. 'You've got to carry this stuff across the gardens.'

The two men yanked their sack full of ripped sails out of the coach, and started the trudge to the back door of the palace.

Once they were on their way, with a wave and a smile from the window, the Countess urged the driver onwards. Then she turned to Alpiew. 'Now, show me this paper you found.'

Alpiew presented the torn sheet of symbols. The Countess gazed at it for a moment before handing it back. 'Incomprehensible. But I'm wondering if that queer chap next door . . .'

'Mr Newton?'

'Correct. Mr Newton might understand it. After all, he wrote that book which none but he can understand.'

'What book?' Alpiew liked a good read.

'A best-seller a few years ago. Everyone has a copy, and

no one has got beyond page four. It's called *Mathematica Principia.*'

'Not a very snappy title.'

'Nonetheless everyone in London bought it. Anyone who can pull off such a coup, must be able to tell you what that thing means.'

When they reached Acton they went first to the tavern, which was always the hub of village life. Alpiew was the first to ask questions. She approached a lone tapster, sitting out in the yard fiddling about with a wooden barrel. He told her he knew of no well-built man working in the village. ' 'Ceptin' myself, that is.' Then with a smirk he gave Alpiew's rump a pat. 'What're you after, lass? Sure, I could perform 'twixt the sheets as well as this 'ere actor chappy.'

Alpiew extricated herself and went in to join the Countess in the warmth of the bar-room.

'And you have never glimpsed Mr Roy?' The Countess was perched on a high stool, leaning over the bar counter, with a pint of ale and a Ploughman's before her.

'No, I haven't, and if you ask me . . .' The landlady leaned forward in an intimate way. 'We're not meant to see him. That's for sure. No one has, and there's been a mighty few peeping, I can promise you. The fellow always arrives in an unmarked coach with the blinds down. Usually in the middle of the night.'

The Countess nodded to her to continue. She had a notion the woman knew more. 'But . . . ?'

'But . . .' The landlady came even nearer, the lace lappets from her headgear almost dragging in the Countess's beer. 'I was out one night, trotting across the fields to see my friend who lives the other side of the village.

It was dark. No moon, or nothing, so he couldn't see me, I hope. But I saw her waiting at the gate . . .'

'The one she keeps padlocked?'

'Yes, that's right.' She gave the Countess a nudge. 'And that's another weird thing about them. Who locks a garden gate?' She pulled her lappets from the drink and started wringing them out behind the counter. 'Well, she was just standing there. And it wasn't a warm night neither. Back in January it was. River frozen over, that sort of thing. And up comes this coach and out he gets . . .'

'Big fellow?' said the Countess licking her lips. 'Dark clothing? Thick neck?'

The landlady drew back, shaking her head. 'No. Whatever gave you that idea? Nothing like that. Strange little thing, he was. Tiny. And walked funny. But that might just have been the cold. Making it slippy like.' She drew her lips closer to the Countess's ear. 'I almost laughed out loud it was so odd. She being so tall, and he so short. But that's how it was. Snow White and the Dwarf.' She let forth a violent laugh that caused the Countess to recoil for fear of damage to her eardrum.

'And his face?' asked the Countess. 'What was that like?'

'Couldn't see it. Big wig, you see. And a feathery hat.'

'And the woman herself – Mrs Roy?' Alpiew joined them. 'What do you make of her?'

'Strange creature altogether.' The landlady seemed pleased to be asked. 'We glimpse her in the garden, digging and planting. Strolling down to the river with a rod. That's it. Never been in here once. Doesn't speak to people who try and address her.'

'Is she seen around the village? Taking walks or . . . ?'

The landlady slammed her hand down on the counter. 'Never leaves the house. Has no coach of her own, and never hires the hackney carriage in the village. Nor catches the post-coach from here. We hire out horses too, but she's never been known to use one.'

'So how does she get up to the theatre?'

'What theatre?' snapped the landlady. 'There's no theatre here. This is Acton.'

'But she goes to the theatre in London.' The Countess took a slurp of beer and wished she hadn't. Never had anything tasted so foul. 'We have seen her there. Sitting in a side box.'

'Seen her! In London!' the landlady bawled. 'But that is impossible. She moved here late last autumn, and so far as any of us in the village know, she has never left the place. Not once. Not even to stroll into the village to buy a pat of butter or a dozen eggs.'

'Not to take a letter to the posting house?' Alpiew tore a hunk of bread and chewed. 'Nor to take tea in the tea shop?'

'No,' the landlady dabbed at the crumbs left on the top. 'She sent her servants for errands. Never went herself.'

'The little moorish boy and the flaxen-haired girl?' The Countess chased her pickled onion round the pewter plate, before giving up any hope of gentility and using her fingers to pop it into her mouth.

'Sometimes the girl, yes. The boy is too young.' The landlady broke off a piece of the Countess's cheese and ate it. 'But she sometimes sent her handyman.'

'Handyman?' Alpiew sat upright. This was it! Surely

they had pinned down Scum. 'Well-built, thick-set cove with a broken nose?'

'Oh, no. The contrary.' The landlady shook her head. 'Tall. Thin. Willowy. Auburn hair, cut short. Never wore a periwig. You'd see him coming to and fro, carrying parcels, galloping off on the horse he arrived on, sometimes carrying the girl or the child.'

'And you know of no other fine lady who keeps a manservant of that description – well-built, thick-set?' Alpiew couldn't believe that the search for Scum would go cold like this, but the landlady shook her head.

'And what is he like to talk to, Roy's handyman?'

'Never spoke anything apart from, "A loaf of sugar, please", or "A quart of whey." Most taciturn lad. Very aloof. Sneery sort of looks.' The landlady wiped down the bar-top. 'So why the interest to you ladies?'

'Mrs Roy insulted me yesterday. After we took lunch in here my friend and I were in a coach which broke down, and she took the occasion of our misfortune to call us names.' The Countess gave an enigmatic smile. 'So I want to find out her vulnerabilities.'

'In that case, I wish you good luck.' The landlady laughed and cleared the plate from the counter. 'We don't need proud City folk like that here in our lovely village.'

'Exactly,' swooped the Countess, making her way towards the door.

The landlady held up the Countess's brimming glass. 'Aren't you going to finish your beer?'

The Countess teetered. She knew she would vomit if she took another sip. 'You have it, my dear. On me. For all your help.'

On leaving the Cock tavern the Countess ordered the coach straight back to the home of Mustafa and his mistress, Mrs Roy.

'But, milady,' Alpiew protested, 'we are searching for Scum. We should be asking at the shops, at the tea house.'

'Yes, yes,' snapped the Countess. 'And so we will. But first I have a debt to pay. Then I will be happy.'

Alpiew curbed her tongue. But greatly regretted the waste of time, for Mrs Wilson was surely going mad for lack of news about their inquiries.

'This will be fun,' said the Countess, tying pattens to her feet and striding out on to the meadow before the house. 'She will not expect to see me back so soon!'

Alpiew held the Countess's elbow and the two women made it over the stile and waded through mud and cow-pats to the padlocked gate.

In the little garden nothing was stirring.

'Well, it's cold,' said the Countess, clambering nimbly over the cross-bar of the padlocked gate. 'Why would she be in the garden? Come, Alpiew, let us surprise her. Perhaps we will get a sight of the mysterious Mr Roy.'

Alpiew leapt down on to the camomile lawn and looked around. It all seemed quite ordinary. A lawn, some flowerbeds, a path leading down to the river, a pretty cottage with plants growing up the front. A typical country retreat.

The Countess had started battering at the front door. There was no reply.

After a few moments Alpiew stepped to her side. She tried the handle, but the door was locked. 'Perhaps they are out? Gone to Town.'

'Probably at the theatre, seeing Monsewer Balloon, the dancer.'

Alpiew moved to the front of the house and peered in through the leaded windows. 'Madam?' she called, waving the Countess over. 'The shutters are closed.'

'My word!' The Countess scuttled to her side and applied her face to the glass. 'How strange!'

Alpiew stood back to take in the whole frontage. The upstairs windows seemed equally dark. 'I will compass the house, madam.'

The Countess sat on the garden bench while Alpiew circumnavigated the cottage. Her toe toyed with a loose piece of camomile. It looked as though someone had been doing repairs to the lawn since yesterday, for she had not noticed the piece of turf, cut square, beside the bench before.

Alpiew returned in a few moments. 'I see nothing. The place is better secured than the Royal Mint.'

The Countess gave a little grunt. 'How disappointing. I wanted to show you the dining-room fountain.'

'I didn't say the place was impenetrable, madam.' Alpiew wiped her hands down her bodice, then pulled a pin from her hair. 'Give me a minute with the backdoor lock and we shall be inside.'

'What fun!' The Countess giggled as they tiptoed round the side of the tiny house. 'I only wish I could imagine a good way to repay the foul strumpet for the insults she screamed at Pigalle and me yesterday.'

Alpiew took two minutes to get inside, where they both marvelled over the kitchen which had all the latest nick-nacks, and a large bread oven. 'It seems strange, though,' mused Alpiew. 'The lady at the inn said she never left the house but there seems to be no one here.'

The Countess turned and frowned. 'You are right, Alpiew. If she never leaves, how comes it that she is not here?'

'And how come we have seen her in Town?'

The Countess led Alpiew to the dining room and waddled over to the fountain. 'Look at this!' She pulled a lever and water gushed out. 'It's a miracle, don't you think? So useful.'

Alpiew couldn't imagine what for, and was anxious to get out of the place, and get back on to the trail of Scum. She left the dining room and stood waiting in the hall. The paintings hanging on the walls were obviously very valuable and the wall hangings were of the finest silks, more like an elegant house in the fashionable part of Town.

When the Countess joined her they both turned back towards the kitchen, but the Countess gave Alpiew's hand an impulsive little tug. 'Oh, come, Alpiew. Now we are inside and undisturbed, let us creep upstairs, just for a minute, and see what style of *à la mode* bedchamber the trollop inhabits.'

Reluctantly Alpiew climbed the stairs behind the Countess, who bolted straight into the back room.

'Oh, Alpiew, do hurry,' the Countess called. 'See! It is splendid, is it not?'

'Very fine, for a country cottage,' said Alpiew, fingering the silk drapery, and admiring the expensive-looking glass mirror over the fireplace. 'And very strange. Where are the servants, and it come to that?'

'Not in here.' The Countess was pulling open empty drawers, and peeking inside. She opened a painted door in the corner near the bed. 'The garde de robe, Alpiew,' she squealed. 'My word, look at this collection of mantuas!'

There were a number of fine dresses hanging inside. Alpiew and the Countess touched the delicate beadery and flamboyant flounces, pulling out sleeves to inspect the dainty stitching. 'They're even better than mine, in my heyday,' sighed the Countess. 'So the dwarf must be very rich.'

Alpiew was tugging at a dress tucked in behind the others.

'Peach. How lovely,' said the Countess. 'Though I'm not sure that Burgundy is right for the ribbons.'

Alpiew sniffed the dress. 'It's the scent I'm picking up. Smell.' She thrust the fabric towards the Countess's nose. 'Lily of the valley and musk. Do you get it?'

But the Countess was pointing down, her mouth open, aghast. Alpiew turned the dress back to take a look at what was upsetting the Countess. It was ruined. Down the front of the bodice, spreading along to the cuffs was a large brown stain.

'Oh my Lord,' gasped Alpiew. 'It's . . . It's blood.'

ELEVEN

Elevation

*The raising of the subtle parts of the substance
upwards, away from the bodily residues,
into the upper parts of the vessel.*

'Oh Alpiew, let us leave this dreadful place.' Alpiew stood
fanning the Countess, who now reclined on the bench
outside the front door of the cottage. 'What does it mean?
Has someone come in and killed Mrs Roy and cut her
up into a thousand pieces?' She crossed herself, then
winced. 'Sorry. Old habit, from living in France, you
know, but when I think of yesterday . . . Pigalle and I
were here, and she was alive . . .' She gave a little shudder
and started to shake. 'And, now . . . Now . . .'

Alpiew laid her hand on the Countess's lap. 'Quiet,
milady. There is another possibility.'

'Oh, and what is that? Perhaps the woman stabbed
herself, and when she was dead she stuffed that dress at
the back of her own garde de robe?'

'There was no hole where a knife might have pene-
trated the fabric.' Alpiew had had a good look at the
dress before thrusting it back into its hiding place. 'The
blood on that mantua did not come from Mrs Roy, but
from another.'

'You mean . . . ?' the Countess made a retching sound. 'That Mrs Roy is herself a murderer?'

Alpiew nodded. 'The dress is oddly familiar to me. Is it not strangely like the dress worn by that masked woman in the churchyard on the night Beau Wilson had his throat cut?'

The Countess gasped so loud that a couple of crows pecking at the lawn took instant flight.

'Oh, Alpiew, if you are right, to what danger did Pigalle and I expose ourselves yesterday? Not a soul would have ever found us out here. She could have despatched us and buried us under this camomile lawn . . .' Her toe tapped at the loose piece of lawn beside the bench. 'Oh Lord!' She held her hand to her mouth and gazed down. 'Maybe someone *is* buried here. For I'll swear this turf was uncut yesterday.'

'It would have to be a very small person, milady, for the cut turf is a mere six inches square.'

'They could be buried standing up, like the poet Ben Jonson in Westminster Abbey.'

Alpiew shot her a look and reached into her pocket for her small penknife, got on to her knees and started hacking at the lawn. 'Perhaps we will find an instrument of murder.'

'A what?' The Countess shrank down on the bench.

'Keep a watch-out!' cried Alpiew. 'If anyone comes back we will have some hearty explaining to do. And with the discovery we have just made we don't want to linger here any longer than we have to.'

'We should leave instantly.' The Countess jumped up, realising the truth which Alpiew spoke. 'Come along, Alpiew.'

'If we 'find the dagger that killed Beau here . . .'

The Countess was already half-way across the lawn.

'Make your way to the gate, madam. I will be behind you.' She parted the earth and pulled up a carpet of camomile, scooping up the soil beneath with her knife all the while.

Suddenly the knife made a hollow sound.

'Madam!' Alpiew looked up in terror, and called the Countess back. 'I have hit something. It seems to be a wooden box.'

'Mary, Mother of God, save our souls!' The Countess crossed herself three times. 'Not a coffin?'

'No. Too small.' Alpiew sawed at the lawn, scraping away the soil with her bare fingers. 'It looks like a ditty box of some kind.' She brushed the soil from the lid.

'Looks like an Indian trunk!' said the Countess leaning down to inspect it. 'What do you think?'

Alpiew was tugging the box from its hiding place. 'I think we must make good the lawn, stick the box under our cloaks and let us get away from here.'

They decided to leave the Acton inquiries about Scum for another day, while making the most of what they had discovered. Alpiew prodded at the box's lock with her penknife and then a hairpin, but to no avail.

'Give it to me.' The Countess laid the box upside-down on her knee and pressed her fingers in while holding tight to the edge. A spring gave way and the lid popped open.

'How did you do that?'

'It's a secret panel. You find them in many a piece of nick-nackery made since the start of the Civil War.' The Countess pulled back the lid and peered inside.

The box contained very little. A handful of letters. The Countess held one up, indicating the spidery writing. 'A man, if I'm not mistaken.'

'Are they all in the same hand?'

'No, but whoever writ this one has a hand like a foot.' She pulled out a piece of paper scrawled over with a very heavy script, which appeared to be a laundry list of some kind.

'Mercy!' Alpiew took the list and scrutinised it. 'Can this be the lady's writing?'

'No.' The Countess wrinkled up her nose. 'That too is definitely a man's writing. Lower class. Uneducated.'

'Our friend Scum?'

The Countess passed Alpiew the list, and she read aloud: '"Dress, gloves, corset, stockings, shoes, pattens, nightwear . . ." What is it? A shopping list?'

'Something like,' said the Countess, already at the letters. 'For look, most of the items are ticked off.'

Alpiew turned the list over. On the back was written the letters KGW which was heavily underlined. Alpiew placed the list carefully at the bottom of the chest and took a wad of the neat letters.

They both sat in silence for a while, skimming through them. The coach took a lurch and rattled wildly as they crossed a small wooden bridge.

'No address, I note,' Alpiew flicked through. 'And no name.'

'But they are dated. Mine are all of love and hearts, unimaginable softnesses, transporting passions and

273

etceteras, all since January this year . . .' The Countess laid hers down. 'Yours?'

'Same.'

They thrust them all back into the box and snapped it shut.

'Now, madam,' Alpiew took a deep breath, 'we must make a plan of action. Time is against us. Mrs Wilson's hopes are dwindling, and if she is truly hanged, then we will have nothing for our pains. Not to mention we have let an innocent woman go to the gallows.'

'I've been thinking, Alpiew, about Mrs Wilson.' The Countess brushed the soil from her skirts. 'If she is confessing to murdering her husband she won't be hanged. Murdering a husband is Petit Treason. It is like a smaller version of killing a king.'

'So what will happen to her?'

The Countess took a deep breath. 'She will be burned alive.'

'How awful,' Alpiew gasped. 'Burned alive. What can we do?'

'If she has made a voluntary confession, the system will speed up. There need be no trial. I've known cases like this go from murder to execution in a very short time.'

'How short?' Alpiew started mentally to count the days.

'Sometimes a week, ten days.'

'And Beau has been dead for four days.' Alpiew gripped hard to the leather strap as the coach took a sharp turn from the stony Shepherd's Bush Lane on to the main Kensington Road. 'For Mrs Wilson to face death so young and in so unnatural a manner puts me in mind of the fragility of our own existence.' Alpiew clung on with white knuckles and gritted teeth as the coach lurched again, though her fright was more at how deeply they had got themselves concerned in an enterprise fraught with so much danger. 'This is a hazardous and terrifying world we have entered, Countess. I do not want to risk either your or my safety. It is important' – she lowered her voice, already a whisper, so that the coachman would not hear – 'that no one should know where we are, or what we are doing. And that we should take great care how we proceed from now on.'

'But Godfrey, Pigalle, my husband . . .' The Countess laughed. 'Surely . . .'

'No one.' Alpiew turned and grabbed the Countess's hands in hers. 'My lady, I saw Betty's body. The girl must have died in an agony. Whoever did that probably killed Beau Wilson too. And you saw him dead. We have been very close to the killer. For all we know, they know about us already.'

'I see what you mean . . .' The Countess let out a dry gulp. 'But my husband . . .'

'No, your ladyship,' Alpiew looked out of the window at the glowing shape of Kensington Palace in the afternoon sun. 'Nobody.'

'But how will I keep it from him?'

'You carry on as normal, Countess. And I will proceed alone, as best I can. When he has business elsewhere you can join me.'

'So how do we talk, plan where we are to go next?'

'It will have to be outside of your house.' Alpiew considered for a moment. 'We could sit in a park.'

'Pshaw! A park? But it's winter.'

'Then we tell Godfrey and Sir Peter that we are going out and instead we creep up to your top room.'

'Godfrey's chamber?' The Countess looked appalled. 'But that is colder than the park. And there are pigeons up there.'

'Pigeons.' Alpiew shuddered. She detested birds. 'So what do we do? Where do we go?'

'I don't know. Tomorrow I will come up with an idea.'

'It's quite a pretty palace, isn't it? Kensington. But Whitehall was more regal somehow. Pity it burned down.' The Countess rested her foot on the Indian box which had slid across the floor when the coach turned. 'What on earth can have been going on between that woman and Beau Wilson? And how is this Jack Fry creature involved?'

'And who is Mr Roy?'

Suddenly the Countess let out a wild yell. Alpiew leapt from her seat.

'STOP!' cried the Countess, banging the ceiling with her fist. 'COACHMAN! STOP!'

'Milady?' Alpiew peered around her. 'What's the matter, madam? What has happened to you?'

The Countess was pointing out to the roadside. In the frosty evening sunlight, Sir Peter and Godfrey trudged, trailing along the marshy pathway, with yards of sailcloth dragging behind them.

'Husband!' yelled the Countess. 'Godfrey!'

The coach rattled to a stop. Recognising the coach, the two men broke into a trot, and clambered aboard. Godfrey shoved the sailcloth before him.

'No,' said the Countess. 'You can come in, but not that stinking stuff. Never!'

'But we can't leave it here . . .' Sir Peter had jumped out to gather the cloth into his arms.

'Then walk, sirrah.' The Countess pushed him by the shoulder. 'And may I remind you that it's a good two miles.'

'All right.' Sir Peter raised his hands, dropping the sailcloth on to the verge, and climbed in. 'You win.'

Godfrey sat between them, Sir Peter perched on his knee.

The Countess was waiting for an explanation. 'So what happened?'

'Princess Anne! What a termagant!' Sir Peter pulled a face of horror. Squashed underneath him, Godfrey emitted a high-pitched whimper. 'I hope to God King William finds another wife to bear him an heir. Princess Anne is a veritable virago. God help all of us if she becomes queen.' He looked round at them, hoping to change the subject. 'So what about you? Good day?'

'Interesting,' said the Countess, who understood the look she received from Alpiew, and decided to give no more information. 'But we didn't find Acton as verdant as you gave us to believe it would be.'

They all sat in silence until they reached German Street.

Alpiew spent the night at Pigalle's. She had some difficulty explaining to her why the Countess had suddenly wanted to return to the country, but explained it away by saying they needed to talk, away from Sir Peter.

'Zat is good, Alpiew. I hope you got her to see sense.'

Pigalle gave a pout and Gallic shrug and changed the subject. 'So what do we eat for ze dinner?'

Alpiew ran through the contents of the Duchesse's larder in her mind. 'Gammon and grilled cheese?' she ventured.

Pigalle beamed. 'Excellent. And while we eat you can tell me when zat miserable little bearded freak, Sir Peter, is going back to ze New World.'

'That I wish I knew, Duchesse.' Alpiew rolled up her sleeves ready to tackle the dinner. 'But it looks to me that he hopes to settle here.'

'*Quel horreur!*' Pigalle was so aghast that she collapsed on to a kitchen stool, and sat hunched up near the oven, softly moaning to herself. '*Quelle horreur! Quelle horreur!*'

'I agree. But perhaps he is turning over a new leaf. He has promised her ladyship an outing tomorrow.'

'Some free-loading junket, no doubt?' Pigalle ran her long fingers through her hair, raising it to an upright position, thereby heightening the impression that she had seen a ghost, and repeated, '*Quelle horreur!*'

'No, indeed,' said Alpiew, hacking some gammon from the large haunch in the larder with a blunt carving knife. 'He is taking her to the Herald's Office.'

'Ze Herald's Office?' exclaimed Pigalle. '*Pourqoui?*'

'Sir Peter is going to buy his wife a coat of arms.'

The Countess surveyed the large illustrated book with enormous excitement.

The pursuivant of the College of Arms smoothed his hand over the ornate shield depicted on the page open before him. 'Very beautiful, this one – sable, a bend, or, between two horses heads razed, argent. With three fleurs-de-lys sable on the bend.' He turned the page. 'But you can't have that, it belongs to the former secretary to the Admiralty, Mr Pepys.'

The Countess gulped. Was the man speaking English? Her husband, eyebrows knotted in a sincere fashion, nodded. 'I understand. So what would you suggest for our charge?'

The pursuivant screwed up his face in thought. 'As recipients of a relatively new earldom, with no particularly famous achievement behind you, I would suggest canting upon your name.'

The Countess puffed a little at the bluntness of the man's remark, and was beginning to regret her husband's sudden decision to grace them with a coat of arms. After all, if they hadn't bothered to pick one up back in the sixties when they were first given their titles, why had it suddenly become so important now? And what would it give her she didn't already have?

'Canting?' inquired Sir Peter.

'In common parlance I suppose you might call it punning.' The pursuivant bestowed a patronising smile upon them both. 'It's great fun. The really creative part of heraldry, in my opinion.'

Sir Peter flicked through the pages of the great book. 'And how does that work?'

The Countess, regretting she had agreed to it, and utterly bored by the whole process, was wandering round the room, admiring the many shields and armorial bearings of knights gone by.

'The family Tremain has three hands,' said the pursuivant. '*Trois mains*. You see?' He pointed at the shield in his book. 'That is what we call a single rebus, rebus being our word for a pun. A double rebus might be, for instance, the family Beestone, who have . . .'

'A bee and a stone?' Sir Peter was proud of the quickness of his wits. 'I get your drift.'

'Good, you're catching on.' The pursuivant pushed the book aside and grabbed a quill and some paper. 'Penge? Penge. Hard to cant that one.'

'Can't we have one of these?' The Countess was pointing at a red fish on one of the wall shields.

'I'm sorry, Countess, but the mullet is reserved for those bestowed from the Lord Above with Divinity. A bishop, for instance.'

She wandered back to the desk and now surveyed a page of names and squiggles.

'Nothing on that page is appropriate either, Countess. They are marks depicting the place in a family; for instance, the battune sinister, reserved for those of royal descent barred by illegitimacy, and that –' he pointed at a little circle with a dot – 'indicates to us the sole surviving child of a particular family. The sole heir. It's a rebus on an astrological sign. A cant upon Sun, you see. Son!' He cocked his head. 'Or come to that sole – sol!'

The Countess, bored out of her wits, gave him a withering look and returned to studying the walls.

'So, uh, for my wife we might have . . .' Sir Peter coughed. 'Ash is easy: a tree. Bee. Ashby. Is there a short-cut for de la?'

'Even if there was, sir, I think you might consider it a trifle difficult to find a rebus for Zouche!' The pursuivant had a wicked glint in his eye. 'No. No. I think I have hit it.'

Sir Peter leaned forward. 'Come along, Ashby, old girl, let's see what the fellow has for you.'

The pursuivant scribbled some drawings on to a piece of paper. 'I think two hands conjoined at the wrist, as though in the act of applauding, and a leg of pork.' He slid his illustration across the desk and made a little bow. '*Voilà*, a double rebus, unique to you. Do you see?' He pointed at the hands. 'Clap.' He pointed at the pork. 'Ham!' He held the paper up. 'Clapham!'

'Buy my cure-all,' yelled a quack at the row of stalls selling medicines at the side of the road leading up to Gresham College. 'It has neither taste, nor smell, cures sickness to the stomach, striving to vomit in the morning, consumptions, sinking of the spirits . . .'

'I doubt it would help ours,' said Alpiew.

'Unless strong cordial water is the principal ingredient.' The Countess was still reeling from her experience at the Herald's Office.

'For palpitations of the heart, twisting of the guts, intermitting fevers, hot and cold fits, quinseys, violent colics, convulsions, rickets, wasting and weakness in children, and the green sickness . . .'

The Countess and Alpiew were trudging through the City, past the rows of stalls run by medicine sellers and masters of physic, in the direction of Gresham College.

'It opens obstructions,' croaked an old fellow who looked as though he was on his last legs, '. . . and creates a good appetite, prevents fearful dreams, adds a lively colour to the face, and brings away all kinds of worms, whether of the teeth or the guts, leaving the body in perfect health. Six pence a bottle.'

Alpiew was carrying a large canvas bag. Inside were all the amassed clues and papers relating to the Beau Wilson and Betty murders. It also contained a finished copy of their week's scandal items for delivery at the Cue Printing House.

'An investigation into these scoundrels might be good for us at a future time,' said Alpiew, glancing at a stall laid out with all sorts of pulverised ingredients, and rows of green bottles, manned by a man with a long white beard, who resembled Merlin the magician.

'There was a verse about, a few years ago,' the Countess gave a little giggle.

> *'Before you partake of my potion or pill,*
> *Take leave of your friends and draw up your will.'*

'A safe and easy cure for the secret venereal disease, the scourge of Aphrodite,' yelled Merlin. 'Effective in either sex, by three doses of a wonderful chymical bolus, prepared without mercury . . .'

'I can't believe these scoundrels shout aloud about such things.' The Countess threw the bearded stallholder a filthy look. 'I was thinking for a moment that they might be able to help us with the coded page, but I think your idea is better.'

'Doctors of physic and medicine sellers would only give us the same as we had from the apothecary,' Alpiew pointed out. 'Besides which it is important to get the alchymical side of it clear. That was Beau's interest, after all.'

'We will surely grab the attention of one of those

experimental philosophers at Wiseacres' Hall,' said the Countess, neatly side-stepping a pile of horse manure and wondering whether she shouldn't gather it up for her husband. 'Perhaps they will understand the code.'

'Your ladyship?' said Alpiew, noticing the Countess's lingering look at the equine droppings.

'Yes, Alpiew?'

'I was just wondering about Sir Peter . . .'

'Isn't it wonderful!' The Countess stopped to face Alpiew, holding her by both elbows. 'He told me last night that he is moving back in with me for good.' She rested her hand on Alpiew's arm. 'We can all be a family again, like we were in the good old days.'

Alpiew tried to smile. But her cheeks seemed frozen, by emotion for once rather than cold. 'Oh, good,' she said with no particular emphasis. 'I'm very glad for you, if you're happy.' How on earth they were going to continue their job together with him poking his nose in she couldn't imagine. And she would have to find other lodgings. The kitchen was comfortable for three, but impossible for four. Especially when one of those four was Sir Pompous Braggadocio, alias Sir Peter.

They started to walk again, the Countess babbling away. 'It's very exciting. He says he wants to renew his vows to me before a priest, so that no one can come between us. And he's got me a coat of arms.'

And what, wondered Alpiew, is the reason for that public show? What could the wretched man possibly gain by it? Alpiew had heard tell of a nasty rogue who had a coat of arms hung in his dining room till his wife died, and then, once she was safely out of the way, he transported it to the outside of his house to attract a rich widow to marry him.

'So, Alpiew,' the Countess jolted her out of her reverie as they came up to the paved entrance to Gresham College, 'tell me, is that man standing over there the blue boy with whom we conversed last time we were here?'

She was pointing at a baby-faced fellow, today dressed in a fawn velvet suit.

'That's him, milady. You spoke to him last time, so go on. Do your work.'

Today the college was deserted. Alpiew and the Countess marched through into the echoing little brick court and followed the boy into the spacious quadrangle leading to the lecture theatre.

'Heigh ho, there!' she called. The boy turned.

'No ladies allowed, I'm afraid.'

'I know, I know,' panted the Countess, winded by trying to keep up his pace. 'I just wanted a little chat with you.'

The boy looked anxiously around him. He leaned forward and whispered. 'I'm trying for a fellowship. They won't like it much if I'm seen flouting the regulations.'

'Oh, pish to the regulations!' flapped the Countess, applying her fan at an alarming rate. 'I am the one who saw Boyle's air demonstration, remember?' She threw him what passed for a coy look.

'I realise that.' The boy took her by the arm and led her back out towards the street. 'I do remember you, but, really, I mustn't let you in here.'

They stood by the portico.

'We have a difficult puzzle to solve.' Alpiew dragged

the page of log-book from her bag. 'And discovering the solution is a matter of life or death. Two people have lost their lives over it already.'

The boy surveyed Alpiew and wondered if she was quite sane. For the first time he began to understand the rule which forbade women from this seat of learning. This one was clearly suffering a bad case of suffocation or even frenzy of the womb.

'I'm sorry,' he said, handing the paper back, 'but I can't help you. We deal here in the higher end of experimental philosophy. I can see from a glance that this is an impure equation. Have you tried the medicine sellers along the road? They might know more than I.'

'Boy!' The Countess snapped her fan shut and stood with her hands on her hips. 'You were pleasant enough last time we met. Why the sudden change in your manner?'

'Really . . .' The boy rubbed his forehead with his hand. 'I am in a terrible rush.' He turned and trotted off, calling back over his shoulder: 'Try the medicine stalls.'

'Well, how about that!' Alpiew turned back down Broad Street.

The Countess was still staring after the disappearing figure of the blue boy. 'We're going to speak to Mr Newton!' she called after the boy, who was now out of earshot. 'Mr Isaac Newton!'

'Come along, milady,' Alpiew tugged at her arm. 'We don't have much time left. They can stick their all-male societies of experimental fiddle-ology up their fundaments.'

'Newton's not a bad idea though, Alpiew. We'll try him when we get back home.'

They walked up and down the stalls a few times before deciding on Merlin.

'He has the appearance of an alchymist,' said the Countess.

'How would you know that?' asked Alpiew. 'How many alchymists are there in your acquaintance?'

'The playhouse, of course, Alpiew. I told you before, alchymists are a great favourite in comedies.'

'. . . a medicine of no equal, it producing more manifest effects of its wonderful efficiency by one dose than probably many other good medicines may by ten,' he was crying as they approached. 'And is in truth what may be depended on for the most expeditious and effectual cure yet known, even when all other medicines have failed, and as it exceeds in goodness all other remedies whatsoever . . .'

'But, madam . . .' Alpiew hesitated before speaking to him. 'He is incomprehensible . . .'

The Countess shoved her on. 'Try anyway. Go on.'

'Sir,' said Alpiew, picking up a bottle to grab his attention. The device instantly worked. He stopped his rant and addressed her directly.

'Madam, may I interest you in a bottle of that excellent elixir? It soothes and cures all afflictions and indispositions as weeping sores, pains, swellings, breakings out . . .'

Alpiew hastily replaced the bottle. It was a cure for the pox.

'Sir . . .' She leaned over the counter and spoke in a confidential tone. He leaned over to meet her lips with his ear. He knew all about stall-side manner and patient confidentiality. 'It is a matter of some urgency and of great secrecy.

But do you know of either an alchymist, or a learned man who understands the symbolism of alchymy?'

The stallholder pulled back and stared at Alpiew through long curly white eyebrows. She began to feel quite dizzy and could not remove her eyes from his. His stare was so effective she wondered if he was doing something with magnets. She stood transfixed in the power of his gaze until at last he disengaged his eyes from hers and glanced in the Countess's direction. 'She with you?'

Alpiew nodded.

'Paul!' he cried into the air, and a young boy emerged from under the canopy. 'Watch over the stall till my return.' Then he strode away down the street with Alpiew and the Countess at his heels. He turned a corner, then stopped suddenly at a small door under the swinging sign of Seneca's Head.

'Most people think of Seneca as a Roman, having taught Nero and Caligula, but he was from Spain.' The man bobbed his head and disappeared through the door. Alpiew and the Countess followed. The Countess realised she had never spared a thought about Seneca's nationality, and Alpiew had never even heard of him.

The interior of Merlin's den was small but busy. The first thing they noticed was a stuffed crocodile on the floor. At least they hoped it was stuffed, because it was very large and lay just by their feet.

Like Beau's elaboratory, the walls were stacked with pieces of equipment, jars, pans and books. From the ceiling hung a star-shaped lamp with seven points, a small flame issuing from each. In one corner a furnace burned, in another stood a small organ.

'Sit.' Merlin swept his arms indicating a small window

seat. He perched on a wooden stool by the organ. 'So what is your problem?'

'We have to work out what this means.' Alpiew thrust the paper at him. 'To save someone's life.'

Merlin gave Alpiew another penetrating look, then took the log-book page and glanced at it briefly before starting on his interpretation.

$$\odot : \; \text{♀} \; \text{♂} \; \text{⚒} \; = \; \text{☥} \; (\text{♀}/\text{☉}) \; (\text{☉}/\text{♄}) \; \text{♄} \; @ \; \bullet \; \text{♎}$$

'Well,' he said, running his hand down his beard. 'The first is *Caput Mortem* – the death head.' He turned to the organ and played an ominous chord.

'Then we have, following in brisk succession, mercury – Wednesday, copper – Friday, per diem, and this crown-like thing, that's the star regulus.' He fingered the organ again. 'It would sound something like this.' A cacophony of disharmony issued from the instrument.

'Star regulus, as in a star in the sky?' asked Alpiew, trying to end the concert and drag him back to the log-book.

Merlin glared at her again. And his look said No interruptions! No suggestions! 'It is the star regulus of antimony, the result of one of the important processes in alchymy. The product is a sort of lead-grey ore extracted by heating antimony with iron and charcoal. Let us say it is the seed of the metal. But a seed is useless and impotent unless put in its appropriate matrix.' He looked back at the paper. 'A pure womb gives birth to a pure fruit. Equals. Balance. Harmony.' He smiled, radiating benevolence. 'After the equals sign we have the symbol for chaos . . .'

'Chaos?' The Countess leant forward and looked at the symbol under discussion, thinking it pretty well summed up the whole business.

'The earth over the sun?' asked Alpiew. 'Is that a form of chaos?'

'Inevitably. The Sun governs the Earth, so when the Earth takes the upper hand, something is wrong. Out of control. A process to rock natural stability. Chaos.'

He splayed his long bony fingers across the organ keys, and, pumping frantically with his feet, produced a noise loud enough to drown out the bells of Old Bailey.

Alpiew kept her eyes on the paper till he had finished. She knew if she caught eyes with the Countess she would explode with laughter. 'And then? In the brackets?'

'An amalgam of iron – Tuesday and copper again – Friday, then a small gold.' He sat bolt upright and scratched his head. 'What can that mean? Can one divide an alloy of iron and copper by gold? It sounds positively lunatic. No tune at all. An experiment like that could land you in Bedlam.'

'Go on,' said the Countess, feeling that Bedlam was closer to home in this place than she would have liked.

He laid his hands over the organ and shook his head. 'No. I was right. No harmony there whatsoever. Quite an impossible melody.' Without playing a note he pulled his hands away and glanced down at the log-book again. 'Bracketed gold and a sword? Perhaps a sword of gold? I don't know.' Another burst of music, this time rather reminiscent of the nobler refrains of Purcell. 'That which kills produces life,' pronounced Merlin over the pretty tune. 'That which causes death causes resurrection. That which destroys creates.' With a flourish he turned back to the equation. 'We are nearing the climax now. Do you see?' He presented the paper for Alpiew's inspection. 'This noble sign represents sublimation.'

'Sublimation?'

'The process by which a solid is heated and the resulting vapour condenses as a solid. The process of making sal ammoniac, for instance. It is a similar process to distillation.'

Distillation the Countess knew of. 'That's how the Scots make ushque baugh,' she said, hoping to keep Merlin on side.

'Ushque baugh?' asked Alpiew.

'A delicious strong cordial which Pigalle occasionally has sent down from . . .' All she remembered was that it came from a Scottish place Pigalle called Edinbugger, though she suspected that Pigalle had got that wrong.

'Ah yes,' Merlin sighed. 'Ushque baugh. It is a perfect example of Art. Art begins where Nature ceases to act. So by taking the seed of the barley and distilling its essence one arrives at the water which contains heat and fire. A miracle of Art.'

This produced another flourish from the organ, only this time Merlin sang along. 'At eclipse in astronomical sign of Libra.' The tune underwent a modulation. 'He who does not know motion does not know Nature.' Up another semitone. 'No subject can be made without long suffering.' And another. 'There is only one Truth.' Merlin was almost singing soprano now. 'Whatever may be accomplished by a simple method should not be attempted by a complicated one.' He ran an arpeggio up the keys. 'Nature must be aided by Art whenever she is deficient in power.' And down again. 'Nature cannot be amended except in her own self.' Then Merlin collapsed down on to an enormous chord spanning three octaves. He lay there, panting from his exertions.

'Do you see?' he gasped, hauling himself up from the instrument and stretching. 'What a wonderful equation! The Music of the Spheres is encapsulated within it. You see, this is my new theory: Experimental Philosophy is the Male Principle. Music, as we know from the muse, Terpsichore, and Saint Cecilia, the patron saint of music, is the Female. The two needs must be mixed. For everything on earth is multiplied and augmented by means of a Male and a Female Principle.' He came over to them and shook their hands. 'Excellent. I feel wonderful after that. Thank you so much for bringing me your little tune. Most original.'

The Countess was already backing towards the door, hoping that now he was away from the organ he wouldn't lose his faculties entirely. Alpiew gingerly picked up the log-book page and dropped it into her canvas bag.

'Thank *you*!' She gave Merlin a manic grin, and sidled to the door.

He cocked his head, staring at Alpiew with that odd, penetrating stare again. 'You are not troubled with lethargies, vishegoes, megrims, quinseys, imposthurns, vapours or loss of memory?'

Alpiew, still backing up, shook her head. 'Not at this present moment.'

'If you are, my dear maid, stop by at my stall and I can provide you with a cephalick elixir which dropped in a cup of bohea tea is virtually tasteless. Free and gratis, of course.'

Alpiew and the Countess were safely out in the street.

Merlin clicked the door closed behind them and as they walked away, for the length of the street, they could hear him laughing.

The two plodded up to the Cues' print shop in Shoe Lane and deposited their week's copy. Mrs Cue stood by the typesetting board, ruddy-faced and covered in printing ink while she read it.

She chortled a little, and raised her eyebrows while she read. 'Robert Smith! Who would have thought it? He's such a prim thing, with his family values and undying support for the Society for the Reformation of Manners. A cully who pays to be flogged, indeed.' She lay the paper down. 'It's short but it's good.' She plunged her hand into her apron, pulled out a bill of exchange and handed it to the Countess. 'A week till your next.'

Both Alpiew and her mistress sighed with relief as they came out. 'I thought she'd send us off for more,' Alpiew giggled.

'Me too!' The Countess grabbed her by the hand. 'Come on, let's get away before she changes her mind.'

They ran down Fleet Street and, plunging through the busy market on the bridge, turned up the Fleet Canal. Once safely out of earshot of the busy shoppers and costermongers, they leaned against the fence and looked down over the canal.

'Plan of action for the rest of the day?' asked the Countess. 'My husband does not expect to see me till late this afternoon.'

'Good.' Alpiew shook her bag. 'First let us pay a visit to poor Mrs Wilson, and see whether she recognises the writing on the letters or the list.'

'I had not thought of that possibility.' The Countess kicked a pebble into the water. 'You think perhaps that the gentleman in the coach who visited Mrs Roy, and whom I suppose we can presume to be Mr Roy on one of his infrequent visits from Town, was one and the same as Mr Wilson?'

'Why not?' asked Alpiew.

'The landlady of the tavern said the man was short. Beau Wilson was tall.'

Alpiew hung her head. Then clicked her fingers. 'Yes, but the letters aren't signed. Perhaps there are two men, Mr Roy and Mr Wilson, and these are not Mr Roy's letters at all. Perhaps they are from Mr Wilson? That woman sounds the type to have a string of men chasing after her.'

'And of course the rough scrawl of the list could be Mr Roy's work. For certainly that is a man's hand.'

They waited for a good half-hour outside the grille at the Fleet Prison. Eventually word reached Mrs Wilson and she pushed her way to the front, and without any word of greeting shouted at them. 'What does my fool of a lawyer say?'

Alpiew froze. In the flurry of Betty's death she had forgotten all about her promise to visit him.

'Nothing, I expect. He's a genius when it comes to property law, but clearly not the best when you are an innocent woman accused of killing your husband.'

'He had a few leads on the case,' stammered Alpiew, diving into her canvas bag and whipping out one of the letters they had found in Acton. 'He says do you recognise the writing on these billets-doux?'

Mrs Wilson took one look at the letter and let forth a hearty, 'No.'

'Or this? It's a list of clothing' Alpiew shoved the paper through.

'My days are numbered, you pair of fuddle-headed fools,' screeched Mrs Wilson, screwing up the paper and throwing it at them. 'Why are you fooling around with love-letters and laundry lists?'

Alpiew tried to speak, but the enraged Mrs Wilson ploughed on. 'Go to my house. Get my servants organised. Send Betty to me.'

'But Betty . . .' Alpiew hesitated and Mrs Wilson cut in on her again.

'Get up to Cowley's office now. I pay him to look after my legal interests, so why is he doing nothing?' She squeezed her face to the cold black iron bars. 'Someone in here has told me I should apply for something called Benefit of Clergy.' She kicked a boy of about fourteen to the side to keep her position at the front. 'It's some kind of legal loophole. It might help me.'

All around her men were thrusting their hands through the grille hoping for gifts of money from passers-by. Mrs Wilson was constantly elbowing them out of her way. Her knuckles were white with the exertion of gripping the bars.

The Countess leant down to be nearer her so she didn't have to shout over the cat-calls. 'We were thinking of getting you a Tyburn Ticket, Mrs Wilson. It's another loophole. It would give you immunity from execution.' She leant forward in an intimate way so as not to be overheard. 'All we have to do is catch a highwayman.'

Mrs Wilson, grabbed at the ruffles of the Countess's dress and pulled so that her face too was squashed against the metal. 'Listen, you superannuated harridan,' she screamed, 'you're so useless you couldn't catch the pox, let alone a highwayman.' She shook her hand at Alpiew, trying to grab her too. 'So stop fucking about and get me out of here.'

The Countess froze to the spot, and even when Mrs Wilson had been swept away by the seething body of prisoners trying to get their turn, she remained squatting on her haunches, facing the prison wall.

'Come along.' Alpiew stooped and put her arm round her mistress's shoulder. 'She's in grave trouble, milady. She didn't mean anything by it. Remember, if we don't get her free she only has one other way out, and that is by being burned alive or swinging at the end of a rope up at Tyburn.'

Slowly they walked away from the prison.

'And she doesn't know the dangers out here. Mrs Wilson doesn't even know of Betty's death, or Beau's liaison with that woman, and his great discovery.'

'You are right, Alpiew.' The Countess gritted her teeth. 'It is a desperate situation for her. And even worse than she believes. And frankly, from what I know of the law, she will not find much comfort there.'

They climbed the stairs up to the lawyer's office on the corner of Fetter Lane and Magpie Yard. It was a large building full of cramped offices. From the clutter of painted signs on the two doors, one leading to the upper floor, the other to the lower, it was clear that the small building housed lawyers, scriveners, and merchants of every item imaginable: spice from the Indies, pearls from the Orient, books, writing implements, sugar from the Americas, plate from Holland, wines from France.

'How do they keep all these things in such a small place?' asked Alpiew pushing open the door and ascending the wooden stairs.

'They don't,' said the Countess. 'The place will be full of pen-pushers, clerks processing the paperwork.'

Passing the door of a Spanish fan merchant, Alpiew knocked at the door labelled Mr John Cowley, LLB, and a gruff voice called, 'Enter.'

The office was very small, barely big enough for the desk and three chairs. Cowley was scribbling with a feather quill. He glanced up, snapped, 'Sit!' and returned to his writing.

Alpiew and the Countess lowered themselves on to two creaky wooden chairs and looked round the room. One wall was solid with books. The Countess recognised many of them: Bracton, Hale, Littleton, Coke, and stacks of yearbooks. Upon the other walls hung drawings and certificates. The small grimy window was framed by a tatty cream curtain, and a similar floor-length drape hung behind the desk.

The desk was stacked with folders, each bulging with papers and tied up in a pink ribbon.

Alpiew was inspecting Cowley himself. How different he looked when he was in control of the situation. She remembered his white sweating face that morning when Mrs Wilson almost died of antimony poisoning.

Sprinkling the wet ink with sand, Cowley tilted the paper and blew it off before asking, 'What can I do for you, ladies?'

'Mr Cowley . . .' The Countess pushed a pile of documents aside and rested her elbow on the desk. 'We are here on a matter of life or death.'

Cowley sighed and pulled a small tinder-box from a drawer. He lit a candle and held some sealing wax over it until it started to drip. 'Really. I have heard that before.' He glanced up, shook his head and dripped the wax on to the document he had just written. Applying his seal to the hot wax, he put the document to one side and then started shuffling papers, opening drawers and putting things away. 'I suppose your landlord has poisoned your monkey?'

The Countess was amazed at his off-hand way. 'I am Lady Anastasia Ashby de la Zouche, Baroness Penge, Countess of Clapham. I have neither landlord nor monkey. I am here on behalf of Elizabeth Wilson.'

'Mrs *Beau* Wilson,' added Alpiew.

'You're wasting your time.' He looked up then, scrutinising both their faces. 'She's guilty. Guilty as sin. He was a friend of mine, Beau. He should never have married that woman. She's a termagant. Social climber. Exceedingly unpleasant.'

'But Beau loved her.' Alpiew was furious at his attitude, even though in her own short acquaintance with Mrs Wilson she had found her to be all the things he claimed. 'And she is very pretty.'

'Oh, pish to that,' said Cowley. 'Beau can't have been so smitten. He'd taken some sort of mistress, I gather. It doesn't take a genius to assume that pretty Mrs Wilson discovered this new amour, and, consumed with jealousy, lured her husband to a make-believe assignation and there rent his throat from ear to ear. It's a classic case.'

Cowley upended a file, tapped it down on the desk a few times to align the papers, then placed it behind him on a shelf. 'Wives murder husbands, husbands murder wives. It's the whole point of marriage, it seems to me, and a lot more common than divorce (unless you have friends in the House of Lords, that is). Still, income for lawyers like me, either way.'

'I don't think, Mr Cowley,' the Countess spoke firmly, 'that you are painting an entirely accurate picture of what happened.'

'Really, madam?' He leant back in his chair and flicked at the tinder-box. 'If it was not how I suggested it to you, then what explains the wretched woman's subsequent behaviour? Why did she take poison that night? The answer is simple.' He pulled open a drawer and put the tinder-box away. 'She tried to kill herself because she was feeling guilty, and sorry for what she had done. She'd had her revenge, and had thereby thrown away her meal-ticket.' Cowley laughed, pulled a book from the shelf behind him and flicked through it. 'It is against the law to kill anyone, you know. Including yourself. So even if you are right and Mrs Elizabeth Wilson is innocent of Petit Treason, she is still guilty of Felo de Se.'

'Felo de what?' said Alpiew.

'Self-murder,' replied the Countess in a whisper.

Cowley stabbed at the open page. 'Hale is clear on the point: "Felo de Se constitutes a murder committed by a man upon himself." And may I remind you there is no mitigation in this crime. There is no such thing as self-manslaughter. Mrs Wilson will be executed, one way or another, and if on the charge of attempted suicide, her body will not be welcome in sacred ground and she will have to be buried at a crossroads in the public highway.'

'And you are telling me Coke does not pronounce any reformation upon this medieval way of thinking?' said the Countess.

Cowley gave her a filthy look. 'What do you know of Coke – you, a mere female?'

'*Coke upon Littleton* has been at my bedside for many years. I am an avid enthusiast on the subject of law.'

'An amateur,' said the lawyer. 'And I, madam, am a professional.'

'I can tell you now, Mr Cowley, that Mrs Wilson didn't try to kill herself,' said Alpiew quietly. 'It was an accident. And we have the evidence to prove that.'

'I was there that morning.' Mr Cowley smiled. 'The apothecary confirmed it. She took a dose of antimony.'

The Countess rose and started peering at the drawings on the wall.

'You may have forgotten me, sir.' Alpiew leaned over the desk. 'I know servants do not exist in some people's eyes. But I have not forgotten you. I too was there in the apothecary's shop that morning. I will remind you that you were so shocked you couldn't even go back into the house to fetch the offending drinking vessel. That task was left to me. Don't you remember that?'

'How can I recall the countenance of every serving wench I encounter?' Cowley scanned Alpiew's face. 'I have more important things to think about.'

'Like getting someone to swear on oath that they'd seen Mrs Wilson at the churchyard when Beau was killed.'

Cowley shifted in his chair. 'Why would I do that?'

'You tell me.'

The Countess had moved across to inspect the items upon the mantelpiece. 'I agree with you, Mr Cowley, that Mrs Wilson is a very difficult woman,' she tossed back over her shoulder. 'But a man of the law must uphold his sacred task to the letter.'

'You know that Mrs Wilson is not guilty.' Alpiew took up the lead the Countess had given her. 'What have you to gain by her death?'

'Nothing.' His lips were tight, his face set.

'And yet you seem perturbed that she did not succeed in her attempted self-murder.'

'That is nothing to do with me.' The curtain at the back of the room rustled, and the 'footboy' Alpiew had encountered outside the Wilson house popped his head through.

'Do you need any assistance, Mr Cowley?'

Mr Cowley spun round. 'It's all right, Nathaniel. Have you taken those letters up to Doctors' Commons?'

Nathaniel shook his head.

'Then do it.' Cowley rose and shouted, pulling the curtain across, 'Now.'

Nathaniel disappeared. Cowley was looking anxiously towards the Countess, who was picking things up from the mantelpiece – the clock, a china ornament, a vase – and checking their undersides.

'To continue . . .' Alpiew was not to be put off. 'I suggest that you wanted Mrs Wilson to die.'

'She herself took the powder, no one forced her to.'

'No. It was a mistake. She misread the wrapper. She took a powder Mr Wilson had bought for his own purposes, instead of her usual nightly dose.'

'Now I know you are lying. Mrs Wilson cannot read or write.'

Alpiew still faced him eye to eye. 'And that is how she misread the symbol. The same sign as Beau put on the powders he prepared for her, if read upside-down, is the sign for antimony, something he had bought the day before his death at the apothecary's shop opposite.'

Mr Cowley sat again. He was cornered. 'So how do you know all this?'

Alpiew drew a deep breath. 'From Betty, Mr Wilson's maid.'

'I need to find Betty.' The lawyer leant forward and started anxiously to fiddle with his quill. 'Where is she?'

Alpiew and the Countess exchanged a glance. 'She is in hiding.'

'Where?'

'If I told you, she wouldn't be in hiding any longer, would she, sir?'

'It's important to me,' said Cowley, his voice trembling. 'I must speak to her.'

'Why is that, then?' The Countess spoke in a dainty, childish coaxing tone.

'You don't understand,' he said. 'It falls to me to complete the formalities on the estate of the late Mr Wilson. I know, several people know, that he owned another property. A warehouse of some kind. I cannot possibly complete my duties to probate his estate until I find out the address of that warehouse. He told me Betty was the only one of his acquaintance who knew about the place. Thus I must find Betty . . .'

Alpiew shrugged. 'Well, we know nothing of that,' she said. 'We are only here for one thing. To convey to you a message from Mrs Wilson, who, whether you like it or not, is still your client.'

'And that message is . . . ?'

'Try "Benefit of Clergy".'

John Cowley started to laugh. 'Then the woman is completely mad.' He pulled another book from the shelf behind him. ' "Benefit of Clergy: applicable to criminals on first offence only," she'd qualify for that. "To persons not strictly in the religious orders, but assisting in divine offices: doorkeepers, readers, etcetera." This law was widened in scope last century to include any person who can read.' He slammed the book shut. 'Mrs Wilson cannot read. Ergo, Mrs Wilson cannot even attempt to apply for Benefit of Clergy. She must face facts. She will die.'

TWELVE

Foliation

Making the substance puff up in layers,
like leaves lying on top of one another.

Alpiew and the Countess walked down to the waterside at Dorset Garden, taking care to avoid the lane where Beau's elaboratory and Betty's body lay. They stood on the deserted quayside, in front of the gloomy neglected theatre with its peeling paint and smashed windows.

'He is Beau's lawyer,' said the Countess. 'He could not be unaware of the warehouse. He must have drawn up the conveyancing papers or the lease.'

'He burgled the Wilson house, did he not? While the servants were carousing on the dead man's wine cabinet.'

'Certainly. I was about to tell you that. But how did you know?'

'It was just a guess. He seemed so uneasy when you started looking at those nick-nacks on the mantelpiece.'

'Very perspicacious, mistress. First I recognised one of the drawings. I knew I had seen it before. Then it dawned upon me *where* I had seen it.'

'Mrs Wilson's bedchamber.'

'Correct. Then the clock. It was quite distinctive. The

ormolu, and the face. Definitely taken from Mrs Wilson's mantelpiece.'

'Strange behaviour in a lawyer,' said Alpiew, kicking a stone across the disused theatre's forecourt and into the Thames. 'Stealing from his clients.'

'Everyone is so unpleasant, don't you find, Alpiew, in this business?'

'Struggling people never have much time to be entertaining, that's true enough.' Alpiew flopped down on to the paved theatre forecourt.

'Look at the river,' said the Countess, settling herself on an empty horse-trough. 'What is the fascination? There it goes all day, flow, flow, flow. Always the same.'

Alpiew was routing through the contents of the bag. 'Let us lay out what we have, and try to think what we might do next.' She had assembled a pile of stones to make sure nothing flew away. 'So we have . . .' she flicked through the letters from the Indian trunk. 'Item: ten love-letters in an unknown hand, written between January and March of this year.' She put them down and placed a stone on top. 'Item: one list cataloguing various pieces of women's clothing, writ in a wild and unregulated hand, not the same as the other.' She put down the list under a separate stone. 'Item: one page of the log-book of Beau Wilson. Indecipherable to all, save Beau.'

The Countess clucked and shook her head. 'And Betty!'

'How do you make that out?'

'If Betty did not understand it, why did she take the bother to tear it out of the log-book and hide it? Whoever killed her must have been after that page. As it turns out, all he got was the log-book. Between the time when we left Betty and when you found her dead, she must have put two and two together.'

'If only the answer was as easy as two and two.' Alpiew placed the coded page under another stone. 'Then there's the apothecary's invoice. But now we know all about that.' She turned the page over and put it under another stone.

'Wait a moment,' said the Countess, leaning down and peering at the back of the invoice. 'What's that writing on the back?'

'"*Alles Mist*",' read Alpiew. 'Whatever that might mean.'

'Yes, but look –' the Countess pushed the stone away from the badly written list with her toe – 'the same bad hand! The same writing.'

Alpiew placed the two together. 'You're right. Look. The *m*, the *s*.' She put both together under the same stone. 'So whoever wrote *Alles Mist* on the back of the invoice Beau was carrying to his fatal encounter, also wrote the list we discovered at Acton.'

'Ergo,' said the Countess, 'there is a definite link between Acton and Beau.'

'We have other bits of evidence which are in our knowledge rather than our possession.' Alpiew pulled a pencil and a sheet of paper from the bag. 'One: we have the blood-stained dress, also at Acton.' She scribbled the word dress and put it under a stone. 'There may be another explanation for that stain, but how could a woman get so much blood down the front of her bodice?'

'Other than murder?' The Countess gazed out across the river. 'Also we have a woman, late of Acton, going

305

by the name of Mrs Roy, who has disappeared from her country retreat.'

'And we have the well-set gentleman player who took the row-boat out from this place. And Betty told us, remember, that the boat journey was only short.'

'So why use the river at all? We know that Lambeth is no quick route to Acton!' The Countess gazed out at two scullers shouting the usual abuse at each other over their oars. 'It's all very confusing.'

'That's it, milady! It must be.' Alpiew spun round. 'That particular night Scum used the river in order to deceive and mislead.'

'But why?'

'From what Betty said, Beau knew we were following him. All I can think is that Beau warned Scum, and so Scum took to a row-boat, knowing we could not follow.'

'I'm sorry,' said the Countess. 'But I don't understand.'

'Beau wanted his plan to work. He was hoping to get a lot of money from this mystery woman. And he knew the money was dependant on secrecy. How would it have worked out if we had shown up at the place? It could have ruined his big chance. So if Beau wanted his meeting that night to go without a hitch, it would have been important that we were shaken off.'

'But he could have shaken us off if he went by coach . . .'

'No, milady. Beau was not to know that we had no money. If he took a coach, what was to stop us taking a hackney carriage to follow him wherever he went?'

The Countess laughed. 'What was to stop us taking a boat?'

'That rude fellow told us. It was icy, the tides were

bad. There were few boatmen on the river. Scum took a chance.'

'So tell me, Alpiew, what do you think happened, that I may better comprehend?'

'I think when Scum went into the coffee house to meet Beau, Beau told him he thought he was being followed. So Scum arranged a meeting which would throw us off the scent. He took Beau by river a few hundred yards along the way, let us say to Somerset House steps, for instance, where his usual coach was waiting to take Beau to meet the mystery lady.'

'Alpiew, you are a genius!' The Countess leapt up and waved her hands in the air.

Simultaneously a gust of wind whipped the pieces of paper up and Alpiew had to throw herself over the whole collection to stop them blowing away. The Countess stooped down and grabbed at the equation. 'I'll tell you, Alpiew, we should go home and copy this out. And make a list of all the interpretations we have received so far.'

'And in the light of our alchymist friend's reading . . .' Alpiew was busily shoving the papers back into her canvas bag. '. . . if I can get myself a fiddle I'll play it to you!'

When they arrived back at German Street there was a group of people standing on the front step.

'What on earth?' The Countess tottered forwards. 'It's not the constables is it, or a magistrate?'

'Doesn't look like it. They look like quality folk.' Alpiew grabbed her arm. 'Wait here. I'll see to them, and if anything nasty happens at least you'll be free, if necessary, to save me.' She swung forward, and approached the steps in a nonchalant fashion, pushing through the crowd. 'Excuse me, ladies, gentlemen.' She tried to squeeze through to get to the front door, but they were jostling one another, leaving no room for her to pass.

'It's a trick,' cried one.

'She's trying to get in first . . .' shrieked another.

'Block her, block her!' they gaggled in unison.

Alpiew stood in the street, her hands on her hips, and bellowed, 'Do you mind getting out of my way! I live here.'

The group rounded as one and gave her the once over.

'Are you the Countess of Nasty Bella Russe?' said an imperious woman with a sneer.

'Do I look like a nob?' Alpiew screeched. 'No. I am not the lady to whom you refer, but I am her maid, and I would suggest that you let me through, and tell me what you think you are doing bellowing like Smithfield cattle on her ladyship's doorstep?'

The tone of the crowd changed instantly from unified fury to disparate grovelling.

'Might your lady favour me . . .' 'My offer will be unbeatable . . .' 'I would be able to close the deal quickly . . .'

When Alpiew reached the front door she turned to face them again. 'Well? Are you going to answer my questions? Why are you here, and what do you want?'

A flushed lady at the back of the crowd shouted. 'We're here to view the house, of course. And it's cold out here, so if someone might start the proceedings . . .'

'View the house to what purpose?' Alpiew yelled back.

'To buy it,' said a grinning man with long yellow

horse-like teeth. 'The sale was announced in this morning's *Gazette*.'

In silence Alpiew waved at the Countess to come forward. It was clear from the startled expression on her face that the Countess had heard the incredible news. Alpiew indicated with a finger to her lips that the Countess should not speak to the potential buyers. Once the Countess and Alpiew had pushed their way inside, they went looking for Sir Peter.

He was out, but Godfrey was, as usual, curled up asleep by the fire with a book.

'Godfrey?' Alpiew whipped the book out of his lap and threw it across the room. 'What's going on? Who has advertised this house for sale?'

The hammering at the front door started up again. 'Oh Lord!' Godfrey leapt up. 'The people are already here. I'm supposed to be showing them round.' He shuffled off towards the hall.

'Not so fast, wobble-shanks.' The Countess barred his way. 'You'd better tell me what's happening. In detail.'

Just then she was almost knocked to the floor as the kitchen door flew open, and Sir Peter burst into the room.

'Oh, wife, wife!' He was holding a bunch of flowers and a large picture-shaped parcel. 'Please don't say that this old nincompoop has ruined my surprise.'

'I'll say it was a surprise!' The Countess had picked up Godfrey's book and swung it upwards. But before she could bring it down on her husband's head he had dived out of the way.

From behind him someone else stepped forward, had the time to say, 'I cannot work with all this commotion!'

before receiving the full force of the book as it came down. The man, his brown shoulder-length hair swept back from his aquiline features, teetered forward, rolled his eyes to heaven and slumped to the ground.

Aghast, the Countess looked down at his prostrate body. 'What have you done?' she screamed at her husband, who was already in the far corner brushing himself down. 'Do you know who this is?'

She knelt down and started to fan the unconscious man. 'Please God, he's not hurt.' She waved at Alpiew. 'Quickly, Alpiew, some water. Hartshorn, sal volatile, anything to revive him . . .'

'He's only one of the punters, isn't he?' Sir Peter was flicking the ends of his moustache. 'There's plenty more where he came from.'

'First an apple,' sighed the Countess, 'then Jeremy Collier's *Short View of the Immorality and Profaneness of the English Stage*. Poor Mr Newton is always getting bashed on the head.'

'Mr Newton?' gasped Alpiew, running forward with a brimming cup of water. 'Mr Isaac Newton?'

'My neighbour,' the Countess nodded. 'And it's the first time I have had the honour of a visit.' She put out her hand for Alpiew to help her up. 'I think for the moment I'll make myself scarce, Peter, dear. I have no desire to be in confrontation with my neighbours. You got me into this mess. You get me out of it.'

Newton's eyelids flickered. Alpiew handed him the glass of water, aching to hand him Beau's equation too.

'Don't worry,' said Sir Peter with a smile. 'He won't be your neighbour for long.'

'Why?' hissed the Countess. 'Is he moving?'

'No,' said Sir Peter. 'We are.'

The Countess raised her fist. Sir Peter ducked. 'Don't worry, wife. I'll get us a good profit.'

'I don't want a good profit,' hissed the Countess. 'I want to keep my dear house and home.'

At this moment a dozen heads appeared round the kitchen door, Godfrey at the vanguard.

'Godfrey,' barked Sir Peter, grabbing his wife by the hand, 'when you've finished showing this lot round, get rid of the mad scientist and meet us at the' – he gave Godfrey a wink – 'new place.'

Sir Peter seized Alpiew's arm, and with both women in tow, rushed through the hall and out into German Street.

'It's the most beautiful place,' he shouted as they trotted along the street. 'Built after the newest fashion. Ready for us to move in. Up-to-the-minute kitchen, with oven, water pump and turn-spit. There's even a little ice-house.'

'And where will we get the money for a place like that?' the Countess blustered, exchanging panicked glances with Alpiew whenever she could.

They ran across the main road and into a half-built street north of Pickadilly.

They walked up past some inhabited houses, some half-finished, some which were still merely holes waiting to be filled with new foundations. Through the odd-looking building site the Countess noticed you could see Burlington House in one direction, the newly named Devonshire House in the other, and straight before them to the north miles of rough uncultivated land.

Sir Peter had stopped outside a new-built brick-faced

house with stone corners and keystones. ' 'Tis paid for, wife, and ours for the taking. The rooms wainscoted and painted, there are fine sash windows, large half-paced stairs, and behind a pleasant court planted with vines, jessamine and other greens.' He pulled a key from his pocket and opened the front door.

'What is this dreadful place called?' inquired the Countess, surveying the rest of the street, the mounds of building materials, weed-covered strips which were as yet untouched, the partially dug foundations of the next-door house.

'It's called Bond Street, wife.'

'It looks like the ruins of Troy.'

'I assure you it will soon be the most fashionable street in all of London.'

'Phough!' said the Countess mounting the steps, observing that none of the houses opposite had roofs. 'And when the sky falls we will catch larks.'

Sir Peter was already in the echoing hall. 'It's part-furnished, as you see. New-fangled wallpaper too, for those of us who wish to be *à la mode*.'

The Countess's face changed once she was inside, for the interior was indeed beautiful. A delicate curved stair-case led up from the chequered, elegantly proportioned marble hall. She turned to scrutinise her husband's face. 'And you have paid for this?'

'What's the point of hanging on to your money? I don't want to be the richest man in the graveyard.' He nodded. 'Signed and all but sealed.' He turned back to Alpiew, whose face betrayed an incredulity he wished to inhibit. 'And for you, Alpiew, seeing as you have become almost a daughter to my dear wife, I have made sure there are excellent accommodations. The top storey, lofty quarters to be sure, is all yours. If you'd care to skip up the stairs on your oh so nimble trotters you may peruse it, you little jilt, while I escort my wife around our handsome new abode.'

The Countess had wandered off and was touching everything as though to ascertain it was real and not a dream.

'But the money?' she stammered as her husband followed her into the dining room.

'May I remind you, wife, or perhaps tell you, for I fear I may have omitted to do so,' he said, taking her hand in his, 'that my business dealings over the last few years both in the Americas and the Indies have made me one of the richest men in London.'

They moved into the kitchen and the Countess gasped at the gorgeous sight. She ran over to the fireplace and started stroking the cast-iron turn-spit. 'We could have a whole pig!'

'With all the trimmings. A great pal of mine, a Cherokee chief whom I befriended over there, gave me a wonderful recipe for roasted pig with chestnuts and spiced apples. He frequently made it, in his wigwam.' He turned and displayed the other pieces of equipment. 'The water supply is plentiful. There's even a little fountain running through to the dining room.'

The Countess had her head up the chimney and was inspecting the multitude of hanging hooks with their potential for cooking with more than one pan at a time. She ducked out and ran over to the bread oven by the back door.

'It will be like old times, only better.' Sir Peter stood

with his hands on his hips, grinning as his wife scampered round stroking all the equipment. 'We can entertain royalty. Think of the menus our servants can prepare in here: duck ragout, stewed oysters, battered rabbit . . .'

The Countess, as though in a dream, continued the litany: 'Pickled pigeon, Spanish puffs, gravy soup, brill cream . . .'

'So, dear wife, what do you think?'

'Let's look upstairs.' The Countess blushed. 'At the bedchambers.'

They met Alpiew on the landing. She gave Sir Peter a look intended to frighten him. She knew the whole scheme was too good to be true, but only wished she could work out what the man was up to.

'So what do you think, Alpiew?' Sir Peter kept her on the landing while his wife wandered into the master bedchamber.

'Seems wonderful beyond belief, sir.'

'Well, that's me all over, isn't it?' he crooned. 'Never knowingly understated.'

His eyes seemed to challenge her to contradict him. She decided to stay quiet.

'You should take a look at the kitchen,' he smiled. 'It has all the latest gadgets.'

It was an order rather than a suggestion, so Alpiew loped downstairs, while Sir Peter strutted after his wife into the master bedchamber.

'When can we move in?' asked the Countess as she stroked the satin coverings on the ultra-tall four-poster.

'As soon as the sale has gone through on German Street.'

'But I thought' – the Countess cocked her head – 'everything was paid for?'

'Every single brick, roof-tile and stair-tread.' Sir Peter put his arms round the Countess and kissed her cheek. 'But I thought with a bit of extra money in the bank we could get a coach, and some servants, and you can run a full equipage again.'

'Oh, I don't mind about that.' The Countess looked up and noticed the beautiful display of ostrich plumes topping each post of the bed. 'Why don't we move in tomorrow?'

'It was going to be a surprise, but . . .' He stroked his wife's wig. 'I've got the painters coming in tomorrow to emblazon all the doors with our new coat of arms, including the front door, so that everyone will know this house is ours. It'll take a week or two for the painters to get that finished. We don't want to live with the smell of linseed oil, turpentine and varnish, do we?'

The Countess smiled and shook her head.

'So, there we have it. Let's wait a bit, and do it in style, eh, wife?'

The Countess lay her cheek against his shoulder. She was utterly content.

Alpiew had taken the few moments she had alone in the kitchen to copy out the equation from Beau's log-book on to a spare piece of paper. And on her way back to German Street she knocked at Isaac Newton's door. After a few moments he opened up, holding a large piece of steak to his forehead.

'Yes!' he grunted.

'I have a puzzle,' said Alpiew, thrusting the paper into his hands. 'It has foxed everyone in London, from the cleverest chymist to the busiest apothecary. I thought maybe you . . . ?'

He took a step back. 'You're from next door, aren't you? From the Bedlam which is Anglesey House.'

Alpiew said nothing, just held out the piece of paper with the equation on it.

'Bugger off,' shouted Newton, and slammed the door in her face.

Undeterred, Alpiew crossed her fingers and slid the paper beneath Isaac Newton's front door.

The Countess was at home, pulling open cupboards and drawers which had not been opened for many years. 'I don't have any trunks or travelling cases. How am I going to get all this stuff to the new house?'

Sir Peter sat nursing a bottle of Burgundy near the fire and gazing lovingly upon the coat of arms which now hung proudly on the chimney breast. 'Don't think of packing yet,' he said, thrusting the corkscrew into the top of the bottle. 'I'll get you servants to do all that. All you have to do now is sit by the fire and have a drink to celebrate.' He pulled the cork with a swagger and filled two bumpers. 'I should have acquired champaign, I know. But no problem, we can have champaign tomorrow, after I have seen to a little business matter.'

The Countess stood scratching her head and staring down at the pile of things which had tumbled from the cupboard: a spinning top, a wig-stand, a pile of unfinished play manuscripts, an ebony and ivory chess set, a broken lantern.

Sir Peter strolled across to the back door and yelled

out. 'Godfrey! Get your arse ready. We've to be there shortly.'

The Countess craned around. 'Are you going out?'

'I'm sorry, my love, but needs must when the devil drives.' Sir Peter was throwing on his cloak. 'I just have a few more things to organise and then . . .'

'But it's dark outside. Everything will be closed. What can you possibly need to do at this time of the evening?'

'I've a few old chums to look up, curry favour, you know. I'm off to one of the gaming clubs round the corner. See who I can cultivate.' He tapped the bridge of his nose. 'As I always said, "It's not what you know – it's *who* you know."'

He placed his beaver hat atop his periwig, carefully arranging it to best display the multicoloured feathers. 'No need to worry, my dear. I've sent Alpiew along the road to fetch your friend Pigalle.' He jolted the hat to give it a rakish tilt. 'Though why you want to knock around with that antique French harridan, I shall never know.'

The front door slammed and Alpiew came into the kitchen rubbing her hands together and blowing on them. 'I think spring will never come this year.'

Sir Peter stood before her, waiting for an answer. Alpiew shoved past him. 'Yes, yes. She's coming later. She's busy.' She stopped short, looking down at the pile of rubbish littering the floor. She got straight on her knees and started to put the chess pieces back into the box.

'Ah my old chess-set, i' faith!' said Sir Peter. 'I was given that for bravery during the war, you know. It belonged to Prince Rupert of the Rhine. Chess!' he repeated, pronouncing the word as though it was an

317

insect he was catching mid-air. 'The noble game of kings. Do you play, Alpiew?'

'You know perfectly well that I do.' Alpiew did not look up, just went on putting the pieces back into their box. 'You taught me yourself.'

'Ah yes, of course.' He tickled the back of her neck. 'When you were practically an infant in arms. May I challenge you to a game?'

'I thought you were in a hurry.'

'When I get back, dolt.'

'I'm no dolt, sir. I could wipe the board with you.'

Looking at her backside, raised up while she reached under a cupboard to pull out a stray pawn, Sir Peter pulled delicately at the point of his beard. 'Yes, you did always have a fine end-game. I'll give you that.'

'I checkmated you frequently, sir, if I remember.' Alpiew had gathered all the white pieces and had only three black pawns to find.

'Only because I let you win. Being a child, you know. It seemed unfair for me to beat you.'

Alpiew was bubbling with anger. She had won fair and square, and longed to do it again. But before she could reply, Godfrey stood at the door, his boots pulled on, his cloak thrown about his shoulders and a large hat pulled down over his eyes.

'Oh, Godfrey,' the Countess laughed, 'you look like one of the villains at the playhouse.'

'Come on then, Godfrey, you old bastard,' said Sir Peter, picking up his sword and slinging it at Godfrey. 'Let's be off.'

Godfrey trotted across the room and followed Sir Peter out.

'Where are they going?' Alpiew asked, looking up with horror at the coat of arms and deciding not to comment.

'Gambling at some men's club.' The Countess followed Alpiew's gaze and looked up at the great shield hanging above the fire. 'Aren't I lucky?'

Alpiew gulped and moved over to sit next to the Countess. 'I didn't go for Pigalle, by the way. I just loitered round the corner till it seemed a decent time to have been gone.' She leant forward and poured herself a beaker of wine. 'I thought we could have another go at sifting through what we've got on the Beau Wilson case.'

While she unloaded the contents of her bag, the Countess knocked back the remains of her wine. 'Why are you still worried about all that stuff, Alpiew? We don't need to work for money any more.' She refilled her bumper. 'You heard Sir Peter, he only has to tie up a few loose ends and we will be rich again. No more grubbing about for scandal in emporia of flogging, no chasing after thugs, and blood-stained dresses. We can just sit and enjoy ourselves.'

'And what?' Alpiew had the papers out before her and was sharpening her quill with a penknife.

'And what, what?' The Countess stared at her over the glass of wine.

'Sit and what?' Alpiew put the penknife away and placed a jar of ink by her feet.

'Sit and nothing, Alpiew. Just sit and feel rich.'

'Has it never occurred to you, milady, that that would be incredibly boring, just to sit and do nothing?'

'No,' snapped the Countess before taking another gulp of wine. 'I would rather like it.'

'You'd die of boredom within a week.' Alpiew had the equation on her knee. 'And anyhow, I feel a bond of loyalty to Betty, if not to Beau. Remember, as things stand, we are the only people who can bring their murderers to justice. And Mrs Wilson does not deserve to hang or burn, however rude she is.'

'Well, you do as you like, my dear.' The Countess refilled. 'I am going to be a lady of leisure.'

'How does he know Acton?' asked Alpiew, fiddling with the feather end of her quill.

'Who?' The Countess was kicking off her shoes, ready to apply her feet to the rail in front of the fire.

'Sir Peter?'

'My husband?' The Countess blinked at Alpiew. '*Does* he know Acton?'

Alpiew nodded. 'He called it an arboreal delight.'

'Did he? How poetical of him.' She leant back and supped from her glass. 'It's just a bunch of trees in the middle of nowhere as far as I'm concerned.'

'He's not tall, though, is he?'

'Who?'

'Sir Peter.'

'Alpiew.' The Countess sat up, suddenly sober. 'What are you trying to imply?'

'He's been away for years and years . . .' Alpiew shrugged. 'We don't know where, or what he has been doing. He is not always with you since he reappeared. And you told me he goes out at night as well.' Alpiew drained her beaker, and dipped the quill, ready to start writing her notes. 'And the locals of Acton talk about that woman, Mrs Roy, having a mysterious husband, who was not tall.'

320

'Well, that just about does it!' The Countess slammed her glass down, and rose from her seat. 'Out of my house, thou viper! Thou serpent that I have fostered . . .' She stood, swaying slightly, pointing at the door. 'Thou bosom traitress, that I have raised from nothing . . .'

'But Countess, I only –'

The Countess raised her skirt and chased Alpiew round the table. 'Begone! Out! Go, go, starve again, alone and forgotten!'

'Dear madam, I . . .'

The Countess picked up a broom and waved it in Alpiew's direction. 'Go, go, you treacherous trull.'

Alpiew gathered up her papers, and dashed from the room. 'Do but hear me, madam . . .' she called from the hall.

'Hear you? Thou frontless impudence, begone!' The Countess's voice became a tremulous wail. 'Begone!'

But Alpiew was already out of the front door. She made her way to Pigalle, who welcomed her as she had done before. 'How perfect, Alpiew. I was yearning for someone to play with.'

Alpiew shuddered. She knew all about Pigalle and her playthings.

'I was just going to offer to cook for you tonight, Duchesse.'

'*D'accord, d'accord*. But only after you have a quick game of chess, with me. You do play?'

'Everyone is wanting to play chess tonight.' Alpiew was relieved that's all it was. 'I was taught by a master, Sir Peter!'

'A master of deception, you mean.' Pigalle swished into her large gaming room. The monkey let out a shrill squeal, clambered to the top of the curtains and set the parrot a-squawking.

'Yes, *mes enfants*, we have a little friend to play with. Isn't it *merveilleux*?' She sat before a marble table where a gigantic chess set was perpetually laid out.

'I was only talking about chess a few moments ago,' said Alpiew thrusting her pawn forward.

'Why so?' inquired Pigalle, hastily meeting Alpiew's white pawn with her own black one.

'A chess set had tumbled from a cupboard which my mistress was going through.'

'Ashby! Going through a cupboard! How extraordinary! What on earth for? She has you for such things.'

'She is excited,' said Alpiew, jumping her knight on to the chequered field, 'because she is moving house.'

'Moving?' Pigalle placed her knight in opposition. 'Has she taken leave of her senses? She has an excellent address.'

Alpiew slid her bishop along the diagonal. 'Sir Peter has bought her a new one. A better one.'

Pigalle hesitated for a moment before moving her bishop too. 'Might I ask where? Tottenham Fields perhaps?' Pigalle was referring to one of the roughest areas in London, where the cinders and rubbish of the city were tipped. 'Or is it a dive in Alsatia perhaps, or the Rookeries?'

'Bond Street,' said Alpiew, bringing another pawn into play. They played a few moves in silence.

Pigalle muttered some French expletives under her breath. It gave Alpiew an idea. 'Do you know the phrase "*Alles Mist*"?'

'Never heard of it.' Pigalle looked up, shrugged and

looked back at the board. 'Sounds German. Is it ze name of a race-horse?'

Alpiew took one of the black pawns.

'You are playing a strategic game, mademoiselle,' said Pigalle, moving another of her pawns away from the white queen. 'By ze way, houses in Bond Street cannot be bought.'

'Sir Peter seems to have done it.' Alpiew looked up at Pigalle while making her move. 'I've seen the place. It is wonderful. A palace.'

'Which house?' asked Pigalle, taking Alpiew's knight.

'It's one of the three finished ones.' Alpiew's eyes darted up and down from the pieces to Pigalle. 'Blue front door.'

'Blue front door? But zat belongs to Sir Cloudesly Swinnerton.'

'Then maybe he is selling?'

'*Au contraire*, *ma petite*. He has only just bought ze place. He has gone to Italy on business for ze government. He left only zis morning for ze coast.' Pigalle swooped a bishop across the board. 'Check!'

Alpiew stared at the board. She moved her queen into defence. Pigalle gazed in silence at the board for a moment then slid her rook two squares.

'And checkmate, my dear Alpiew. The king is dead. The game is over.'

Alpiew gazed at the board. Pigalle had definitely won.

Pigalle rose and rubbed her hands together. 'So, what will we eat?'

Alpiew got up, and without thinking, curtseyed before leaving to inspect Pigalle's walk-in pantry and larder. She rifled about in the cold cupboard. What was going on?

What was Sir Peter's game? She knew that the Countess was being duped, but how to prove it? She leapt into the air as a cat wandered out from behind some jars. He was licking his lips. No doubt he had found the butter.

Pigalle had a pigeon, and the ingredients for pastry. So that was supper. Pigeon pie.

While Alpiew plucked and chopped and beat and kneaded she thought hard.

What if Sir Peter *was* the mysterious Mr Roy, and, like his enigmatic wife, had pots of money? Perhaps he really had bought the house before this Cloudesly Swinnerton left for Italy. Perhaps he really had struck it rich in the Indies – many others had before him. Maybe his mad deals were bringing in pots of money this time.

She shuddered as she beheaded the pigeon. If Sir Peter was Mr Roy, then what part had he in the murder of Beau? And even worse, of Betty.

The frying onions sent a comforting bouquet throughout the house, eventually enticing Pigalle herself down to the kitchen. She perched on a tall stool, and smiled at Alpiew.

'You are a better cook than Azis was.' She sighed and breathed deep of the mixed aromas of onion, gravy, baking pastry and herbs. 'Ashby is very lucky.'

Alpiew looked up. 'Why does she never use her Christian name?'

'Simple, my dear.' Pigalle brushed some cat hair from her bodice. 'Her name is Anastasia. Everyone in England insists on shortening Christian names. Ze abbreviation for her name when she was an *enfant* was Nasty. She didn't like zat.'

Alpiew laughed. How very like her lady. 'I am very

worried for her,' said Alpiew, taking a wooden spoon and beating at a nearby pan. 'I must protect her.'

'No need to say it, Alpiew, dear.' Pigalle winced. 'Anyone knows zat. And zat is why ze horrible little husband is so frightened of you.'

'What are we to do?' Alpiew realised her tears were spilling into the sauce.

Pigalle went to the pantry and brought out a bottle of Spumanti. She tore at the foil and tugged off the cage. She then shook the bottle a little. 'Alpiew!'

Alpiew turned as Pigalle popped the cork, spraying the table with a gush of foam.

'I make myself happy when I am near zat *charognard* by remembering zat his name in French means to fart!'

'Peter?'

'*Oui, péter* – to fart!'

Alpiew smiled through her tears.

'Don't worry, my dear child. If something is going on, something bad, together we will save her. Have no doubt about zat. But first we will eat.'

The Countess sat alone and prodded at the glowing ashes of the fire. She wished she had not sent Alpiew off. The silence in the house was putting thoughts into her head. Thoughts that she did not wish to entertain. Where *had* Peter gone each night? He and Godfrey were always up and out when she woke. Even this morning, when she woke at five because a night-watchman fell over a travelling trunk which must have fallen off a passing coach and let out an almighty wail immediately preceding his, 'Five o'clock and all is well,' Godfrey and Sir Peter were not in bed. So where had Peter gone before dawn's rosy blush painted the morning sky?

And how *did* he know about Acton? She herself had never even heard the name until Pigalle dragged her out there. And if he was acquainted with that awful Mrs Roy, what then? Was he a murderer, or a murderer's accomplice? Would she have to turn him in to the authorities?

It was too awful to contemplate. She swigged down the rest of the glass. The bottle was now empty.

It was almost midnight. Alpiew had gone hours ago now, and she was ravenous.

She tried to drain a few more drops from the empty bottle, and went to forage about in Godfrey's pantry to see what he had in store. She grabbed a piece of dry bread and some greasy-looking cheese.

If Alpiew was still here the wench could have prepared something and they would both have made up their quarrel while preparing their food, and had a hearty meal together. She slid the jars around, searching for some chutney or pickles, then she could imagine it was a real Ploughman's, which she found she had rather enjoyed. She pulled the top from one jar labelled 'chutney of apple', but the contents were covered in a thick fur of green mould. She shoved the jars around. Most looked empty or rancid. She grabbed a bigger jar labelled 'pickings' and grasped at the lid. It was jammed tight. She carried it over to her seat by the fire to see if she could prise the thing open with her knife. It was surprisingly heavy. She flopped down and tried to lever the end of the knife between the cork and the glass, but all she got was a shower of glass splinters. She thrust the knife deeper this time, dislodging a wad of cork. Then she wiggled her finger down the resulting hole and pulled out the remaining cork stopper.

The inside of the jar had been coated with material, some sort of dark felt, but it was not filled with any kind of conserve. The jar was crammed with jewellery.

The Countess plunged her hand deep into the jar and tumbled everything out on to her chair, then she knelt, back to the fire, and rifled through it all. There were sparkling brilliants of all shapes and sizes, rings, bracelets, necklaces, diamonds, emeralds, rubies and pearls. Brooches, bodkins and cravat pins in ivory and silver. A cornucopia of valuables. She cocked her eye closer to one piece, thinking perhaps it would be fake, coloured glass, but no. It was the real thing. She bit another, held another to her cheek. It was all genuine.

It must be worth a fortune.

Behind her, as she sifted through the pearls checking them out for size and flaws, the kitchen door opened slowly.

The Countess realised too late. She threw herself across the seat of the chair, and took a sideways look towards the door. 'Hello? Who's there?'

It was Alpiew. 'My lady?' From her point of view the Countess, on the floor and splayed out over a chair, looked as though she had been taken by a seizure. Alpiew dashed across the room and started tugging at her, hoping to get the woman into a lying position so she could loosen her corset before calling for a physician. 'Are you unwell? What has happened to you, madam?'

'Alpiew, Alpiew! It's terrible!' The Countess raised her bosom from the cache of jewellery. 'Regard!'

Alpiew joined her mistress on her knees. The fire made a great crack, and as though by instinct both women lowered their bosoms over the jewels. 'If someone comes in now and sees us we'll have to say we're turned Mussulmen and are praying to Mecca.' She lifted a diamond ring and started the same procedure as the Countess had been at, testing the gems to see if they were real. 'Where did you get this?' She heard an awful crunch as one of her teeth succumbed to the diamond. 'Ouch!'

The Countess pointed to the jar. 'It was in Godfrey's cupboard.'

Alpiew started to shove the stuff back. 'Then it had better be still there when they return.'

'They!' moaned the Countess. 'You don't think?'

Alpiew dared not utter any deprecations regarding Sir Peter again. 'Just safer.' She went to the pantry and returned the jar. 'It was at the back? Am I right? Hidden by the others.'

The Countess stood in the doorway and pointed. 'There. How do you think he . . . ? What was . . . ? Where did . . . ?'

Alpiew slid the jar into place. 'That we will have to find out when they return.'

Alpiew jolted to silence and grabbed the Countess by the elbow. Behind them the kitchen door had creaked open again. Trying not to look guilty, both emerged from the pantry to find the Duchesse de Pigalle leaning against the side-table, pouring herself a bumper from an open bottle she had brought with her.

'Bottoms up!' she cried and pulled a seat towards the fire. 'Now, Ashby, dear, I know it's very late. Ze watchmen are stalking ze streets and ze owls are fluttering about after rats, or whatever it is zey do at midnight, but . . .' She sat and took a swig. 'I have something very important to tell you about zat house in Bond Street.'

The Countess came to sit beside her. 'Yes?'

'Now, Ashby, you know I adore you. I do not want you to be hurt.' Pigalle shifted uneasily. 'And zat is why I must tell you what I know.'

Alpiew decided to use the moment to visit the privy in the garden. She had been with Pigalle, before she had gone off to make her inquiries, and suspected she knew what was coming.

'In ze last hour I have been to see a friend at St James's Palace. He organises ze travels for the ambassadors. And he has told me some disturbing news about the owner of zat house.'

'Which house?'

'Where he took you today, your husband: Bond Street.'

'Ah, our new house, you mean.' The Countess tutted and held out her glass for some of Pigalle's Spumanti. 'I knew you'd be jealous.'

'Ze house is beautiful. A city goldsmith sold ze plot to Sir Cloudesly Swinnerton a few years ago. Ze builders . . . Well, you know how it is in England. Nothing happens for years. So ze house is finally ready when, oplah!, ze poor man is called away to Italy.'

'Swinnerton? Italy? But what has this to do with me?'

Pigalle pressed on. 'Ze man Swinnerton left English shores zis morning, after travelling to Portsmouth in ze early hours. But, on ze road Sir Cloudesly met with an unfortunate fate for he was held up by two highwaymen. The men were buffoons he said, but they did manage to get his wife's jewellery box, which was at the back of

329

ze coach with ze other cases, and the gentleman's *étui*.'

'*Étui*?' murmured Alpiew, who had come back into the kitchen and was sitting quietly on Godfrey's bed.

'It's a small bag that men carry penknives and manicure sets in,' said the Countess, aching for Pigalle to get on with her story. 'Very continental.'

'In zat *étui* was ze key to ze gentleman's house, which will be empty for a few weeks till his return. And zat house is in Bond Street, ze only one with a blue door.'

The Countess stared into the glowing coals of the fire. 'So someone stole a lot of jewellery?' Her lower jaw started to tremble, and tears filled her eyes. 'And a front-door key?'

Pigalle threw a look in Alpiew's direction. 'Bring me over ze bag.'

Alpiew fetched the bag which Pigalle had left by the side-table. Pigalle dived in and pulled out a bulky folded napkin.

'I took ze liberty of slipping some sweetmeats into a napkin for you. At ze palace no one notices such stuff going missing.' She unfolded the napkin, exposing some marzipan, a few wafers and some pieces of fruit-flavoured boiled sugar, called sucket.

The Countess's eyes lingered on the pretty package, her chin gave another wobble, her eyes roamed from marzipan to sucket. She picked a piece of marzipan decorated with a date.

'What shall I do, Olympe?' She chomped away at the sweet and popped another in her mouth. 'Tonight I have myself made another discovery which reinforces the truth of your story.' She nodded towards Alpiew. 'The jar, Alpiew.'

Alpiew vanished into the pantry.

'You must be careful, Ashby.' Pigalle took the Countess's hand and squeezed it. 'It is a dangerous position zat you are in.'

'When he returns I will challenge him, Pigalle.' She wiped a tear away from her cheek. 'You will stay with me while I talk to him?'

Pigalle patted the Countess's hand. '*D'accord!*'

As Alpiew returned with the jar, the front door slammed. Alpiew darted back into the pantry and slammed the jar back into its position, before returning to the kitchen clutching a jar of mouldy chutney.

Ready for battle, the Countess and Pigalle jumped to their feet.

A head bobbed round the kitchen door, lanky brown hair hanging loose. 'I heard voices. Knew you were up. Thought I'd pop round.' It was Mr Newton. 'I've been working on that equation all night long. I can't take my mind off it.' He pulled the crumpled note from his pocket and waved it in the air as he dragged a chair across to the fire. 'This is a good idea, living in the kitchen. Very economical.' He sat. 'Good evening.' He shook Pigalle's hand, then smoothed the paper out on his lap.

Wondering if he was drunk, the Countess offered him a sweet. 'It's fascinating, you know.' He took a wafer, and scratched his head. 'Harder to puzzle than the workings I used to ascertain the speed of light.'

'Sorry, Mr Newton, if this is an impertinent question' – the Countess cocked her head – 'but why did you *want* to find the speed of light?'

'Unless it's running in ze maiden filly stakes at Newmarket,' cried Pigalle, crunching on a piece of red sucket.

Ignoring them, Alpiew perched on a footstool near Mr Newton's feet.

'Mercury and copper are very difficult to fuse,' he muttered, poring over the paper. 'It's what they call a "vegetable process". You get a sort of useless stone . . .' He stabbed at symbols. 'And as for iron and copper, they will fuse, with some difficulty, but produce nothing more than a metallic stone of rust-resistant greenish-colour.'

The Countess and Pigalle raised their eyebrows and crossed their eyes at each other. 'Alpiew, darlink, is ze fire lit in ze front room?'

'It was when I left.' Alpiew nodded. 'May need a top-up.'

'Perhaps if you and Mr Newton want to work . . .'

'No, no,' said Newton, popping a marzipan almond square into his mouth. 'I'm most comfortable here, thank you. It's very cosy.'

The Countess indicated to Pigalle to join her for a quiet chat in the pantry.

When they were out of earshot Alpiew ventured: 'Mr Newton, do you know the phrase "*Alles Mist*"?'

Newton groaned. 'That old chestnut!' He slapped his thigh and appeared to be angry. 'When will they realise they are not being at all clever? Either scientifically or grammatically. The lowest poet will tell you it's not even a decent pun.'

'What do you mean?'

'*Alles mist* equals alchymist.' Newton sighed. 'Although only a drunken Scot might pronounce it thus. But it is also a German phrase meaning, "It's all shit". And every witless buck in town screeches it at anyone thought to dabble in the hermetic art.'

'That's another thing I've been wondering about.' Alpiew flipped a wafer into her mouth. 'Why hermetic?'

'Hermes.' Newton smiled. 'The winged messenger of the Gods.'

Alpiew pointed to the symbol: ♎ 'And sublimation occurs at the eclipse in Libra?'

'Oh, Libra!' Newton gave her a puzzled look. 'I was reading that as chloride of mercury, or corrosive sublimate.'

'It means those things too?'

'Yes, and sublimed mercury, calcined green vitriol, and the mixture of common salt and nitre.'

'There are so many possibilities,' Alpiew sighed. 'I will make a chart. That might help us.'

'Exactly,' said Newton, screwing up his face and pondering the equation again. 'It's worse than a game of chess for possible options.' He ran his finger along the equation again. 'Talking of which, that cross could be the sign for checkmate.'

Pigalle drew the pantry door shut when she saw the contents of the jar.

'It does not look too promising for you, Ashby, darlink.' She sifted through the jewels, pulling one out and biting it. 'Real too! Perhaps you should make a call on ze constable. Raise ze hue and cry.'

'Do you know' – the Countess thrust the cork stopper back into the jar – 'for once, I believe you are right.'

*   *   *

333

Alpiew could hear the low hum of the two women talking in the closed space of the pantry. From the other side of the room there came a sudden creak. Someone was in the hall.

She crept over to the pantry to warn the Countess of her husband's imminent return. 'Countess!' She knocked gently on the door, then pulled it open, pulled a face and scurried back to the fireplace.

The Countess and Pigalle, puffed up for battle, sidled round the pantry door. But both stood transfixed when they looked across the room to see, standing before them in the doorway with an axe raised above his head, Jack Fry, the man they called Scum.

THIRTEEN

Fulmination

*The preparation of a fulminate –
applied to any process in which
a sudden eruptive event occurs.*

Everyone screamed, Newton included, as Scum brought his axe down on the table, splintering it in two.

'Is this one of your husbands?' screamed the famed mathematician. 'Tell him I'm only a neighbour. And I don't even like women.'

Scum growled and pulled the axe out of the table.

'Please, not me. Let me go.' Newton dropped to his knees, sobbing. 'I didn't touch her. I promise. I didn't touch *anyone*. I'm a dried-up old brain-box. No sexual equipment worth mentioning . . . Really. I prefer boys.'

Scum was humming, his eyebrows lowered in a black knot. The low hum rose and increased in volume till it turned into a roar and the axe slammed down into the sideboard and stuck. While Scum struggled to remove it, Pigalle sidled back into the pantry and started pulling jars from the shelves. One by one she tossed them to the Countess who hurled them at Scum.

'Take that, you bully!' cried the Countess, lobbing a paper packet of tea his way.

Growling, he turned and advanced on her while Alpiew hurriedly slid her chair across the tiled floor in an attempt at blocking the way.

'Stand back, blackguard!' said the Countess, trying to imitate the tone which always worked when employed by actresses in scenes involving rape and pillage. Utterly unmoved by her performance, Scum loped towards her. In defence, she pitched a packet of flour at him. It fell short and exploded at his feet.

Less than a yard from Scum's heavy boots, Newton was prostrate, trying to slide himself under Godfrey's bed. Dredged with flour, he now resembled a pretty winter landscape. With a slither, he disappeared under the bed, then, nestling next to Godfrey's chamber pot, he started pulling piles of books and manuscripts round himself for protection, whimpering all the while.

By the pantry door, Pigalle and the Countess had a good rhythm going, and jars were flying through the air like swallows in an autumn sky.

Scum kicked a stool out of his way. It fell apart. Picking up a wooden side-spar, he let out a roar and lashed at Alpiew, who had crept up on him, hoping to prong him in the posterior with the toasting fork.

He grabbed her hand, peeled her fingers back and threw the fork into a corner with a roar.

From the pantry corner, a shower of jars of beans, peas, rice, nuts and bolts, upholstery pins, and mouldy chutney sailed across the kitchen. When one actually hit him on the arm, Scum let Alpiew go and advanced again on the Countess.

'Make a dash for it, milady,' screamed Alpiew. 'Lock yourself in the privy . . .'

'United we stand,' panted the Countess, sliding to the floor on a melted lump of butter.

'You arse-worm,' bellowed Alpiew in Scum's direction. 'You big Molly! You madge cull!'

Scum stopped in his tracks. His face went a deep shade of purple, his bloodshot eyes glared through his knotted brow. Baring his teeth, he loped back towards Alpiew. With a sudden cry that could be heard in Wapping he flailed the wooden spar before him and jumped in the air before Alpiew, who, with a new-found talent for steeple-chasing, jumped over the Countess's bed in one bound. Scum followed. One by one she grabbed books, papers, pillows and hurled them at him, ducking out of his way as he lurched at her with the wooden spar.

Now that the pantry shelves were bare, Pigalle had crept back into the kitchen and was at the sideboard, tugging at the axe, which was deeply embedded. The Countess dropped the remaining jars and joined her.

'*Rien à foutre*,' howled Pigalle. 'It won't budge!'

With a flourish the Countess pulled open a drawer, exposing a meat cleaver. But before she or Pigalle could grab it, Scum had swung round, bellowing, and vaulted across the room. Pigalle and the Countess backed away, and Scum seized the meat cleaver.

A continuous high-pitched whine was coming from under Godfrey's bed.

Grabbing an iron poker from the grate, Alpiew marched into the centre of the room behind the vast square shape of Scum. As she raised the poker to bring it down on the villain's head, someone grabbed her from behind and threw her to the floor.

'What the devil's going on in here?' It was Sir Peter,

the worse for a few drinks. 'Can a man not return to his own bedchamber without experiencing a reconstruction of the antics of a full moon at Bedlam?'

Growling, Scum thudded in Sir Peter's direction.

Taking one look at the madman, Sir Peter let out a shriek and revolved, heading for the door. He stumbled over Alpiew's prostrate form, and flew in the general direction of the fire.

Now that Alpiew was down and Sir Peter tumbling, Scum turned back to take on the others. Raising the cleaver above his head he lurched forward.

Staggering amongst the broken furniture like a pair of elderly Siamese twins, the Countess and Pigalle clung on to each other, ducking out of the way of the cleaver's downward strokes as though bowing to Mecca, popping up only to fling the occasional jar over their shoulders.

Alpiew's feet had already slammed the hall door shut. Now, as she climbed to her feet, she knocked down a chair which effectively blocked the exit altogether.

Regaining his equilibrium, Sir Peter flapped his singed hands, which had saved him from falling into the fire.

'What is zat funny smell?' hissed Pigalle, lunging towards the door. It was the feathers on Sir Peter's hat, aflame on his head and making him resemble a flaming Christmas porridge pie.

'Get that bloody door open,' he shouted to his wife and Pigalle, who were tugging with all their might at the chair blocking the way out.

But seeing Scum, trailing Sir Peter, heading their way, Pigalle and the Countess left the chair and pursued Alpiew, who, having retrieved the toasting fork, was heading towards Scum.

Like a game of ring-a-ring-o'-roses the room was now full of people running in a circle. Scum chased Sir Peter, who was catching up with Pigalle and the Countess; ahead of them was Alpiew, who in turn was pursuing Scum.

In the middle of the room, Godfrey's bed was screaming at a very high pitch.

Hat aflame, Sir Peter darted out of the circuit, grabbed Alpiew and, using her as a shield, backed towards the pantry door.

'I have influence,' shouted Sir Peter. 'How much do you want?'

Scum roared and whacked a pillow in half with the cleaver.

As the feathers settled, it took Scum only a few seconds to have all four of them cornered, Pigalle, Sir Peter, Alpiew and the Countess quailing together, their backs to the pantry door, the smouldering hat towards the rear.

'We are not cowed,' whispered the quivering Countess. 'You don't frighten us!'

The meat cleaver thumped down on a bed-post. They all shrieked.

'*Vous êtes jetée, epèce d'ordure!*' Pigalle tried to spit, but her saliva had dried up. She looked as though she was blowing kisses.

Alpiew was trying to reach the door handle but three trembling bodies were in the way.

'Will somebody tell me what the hell is going on,' wailed Sir Peter, clouds of smoke billowing round his head.

Scum pulled the meat cleaver up.

'*Couillon!*' barked Pigalle. '*Bordille!*'

On the floor at her feet, where the Countess had dropped it, was the jar full of jewels, still intact. She stooped to pick it up, narrowly missing the cleaver's blade as it hissed past her shoulder. Retrieving the heavy jar, she hurled it with all her strength at Scum's shaven head. It hit him square on and smashed into bits, spraying sparkling bracelets, necklaces, rings and brooches round the room. At the same moment Newton's floury hand darted out and pulled Scum by the ankle, and someone started bashing at the front door.

As Scum teetered, swayed and fell to the ground, the kitchen door was kicked open and four constables stood there, frowning.

'We've come to return a drunk, who claims he works here for Lady Asti Scaramouch.'

In the doorway, between two young watchmen, swayed Godfrey.

The chief constable looked round the room: the air was heavy with feathers, drizzled with flour; smashed furniture and torn papers lay everywhere and jewellery hung from each cross-bar. Resting on a carpet of smashed bottles, a huge unconscious man was splayed out on the black slate tile floor, four people huddled in a haze of smoke against the pantry door and the only thing standing upright was an axe in the sideboard.

A brief silent hiatus was shattered with a unified sigh of relief. All four people by the pantry door charged towards the constables, babbling.

'Might it be safe to say there has been a serious incident here tonight?' inquired the chief constable, trying to pry himself free of Pigalle who was kissing him passionately on both cheeks.

Scum stirred. He raised himself on to his elbows, looking round as though he had no idea where he was.

Newton had kicked the books out of his way, crawled out from under the bed and got to his feet. 'There has been a spot of bother here tonight, Constable . . .' He brushed himself down and placed his boot upon the recumbent axeman's back. 'Your deductions are completely accurate. And now we would appreciate it if you would take this lunatic and have him safely locked away from civilised society.'

The chief constable inspected Newton, whose face was white but for the areas round his eyes and mouth, which were puce. 'Are you a player with the Italian Comedy?' he asked.

'I most certainly am not,' said Newton firmly. 'I am Isaac Newton, Esquire, eminent academic and an officer of His Majesty's Government. I am the Master of the Mint.'

'Not in mint condition tonight, though, sir,' said the constable. 'If you'll pardon the pun.'

Above Newton, a shelf, seriously disturbed by the many missiles which had lately flown around the room, started to list forwards. Upon it stood a hat. The hat was large, a multicoloured feathered affair which the Countess wore for fancy occasions during the summer months. As the shelf tilted, the hat fell, and landed with perfect aplomb upon Isaac Newton's head. Without moving, he mumbled the incomprehensible phrase: 'G equals twice H over T squared.'

'Certainly, Mr Newton, sir,' said the constable.

The thug known as Scum shook his head and spoke: 'But I didn't do nothing, constables.' His voice came out in a strange high-pitched squeak. 'Truly! I only came 'ere to give 'em a fright. Honestly, look around you. I didn't hurt no one, did I?'

When the constables had gone, taking Scum with them, the Countess rounded on her husband, accusing him of fraud, of offering her a house which was not his to give, of highway robbery, of adultery, deceit, general skul-duggery and every crime barring treason, murder and sodomy.

At her side, Pigalle threw in a few incomprehensible phrases in French, and hawked up a monstrous amount of phlegm. Godfrey collapsed on to his bed and started snoring, while Alpiew and Newton resumed their places at the fire, poring over the equation. Newton was still wearing the Countess's hat. Sir Peter put out the fire in his own with a glass of water.

'This house is sold.' Sir Peter poured himself a brandy from a flask in his pocket.

'Sold!' screamed the Countess. 'You can't sell my house.'

'I can, you know. Completed the deal this evening. As soon as the stamps and seals are applied tomorrow evening it belongs to a property consortium in the City.'

'Ah, Ashby!' Pigalle clutched her forehead and reeled backwards. '*Tu es foutu, mon vieux.*'

'I thought you loved me.' The Countess's top lip was starting to wobble. 'Over my dead body will you take my house from me.'

'May I remind you, madam, that you are my wife. We

have not gone to the House of Lords and been granted a divorce. And in the ceremony of marriage you swore to obey me.'

'But I was given this house by King Charles. It is mine.'

'I am your lord. I am your master. What is yours is mine. Mine to sell, if I so desire. And I have sold it.'

'And where will I go? How will I live?'

'That is your problem, madam.'

'Oh, Pigalle,' cried the Countess, reaching out towards the knife drawer. 'Pass me the largest blade I own, so that I can murder him at once.'

'I wouldn't even attempt it, madam.' Sir Peter grabbed her by the wrist. 'By law I am a Petit God to you. You are to me as a citizen is to their king. If you kill me, 'twill be Petit Treason and the law will show no mercy. I am to you a little king, and this house is my kingdom, to dispose of as I wish.'

Newton slammed his finger down on the paper. 'Little king! It runs right through it. The little king.' He pointed at the small dotted circle in the first bracket. He banged his forehead with the palm of his hand. 'It's everywhere. Look, Alpiew.' He held the paper up.

$$\odot : \female\female \male \text{ \Large⛢} = \overset{\male}{\circ} (\male\female / \odot) (\odot / \dagger) \text{ } \Large⚓ \text{ } @ \text{ } \male \text{ } \libra$$

'It goes thus: Caput Mortem: the mysterious amalgam of mercury and copper, conjunction with the regulus. This crown –' he pointed at the ⛢ – 'this is the regulus. I took it as regulus of antimony, but maybe it is not. Maybe it is simply the regulus – the little king.' He wiped his hair back from his face, pushing the Countess's hat to a rakish angle. 'After the equals sign we have chaos. Bracket, amalgam iron copper, line, a little sun – the sun: the ruler, therefore the little king. New bracket, Gold – the sun, the ruler, the king – line, checkmate – the king is dead, the game is over. Sublimation at eclipse Libra.'

He rested the paper on his knee and leant back, his eyes closed. Alpiew gazed at Newton with adoration in her eye, and gently took the paper. She ran her finger along the symbols. 'So what does it all mean?' she asked in an awed voice.

'What does it mean? What does it mean?' Newton lifted his hands out in front of him, palms upwards and stood. 'What does it mean?' He moved to the door, and bowed, removing his hat and tossing it to Alpiew. 'I'm buggered if I know.'

'Who is that vulgar man in make-up?' said Sir Peter, as though he noticed Newton's presence for the first time only after he'd gone.

'Mr Newton,' echoed everyone in the room.

'Yes. But what *is* Mr Newton, exactly?'

'He's famous, didn't you hear him?' said Alpiew.

'And he lives next door?' Sir Peter's eyes lit up, and he rubbed his hands together. 'That'll put a few hundred on the price.' He surveyed the room. Smashed chairs, tables split in half, broken glass, flour, feathers, rice and pieces of jewellery lay everywhere. Chaos. Sir Peter got on his knees and started gathering the jewels. 'These are mine, I believe.'

Pigalle loomed over him. 'Not, by any remote chance, Sir Cloudesly Swinnerton's?'

Sir Peter ignored her and went on stuffing necklaces and brooches in his pockets.

Alpiew came up behind him and gave his backside a good kick. 'I should have done that years ago,' she said. 'Now get out of this house before I get the constables back here and turn you in for a highway robber.'

'Upon what proof?'

Silently Alpiew pursed her lips, pointing at his armful of booty.

'Bought it off a mate down the tavern,' said Sir Peter with a nonchalant shrug.

The Countess was sobbing, Pigalle trying to make good the damaged furniture.

Sir Peter gave a wide smile. 'Goodnight, all.' He tipped his hat, the charred plumeless spines of his feathers vibrating in the air like the antennae on a moth.

Godfrey was still snoring in his broken bed, as Pigalle, the Countess and Alpiew stood silently listening to Sir Peter's footsteps going along the hall and out to the street.

'We should have turned him in,' said Alpiew. 'Got the Tyburn Ticket.'

'No, Alpiew, he's right,' said Pigalle. 'He would have wiggled out of it.'

The Countess let out a loud wail. 'Please, Olympe, let me come and sleep at your house tonight. I am so unhappy.'

Pigalle pointed out that by leaving the house the Countess would have quite surrendered the place, promised to get her a locksmith, and instructed her on no account to leave. Any business outside the house could be undertaken by Alpiew.

The three women sat and polished off a bottle of wine which had rolled into a corner, and when Alpiew had tucked the Countess up in bed, Pigalle left.

Alpiew stoked up the fire for the night, and slumped down on a chair to carry on piecing the code together.

FOURTEEN

Ablation

*The separation of a component by removing
the upper part, by skimming,
or fluffing up with a feather or cloth.*

Early in the morning Alpiew left the house. She had a
busy day ahead. Scum was being held at Newgate Prison
on charges of causing an affray. Alpiew wanted to use
the opportunity to try to get something on him. To make
sure he was kept locked up.

'Did he ever talk about Acton, or what the house was
like?' Alpiew was back at Rose Court talking to the actor
who had told her about Scum.

'No. He never went there.'

'What do you mean?' Alpiew blinked in disbelief. 'But
you said . . .'

'I said he was working for a woman who lived in Acton.
He never *went* to Acton though. He was a sort of general
messenger, I gather, and her bully boy.'

Alpiew felt utterly deflated by the news. 'So what made
him give up his job here for that?'

'My dear, it's all the rage. Some people mistake a career
on the stage for a shop window in which they can display
themselves, in their search for a wealthy lover. Look

at them all: Mary Lee became Lady Slingsby, Hester Davenport Countess of Oxford, Margaret Hughes was kept by Prince Rupert . . .'

Alpiew interrupted. 'But they're all women . . . Men wouldn't . . .'

'Don't you believe it. Look at Charles Hart and Lady Castlemaine.'

'I take your point, but with respect all of those are a good thirty years ago.'

'Maybe, but they're all still at it, believe you me. There are dukes in every night: Clacton, Brighton, Blackpool . . . and the actresses love it. They're all desperate to have their own peer.' The actor leant forward in a conspiratorial way and whispered. 'Between you, me and the bedpost, the Earl of Scarsdale is after Mrs Bracegirdle at this very moment . . .'

Alpiew's jaw dropped. 'But she's a professional virgin!'

The actor sat back in his chair, raised his eyebrows and pursed his lips.

Alpiew made a mental note to get that information into their next copy for the Cues, and dragged the conversation back to Scum.

'But this man Fry, you're telling me he left the company just to be a servant of an untitled lady? Why would he do that?'

'Oh, he was a total failure as an actor, didn't I say?' The actor smiled that bland practised self-regarding smile of the supporting player. 'That silly little voice! Sounded like a child. And the accent, my dear. Incomprehensible to all but the inhabitants of the moon.'

'So why was he employed here?'

'With that ridiculous voice he was excellent as eunuchs. And looks, of course. He had a threatening air.'

'Just an air. Was no one frightened of him?'

'Oh yes, we were all terrified. He was a monster.'

'But what on earth happened when he spoke? Did the audience not laugh?'

'He couldn't act, that's true. But he was always given roles where the lines were spoken during fights, or while running, or garrotting someone. It came across as strain.' The actor sighed. 'Truth is, he always had a small part.'

'Like Signior Fideli,' said Alpiew, somehow shocked at the possibility.

The actor let forth a shriek, holding his sides while he laughed. 'Quite the contrary, from what I glimpsed in the tiring room! No, I mean his roles. They gave him a medium-size part once and he couldn't do it. Some like him do manage to get by, I'll wager, but not him. He couldn't pull it off at all.'

'There are others like him?'

'Of course, many. There was dear old Nell Gwyn for one.'

'Nell Gwyn!' Alpiew's mind was racing. What could he mean by that?

'Yes,' said the actor with a flounce of the cuff. '*Identical* cases. Just the same.'

'Nell Gwyn and Scum?'

'Oh yes. Indistinguishable. Poor old Nelly couldn't read either. Not a word. Had to learn it all by rote.'

'Oh.' Alpiew was deflated by the news. 'Is that all?'

'Quite a serious disadvantage in an actor, wouldn't you think?' The actor gave her a huffy look. 'Not to be able to read in a profession which is the apotheosis of the word?'

'Utterly.' Alpiew smiled and made herself scarce.

Alpiew went back to German Street to take watch while the Countess visited the lawyer, to see what options were left to her, and if it would be possible to save her house. Pigalle had lent her the coach and coachman for the day.

When Alpiew came in, Godfrey was awake and looking the worse for the night before. 'You cuckoldly, whiffling, lying son of a whore, begone.' Alpiew shooed him out into the hall with a broom.

'But I . . .'

'Stop your smoke-hole, nincompoop! You nasty traitor to our lady, you fumbling rogue, get you gone.'

Godfrey grouched and mumbled obscenities under his breath.

'Godfrey –' Alpiew grabbed him by the jacket – 'don't you see that by aiding and abetting the master, what you have done is made us all homeless?'

'How can that be? We can go on living with the mistress when he sods off again.'

Alpiew hauled him back into the kitchen and thrust him down on to one of the two remaining chairs. 'Godfrey, by then the mistress will be living on the street.'

Godfrey let out a low growl. 'I ain't living on no street.'

'Hasn't Sir Peter offered to take you with him?'

'Take me where?'

'Wherever he's going to?'

'The New World! I can't go there. I hate boats. Anyhow, I don't speak the language.'

'But you went riding out with Sir Peter in the dark, morning before last, am I right? Out of London. Just before dawn.'

'And what if I did? It's a free country.'

'Come on, old boy.' Alpiew decided to change tack. 'Let's clean up the kitchen together, and see if we can think of a way to keep hold of this place.'

For a few minutes they worked in silence, mopping up spilt wine, flour, feathers, peas and mouldy chutney.

'You know, Godfrey,' said Alpiew, dropping a large black lump of congealed mildewy marmalade into the rubbish sack. 'They could hang you for a footpad.'

'I ain't no footpad. We had horses.'

'So it *was* you?'

'I didn't say that. I don't know nothing about no highway robbery.'

'But you rode out on the Kensington Road, and beyond?'

'Yes, and we overtook a coach, an' Sir Peter, he said, "There's some friends o' mine. Let's stop while I go talk to 'em. You 'old the horses." ' Godfrey unstuck a piece of sucket from the flagstones and popped it into his mouth. 'So I did.'

'And?'

'And what?'

'What happened next?'

'Well, he told me to hold my hand out under my cloak, thus. This was meant to frighten off any robbers who might be lurking in the woods and take the horses while he was busy by the road.'

Alpiew looked at him and pictured it. In the dark, in the distance, it would have looked as though Godfrey was holding a musket under his cloak.

'And then?'

'Nothing. They had a little chat, then the gentleman gave Sir Peter some things for safe-keeping, he said, and we rode back here. And Sir Peter hid them, for safe-keeping, as he'd promised. And that's all I know.'

The Countess climbed the steps to the lawyer's office. She had decided on visiting John Cowley. Her own lawyer had died years ago. Too much port at lunch. And tea, and supper. She remembered Mrs Wilson saying Cowley was a genius at property law. And who knew, perhaps he would let something slip regarding the Wilson case while they were talking about unconnected business.

The lawyer sat at his desk, as before, scratching away at indentures and deeds with a quill.

The Countess sat demurely on the seat before him.

'What can I do for you, today, madam?' Cowley pushed the document he had just finished to one side.

'I believe you are a prodigy in the field of property?'

Cowley nodded. 'No more nosing about into other people's business?'

'It's my husband,' said the Countess, ignoring his rude remark. 'He has sold my house.'

Cowley nodded. 'And . . . ?'

'And I don't want to sell. It was given me by King Charles.'

'Under what agreement? A tenancy agreement? A leasehold?'

The Countess shook her head. 'I can't remember the exact details but it was for my lifetime.'

'It's almost certain that it wouldn't have been a free-hold. Charles only ever gave one freehold in St James's and that was in Pell Mell, to that actress with the big . . . oranges . . .'

'Nell Gwyn,' muttered the Countess. 'Trollop!'

'Even if it is a leasehold, I doubt there's any reason why your husband couldn't sell the remaining time.' He chuckled. 'And of course it would then be in the interests of the purchaser to keep you alive as long as possible.'

The Countess was scowling at him. He returned to doodling with the quill. 'And why did His Majesty give you such a gift?'

The Countess blushed. 'Because my husband deserted me.' Discretion was important in these matters, she knew. 'The King was a very generous man. Couldn't bear to see human suffering.'

'But your husband is back now?' Cowley was taking notes. 'How long since he returned?'

'A matter of days,' sighed the Countess. 'I knew he was a scoundrel. I cannot believe I have been taken for such a dupe.'

'The law says . . .'

The Countess snapped at him. 'I know what the law says. I want you to find something above the law.'

'Then I cannot help you.' Cowley lay down his pen. 'No one is above the law.'

'Even the King?' said the Countess.

'Interesting point, madam. I would say that the King is the law. But that is a different thing.'

The Countess stared at the mantelpiece in silence. She had to find a way to intimidate this man. The clock struck the half-hour. The clock! That was how she could frighten him. 'Nice clock, you've got, Mr Cowley.'

'Yes. It was a present.'

'Oh, really? From Mrs Wilson, by any chance.'

'No.' Cowley cocked his head. 'What makes you think that? It was given me by my apprentice. My footboy, Nathaniel.'

Well, thought the Countess, there was a rum explanation! 'You must pay him a great deal over the norm, Mr Cowley, if a footboy can afford a clock of such splendour.'

'The boy is practically my adopted son.' Cowley glanced at the clock and shifted uneasily in his chair. 'He used to work at the palace. Since he was an infant. He was given the clock by the Queen before she died. And last week he gave it to me. For my birthday.'

What a tale of a cock and bull! The Countess gave a polite smile and decided she had better look elsewhere for advice.

'I hear there were constables called to your house in the middle of the night.' Cowley leaned forwards. 'What was all that about?'

'I thought you might know.' The Countess eyed him. 'Some big fellow came in and started smashing up my kitchen, for no reason whatsoever. Luckily, the constables were returning my groom, who my husband had taken out purposely to get drunk.'

Cowley showed no reaction. 'Has your husband any . . .' He paused, raising his eyebrow, '. . . *tendencies* we might use to your advantage?'

'Oh, yes.' The Countess leant forwards and whispered. 'I believe him to be a highway robber.'

'Can you prove it?'

'He had a key to someone else's house.' She leaned

354

forwards again eagerly. 'Someone who had been robbed on the Kensington Road. He also had a kitchen jar full of jewels.'

'And where are they now?'

'With him.'

'And where is he?'

'How should I know? He ran off.'

Cowley toyed with the tip of the quill. 'But if we could find him . . .'

The Countess 'Yes . . . ?'

'We could get him arrested, and he would be unable to complete the legalities of the sale, and his power of attorney should pass to you.'

'Is that what they called a Tyburn Ticket?'

A slow smile spread across Cowley's face. 'I see what you mean. To save Mrs Wilson?'

The Countess had meant no such thing, but . . . if both things could be pulled off by the same action, then so be it.

Pigalle popped round with the locksmith. She left him tinkering at the door while she went into the kitchen to see Alpiew and Godfrey.

'Zut!' she cried, observing the disordered scene before her. 'It looks even worse by daylight.' She rolled up her sleeves. 'Godfrey, have you a hammer?'

Godfrey, still in a haze of tiredness and alcohol, was on his knees cutting pieces of marzipan from the flag-stones with a penknife. He looked up, came face to face with Pigalle in her black and gold mantua lined with black lace, her bright ginger hair piled high on her head, her white make-up fresh and flawless, her smiling blood-red lips framing yellow teeth, her long curled nails, and let out a blood-curdling scream. Pigalle slapped him across the face. 'You're hysterical, man, it's not so bad. I only want it to mend ze bed-post.'

Godfrey loped off towards the garden in search of tools.

'No help for zat, I'm afraid.' She tossed the splintered remains of a chair on to the fire, then cracked the remaining spars across her knee and tossed them into the log-basket.

The floor was strewn with broken crockery, Godfrey's books, pages from the Countess's old play and assorted papers which had flown around during the fight. 'So many papers! Why she keep all zese?' Pigalle knelt and started putting them into piles.

Alpiew wrung out the cloth in a basin of water. 'I hope that horrible lawyer gives her good advice.'

Pigalle sighed. 'It does not look good, I'm afraid.' She rustled through a pile of jam-smeared papers. 'One would have to go very high up to countermand ze sale. It's true what zat *raclure*, Sir Peter, says about husbands. Zat is why I have been so careful not to have one since I was widowed, mercifully young.' She pulled a sealed paper close to her face and screwed up her eyes. She pulled the letter open and scrutinised the writing for a moment. 'Whose is zis *billet doux*?' she called, tossing the letter across to Alpiew.

Alpiew took one look and tried to make little of it. It was one of the love-letters they had found at the lady's house in Acton. 'Oh, this. It belongs to my lady.'

'Really,' Pigalle's eyes were popping out of her head.

'I am amazed! I wouldn't have thought she was his type.'

Alpiew got up. 'You know who wrote this letter?'

Pigalle puffed a little, as though she was caught out in an indiscretion, and gave a Gallic shoulder shrug. 'Why yes, of course I do.'

Alpiew stood over her, hands on her hips. 'Well?'

'It was written by ze King.'

Alpiew didn't quite understand the implication. 'King Charles?'

'King Charles! Don't be ridiculous,' guffawed Pigalle. 'Zat old darlink has been rotting in his grave for years. No, ze *Petit Roi*, William.'

Alpiew snatched the letter from her and stared down at it.

'My darling secret, I adore you above all...' She turned the page over. 'Mr Roy!' she whispered. 'Of course. Roy. *Roi*. The *Petit Roi*.'

'The Dutch dwarf...' Pigalle snorted with distaste. 'How could she?'

'Oh, my God!' Alpiew grasped Pigalle's wrists. 'That's it. You have hit it! Mr Newton was right. It's all about the little King.'

Alpiew excused herself and begged Pigalle to guard the house in her absence, she had an urgent errand to run. Pigalle was all questions – how long had the Countess been getting love-letters from the King? How far had she gone with him? How had she kept it a secret all this time?

Alpiew explained, as vaguely as she could, that Pigalle had misunderstood. The Countess had possession of the letters, but they had not been written *to* her. Pigalle leapt up and down. 'Even better! Zey could save her. She could blackmail ze King to overturn the sale of ze house – it must be within his powers so to do.' Alpiew hesitated. It was a possibility. But then what of Mrs Wilson? Would she have to hang to save the Countess's house?

But Alpiew knew she was close to a solution now. Close to unravelling the thing that Beau had discovered and which had led to his murder. Mrs Wilson need not die.

'We can do nothing until the Countess returns,' said Alpiew, throwing on a cloak. 'Please excuse me. I will be back.'

She grabbed the attention of a cart driver in the Hay Market and persuaded him to let her ride on the back of his wagon for a small fee. Once comfortably wedged between bales of straw she pulled the equation from her pocket. Damn! She realised that she had left the list of meanings she had drawn up under her pillow in the Countess's kitchen. Still, most of it was in her head and easy enough to summon. She set to.

She was so absorbed she almost forgot to jump off at the Fleet Bridge. Picking up her skirts so she could run faster, she pushed her way past the women selling socks and furmity, nightcaps and pudding, and made her way up to the grille at the Fleet Prison. She had to talk to Mrs Wilson, ask her whether she or her husband had any dealings with the King, or for that matter anyone at court. On her knees she screeched into the grille from the pavement for about half an hour. She received many leering comments about her bosom, and offers of marriage, but no one responded to her calls for Mrs Elizabeth Wilson.

Alpiew was not going to give up that easily. There

were other ways of getting to the woman. She called through the wicket gate, banging it with her fists until a guard came and answered her. 'What do you want?' he snarled. 'Getting married or something?'

'No,' said Alpiew as demurely as she could. 'I have urgent business with the keeper.'

The guard raised his eyebrows. 'He knows about it, does he?'

Alpiew smiled. 'I'm sure if you tell him I am here, he will let me in.' She crossed her fingers and hoped to God she wouldn't be expected to give him sex, though the anticipation of it on his side might get her inside the prison.

The guard shuffled off, then returned and opened up. 'Know the way, do you?'

Alpiew smiled and pushed past him into the prison and the keeper's office.

'Mistress Alpiew,' the keeper beamed. He was sitting, fiddling with the buttons to his breeches, and obviously wanted to get straight down to business. Alpiew remained standing near the door.

'I need to speak to Mrs Elizabeth Wilson, on a matter of life and death.'

The keeper grinned, patting his lap. 'Of course, of course. Now let's have a little cuddle first, shall we?'

Alpiew shook her head. 'I speak to Mrs Wilson first, then a cuddle.'

The keeper pouted. 'No. Firkytoodle first, then you see Mrs Wilson.'

There was a knock on the door. 'Yes?' The keeper gave a grunt, and the door opened. A tipstaff was standing in the passageway.

'Wait one moment,' the keeper yelled, fastening his buttons.

Alpiew took the opportunity to walk out of the office. The keeper shouted after her: 'You can't see her, anyhow. She was taken away from here late last night.'

'Away?' Alpiew spun round. 'Where to?'

The keeper rose and put his hand out to grasp Alpiew's bottom. 'Newgate. They're getting her ready to take her up to Tyburn.'

'Tyburn!' shrieked Alpiew, removing his hand.

He nodded. 'To be executed. First light tomorrow.'

Jogged into cramps by the violent ride home in the coach as it ran along a street which was being re-cobbled, the Countess limped up to the front door and pushed. She had forgotten about Pigalle's plan with the locksmith, and banged her shoulder dreadfully. She looked around for the bell-pull, which she had never had occasion to use before. She found it and gave it a sharp tug. Inside she heard the dull thud of the rigged-up drum.

She waited a few moments. No one came. Well, this was a pretty pickle! Locked out of her own home. She called through the letter box.

'Alpiew! Godfrey! It's me, your mistress. Open up, at once.'

A few minutes later a very dusty Pigalle turned the key and pulled the door open.

'Why didn't you tell me you 'ad zat thing for a bell?' growled Pigalle, who, hearing the banging, took it for Sir Peter or Scum trying to break the front door down and had flung herself under Godfrey's bed for shelter.

'It's solved!' The Countess wafted in. 'If we can find my husband.'

Pigalle rolled her kohl-lined eyes. 'Pick up ze nearest stone,' she muttered. 'Or look in any cess-pit.'

'The important thing is not to let him in here, in case he takes possession. Where's Godfrey?'

'Gone out,' snapped Pigalle. 'To dispose of ze rubbish.'

'And Alpiew?'

'On what she called important business.' Pigalle picked up the glass of wine to which she had helped herself. 'So, now we are alone, you can tell me all about him?'

'Who?' The Countess removed her cloak and gloves and sat down. Pigalle fetched her a glass too. 'Don't be so mysterious! King William, of course.'

The Countess spluttered her mouthful of wine back into the glass. 'You know perfectly well what I make of that priggish little Hollandaise.'

'So why do you have his love-letters?'

The Countess blinked and re-ran Pigalle's question in her mind. 'Take it a little more slowly, Olympe, I am mystified.'

Pigalle explained about the letter she had found while clearing up and how she had recognised the writing.

'Oh!' The Countess looked around trying to see them. 'The Acton letters.'

'Acton?' shrieked Pigalle. 'What about Acton?'

The Countess did not want to explain the story any further to Pigalle. 'It was blowing along the road, near Kensington Palace. Alpiew saw it and picked it up, hoping it might be money.'

Pigalle was deflated. The Countess tried to divert the

subject matter a little. 'That day in Acton, Pigalle. Wasn't it funny?'

'Zat frightful woman, going on and on about her dresses,' squealed Pigalle 'Have you ever heard anything like it?'

The Countess shook her head. 'Not since Monsieur.'

'Monsieur who?'

'Le Grand Monsieur, you remember: King Louis's brother.'

'Oh, *Monsieur*!' screeched Pigalle. 'Poncing around Versailles with his powdered cheeks and eyelashes stuck together with blackener.'

'And his clothes plastered with diamonds!'

'And for all zat,' said Pigalle, sticking her tongue into her cheek. 'What about l'Abbé?'

'Oh, l'Abbé!' the Countess howled. 'Do you remember in the confessional? You'd be kneeling there, peeling off your sins and, glinting through the gauze, you could quite clearly see his diamond earrings.'

'Ah!' sighed both women in contented unison. 'Men!'

'Talking of which, I must rush away now, darlink, or I will be late. I have a meeting with a dressmaker at my house for an hour, then I am meeting a trader in ze piazza. He is going to sell me a pair of marmosets to replace my poor George.'

'George?'

'My squirrel who died, darlink. You remember? My darlink George.' She kissed the Countess, leaving a scarlet gash of paint on her cheek.

*   *   *

Alpiew scuttled along the City street, ploughing through mud puddles and lumps of congealed ordure. The thaw had begun. Everything was brown with mud. A flock of sheep was crossing Warwick Lane on their way to the Newgate Market. She pushed past the street food stalls, and women with trays screaming their wares. She was going to Newgate Prison to see what she could discover. She side-stepped a big hole in the road and collided with the large frame of a tall man. 'Sorry!' she exclaimed and pressed on. But a heavy hand fell on her shoulder.

She looked up. It was Scum.

She started to run. He loped along behind her.

Alpiew darted in and out of the traffic, nipping round food stalls. Every now and then he caught up and grabbed at her clothing. She dived down an alleyway, knocking a porter carrying a head-high pile of baskets to the floor, effectively blocking the way. But, after a crunch and a mouthful of invective from the porter, she heard those heavy footsteps pounding behind her again. Alpiew took a sharp turn down an even smaller passage, squeezing past mounds of rubbish. The footsteps stopped. Perhaps he had fallen, or given up. Keeping up her speed she leapt out into the main road.

And there Scum stood, in front of her, grinning, pushing her back into the passage with his huge blunt fingertips. 'Got a message for you.' He leant forward and grabbed her by the ribbons at her cleavage. 'Back off on the Wilson case. Let what is ordained come to pass.'

Alpiew wiggled a bit and tried to run, but using his other hand he simply leaned forward and seized her by the arm. Then, letting go of the ribbons, he grabbed her hand and splayed out her fingers. 'I could break each one of these.' He made a sudden movement causing the bones in one finger to emit a loud crack. Alpiew screamed.

Passers by turned and stared. 'Who hasn't been troubled with a bothersome wife?' he yelled at them with a grin. They walked on. Alpiew spat in his face. Leaving the saliva to drip slowly down his rough cheek, he bent and whispered into her ear. His head was so close that she could feel his hot wet lips against her skin. 'Did you hear what I said, Mistress Alpiew?'

Alpiew nodded and tried to look penitent. 'Yes. I'll leave it alone.'

He pulled his lips back into a lazy but terrifying smile. 'Good.' He did not let go his grip of her.

Alpiew decided: nothing ventured, nothing gained. 'You should be in prison,' she stated. 'How did you break free?'

'I didn't break anything.' Scum let forth a sneering laugh. 'I was released by legal warrant.'

Alpiew's face betrayed her puzzlement. Scum was proud of the effect he was having. 'Friends arranged it for me. Important friends,' he leered. 'Ancient law, called Benefit of Clergy.' He clacked his teeth together, then wiped his hands down his jacket, as though touching Alpiew had dirtied them. He reached forwards and pinched her chin between his finger and thumb. 'Cheer up, sulky-puss!' He turned and strolled away.

Alpiew considered for a moment sneaking after him, trying to tail him, to find out where he lived, anything that might lead her to his mistress. But it was too dangerous. With no one who knew where she was, and less than a day to Mrs Wilson's execution, Alpiew decided to stick to her original plan.

She hurried along in the direction of the prison. She knew no one here, and there was no convenient grille through which to contact prisoners. She hollered through the wicket gate but no one came. She walked round, amazed at the elaborate decoration of the outer walls: Tuscan pilasters, statues, elaborate battlements. A nearby clock showed that it was nearing the end of lunch-time, officers would be coming and going again soon. She stood close to the gate, trying to squeeze her face into the gaps in the great ironwork to get a better look inside. There was a tap on her shoulder. Terrified it would be Scum come to give her a second warning, she let out an involuntary scream, and leapt about six inches in the air.

'Bless you, my child, of what are you so frighted?' It was a priest.

'Oh, Reverend, I am so sorry.' Alpiew couldn't remember going to church once in her life, but had watched with beady eyes how women treated priests. She inclined her head towards the floor, and forced a tear into her eye. 'I need your succour, sir, for my cousin, an elegant lady, is inside, and due to die tomorrow, and I needs must speak with her about a grave matter.'

'And what would that be, maid?' The priest pulled a bell-rope which Alpiew had not noticed.

Alpiew's mind raced. What would a priest believe worthy of aid? All prisoners must try the wrongly accused tack. She knew that would not work.

A lumbering turnkey was busily unlocking the padlocks to the two giant bolts.

'The welfare of her children, sir, who will become orphans tomorrow.'

The turnkey slid the bolts across and rattled about with

his enormous ring of keys, trying to locate the correct one for the main lock.

'Truly, child, I am engaged to preach to those doomed to die tomorrow. Perhaps you would carry my prayer book for me?'

Alpiew saw the ploy he was suggesting. She grabbed the book and bowed her head.

The turnkey looked them both over. 'Who's this?' He was pointing at Alpiew with his key.

'This, my friend, is a penitent sinner who is obliging me for the day by assisting me, carrying my goods, etcetera. May we pass? Or I shall be late.'

The turnkey grunted and let them through.

As they walked through the stinking rooms crowded with felons and debtors of all ages and types, the priest spoke. 'You were lucky I am standing in today. The prison's own ordinary is ill.' The priest looked around. 'And living in this squalor, no wonder. They sent for me this morning to fill his place until he recovers.'

Another turnkey let them through into the Press Yard. 'It's a bad business, this ceremony. No one pays much respect. Last time I was here, during the service a number of prisoners strutted through and relieved themselves in the chapel, so that there was an evil smell all around us.'

A dog belonging to one of the prisoners came up and sniffed at Alpiew's skirt. She pushed it away, chickens scattering in the wake of the dog.

'Of late the governor has made a healthy trade in offering tickets to the public, who for some reason crave to see people who know they are about to die.' He nodded to the turnkey to open up the chapel. 'I do not permit such a thing when I officiate.'

They were let through into the chapel. An empty coffin was laid out in the centre of the room, and gathered around it, within a railed enclosure, sat a handful of poor souls who, from the expression on their faces, were the condemned prisoners.

Alpiew saw Mrs Wilson at once and went to sit behind her.

The priest took the prayer book and went up to the altar.

'To those of you condemned to die, I say to you: repent,' he declaimed, opening the book and laying it before him on an ornate oak lectern.

'What is happening?' hissed Mrs Wilson. 'What is Cowley playing at?'

'I need to know a few things,' whispered Alpiew. 'First, do you or did your husband have any dealings with the King?'

'Are you mad?' Mrs Wilson span round. 'If I knew the King, don't you think I would have appealed to him first for clemency?'

'Second, when did your husband start acting strangely?'

'January,' said Mrs Wilson. 'The start of January.'

In the pause while Alpiew tried to remember what other questions to ask, the priest rattled on: '. . . so by continual mortifying our corrupt affections we may be buried with him; and that through the grave, and gate of death, we may pass to our joyful resurrection'

'Do you know anyone living in Acton?'

Mrs Wilson looked Alpiew up and down. 'What is this? Are you trying, by making up these bizarre questions, to make me think you deserve paying anyway, even though you are letting me go to my death for something I did not do?'

Alpiew pressed on. She didn't want to remind Mrs Wilson that she herself had pled guilty to the crime. 'Do you know anybody living in Acton?'

Mrs Wilson shook her head.

'. . . wise men also die,' droned the priest, 'and perish together: as well as the ignorant and foolish, and leave their riches for other. And yet they think that their houses shall continue for ever: and that their dwelling-places shall endure from one generation to another . . .'

'Do you trust your lawyer?'

'Cowley?' said Mrs Wilson. 'I've known him since I was a child. Though after this debacle I wouldn't recommend him in criminal cases.'

'Did you know that he has taken various items from your house?'

Mrs Wilson's face clouded. 'Has he indeed? To cover his costs, I suppose.' She let out a deep sigh. 'Most important that a lawyer should not be put in danger of starvation. It's a pity he has done so little work for his fee.'

'He has your clock on his mantelpiece.'

'Well, better that than it is claimed by the state. I have no children, no heirs. Despite Beau's powders. And no relatives. I had only my husband. Now I have nothing. And tomorrow . . .' Her head fell forward and tears rolled down her cheeks. 'I will cease to be.'

'They lie in the hell like sheep, death gnaweth upon them, and the righteous shall have domination over them in the morning . . .'

'Do you know of anything that will happen in mid September?'

'Why should I care about a future I will not see?'

'Mrs Wilson, please try to help me. There is still a chance. I feel so near to finding out the key to the secret you need to save your life, but you have to help me.'

'. . . Such as sit in darkness, and in the shadow of death: being fast bound in misery and iron; Because they rebelled against the words of the Lord: and lightly regarded the counsel of the most Highest; He also brought down their heart through heaviness: they fell down, and there was none to help them . . .'

'Listen to the priest, Mrs Wilson. There *is* someone who can help you, and it is me . . .'

'Minister,' cried Mrs Wilson, rising from her pew, 'please take this wretched woman away. She is only trying to sell my story for a broadsheet to be printed and sold at Tyburn tomorrow.'

'A grub street hack!' The priest lowered. 'Never have I been so deceived. Out of my chapel now! You vermin on the dung-heap of life.'

Alpiew tried to plead her case but two burly gaolers had picked her up and were carrying her out before she could open her mouth. They dumped her with no ceremony on the street.

FIFTEEN

Coagulation

*The conversion of a thin liquid into
a solid mixture through some inner change,
by the addition of some other substance, by heating or
cooling. For example, the curdling of milk.*

When Pigalle had gone the Countess fiddled about, straightening this and putting that back into place. She poked at the fire and cut herself a slab of bread to make some toast. She prayed she would win this battle and keep the house. But where to find Sir Peter? She could send Godfrey into every whorehouse in London, but who was to say that Godfrey wouldn't be seduced by his treats and promises and betray her again?

She took a bite of toast and flopped down on to the bed. Where was Alpiew? What was she out doing that was so urgent?

And what was it that Pigalle had said about the love-letters they'd retrieved from the camomile garden out in Acton being from the King? The King indeed! Writing love-letters to that awful woman. It put a whole new slant on things. She had almost convinced herself that the mysterious Mr Roy had been Sir Peter, and now it seems it was the King. But if Mrs Roy's weekend and night-time husband was the King, where did Beau Wilson fit in to the scene, and who had killed him? And why?

She shuddered at the thought of the blood that night in the churchyard dripping from her hands. The thought drew her naturally to the blood-stained dress they had found in Mrs Roy's garde de robe.

She sat up in horror. Of course. That was it! The whole thing was political. Something to do with the King. Perhaps Mrs Roy had not killed Beau, but, even if she had, the dress proved nothing. What if the blood soaked through that peach dress was Mrs Roy's own life-blood? That would explain why the woman had disappeared so suddenly. Alpiew had said there was no rent in the dress. But the hole made by a stiletto blade or rapier would be so small perhaps Alpiew had missed it. Beau and Mrs Roy had both stumbled on a secret concerning the King, and some secret lover of his, and as a result they had both been killed. Mrs Roy probably was murdered out at Acton and her body cut up and flung in the river for all they knew.

The Countess plumped up the pillow. Something was peeking out underneath it. It was Alpiew's list of possible explanations of Beau's fatal code.

She decided to take a stab at solving the thing for good and all.

☉: Easy. This was just a warning to Betty, that the message which followed was astonishing. Promising dangerous change. Nigredo. Caput Mortem, the skull. Gloom and decay.

☿ Mercury and Venus. Or quicksilver and copper. But that seemed unlikely after what Mr Newton had said. Or Wednesday and Friday. But that was simply ridiculous.

♂ Conjunction. A getting together, lying closely with.

♌ The Little King. Regulus. The Lion's Heart. Cor Basilisk.

So, that must mean that someone was lying with the King. They certainly had one side of the letters to prove that.

☿ Well that was easy enough. Equals.

☿ That too. Chaos.

(♂/☉) Another mystifying one. Mars and Venus. Or the unlikely amalgam of iron and copper. Or Tuesday and Friday. Bracketed with the little circle with the dot in the middle. Maybe another little sun or gold or king.

(☉/♄) The large circle, and that was certainly gold, or the Sun, or indeed, the King. Together with the cross, poison or checkmate – the king is dead, the game is over. So it must be king. Something to do with the death of the King.

The Countess shook her head, and scratched under her wig. How confusing. It was like one of the puzzles in the newspaper the ladies at Versailles were always doing to pass the time. The Countess looked up from the sheet of paper. Now there was an idea for the Cues: she and Alpiew could put a puzzle into the paper to amuse London ladies.

It would be worth pressing on with this one just to bide the time, and see if she could solve it alone and pick up the knack of how to set such a conundrum.

♁ Then sublimation. A pox on these terms from the hermetic arts!

@ ♂ ♎ And finally a rush of common sense: at the

eclipse in the sign of Libra, which was due on 12 September of this year 1699.

Taking the most human interpretation of all this it read: Watch out! Mercury and Venus lie together with the little king. This equals Chaos. Mars and Venus with the little circle with dot.

'One minute!' The Countess pulled at her chin. Hadn't the herald said something about those little circles? It looks like a little sun, and in that lunatic world of heraldry where creative abuse of the homonym rules, that would pass for little *son*. And the symbol meant, in heraldic terms, the only surviving child.

She applied herself again to the paper. Mars and Venus, the only surviving child.

She spat. 'What utter rot!'

She moved along to the second bracket. The King. The King is dead, the game is over.

That wretched sublimation again. At the September eclipse.

Perhaps if she could free the thing of experimental philosophy it would make sense. Sublimation, for a start. What did that mean in ordinary terms? To make sublime, to elevate, to raise above the ordinary, to come to fruition. That must be it. So the whole business was due to come to a climax in September.

She flopped back on to the bed again and put her fingers to her temples with a sigh. What whole business? She was none the wiser.

Alpiew picked herself up from the cobbles outside Newgate and wondered what to do next. There was so little time. Even though Mrs Wilson was so unpleasant to her, Alpiew knew she was very near a solution and was determined to save her. Then she would need to deal with the Countess and the mess *she* was in with that wretched husband of hers, but first Alpiew decided to take the short walk to the lawyer, John Cowley. He could make a last-minute plea to the King for pardon, or leniency or whatever might work. She might even get him to help her with the sale of the house.

'Alpiew?'

Alpiew looked up to see her old friend Simon, dressed in a very fancy livery, standing before her, beaming from ear to ear and clutching a fistful of large white ostrich feathers.

'Lord, Simon, you made me jump out of my seven senses.' She looked him up and down. 'What sort of rum-togged cove have you become, boy?'

'I got myself a job at the palace.'

'St James's?'

'No, Kensington.'

'How did you manage that?' Alpiew knew that Simon had no contacts in that world.

'Lots of the old workers left. There's been some rumpus about lost perquisites and so on. But what you've never had ... I'm very glad to get paid for doing anything, without getting free meals or old candle-stumps and the like.'

'What do you do there?'

'I work for the Lord Chamberlain. I am runner to the Page of the Privy Wardrobe.'

'The what?'

'I work under the groom, who answers directly to the

yeoman, and he to the gentleman, and he to the sergeant and he to the Lord Chamberlain himself.'

'And who does he report to?'

Simon looked worried. He had not thought that far up.

'I'm only joking, Simon.' She looked at the nodding bunch of ostrich feathers. 'I suppose they are part of the job?'

'Indeed yes, Alpiew,' the boy said with some pride. 'I am third in command with special responsibility for the purchasing and primping of ornamental feathers.'

A rough carter swiped past, almost breaking the lolling plumes from their spines. Simon whisked them out of danger. 'If I lost these I'd be a ruined man,' he said. 'They cost a fortune, and if they get damaged while in my care I'll have to replace them out of my own money. I'm taking them down to the Royal Wardrobe in Savoy to be dyed and then up to St James's, where I curl them, and dust them, and sew them on to royal hats.'

'I hope you get paid well for this, Simon.'

'Not really. I got better paid working as a pot-boy in Covent Garden. But I do get accommodation and this livery, and at least I'm not working under the Laundress to the Royal Body, or the Strewer of Herbs, or the Rat-Killer, the Mole-Taker, or the Keeper of the Fowl.' The boy looked so earnest and proud of himself, Alpiew decided against making any of the obvious jokes. 'You don't ever see the King himself, do you?'

Simon shrieked with laughter. 'Of course not. Never. But if I work my way up, I may, one day.'

'Would you do me a favour, Simon? When you pass my lady's house in German Street, will you just tell her

I'm paying a visit to Cowley, the lawyer, and then I'll be home. Tell her I've not deserted her.'

'Is something wrong?'

'Oh yes, almost everything.' Alpiew shook her head. 'But it would take far too long to explain.' She planted a big kiss on Simon's cheek. 'I know where to contact you now, at least.'

With a wave Simon trotted off on his way, feathers bouncing before him.

The Countess was still poring over Alpiew's notes. The afternoon was rolling on and she had to light a candle to see properly.

If only she could work it out.

She started again.

Mercury/Venus gets close to the little king; Wednesday/Friday gets close to the little king; Quicksilver/copper gets close to the little king.

'What piffle!' she said aloud to the ceiling, and tossed the wretched paper to the floor, flung her feet up on the bed and lay down. She stared at the familiar white-washed walls and sighed. This might be the last night she would ever spend in her beloved house.

She knew that lawyer Cowley was a no-good, hopeless, money-grabbing swine. They all were. What about that clock? Had he taken it from the Wilson house, or had the footboy, trying to curry favour, taken it while preparing the inventory and then given it to Cowley, or were they both in it together. Lawyers! She wouldn't put any filching twist beyond them.

She looked around the kitchen and felt desperately sad.

She had been happy here. She didn't want to leave, and she knew that there would be no going back. How could she stop her husband, especially when she didn't even know where he was or how to find him? It was too depressing.

Thank God for Alpiew. Even Godfrey seemed loyal again. Though he of course had got them into this mess by bringing that dreadful man here in the first place. But she herself had not helped the situation. How had she fallen for all that sweet talk again? Oh, to be a widow, like Pigalle.

Dear Pigalle! How funny she was with her talk of Monsieur and all those men at Versailles who insisted on dressing in women's clothes, and spoke endlessly about fashions and fabrics and perfumes and make-up and undergarments, and all the things a real woman never thinks about. Except for that ghastly Mrs Roy, of course.

She sat up faster than if she had been bitten in the behind by a rabid dog.

Like Mrs Roy. That was it! Mrs Roy was very tall, had good strong arms, as the fishing expedition had proved, and talked non-stop about every detail of her clothes. Something a real woman *never* does. There was only one explanation. Mrs Roy was not a Mrs at all. Mrs Roy was a Mr.

Alpiew opened the lawyer's door and skipped up the stairs. It was dark. A man passed her on the stairs. He carried a bundle of papers, and had the contented look of someone going home at the end of a day's work.

For a brief moment she thought she got a waft of that

scent again. Lily of the valley and musk. On the landing she knocked.

After a swift rustling of papers Cowley's voice called her in.

'Ah, Mistress Alpiew.' He was sitting behind the desk as before, picking his fingernails with the point of his quill. 'What can I do for you? Is it more nonsense about Benefit of Clergy you're after? Or your mistress and her highwayman husband? Ha!'

Alpiew remained standing. 'I don't know about nonsense, but I do think it pretty unpardonable that you are going to let an innocent woman go to the gallows, while you sit here picking at your nails.'

'Calm yourself, Mistress Alpiew. What is there to do? The woman has told the Justice she is responsible for her husband's death. Who else could be guilty of the crime? And why? Tell me why anyone other than the wife would want to kill the errant husband who we know was whittling away her fortune?'

Alpiew glanced down at Mr Cowley's desk. On his blotter was a scribbled note. Alpiew thought she had seen the handwriting before but could not be sure. She needed to get a closer look.

'And what of Betty?'

Cowley bristled. 'Betty who?'

'Mr Wilson's maid, Betty. She was killed too, in his elaboratory.'

'What do you know of the elaboratory, and who says Betty is dead? Nobody has told me so!' He started shuffling papers and shoving them into drawers in his desk. 'Perhaps *she* was the other woman, and Mrs Wilson is guilty of murdering her too.'

378

'That is impossible. Mrs Wilson was in prison when Betty was murdered.'

'You keep saying Betty was murdered, but where is the body? And why are the Justices not informed?'

'I know where the body is. I have seen it. It is in Beau Wilson's elaboratory.'

Cowley glanced towards the window. 'If you say so. Although I very much doubt you know where the elaboratory is, as nobody has found it.' It was dark outside. His candle guttered as he coughed. 'So what is your line on this pair of gruesome murders? Who do you think is the killer? Jack o' Lantern?'

'I know of no such person, sir,' said Alpiew.

'There *is* no such person.' Cowley laughed, throwing back his head. 'It is a word for a delusion, for the thing which rises from the marshes, you can see it, but it is always two steps ahead of you. But you can never catch it, because it is merely a flame-like gas of phosphorus.'

Alpiew froze at the mention of phosphorus. 'You knew Beau Wilson practised alchymy, did you not?'

'Maybe I did.' Cowley did not move. 'What of it?'

'Who else did you tell about that?'

Cowley pouted. 'No one.'

'You are lying, Mr Cowley. Beau Wilson came to you to ask you to help him find a sponsor, did he not, for that alchymical work? So who did you come up with to finance him?'

'I really don't know what you're trying to prove.' Cowley rose and turned to inspect the bookshelf behind his chair. 'Yes, Wilson did come to me, but I gave him the advice he should have been given. To stop it at once. To give it up and concentrate on his trade.'

'Did *you* give him money? Was that it?'

Cowley ignored her, moving stacks of papers from shelf to shelf. While his back was turned Alpiew took the opportunity to get a good look at the familiar handwriting on his blotter. It was a clumsy uneven scrawl. But she knew right away where she'd seen it before – in the list they found at Acton and in those words written on the back of the apothecary's bill: '*Alles Mist*'. Everything is shit.

'Mr Cowley, you *did* give Beau Wilson money for his alchymy, didn't you? And he lost it all?'

Cowley spun round, his face purple with rage. 'Yes. I gave him some money, and when he came back for more I told him no. And what business is it of yours?'

'*Alles Mist* – what does that mean?'

'The office is now closed, Mrs Alpiew.' Cowley, beads of sweat glistening on his forehead, pointed to the door behind her. 'Maybe you would like to make your way out, and if you have any further insinuations to make you may come back when I reopen in the morning.'

'You employed that actor Jack Fry to frighten us, didn't you? The man who Beau so aptly named Scum.' Alpiew moved closer to the window. 'And it was you who managed to get him released from prison on the pretext of Benefit of Clergy. How did you do that? The man is an illiterate. Just like Mrs Wilson. He cannot read.'

'He's an actor.' Cowley smiled. 'He has a knack of picking up lines. It doesn't take long to get the 51st psalm into a man's head, and then he can pretend to read it.'

Alpiew was aghast. She had hit it. 'You really did get Jack Fry freed to come chasing after me?'

'The man seems unpleasant, I'll grant you, but it is

not in a lawyer's brief to pick and choose his clients.' Cowley returned to his chair, obviously making a considerable effort to remain calm now. 'I did *not* employ him to come and burst into your house. I would be a pretty poor lawyer if I paid a client to commit a crime and then defended his right to freedom.'

'But you did get him freed, using the ridiculous plea of Benefit of Clergy?'

'I was asked to represent him and I did so, very successfully, and may I say I have your mistress to thank for the idea. Benefit of Clergy is an ancient plea and not one much thought of these days.'

The Countess was nodding off. She had stared at the symbols of the code for so long she was almost cross-eyed. The fire was warm, and she leant back to have a snooze.

A sudden thundering at the door abruptly woke her. She leapt up, frightened that it was her husband, or the potential buyers come to shoo her out of her own home. Or maybe it was another bully boy, like that dreadful man last night. She was terrified and wished Alpiew was here to protect her. Where had she got to this late of an afternoon?

The Countess tiptoed along the hall, staying close to the walls for security. It took her some time to find her way in the gloom. She stood by the door and listened. She could hear someone breathing on the other side. She tried to peek through the keyhole, but all she could see was a man's hand and what looked like a bunch of ostrich plumes. The hand disappeared and there was another rap on the door. The Countess leapt away from the keyhole.

'Is someone there?' called a man's voice which she did not recognise. 'Anyone at home?'

The man lingered for a moment or two and then seemed to depart.

The Countess stood trembling in the dark until the footsteps retreated. Whoever it was had got bored of waiting. But the whole episode had put her into a terrible fright, and she decided she had had enough of being alone here. She pulled on her cloak and headed for Pigalle's, hoping she was not too late.

As she stepped out into the street Pigalle's coach clattered by.

'Olympe,' she screamed.

Pigalle popped her head out and signalled the driver to stop. 'Hop in, darlink. I should be glad of ze company.'

'I was frightened.' The Countess hauled herself up into the coach. 'Someone was hammering at the door.'

'But you are all right?' She looked the nodding Countess up and down. 'Zat is good. Now you can help me choose my marmoset.'

As the coach approached Covent Garden the traffic became unendurable. It was all but stationary for a good half-hour. Pigalle huffed and puffed. 'If I have to gaze on ze tombstones in zat churchyard one minute longer, I will need one myself.' She thumped on the roof of the carriage. 'I will walk ze rest,' she cried and, hoiking her skirts up, thrust a red-stockinged leg from the carriage door. 'Come along, Ashby, darlink!'

The Countess tumbled out into the bustling street alongside the churchyard where she had stumbled over

Beau's body, and followed Pigalle, who was pushing her way through the crowds in Bedford Street, trying to reach Henrietta Street.

On the corner a pair of white-faced idiots were juggling and had attracted a crowd. Cursing, Pigalle ploughed through them, the Countess at her heels. 'Street entertainers,' she cried at the top of her voice, 'should be banned.' Having passed the audience for the jugglers, Pigalle bumped into another crush of spectators, this time ogling a Punch and Judy show. 'My God, how primitive are you in zis country?' she exclaimed to no one in particular. She strode forward to the booth and tugged at the puppet, pulling it clean off, leaving just the puppeteer's hand waving about. The crowd around her booed and she tossed the puppet into the air. 'Since ze piazza has been turned into a circus, it is impossible to get anywhere,' she squawked in the Countess's direction. 'Go home.' She turned on the crowd. 'Make some space for honest pedestrians to walk.'

Pigalle jostled through the mob, the Countess trotted along behind. This was the same street she had trotted along to get into St Paul's churchyard that fateful night. The very same street where Beau's murderer had vanished into thin air. Somewhere in this street she was sure the answer must lie. It was impossible that the woman in the churchyard could have got away without passing either herself or Alpiew unless she had hidden in one of these buildings, waiting for the coast to clear.

Tradesmen carrying stacks of baskets on their heads blocked her way, prostitutes calling their wares even though it was only dusk, shouldered her out of their path, link-boys were lighting up in preparation for the night.

Pigalle was well ahead and almost out of sight. The Countess tried to jostle nearer.

A child bolted between the Countess's legs and got caught up in her voluminous skirt. She stooped to shout at him, but then saw who it was.

'Mustafa! My dear boy, how are you?' The boy was not in his usual costume of satin and silk, but in the brown tweedy clothes he wore at Acton. Acton! He could lead her to Mrs Roy, or should she say, Mr Roy. 'Remember me?'

The boy tried to make a run for it but the Countess grabbed him by the collar. He was the missing link, and here he stood practically on the spot where the crime had been committed. 'Shall I buy you some sweetmeats?' she cooed, before calling out to Pigalle, who did a smart U-turn when she saw who the Countess had collared. 'Pigalle! It is our little friend Mustafa. We are going to buy him some sweetmeats.'

'Zat's right,' cried Pigalle, holding him by the hand. 'We will go to ze sweetmeat stall, and you shall choose anything you like.'

'But my mother!' cried the lad. 'I am on an errand for her.'

'Where does your mother live, darling?' The Countess stooped to talk to the boy.

'Whatever it is she wants, she shall have it,' Pigalle cooed. 'But I will pay. What does she need?'

The child pointed to an upper storey of a house across the road on the southern side of Henrietta Street.

'She wants some sucket. She is feeling sick, you see, because she is going to have a baby.'

'And you both live up above the Rummer Tavern, is

that right?' The Countess looked with horror at the seething public house, which, from the signs dangling outside and the look on the faces of the men passing in and out, obviously doubled as a seedy bagnio. 'Tell me, where is the lady you worked for before?'

The child wriggled out of the Countess's grasp and tried to make a dash for it. But Pigalle caught him in her talons and stooped to whisper to the child. 'I have a secret. Do you like little marmosets?' The boy's eyes lit up and he nodded. 'I am going to buy two, and whenever you want, you can come and play with zem. But you must help me choose.' She put out her hand as though to make a handsel with the boy to close a business deal. Mustafa understood and slapped her hand with his dear chubby little fingers.

The Countess at once noticed scratches on his skin. She patted the boy's head. 'You shall have a lovely present, and so shall your blessed mother.' She exchanged a look with Pigalle.

The Countess spoke quietly to Pigalle. 'Take the child for his presents. I will wait in the Rummer till you return.' She glanced in the direction of the tavern. 'I will take a drink and you come and fetch me when you've done your business with the marmoset man.'

Pigalle strode along in the direction of the piazza, the little moor trotting along at her side, gripping her hand, while the Countess plunged into the seedy tavern.

Alpiew knew she was close to something. Cowley was looking very uncomfortable. And he was sweating. Alpiew could smell it.

'Mr Cowley, you cannot let Mrs Wilson go to her death if you know of anything that might save her. It would be tantamount to murder.'

Cowley shrugged. 'I wouldn't worry too much about Mrs Wilson's welfare, if I were you.'

Alpiew pressed on. 'Who do you really think killed Beau Wilson?'

'Mrs Wilson.'

'And who killed Betty?'

'How should I know? I didn't know she was dead until you told me. Maybe it was a jealous alchymist.'

Alpiew decided to change tack. 'Do you have a customer who owns a house in Acton?'

Cowley blushed, shaking his head.

'So she's dead then? Am I right? Is Mrs Roy dead too? Did you kill her?'

'Mrs Roy is not dead,' said Cowley. 'She is in a delicate state and is in hiding.'

'So you *do* know Mrs Roy?'

'She is a client, yes. But I have never met her. She corresponds.'

Cowley was stabbing at his desk with the tip of his quill, and he kept glancing at the mantelpiece clock. 'Look at the time. I will be last out, and have to lock up the whole building if you don't leave me alone and go home.'

'When I asked you if you had a customer living in Acton you shook your head. Why are you lying?'

'You're trying to trip me up, now, Mistress Alpiew.'

Alpiew fumbled in her pocket. 'What do you know of the relationship between Mrs Roy and the King?'

'Again, you leave me in a maze. I have no dealings

with His Majesty, nor do I know of any relationship between my client and our sovereign.'

Alpiew had dug out Beau's receipt. 'And when Beau Wilson was getting too deeply into debt, you declined to help him?'

Cowley rose and moved across to the rear doorway, as though preparing for a hasty exit into the back room. 'I must lock up. You really have to leave now. If you have any more ridiculous questions, come back in the morning.' He stood facing Alpiew, his back touching the curtain that divided the room.

'Answer my question, Mr Cowley. You refused to help Mr Wilson when he came to you for money?'

'Yes,' said Cowley. 'I told you that I did.'

'And to put him off, you wrote these words on the invoice you were returning to him, unpaid.'

Alpiew held out the invoice for the antimony, with, scribbled across the back, in the spidery scrawl, the words *Alles Mist.*

'Ah yes, *Alles Mist.*' Cowley glanced down. 'No. I did not write that, but there I can help you, those two words were written by –' His mouth fell open and he stared strangely at Alpiew. 'I . . . I . . .' He seemed to freeze, his face the only part of him moving, finally contorting into a mad grimace.

'Mr Cowley?' Alpiew was frightened. He had gone a strange colour and Alpiew feared that some over-heating of the brain might turn him mad and that he would attack her. She took a step back.

With a sudden jolt, John Cowley started jerking, as though in an apoplexy. Then he slumped, slowly, silently to the floor.

Across the centre of the dividing curtain, where John Cowley's back had been, there was a large, red, slowly-spreading stain.

John Cowley had been stabbed in the back. And John Cowley was now very dead indeed.

No amount of questioning the staff at the Rummer Tavern elicited any information about the moorish child and his mother. And when she asked about tall, well-dressed ladies, the Countess received only a guffaw from the landlord. She made one attempt to creep upstairs, but was put off by the number of men lurking in the stairwell cat-calling and whistling at every woman who passed. Also, because it was a tall house, each storey no doubt crammed with rooms housing different families, the Countess decided to wait till Pigalle and the boy came back before exploring. Without further information it would take too long to find Mustafa's mother.

She sat down with a bumper of wine to wait for his return.

' 'Ow much for a fumble?' A filthy man with only two teeth leered down at her.

'You mistake me, sir.' The Countess shot him a withering look. 'I am no whore.'

As the man slouched off, the Countess plunged her hand into her pocket and pulled out the papers Alpiew had prepared about the page from Beau Wilson's log-book. In order to make sure she was not approached again she decided to busy herself with the code.

⊙: ♀ ♂ ♒ = ☿ (♂♀ /☉) (☉/♄) ♎ @ ♂ ♎

Right, thought the Countess. It is almost solved. There were only four symbols which did not make sense in a human way, and those were spaced so closely together they could pass for two. The Countess drew them on the back of a used sheet: ☿♀ and ♂♀.

'Mercury plus Venus, Mercury plus Venus,' she repeated out loud. 'Mercury plus Venus. Quicksilver plus Venus.' She sighed, and looked up. Some of the clientele were giving her strange looks. Good, she thought. If they think I'm mad they'll keep a wide berth. 'Venus, Venus, Venus. Goddess of Love.' She looked down at the paper. 'Goddess of Love. Mercury – winged messenger of the gods.' Now wait a minute, what was it that Newton had said about alchymy and the winged messenger of the gods? The Hermetic Art, after Hermes. That was it. The Greek messenger. Venus was the Roman goddess of Love. Now who was another one, the Greek goddess of Love? She racked her brains. Who *was* she, the Greek? With a click of the tongue she mouthed the name. 'Aphrodite. Hermes plus Aphrodite. Hermes Aphrodite.'

That was as absurd as Venus Mercury.

Try the next one with Greeks instead of Romans: Ares, Aphrodite. No.

But the Countess had seen that sign before. It was on the papers Beau made up for his wife's female troubles. It was the sign for woman. And the sign for Mars was the sign for a man. She glanced down at Alpiew's list again.

It hit her like a thunderbolt.

Man/woman. The man-woman has the sole surviving child.

Quickly her eyes skimmed back to the previous sign. Hermes Aphrodite.

She gasped with the sudden rush of clarity. The puzzle made perfect sense.

Hermaphrodite. A man-woman.

Mrs Roy! A man-woman.

She read the code through, trying to get it into her head.

Warning! The man-woman lies with the king, equals chaos. The man-woman has the sole surviving child. The king, the father of the sole-surviving child, is dead, then the game is over. The game reaches its zenith at the time of the eclipse in September. This baby, the sole surviving child, must be due to be born in September!

It made sense. The King had no heir. The throne would pass to his sister-in-law Princess Anne unless he sired a child. The Countess scratched her forehead. But Charles had sired many a bastard and they had not succeeded him. William would have had to marry the mother. The child had to be legitimate to succeed. The Countess thought of Nell Gwyn's children, of Castlemaine's, and Lucy Walters' doomed child, the Duke of Monmouth. None of them had succeeded to the throne, but, my word, they had had dukedoms and fortunes and estates lavished upon them. And of course hot-headed Monmouth had made a jolly good try at seizing the crown from Charles's brother, James.

All of their mothers had got mighty fine properties too. She and Pigalle had definitely lost out by not producing any offspring by darling King Charles. Just think of Nell Gwyn and her damnable freehold.

The Countess looked back at the paper.

Assuming she was right, the picture was clear. This Mrs Roy was trying it on. She was going to have

William's baby in September and ... The Countess's thoughts ground to a halt.

But if Mrs Roy was a man, how could she? Even if he was a true hermaphrodite, as far as the Countess knew, there was no hope of producing children from such a body. No. She must be wrong. Mrs Roy was a woman. How had she ever thought otherwise?

Whatever was going on, whatever it was that Beau Wilson had discovered, or been part of, was a trick. A trick against the King, and against the nation. But what that trick was, or why Beau Wilson and his maid Betty had to die for it, the Countess could not imagine.

Alpiew stepped over the lawyer's body and pulled back the blood-stained curtain. Ahead of her lay a short windowless corridor lined with shelves which spilled over with papers and boxes. She took a deep breath. The air was charged with lily of the valley and musk. Ahead of her she heard the rustling of fabric, and, running forward into the darkness, saw the bottom of a blue and white skirt swish round the corner. Swiftly she rushed on, desperate to catch whoever it was running ahead of her.

The only light was the flickering candle behind her in Cowley's office. She realised it was throwing her shadow along the floorboards before her, making her every movement visible to whoever lay in wait around the corner. She pressed further in to the wall, squeezing herself against the bookshelves, stepping sideways up to the corner, chasing her own shadow. With a sudden dash she leapt out, not knowing what or who lay ahead. Her heart thudded as she cleared the corner and glimpsed the back of a woman running up to another corner. The blue and white dress. It was an expensive-looking dress. She'd seen it before somewhere. The lady had brown hair, piled high on her head. The whole ensemble was familiar.

Wait a bit! It couldn't be? Alpiew had seen only the woman's back as she rounded the bend, but she remembered exactly where she'd last seen that dress. It was worn by Mrs Elizabeth Wilson, Beau's wife, on the night she first turned up at German Street with her sob-story about an errant husband. Alpiew's head raced. She had only seen Mrs Wilson in prison a few hours earlier. Had she escaped?

Alpiew ran along into the intensifying gloom. As she ran it dawned on her that not only did she have no light with her, but that she was not armed. She had nothing with which to protect herself, and the person ahead cer-tainly had a knife. Not only that but, whoever she was, she knew her way round this maze of corridors.

Alpiew turned the second corner. She could see noth-ing ahead but darkness. She put a foot forward and took a few strides into the black. With one hand out, keeping contact with the wall, she hurried forward as best she could. Then she tripped over something and fell to the floor. Groping around she realised she had stumbled over a stack of books, and there was something in her eye. Clambering to her feet, she thrust her hand into her pocket for a handkerchief. The corridor was suddenly illuminated with a dim yellow glow. It was Beau's bewitched kerchief. Alpiew held it up before her like a lantern and plunged along.

She could see someone ahead disappearing down a staircase. It certainly looked like Mrs Wilson. But how could it be? Mrs Wilson was in prison. But then when she thought Scum was safely under lock and key he was free enough to chase her round Newgate market. Who knows by what ploy the woman could have escaped, or been released? Now that she thought of it, Cowley had told her not to worry about Mrs Wilson. Perhaps he knew she was waiting for him behind the curtain in his very office? Perhaps he was right, and the woman was far more scary than Alpiew had ever believed, and having killed two people, thought nothing of killing Cowley too . . . And now? Her own future didn't look promising.

As she ran, Alpiew considered beating on one of the many doors she passed, but anyone else who might work here during the day would surely be gone by now. Hadn't Cowley worried about being the last one out?

She hurried to the top of the staircase and listened. Silence. Gathering her skirts, she dashed down. It was a stone spiral, with very uneven treads, and she was finding it hard to hurry. Alpiew started to take the steps three at a time, and, as she grasped at the walls to steady herself, she dropped the handkerchief.

As she stooped to fetch it, with lightning speed a hand reached out from a small inset alcove and caught her round the neck. Alpiew lost her footing and teetered on the edge of a step. A second hand tightened round her throat, pulling her up so that her feet left the ground. She writhed and kicked, but the grip grew tighter. She could not breathe, she could not see. The woman had her from behind. Alpiew threw her whole body towards the blue and white dress, causing the woman to lose her balance, perched as she was on what must be a small gothic window-sill set in the outer wall. The woman kept hold of Alpiew's throat, but her struggle unbalanced them, and together they both fell, tumbling down and down, round and round, grazing themselves against the rough walls, flailing as their bodies thumped against the worn stone steps.

Alpiew grappled with the woman, grabbing at her hair. It came away and rolled down the steps ahead of them. It was a wig.

Still wrestling, they both landed with a thud on a wooden floor at the bottom of the stairs. In the soupy gloom it was impossible to see. Alpiew blinked, and screwed up her eyes. The darkness seemed palpable. It was as though something was pressing black felt on her eyelids. Then a fist pounded into her cheek. Alpiew rolled over to protect herself. The woman clambered over her, and ran away along another passage.

Trying to think clearly, to stop the pain in her cheek, Alpiew staggered to her feet and again she gave chase.

Pigalle had placed the new marmosets in the coach under the care of her driver, and come to fetch the Countess. The Countess made it clear that they could not leave the child without inspecting his accommodation.

The clientele of the first-floor bagnio were doing all manner of things on the staircase. The Countess had to clamber over a couple on the stairs *in flagrante*, without so much as a by your leave. As she hauled herself up the final staircase of the Rummer Tavern, Pigalle stood panting at the top. 'It is like climbing ze Matterhorn, no?'

Mustafa smiled. He was used to it. His arms were over-flowing with every kind of sweetmeat, as well as bags of roasted nuts, gingerbread, and spice cake. The Countess was clutching a large bottle of brandy.

Mustafa had pushed through the broken-down door and now stood in the dark attic room, pointing at a small door. 'My mother is in there. But I have promised that no one can see her.'

The Countess looked round at the wretched place and stooped to enter. It wasn't a room, more a tiny roof space. A few boards were laid across the rafters. A slate was missing, and she could clearly see the stars sparkling outside. Despite the fact that the only light came in from the night sky, it was evident that Mustafa and his mother shared the place with rats and pigeons. The only furniture was rickety stuff which must have been retrieved from rubbish dumps.

The Countess creaked down to meet the boy's eye-level. 'Is this your home?'

The boy nodded.

'I would like to help you,' she whispered.

Pigalle knelt and tweaked at the boy's cherubic cheek, totally smitten with his sparkling brown eyes. 'You and your mother. If you come to my house, you will have big rooms, and money.' She shivered involuntarily. The place was freezing. 'You will be warm. And have good food.'

'But we will be rich soon,' the boy said gaily, keeping up the conspiratorial tone. 'As soon as the baby is born, and my uncle gets us the money.'

The Countess thought she might as well pop the important question again. 'Mustafa, what happened to the lady who you worked for before? It's very important. You must tell me.'

Mustafa tilted his head, puzzled. 'There is no lady.'

The Countess smiled, baring her stained teeth in the dim light. 'Don't you remember? At the theatre? Out in the country? When we went fishing?'

Mustafa lowered his lashes in his flirty way, and looked down at his laden arms. 'I must take the sweetmeats through to my mother.'

As the Countess rose to follow the boy, he held up his hand. 'No. It is not permitted.'

Astonished at this strange response, she let him go in alone. She waited a moment, then, shooting a quick look to Pigalle, crept over to the door, and sneaked it open a crack to peep inside.

Lying on the bed, her hair spread across a filthy pillow, lay a white woman. The Countess recognised her at once. It was Mrs Roy's maid, Lucy. The lumpen girl with flaxen hair. She was crying. Mustafa was holding her, kissing her face, holding a sweetmeat to her quivering lips. It was necessary for the child to do this, because the girl with the flaxen hair, Mustafa's mother, couldn't move her hands. Her wrists were held in leather straps, and chained to the bed-head.

Gingerly, Alpiew turned the door handle. Her cheek felt wet and sticky. She knew from the throbbing that she had a gash on her forehead and her eye was sore.

She tried not to breathe as she pushed open the door leading from the short black corridor to an equally dark room. She stood in the doorway listening.

Silence.

All she could hear was her own heart pounding like a

kettle drum at the Lord Mayor's parade. Her eyes scanned the darkness for something, but she could not even see her own trembling hands. She waited almost a minute, listening, desperate to detect any give-away hint of another presence in the room, before she took one cautious step forward.

The slashing hiss of a knife cut the silence. Alpiew screamed. She was cut. The blade had gashed her arm, and now was moving upwards, ready to slash at her again. The air resounded with the vibration of its motion. Alpiew threw herself to the floor, hitting out at her attacker's ankles, grabbing at her feet, trying to pull her down.

Alpiew screamed, almost bursting her lungs with the effort, hoping that somebody would hear. With a shriek of pain, the knife ripped at her calf. Her temper erupted bringing her renewed energy and she pulled so hard at the lunatic's ankles that the frenzied slashing stopped long enough for her to topple the maniac to the floor.

In the black they fought, squirming across the rough wooden floor as one entangled body.

Alpiew could see a glimmer of flickering light in a long line at floor-level. It must be the gap beneath a door. And beyond that door there was light! She scrambled towards it, hollering at the top of her voice. Heavy hands grabbed her head, and crashed it down on the floor-boards.

As her pain became unendurable, the door slowly opened and light from a burning torch flooded the small store-room.

Alpiew looked up, imploring assistance. But there

would be no help for her in that quarter. Standing in the doorway, flambeau aloft, was the one-time hireling actor Jack Fry, otherwise known as Scum.

SIXTEEN

Incineration

*The conversion of a substance to ashes
by means of a powerful fire.*

The Countess and Pigalle sat solemnly in the coach, Mustafa perched on Pigalle's lap, his mother flopped down in the Countess's arms.

'Your brother forced you to have sex with some stranger who was brought to you wearing a blindfold, like a masquerade?' squawked Pigalle.

Beau Wilson, thought the Countess, stroking the girl's blonde hair to soothe her.

The two women had freed Mustafa's mother from the manacles, after calling down for help to the brothel on the floor below. Luckily, for them, manacles are a frequently used piece of equipment in bagnios, so the prostitutes who came to their aid knew how to unlock them. Pigalle rushed to her coach with Mustafa and the coachman carried the sick girl, Lucy, down the stairs.

Now Lucy was blurting out her story in no particular order.

'The man in the blindfold was murdered. And his maid. And it won't stop there. My brother wants to trick the

King.' The girl started to cry. 'He knows the King. It's some kind of blackmail. He wants money . . .'

The Countess's mouth fell open. Her solution of the code was seemingly quite accurate.

'Zen we must go straight to my friend ze Equerry to His Majesty at St James's Palace, and explain ze whole awful story to him.' Pigalle screeched up to the coachman to head straight for the Palace Yard. 'Ah, German Street,' sighed Pigalle, looking out of the window. 'We are almost zere.'

'German Street!' cried the girl. 'An ancient Countess lives here with her maid, Alpiew. He has already sent a thug round to smash things up and frighten them. But now both of these women are in grave danger. He has vowed to kill them.'

The Countess gasped, her head racing. 'But where is Alpiew?' She gripped at Pigalle's sleeve. 'I have not seen her since this morning. Oh, Pigalle, I have no idea where she is.' Involuntarily the Countess crossed herself. 'Oh, Olympe! My own Alpiew, my poor darling. How can we save her? We don't even know where she is.'

'What is zat note pinned to your door? Stop!' Pigalle thumped the roof of the carriage, pointing out of the carriage window. 'Fetch me zat paper on my friend's door.'

The coachman leapt down and thrust the note into Pigalle's gloved hand.

The Countess grabbed it and read quickly. 'It's about Alpiew,' she said, her hands trembling. 'Oh, that's all right.' She smiled and sat back. 'It says she's gone to see the lawyer, Cowley.'

Inexplicably, Lucy sat bolt upright and screamed.

*   *   *

Splayed out on the floor, Alpiew rolled herself into a tight ball to protect herself and started to pray.

'I am going to kill you,' yelled Scum in his high-pitched squeal. 'Prepare, madam, to meet your doom.'

Then there was a silence. Alpiew opened one eye and looked up at Scum. He stood in the doorway as though transfixed, his eyes staring, his mouth hanging open. He looked for all the world like one of Mrs Salmon's waxworks at last year's Bartholomew Fair. But he was not looking at her.

'But . . .' He slowly came back to life again. 'But . . .' His hand was pointed in front of him, the flambeau lighting the room, making shadows jump around the walls. 'You are not . . . Mrs Roy . . . ?'

Alpiew, through her one good eye, watched the slow workings of Scum's brain click into place. He cocked his head to one side, like a puzzled puppy. 'You are a man?'

Slowly, trying to make her movements imperceptible, Alpiew rolled her head sideways to take a look behind her at her quondam assailant.

Standing in the corner, his short-cropped red hair throwing Mrs Wilson's ripped and bloody blue and white dress into stark contrast, stood Nathaniel, the lawyer's footboy. One hand was raised high, gripping the knife he had just used to stab Cowley.

With a sudden lunge he leapt forward, flailing to either side with the knife as though cutting his way out of a thick forest.

At the same moment from the room above, which she thought must be Cowley's office, Alpiew heard footsteps, and then the Countess and Pigalle calling her name.

Then a short duet of a scream. The two old friends had found Cowley's body.

Nathaniel leapt over Alpiew, and Scum tried to grab at him, using the flambeau as a foil in a fencing duel. 'You filthy pervert!' screamed Scum. 'You killed her. I just found the body. You killed Betty.'

'So what?' yelled Nathaniel. 'She was poking her nose in.' He thrust the knife at Scum, but Scum ducked and the knife embedded itself in the wainscoting.

Alpiew dragged herself out of the way as the two men fell upon each other in a fury.

'Milady!' she called towards the ceiling. 'Duchesse! Take care.'

'Why did you go to the elaboratory?' said Nathaniel through gritted teeth. 'I told you to stay away from there.'

'Because the girl was my fancy. I wanted to ask her out.' Scum's vast body pushed Nathaniel against the wall. 'You told me it was play-acting. That no one would be hurt. But I have just touched her rotting body. You, you, you . . .' As he thundered blows down on Nathaniel the flambeau flew out of his hand and landed high up on a shelf stacked with papers and vellum documents tied in pink ribbons. The dry, dusty papers caught instantly, and fire began to lick across the ceiling.

'My lady! My lady Countess,' screamed Alpiew, trying to beat out the fire with her bare hands, succeeding only in swiping mounds of flaming paper down on to the floor beneath her. 'Watch out, milady! Fire below!'

She looked down to see Nathaniel, now wriggling and threshing on the floor under Scum's foot. Scum tilted his head to listen to the women's panicked footsteps above. The wooden ceiling was ablaze, crackling and spitting, and the treads of the wooden stairs, which ran through this room were ablaze too.

'They don't know about the stone steps,' screamed Alpiew, pointing towards the door leading to the spiral stairs. 'They will surely be burned alive.'

But Scum had not heard her, nor seemed to care. Red-faced, veins standing up on his forehead and neck, he pulled open a door and ran up the flaming wooden stairs which led straight to Cowley's office.

Nathaniel clambered to his feet, but as he moved his skirt caught in the flames and began to burn. He tore at it, trying to rip it off, moving towards the door which led out to the street. Alpiew grabbed at Nathaniel's waist, trying to stop him escaping. He whipped round and belted her so hard in the face that she flew backwards across the room and slammed into the wall. As Alpiew tried to recover her equilibrium, Nathaniel, still ripping at his flaming skirts, reached out to retrieve his knife, when, with a resounding crash, the whole wooden staircase collapsed upon him.

Clambering over the inferno which had once been the staircase, Alpiew ran out into the street.

A small crowd had already gathered. 'Help, ho! Fetch the fire engine!' she screamed at them. 'Gentlemen, pierce the water pipes, please. There are three people trapped upstairs.' Then she dived back into the burning building. She ran along the ground-floor passage leading to the spiral staircase and fought her way through the dense choking smoke. As she shot up the stairs she collided with Pigalle, on her way down.

'Save yourself, *mon enfant*,' croaked Pigalle, speaking through a fur muff held to her mouth. '*Allons! Allons!* Zere is a fire!'

'But the Countess . . . ?'

Pigalle pushed her. 'We must get out. Down, down, down.' Reluctantly, Alpiew, coughing and choking, turned and ran back down the stone steps, Pigalle poking at her all the way down and into the street.

When, black with smoke and gasping for air, she stood in the open again, Alpiew turned back to see, right behind Pigalle, Scum teeter out of the building. In his scorched burly arms, her wig frizzled to a wisp, her white ceruse make-up patched with black, giving her the complexion of a Friesian cow, lay Lady Anastasia Ashby de la Zouche, Baroness Penge, Countess of Clapham. She was coughing, but alive.

The whole street was blocked. Pigalle's carriage was slewed across the road at one angle, an even larger one jammed right behind it, and a whole queue of chairs, hackney carriages and private coaches were piling up along the length of Fetter Lane.

'We are the Lord Steward's men.' Two large men with drawn swords stepped forward from the traffic chaos, pointing in Scum's direction. 'Is this the killer?'

'No, no.' Pigalle raised her hand. 'Zis man is a hero! Ze murderer is a tall boy with red 'airs.'

'Red airs?' asked one of the guards.

''Airs! 'Airs, you imbeciles!' screeched Pigalle, pulling at her own frizzy mop.

'I don't think he . . .' Alpiew looked back into the inferno. 'I think he must be . . .'

'Dead,' snapped the Countess, wiping her hands and being set down on her feet. 'So that's the end of the whole nasty business.'

'I shink not,' said a small man, standing at her side.

Alpiew rolled her eyes to heaven. Not another impenetrable foreign accent!

'And what, may I ask, is it to you, sirrah?' The Countess looked down at the little, slightly hunched man with the hook nose. 'My maid Alpiew and I have almost died at the hands of that lunatic. And to our certain knowledge another three people, one of whose bodies is currently being incinerated, have suffered cruel murder at his hands.' She puffed. 'And unless we can move fast, a fourth victim will be taken. At dawn a poor woman is going to the gallows for a crime she did not commit.'

The short man crooked his finger, indicating for the Countess to stoop so he could whisper into her ear.

Alpiew watched the Countess pull faces while the man murmured. First she seemed irritated, then bored, then puzzled, then surprised, then astonished and finally she fell into a sudden deep curtsey. The little man put his finger to his lips, and with a breathless 'Pshaw!' the Countess looked around at the crowd, shrugging and trying to look unfazed. 'Come, Alpiew,' she called, her voice high and strangled. 'To the coach.'

Alpiew, aching in every bruised bone of her body, stumbled to Pigalle's coach and pulled open the door.

The Countess bobbed her head. Sign language for 'Onwards!'

Puzzled, Alpiew walked past Pigalle's coach.

A liveried footman stood before her, bowing, holding open the door of a much bigger and more luxurious carriage. Another footman took Alpiew's hand and gently helped her inside. The Countess, chatting intensely with the little man, followed a few steps behind. They both climbed in, the postilions and footmen took up their positions and the coach rumbled into the night.

'Allow me to introdoosh myshelf,' said the little man. 'I am William.'

Alpiew smiled. Who in God's name was William? 'Oh, I see . . .' she said with a wan smile. 'William who?' Hoping the man would illuminate matters with his surname.

'Alpiew –' the Countess was jabbing her with her elbow, while her head bobbed up and down like a cork at sea – 'it's *William*, Alpiew.' She coughed politely. 'It's His Majesty, the King.'

SEVENTEEN

Projection

*The throwing of a ferment or tincture
on to a substance in order to effect
a transformation of the substance.*

Alpiew and the Countess sat staring at the money bag which lay on the table before them. Outside, the sun was already sending grey streaks to break the black night. Soon it would be morning.

'So explain again?' Alpiew was trying to catch up with the extraordinary developments of the night.

'The red-haired boy, Nathaniel, had been brought up working at the palace. He was one of the great underpaid during that cowardly James's mercifully short reign. His mother was a cook in the Royal Kitchen. The boy was nine and his sister seven when their mother was injured in a freak accident with a turn-spit. William had just been made king. The woman could not work because of her injuries, and was laid off with no pay. Then someone accused her of pilfering from the royal stores and she was thrown into gaol, where she died of a fever.' The Countess's head was buzzing with the stories she'd heard from Mustafa, from Lucy, and the King himself.

Alpiew shook her head. 'I still don't understand . . .'

'At this tender age the boy was thrown into a turmoil and blamed King William himself. He didn't realise that the monarch knows little of what goes on in his kitchens. Anyway, now having to support himself and his sister, Nathaniel worked his way up the ladder. He was quite happy in his work, and a few years later he was promoted to a job at the King's Great Wardrobe.'

'Ah, so that's what the KGW stood for.'

'KGW?'

'On the top of that list of clothing we found at Acton.'

'Indeed,' said the Countess. 'His particular duty was to tend to Queen Mary's clothing. William's wife. He even got to meet her. And he became very fond of the Queen. She petted him, because he was pretty. And for that reason too, she also let him model her dresses, so that she could see what they looked like in motion, and from behind. As a boy he was plain, unmemorable, but he could see that as a woman he stood out. That was the beginning . . .'

'You're telling me the Queen wanted him to be a transvestite?' Alpiew was shocked.

The Countess shook her head. 'No. Nothing like that. He was a child of thirteen, remember. She thought it was simple fun . . .'

'But why . . .'

'Hold your horses, Alpiew. I'm getting there.' The Countess took a sip of champaign and a bite of biscuit and continued. 'A year or two later his little sister Lucy fell in with a Royal Trumpeter, a handsome black fellow, who did not behave like a gentleman. When the villain found that he had got the girl with child he applied for a job with the army in France. He did not come back.

So now Nathaniel not only has a sister to support, there is also a baby. Nathaniel is fifteen. Then suddenly the Queen contracted smallpox. Within weeks she was dead, and the boy was no longer required . . .'

'There was no Queen's Wardrobe any more?'

'Right,' said the Countess. 'So he was let go. Again he felt bitter that King William did not help him. The boy had petitioned and received no reply. But as every senior courtier knew, the King was devastated at his loss. He became a recluse, speaking to no one, going nowhere, just sitting alone, and crying.

'Nathaniel's final job was to clear the Queen's clothing from the palace at Whitehall and put it into storage. It was when he found himself in the enormous store-room in the Savoy that the idea first came to him. He took gloves, shoes, corsets, mantuas, cloaks . . . Everything he would need to pass himself off as a lady.'

'But surely the King would have recognised his own wife's clothing?'

'But the boy was careful to take only clothing owned by Mary of Modena, James's Italian wife. So the stuff was stylish and expensive, but never before seen by William.'

Alpiew recharged their two glasses from the bottle of vintage champaign.

'Nathaniel took his time. To make ends meet, he got a job as a runner to Cowley, and went to the theatre on the afternoons when he wasn't needed. He watched the women in the audience and on stage, perfecting their coquettish movements, their flirtatious ways. At home in the evenings he practised making up his face.'

'A good place for that,' said Alpiew. 'In Covent Garden no one would think twice.'

'That's right. It was in the piazza that he took his first steps dressed in all his female finery, and he realised that as a woman he was a success. He was an eye-catcher . . .'

'A rum blowen . . .'

'He knew his way round the royal palaces, and once he had perfected the art of being a woman, he hung around, dressed to kill, modestly approaching William just as the poor man started to come out of his grief. As a woman of mystery, Nathaniel made himself very attractive to the lonely King. Men enjoy an enigma. And remember, Nathaniel had known Queen Mary well. He took on some of her mannerisms, even wore the same scent. William became fascinated. And eventually promised "the woman" a small cottage in the country where the pair could secretly meet. For the first time in his life, Nathaniel became important.

'In January, to celebrate the New Year, the female Nathaniel got William drunk, and a fumble ensued, during the course of which His Majesty passed out. Nathaniel decided to use this to his own advantage. He realised that if he could present William with a "love-child" he would have an opportunity to get very rich indeed.'

'And I suppose that was where Beau became necessary?'

The Countess nodded. 'With the pocket money William gave him, Nathaniel, in his role as Mrs Roy, spotted Scum at the Playhouse and took him on as a minder. On his days at the lawyer's office he found out about Beau Wilson needing money. He sent his first message to him via Cowley's office. You know the rest . . .'

'So Scum arranged for Beau to come out to Acton to do the business with Lucy.'

'Yes,' said the Countess. 'It was Scum's job to put Beau, blindfolded, into the mysterious hired coach, driven as often as not by Nathaniel himself. At Acton, Beau, still blindfold, lay with the girl, who was tied to the bed. When the wench showed the first signs of pregnancy Beau's services were no longer required and he was given the heave-ho.'

'But . . . ?'

'Oh, yes indeed, but . . .' The Countess sighed. 'Beau didn't want to lose the money he got paid for his sexual services. He didn't realise it wasn't a bottomless jar. He was paid for five trips to service poor Lucy, but then he wanted more. Betty was right. He did peep. And he saw Nathaniel, half-way into his gender transition. And he recognised him from Cowley's office.'

Alpiew gasped. 'And Cowley. Why did he try to put obstacles in our way?'

The Countess shook her head. 'I don't think he had a clue. Nathaniel simply acted in the name of Cowley, and did what he thought fit.'

'And he sent Scum round to German Street that night to scare us off.'

The Countess nodded. 'And I believe Beau told Scum he'd guessed something odd was going on.'

'That was while he was in the coffee house and we sat freezing on the horse trough.'

'How did you know that?'

'Obvious.'

'So that night, as you guessed, the route was changed. And Scum rowed him a few yards along the Thames, from Dorset Garden, where we saw him, to Somerset House, just along the way.'

'So that if Beau tried to work it out he would think the country house was south of the river?'

'Correct. But Beau still hadn't quite realised the enormity of his role in this rig-me-role, not till that last night when he found a wax seal which was unmistakably the King's. It had come from the wrapping on a painting which had arrived that afternoon, and which he heard Mrs Roy boasting came from another of her besotted lovers. Next day at the theatre, Nathaniel-femme was there, in full rig, watching Beau to see how he reacted to getting another assignation so soon after he thought he'd been dismissed.

'Although we lost him that afternoon, "she" had Scum follow Beau to the elaboratory, where he left the coded message in the log-book, before going off to his fatal meeting at . . .'

'St Paul's, New Built, nine.' Alpiew sighed. 'And then, after Beau was killed and Mrs Wilson arrested, in his manly persona of Cowley's runner he searched the Wilson household, stealing some of Mrs Wilson's dresses and taking the clock as a present for Cowley.'

'Why, though?' Alpiew had reached the bottom of the pile of biscuits, so poured herself another bumper.

'I think he was Cowley's lover too. He needed him. And needed to keep him sweet.'

'What about Betty?'

The Countess shrugged. 'The mad boy already had the elaboratory's address from Scum, and the poor girl was a sitting duck . . .' Her voice trailed off.

'But would Nathaniel have made enough money out of this scheme of his to be worth two lives?'

'It seems that reality had gone out of the equation.

He had a mission. He wanted power, he wanted to be important, and . . . oh, you know kings!' The Countess shook her head. 'They have different ways from ordinary mortals. If the boy had pulled this plan off, persuaded King William that one night of drunken passion had led to a royal love child, Nathaniel could look forward to great riches and titles for the rest of his life, and the child's. And with the succession so shaky at present, he could even have persuaded William to marry him and then made an attempt at the throne, on behalf of his "love-child".'

'The child!' Alpiew leapt up. 'What about the child?'

'I'm not going to sleep tonight, are you?' The Countess got up too, glancing at her new coat of arms on the mantelpiece, and drained her glass. 'How kind of His Majesty to issue a Royal edict counteracting my husband's sale and making it impossible for the house to be sold during my lifetime.'

'And for giving us the money,' said Alpiew, gazing with overflowing sentiment at a huge bag full of golden coins. 'It's lucky you kept friends with the Duchesse de Pigalle, for if she hadn't got connections at the palace, things might have turned out quite differently.'

They left the house, locking up carefully behind them, and sauntered along German Street. The watchmen were packing up to go home to bed for the day, and market traders already rattled along towards St James's and the Hay Market.

'Look,' said Alpiew, pointing at the glowing windows ahead, 'she's still up.'

It sounded as though a party was going on upstairs. 'Nice of her to invite us!' The Countess pushed at the front door, and she and Alpiew made their way up the stairs.

Pigalle's great hall was aglow with hundreds of candles, the marmosets scampered along the chair-backs, while the parrot was screaming, '*Merde*!' the monkey hung from the curtains squealing with all its might and trunks of clothing were flung everywhere.

'Ashby! Darlink!' Pigalle staggered across to the door, champaign bottle in hand. 'I thought you two would be asleep. Come.' She pulled the Countess across the room to a table loaded with bottles. 'You must drink. Look! Everything is marvellous.'

Alpiew and the Countess gazed with amazement at the scene. Scum, dressed in full Turkish costume, was dancing a reel with Lucy, who was also in oriental dress. Mustafa, back in moorish satins, perched on a chair-back stroking one of Pigalle's cats, feeding him bits of bacon.

'I have a full household again. Zey are all going to work for me, and live here.'

'It must be hard for Lucy . . .' Alpiew watched the girl, her pale face without expression, dancing with Scum. 'Her brother . . .'

'Her brother was an *aliéné* and a murderer,' snapped Pigalle. 'She hated him.'

'But why did she go along with it? Has she spoken to you?' Alpiew huddled in close to Pigalle.

'*D'accord*! She was frightened of him. When we turned up in ze country, she suddenly saw everything clearly, as though through the eyes of others. And she resolved to tell . . .'

'So he tied her up in that garret!'

'Pigalle, dear, I speak as a friend.' The Countess pulled

414

Pigalle aside. 'You do remember that the girl is with child?'

'Of course.' Pigalle grinned and shrugged. 'Of course.' She led the Countess out of the room and along to Azis's old black bedchamber. Gently she pushed open the door.

'I went with ze steward to get her released while you were with ze King.' One solitary candle burning on the bedside table lit the sleeping features of Mrs Elizabeth Wilson. 'It is Beau's baby. She has said she wants to have it, and Lucy is glad to let ze child go to someone who would love it as she loves little Mustafa.'

'But . . . her own baby?'

'Remember how it was conceived, darlink.' Pigalle gently closed the door. 'Ze girl was bound, and forced to have sex with a blindfolded stranger. She wants to forget all zat stuff.'

They strolled back to the party.

'Aren't you frightened of that big thug?' asked the Countess as they re-entered.

'Jack Fry? He saved your life, darlink. Besides which he is quite simple. You tell him what to do, what to say, he does it. It takes him a long time to work things out for himself, but he seems to have a good character.'

Alpiew winced. 'He certainly showed courage when he ran up that burning staircase . . .'

'And in zat costume,' Pigalle grinned, 'he is some sexy *zigomard, non*?'

It was coming up to noon when Alpiew and the Countess, refreshed with many more glasses of champaign, staggered home.

The Countess pushed open the door, and reeled into the kitchen. As usual Godfrey was snoring in the far bed.

Alpiew flopped on to her bed and started pulling off her stockings. She cocked her head.

'Milady?' She was staring at the chimney breast. 'The coat of arms?'

The Countess looked up. The coat of arms was gone. 'Thank God for that,' the Countess emitted a burp. 'Ghastly-looking thing. A leg of ham indeed! Don't know why that stupid herald didn't go the whole hog and have something altogether worse for the "Clap" bit.'

She pulled off her shoes and threw them under the bed.

'The money!' Unfastening her bodice, Alpiew was gazing open-mouthed at the table. 'It's gone!'

The Countess span round, gripping at the bed-post to steady herself.

The money was indeed gone from the table-top where they had left it.

'That filthy, dirty, whoring, cross-biting cully, that . . .'

'Where is it?' Alpiew gave Godfrey a good shake. 'Where did he go with our money?'

'What money?' Godfrey sat up, dribbling with sleep. 'Who?'

'Sir Peter, of course . . .'

The Countess was screaming. 'Don't even credit him with a name, the poxy, scabby . . .'

'He's in bed, isn't he?' Godfrey pointed at the Countess's empty bed. 'He was . . .'

'And how did you both get in, anyhow?' screamed Alpiew, shaking him. 'My lady has the only key.'

The Countess let out a groan and collapsed on to the

bed. 'He picked the lock, of course.' At that moment the door drum started beating. 'Someone at the door, Alpiew.'

Alpiew started doing up her bodice again and made for the hall.

The Countess followed Alpiew out.

Standing in the doorway were Mr and Mrs Cue.

'Sorry to call without warning,' beamed Mrs Cue. 'But the paper's a bit short this week, and we were wondering if you knew of any extra scandalous things that have been going on?'

Alpiew and the Countess looked at one another, then back to the Cues.

'Absolutely nothing!' said the Countess.

'Nothing at all,' Alpiew reiterated. 'But give us an afternoon, and for two guineas we'll find you something by this evening.'

Alpiew and the Countess stood in the doorway and watched the two rotund figures of the printers waddle away up German Street.

Lurching towards them in the other direction was someone they'd seen before. Head upright, arms swinging freely at his side, his grey hair hanging loose to his waist, came the Naked Man of Pest House Fields.

'Oh Lord, child.' Instinctively the Countess shielded Alpiew's eyes. 'It's that awful creature again. In *puris naturalibus*, as ever.'

When the man in all his glory had swung past, the Countess and Alpiew turned back into the house.

'If only all men were so clearly what they seem, we'd not have had any problem finding Beau Wilson's murderer,' said Alpiew.

'If only all men were so clearly what they seem,' sighed the Countess, 'Beau Wilson would not have been murdered. Come along, child!' The Countess linked arms with Alpiew, and together they returned to the cosy kitchen. 'We're both tired and we have a scandal to invent.'